ALSO BY BENTLEY LITTLE

THE
BURNING

Bentley Little

A SIGNET BOOK

SIGNET
Published by New American Library, a division of
Penguin Group (USA) Inc., 375 Hudson Street,
New York, New York 10014, USA
Penguin Group (Canada), 90 Eglinton Avenue East, Suite 700, Toronto,
Ontario M4P 2Y3, Canada (a division of Pearson Penguin Canada Inc.)
Penguin Books Ltd., 80 Strand, London WC2R 0RL, England
Penguin Ireland, 25 St. Stephen's Green, Dublin 2,
Ireland (a division of Penguin Books Ltd.)
Penguin Group (Australia), 250 Camberwell Road, Camberwell, Victoria 3124,
Australia (a division of Pearson Australia Group Pty. Ltd.)
Penguin Books India Pvt. Ltd., 11 Community Centre, Panchsheel Park,
New Delhi - 110 017, India
Penguin Group (NZ), cnr Airborne and Rosedale Roads, Albany,
Auckland 1310, New Zealand (a division of Pearson New Zealand Ltd.)
Penguin Books (South Africa) (Pty.) Ltd., 24 Sturdee Avenue,
Rosebank, Johannesburg 2196, South Africa

Penguin Books Ltd., Registered Offices:
80 Strand, London WC2R 0RL, England

First published by Signet, an imprint of New American Library,
a division of Penguin Group (USA) Inc.

First Printing, August 2006
10 9 8 7 6 5 4 3 2 1

Copyright © Bentley Little, 2006
All rights reserved

 REGISTERED TRADEMARK—MARCA REGISTRADA

Printed in the United States of America

PUBLISHER'S NOTE
This is a work of fiction. Names, characters, places, and incidents either are
the product of the author's imagination or are used fictitiously, and any resemblance to actual persons, living or dead, business establishments, events, or
locales is entirely coincidental.
    The publisher does not have any control over and does not assume any
responsibility for author or third-party Web sites or their content.

For my son, Emerson Li Little,
who asked me to write a story that included a
haunted train and the two graves marked *Mother*
and *Daughter* in the open land between the towns
of Payson and Pine, Arizona.

Prologue

The Man from the Government stood at the edge of the windswept plain and stared out at the carnage before him.

It was far, far worse than he'd been led to believe. He'd been told the numbers, even had in his courier pouch a description of the worst atrocities, but there was no way that the scope of the massacre could have been conveyed by mere words.

Hardened though he was, he was forced to glance away, looking out beyond the bodies. To the north, he saw barren ground broken by occasional scrub brush. To the south, a series of small hills, beyond which was the lake. Overhead, the sky was full of clouds, their white innocence contrasting sharply with the rent flesh on the field below.

Girding himself, the Man allowed his gaze to fall once again upon the ground. The bodies—or body *parts*—lay strewn in every conceivable position, stacked several deep, human mixed with horse, testifying to the unbridled ferocity of the slaughter. Fingerless hands on the ends of severed arms emerged from the rotting viscera of gutted torsos; butchered legs rested atop mutilated man faces and hairy horse heads. The soil had been stained a deep dark crimson, but it was obvious that before the blood had sunk into the ground, there had been pools, rivers, lakes of it, blood so thick the red tide would have reached halfway up his boots.

As terrible as the sight was, the smell was a thousand times worse, an overwhelming stench of death and decomposition, shit and spoilage, piss and putrefaction.

The only noise on the plain was the cawing of carrion birds and the buzzing of flies, both so loud and overpowering that it was nearly impossible for him to maintain a coherent train of thought.

It was his job to scout the location, however, to determine what was needed and then report back. Holding his breath, the Man stepped forward, attempting to pace off the dimensions of the massacre site, though it was impossible to walk a straight line through the jumble of mangled corpses and the constant startled flight of birds and bugs. He advanced carefully, wincing as he trod upon a man's detached genitals, nearly slipping in a still-sticky patch and pitching forward into a battered chest cavity, saving himself only by crunching a skull with his right boot.

This would not be easy work. The crew would have to be much larger than originally anticipated, and once they were through, their silence had to be assured. If any of this ever got out . . .

But of course it would not get out. President Grant had given strict orders that everything was to be conducted with the utmost secrecy, knowledge restricted to a very few, and it was the Man's duty to carry out the president's wishes and make sure that everything went as planned. Congress was watching Grant like a hawk, but out here in the wilderness there were no overseers and there was still some discretion. The president could deal with the situation in his own way.

Because General Grant knew war.

He knew bloodshed.

He knew horror.

He knew how to handle this.

The Man from the Government kept pacing, marking off measurements. He worked as fast as he could, but it was still close to sundown before he finally made his way back to his horse and took off across the countryside the way he had come.

He returned a month later, after the cleanup, after the bonfire.

Bone fire.

It was the only way to dispose of the evidence, but smoke from the burning bodies had been visible for fifty miles, the foul-smelling black soot falling on homesteads more than a day away. They'd had to post a perimeter of guards to keep away people from the city curious to discover what was happening.

Other than that, though, the cleanup had gone well, and indeed, upon inspection, there appeared to be no evidence of the terrible events that had occurred on this spot. Holding his hat so it would not be blown off, the wind whipping his coattails, the Man from the Government strode over the ground, examining it as he went. He thought that at one point, near a patch of mud, the soil appeared redder than it should, but the variation in hue was so slight that it would be noticed only by someone specifically looking for it.

He was not slow, but he was methodical, and by the end of the afternoon, he was satisfied that any crisis had been averted, that there was no evidence anything out of the ordinary had occurred here.

He climbed upon his horse. It was a two-hour ride back to camp, another two days to a telegraph office. It was fortunate that the atrocity had happened here, far from civilization and the prying eyes of humanity.

He might not return to his camp and his aides until after nightfall, but that inconvenience was a small price to pay for the ease of completing this mission, which could have been so much more difficult.

Tomorrow, they would pull up stakes, and once he reached the telegraph office on Friday, he would cable to Hogue, who would inform the president that all was right, that the field had been successfully cleaned and cleared.

They were safe.

At least for now.

One

Flagstaff, Arizona

Angela Ramos stood in line in front of the university's housing office and, for the fourth time in ten minutes, looked at her watch. The line had not moved. Oh, there'd been a barely perceptible shift forward, but it was the result of students shuffling their feet, closing spaces, pressing ahead incrementally in the hope that it would somehow spur the workers in the office to speed up, and not the result of genuine progress.

She was here because she'd been promised on-campus housing, and she held in her hand a computer-printed form stating exactly that. But when she'd arrived and checked in at Admissions and Records, Angela had received notice that, due to overenrollment this semester, she would not be able to stay in one of the dorms. Preference had been given to upperclassmen and returnees, and spaces for freshmen were allotted based on distance from home. As a student from California, she hadn't traveled far enough to merit accommodations.

This is totally unacceptable, she planned to say when she finally reached the head of the line and got a chance to confront someone from the housing office. In her mind her voice came out firm, resolved and authoritative. She saw herself meeting the eyes of her nemesis and not backing down. It never worked out that way in real life, though, which was why she was using this time to prepare and practice the speech she would give to the university automaton she would have to face.

A kid about her age with a huge halo of retro hair who'd been walking down the sidewalk toward the back of the line stopped when he saw how many students were already ahead of him. "How long have you guys been standing on line?" he asked in a thick New York accent.

"A half hour," a clean-cut young man two spaces in front of her answered.

"Shit," the hairy guy said, and walked away.

Angela watched him go. Why, she wondered, did people from the East Coast say "*on* line" instead of "*in* line"? People in a queue weren't standing *on* a line. They *were* the line. The line consisted of the people *in* it.

Already she was getting annoyed by differences in speech patterns?

This was going to be one long afternoon.

It *was* one long afternoon. Either everyone in front of her had unbelievably complicated problems or the people who worked in the housing office were totally incompetent. By the time she was inside the building and at the front desk, her righteous diatribe had been honed to perfection. After hearing a brief outline of Angela's problem and determining that it wasn't the fault of misfiled paperwork, the secretary at the counter instructed her to go down the hall to office 1A and speak to a housing administrator.

Angela strode purposefully down the corridor, her confidence bolstered by the authoritative click of her heels on the institutionally tiled floor. Man, woman, it didn't matter; she'd been promised a dorm room and she was going to give the housing administrator living hell until her problem was solved.

Only she didn't.

Edna Wong, the elderly woman in office 1A, was friendly, apologetic and understanding, and of course Angela did not have the heart to jump down the old lady's throat as she'd planned. In fact, as always, she eventually found herself apologizing to the housing administrator for being such an inconvenience. She hated herself for backing off even as she did it, but the alternative was to blame this nice old woman for something that wasn't her fault. She was just a part of the machine, a cog in the system.

"I can't tell you how sorry I am that this happened," the administrator told her. "Rest assured, you will get top priority for housing next semester. But there are roughly twenty-five or twenty-six of you who have been displaced because of this mix-up, and despite our promise to you, I'm afraid we simply have no more room in our on-campus housing."

"I understand, Mrs. Wong—"

"Call me Edna."

"—but I have no place to live. I assumed that I *did* because of the letter you sent me, and now I'm . . . I'm homeless. I literally have nowhere to go. I don't know anyone in this state, I've never been here before, I don't have much money. I would have made other arrangements or figured something out if I'd been told ahead of time, but this was just sprung on me today, and . . ." She had to stop, look away and bite her lip to keep from crying.

Mrs. Wong—*Edna*—reached across the desk and took Angela's hand in hers. "Don't worry. Everything will turn out all right."

Angela didn't trust herself to respond.

"I want to help you," the housing administrator said kindly. She rummaged through her desk. "Since you got such a raw deal, and it *is* our fault . . ." She handed Angela a three-by-five card. "Here. We have a bulletin board out front with students looking for roommates, but I haven't put this on the board yet. Why don't you take it?"

Angela read the card:

> *Wanted. Female roommate, no smoking, no drugs, to share furnished two-bedroom, one-bath apartment. $275 per month plus utilities. Call Chrissie Paige. 555-4532.*

"In fact, let me call for you. I know Chrissie."

The old woman not only set up an appointment for Angela to meet Chrissie Paige and look at the apartment that afternoon; she also vouched for her, promising that Angela was reliable and trustworthy and would make a great roommate. Just the fact that she was willing to stick her neck out left Angela feeling so grateful that she almost started crying again.

"Don't do that, dear," Edna begged. She smiled brightly. "Everything's going to be fine. Despite the problems computers cause us, people can always find a way to work things out. NAU's a terrific school, and Flagstaff's a wonderful town. You're going to have a great semester. And next term, if you still want it, you'll be at the top of the list for on-campus housing."

"Thank you," Angela said. "Thank you so much."

"You're welcome, dear."

State Street was located off what must have once been the downtown district, just across old Route 66 north of the railroad tracks, a series of blocks with closely packed buildings of faded brick or rough-hewn stone, several of them three or four stories tall—what passed for high-rises here in Flagstaff. All looked as though they'd seen better days, but at the same time the area seemed on the upswing. There was a small used bookstore, a health-food store and a couple of café-style restaurants. There was even a church with gargoyles lining its peaked roof, and Angela didn't think she'd ever seen gargoyles in real life before.

The apartment building itself was an old Victorian home that had been subdivided and converted. The standout in an eclectic neighborhood that included a couple of California-style Craftsman cottages, a Tudor home, a log cabin and several homes that appeared to be made from chunks of lava, the apartment house boasted not only an incredibly ornate facade but a rolling lawn three to four times bigger than any other on the block.

Chrissie Paige was waiting on that lawn when Angela drove up. Tan and frizzy-haired, wearing a halter top and cutoff jeans, the girl, like a lot of the students she'd seen in Flagstaff, looked somewhat hippieish, which Angela found oddly comforting. That era had always seemed to her to have a greater sense of community than the fractured world in which she'd grown up. There'd always been a few neohippies back in Los Angeles, but as with everything else, that look was inevitably tied to some musical movement or other. Appearance and culture in California were always connected to entertainment. Here the lifestyle seemed somehow more real, more organic. She liked that.

The other girl stood, brushed grass off her cutoffs. "Are you Angela? I'm Chrissie."

"Hi," Angela said shyly. She felt slightly embarrassed, as though Mrs. Wong—*Edna*—had forced Chrissie to see her against her will, but that wore off almost instantly as the other girl led her up the lawn to the house, chatting happily.

"This place was originally built by one of the Babbitts. The Babbitts practically *owned* northern Arizona. You know Bruce Babbitt, who used to be secretary of the Interior? His family. You'll see buildings up here named after them, department stores, almost everything. Anyway, one of the cousins or something built this place fifty, sixty years ago. I think it was empty for a while—no one could afford it—so eventually someone bought the house and subdivided it into apartments. I think that was in the sixties or seventies. And here we are."

Chrissie led her through the front door into an elaborate foyer. Straight ahead was a long wide hallway, to the right a curving staircase of dark wood that led to the second floor. Angela followed Chrissie upstairs, where a hallway identical to the one on the ground floor stretched toward the rear of the house. They stopped at the first doorway on the left. "My place," Chrissie said, opening the door. "I don't know if Edna told you or if you saw the ad, but it's a two-bedroom. We have a small kitchen, one bathroom and a sitting room. As you can see, it's pretty big, though. And the view from the bedroom windows is awesome. You have to look over the roof of the house next door, but you get a perfect view of the San Francisco Peaks. By next month, they'll be covered with yellow when the aspens change. It's pretty spectacular."

Angela peeked through the open doorways of the two bedrooms. Both were larger than her bedroom back home, and though hers was the smaller of the two, it had a full-sized four-poster bed rather than the headboardless twin she was used to, and an oversized dresser that could hold twice as many clothes as she owned.

"Of course, you can decorate it however you want, put up pictures, posters, whatever."

"Wow," Angela said, walking into the room and looking around. She glanced out the window, saw the mountains. "Only two hundred and seventy-five for this place?"

"It's haunted," Chrissie offered.

Angela looked over at the other girl to see if she was joking, but she didn't appear to be.

"It's true. I mean, that's the rumor. I've never actually seen anything. But Winston and Brock, downstairs, say that they've heard stuff. Moaning, mumbling, the usual."

"Here?"

"No. In the house. Not your room in particular. In fact, I haven't heard any stories about our apartment at all. They all seem to be downstairs. But supposedly, that's the reason the rent's so cheap. I don't believe in ghosts or gods or anything supernatural myself, but in the interest of full disclosure I thought I'd better lay all the cards on the table in case you're the type of person who worries about that stuff."

Angela was intrigued. "You don't believe in gods? *Any* gods? Not even . . . God?"

"No." Chrissie smiled. "You do, I take it?"

Angela reddened, feeling embarrassed, though there was no reason why she should. "I'm Catholic," she admitted.

"That's cool. You don't preach to me, I won't preach to you, and the two of us should get along just fine."

Angela couldn't let it go. She was far from a perfect Catholic—she'd engaged in premarital sex, was vascillatingly pro-choice—but she couldn't imagine not believing in God at all. It seemed so . . . brave.

"Just so you know, Winston and Brock are a couple. They're gay. So if you have a problem with that—"

"No, no. Of course not."

"Good."

"But . . . aren't you worried?" she asked Chrissie. "I mean, about not believing in God? What if you're wrong? After you're dead—"

"I'll be worm food. Listen," Chrissie said, "I really don't want to blow this up into a big deal here. If this is going to bother you . . ."

"No," Angela assured her. "I was just . . . curious."

"Are you sure? This is Flagstaff, average snowfall one million feet. We're going to be spending a lot of time indoors together this winter."

Angela smiled. "I'd like that."

Chrissie nodded, satisfied. "Okay, then. I'm the one actually renting this apartment—I'll be subletting it to you—so what I need is first-month's rent and a security deposit of, oh, a hundred bucks. If you can swing it. If not . . ." She smiled. "*Que sera, sera.* I guess that part could be waived."

"Thank you," Angela said. "I'll take it. And I can give you a security deposit. I'm just . . ." She took a deep breath. "You saved me. I was supposed to be in a dorm, and the computer screwed everything up, and I was going to be homeless. So I'm grateful."

"Good," Chrissie said. "I'm glad. I think this is going to work out just fine."

"Me, too." Angela took one last look out the window before following Chrissie back into the sitting room.

Snowstorms and gay neighbors and a haunted apartment and an atheist roommate.

She smiled.

This was going to be an exciting semester.

TWO

Canyonlands National Park, Utah

The sun was angry when it awoke. Henry Cote could feel it through the curtains, see it in the thin sliver of white-hot light that entered through the part in the drapes and reproduced itself on the opposite wall, obliterating his photo of Sarah by the beach. The sun was angry and it was going to take out that anger on him. He knew it, he resigned himself to the fact, and though it was his day off and he'd been planning to sleep in, Henry forced himself to get out of bed. He needed his morning coffee, and he wanted to make it and drink it before the temperature in the cabin rose above eighty-five, before it got so hot that the sweat the steaming Folgers would coax from his pores decided to linger all day.

Lack of air-conditioning could do strange things to a man.

The park service had been promising them new accommodations for the past decade, but the funding bills passed by Congress always provided just enough money for maintenance, none for upgrades. Both Democrats and Republicans were equally guilty of publicly expressing support for the parks—and privately voting to finance pet projects in their home districts at the expense of much-needed improvements at places like Zion and Arches and Canyonlands.

Which was why the American people had to pay to go to national parks these days.

Even though they *owned* the parks.

Fucking country was going to hell in a handbasket.

As he walked over to the kitchenette, he looked at the photo of Sarah, wondering what she was doing now, where she lived, whom she was with. Whoever it was, he could be pretty damn sure it wasn't a ranger or other park-service employee. Not only had Sarah hated the low pay; she'd despised the lifestyle as well, complaining every single night about the heat or the cold, the rain or the snow, the lack of TV or radio reception or, most frequently, the distance from civilization.

Complaining.

Every.

Single.

Night.

Sarah was not temperamentally suited to a life out-doors, was the type of person for whom the lack of a local Nordstrom was considered a severe hardship, while he felt uncomfortable and unhappy in any city with a population greater than four digits.

Which was why their marriage had been so short.

And so disastrous.

He plugged in the coffeemaker, and thought of the dream he'd had last night as he shook the old grounds in the filter and poured in water. It had been a long time since he'd shown any interest in sex. That wasn't a complaint, merely an observation. Hell, if he'd had more of a libido, perhaps he and Sarah could have weathered a few of those early storms and their rela-tionship would still be standing today. But the prob-lem was, and always had been, that he ended up thinking of the parts of a woman's body as . . . well, *parts* of a woman's body. The vagina was a tube not unlike the intestine or trachea. The breasts were fatty tissue covered in skin. The ass, of course, was the hind end of the gastrointestinal tract and the location where waste elimination occurred.

Put simply, it was hard for him to become aroused when his view of sex was so clinical and detached.

But last night, he'd dreamed of two Oriental beauties who had come to his cabin from the desert, twins of indeterminate age who had strolled naked toward him across the sand, their forms gradually coalescing from the shimmering heat waves like the rider in *Lawrence of Arabia*. They were beautiful. He'd fought in Vietnam but, unlike most of his fellow soldiers, had not partaken of any of the local feminine pleasures. No reason, really. Oh, maybe he'd taken the training films about diseases a little more seriously than his buddies, but that wouldn't have deterred him had he really been interested. He just . . . hadn't been attracted.

These two, though . . .

They'd walked all the way to his cabin, moving in a slinky, sexy manner that should have been impossible given their bare feet and the irregular drifts of sand. Their breasts were small, but the nipples were large, and only sparse thatches of pubic hair sprouted between their legs. The two women reached him much faster than expected, as though the desert between his cabin and the horizon had been foreshortened, and they stopped mere inches in front of him. The one on the right reached between her thighs, slid an index finger into her obviously wet opening and then pressed it to his lips.

And he'd awakened completely erect.

That should have been cause for celebration—he

couldn't remember the last time he'd been aroused by a dream or anything else—but instead it left him feeling uneasy. There was something about those identical women that did not sit well with him, something disturbing he could not quite put his finger on.

Having set up the coffee, he turned on the freestanding oscillating fan he'd placed near the fireplace, and looked again at the angry light streaming through the curtain crack.

Angry light.

It was an Indian thing, Henry supposed, this personification of the natural world. He'd heard a lot of tribesmen say similar things about wind and rain and animals and land, and he wondered if the predisposition wasn't in his genes. According to his father, their family was part Papago on his grandfather's side, but Henry wasn't sure how much store he put by that. Everyone on the damn planet seemed to be part Indian these days, every suburban accountant who dragged his family out to the national park bragging that he was one-quarter Cherokee or Choctaw, or was Navajo on his father's grandmother's cousin's uncle's side. Hell, Henry had been born in Phoenix and, except for that stint in the army, had spent all of his life in the Four Corners states. He knew firsthand how Jim Crow this area of the country still was, how whites and Indians didn't mix, lived basically in two separate societies, and he had his doubts that a whole lot of interbreeding had gone on in more enlightened days of yore. More likely, it was all a crock of shit.

Which was why he kept his own suspected heritage a secret.

Still, he sometimes thought that perhaps he *did* have Indian blood in his veins, and that his hidden background had led him to this job, to this place, had made him who he was, caused him to think of things like angry suns and kind rocks and playful plants. Hell, maybe that same inborn sense was at work with his dream, creating that strange sense of dread he felt when he thought of those Asian twins.

By now, the cabin was filled with the smell of coffee, and he walked back over to the counter and poured himself a cup, drinking it while the breeze generated by the fan blew in his direction. The breeze was cool now, but that wouldn't last, and even if he kept all the drapes closed, by noon it would be circulating hot air.

Maybe he'd go into Moab today, give himself a treat, hang out at Arby's or McDonald's or some other air-conditioned fast-food joint. Or maybe he'd get in his Jeep and do a little backcountry exploring; if he was going to be hot, he might as well have fun at the same time.

No, Henry thought, he wasn't going into the back-country alone.

He might meet the twins.

That was ridiculous. It was damn near the stupidest idea he'd ever come up with—and he'd thought up some whoppers in his time.

But . . .

But it wasn't really stupid, was it? He wanted to pretend that such a notion was absurd, wanted to act as though he was being foolish by even considering a thought like that, but the truth was that he was being all too reasonable and realistic.

They were out there.

In the desert.

And they wanted him.

He knew it was true, though he didn't know how he knew, and even in the burgeoning warmth of this summer morning he felt cold, his skin suddenly alive with goose bumps. He was hard again, his erection tenting out the front of his boxers, and that also frightened him.

Ray Daniels lived in the next cabin down from his, but Ray was on duty today, as was Jill Kittrick, who bunked with her husband in one of the newer cottages farther up the road. Ordinarily, he enjoyed being alone and appreciated the solitude Canyonlands offered, but today it made him uneasy, and he decided to eat a quick breakfast and get his ass to town.

It would make him feel safer.

Moab was crowded.

It was always crowded in the summer months, what with the tourists to the national parks and the hordes of extreme cyclists who came from all over the country to off-road on the sandstone, but that usually thinned out after Labor Day. Today, though, the highway was one long traffic jam, and every parking lot seemed to be full. Henry was grateful for that. There was safety in numbers, and though he never thought he'd find himself echoing that trite cliché, those were words to live by now.

He got some gas, stopped by the grocery store for bread and cereal, beans and tortillas, then hit a couple of camping-supply stores to check out the latest gear. He saw some people he knew, stopped for a few moments to chat with each of them, got into a conversation about conservation with a family who'd been on one of his ranger talks out at the park yesterday, and, as planned, spent the sizzling lunch hour at an air-conditioned fast-food joint.

But still he didn't feel comfortable. He found himself looking at the Chinese restaurant with suspicion, eyeing a Japanese family with mistrust. He was not a bigoted man, never had been, but that dream—

nightmare
—had really thrown him off.

He drove around aimlessly for a while, then ended up spending two or three hours at the Boy Howdy Bar, one of his hangouts from the old days, content to nurse a couple of beers through the hottest part of the afternoon. He was settling up his tab and just getting ready to leave when his ear caught part of a conversation from two men at the opposite end of the counter.

". . . swear to God. It was a gook ghost. Someone he'd offed in the jungle, he figured, back in the war . . ."

Chills coursed down Henry's arms as he got his change from the bartender. He walked over to the two men. ". . . and it was crouching by the foot of his bed!"

"Excuse me," Henry said. "I couldn't help overhearing you."

The man closest, a fat guy with a beard and a Cat hat, frowned at him. "Yeah?"

"Was this . . . ghost you're talking about anywhere near Canyonlands? I mean, did it happen around the national park? Is that where your friend saw it?"

Cat hat snorted. "Omaha, dude."

"Oh." Henry backed off, turned around, ignoring the laughter that built behind him as he headed for the door. Outside, the sun was bright, too bright, and he blinked back tears as his eyes adjusted.

Angry.

It was not only the sun that was angry, he realized. Those two twins had been angry, too. Oh, they'd hidden it behind their nudity and their blatant sexuality, and it had taken him until now to realize it was even there, but behind the sensuous attitude was a seething anger, a terrifying rage.

And they were out in the desert somewhere.

Looking for him.

Henry shivered. He no longer saw the two women as figments of his imagination—if he ever had. The reason he had been so excited by the conversation of those men in the bar—

a gook ghost

—was because he believed that the naked twins were supernatural entities of some sort, spectral beings trying to contact him, and he'd briefly hoped that they'd appeared to someone else as well.

What the hell was wrong with him? Was he going crazy?

Henry had never in his life experienced anything like this. He was one of the rangers who made a specific effort to debunk "ancient astronaut" explanations of the cave drawings in Canyonlands rather than let visitors hold to their preconceived interpretations, and he would have thought that it would take multiple objectively verifiable sightings and hard documentation to convince him of the existence of anything as flaky as a "supernatural entity" or "spectral being." Yet he had rolled over like a backseat bimbo and after one confusing dream was now afraid to hike or drive the backcountry alone.

Indian genes again.

The alcohol had not strengthened his courage, had weakened it if anything, and he realized that he still did not want to return to his cabin. Ector was on duty at the visitors' center in Arches today; maybe he'd stop by there, shoot the breeze for a while. Ector was broad-minded, had been into that New Agey shit back in the 1980s. Maybe Henry would hint around about the naked Asian babes, test the waters. It couldn't hurt.

Feeling more confident now that he had a plan,

Henry got into his Jeep and turned onto the highway, heading north. But once outside the city limits, he kept his attention focused squarely on the highway, on the double lanes of blacktop, not looking at the desert, not wanting to see the sand, and it wasn't until he had pulled into the visitors' center parking lot and was faced with the building and the enveloping cliffs behind it that he was finally able to relax.

Three

Bear Flats, California

Sawdust and wood chips. The smell of sap and freshly cut trees. The fragrance of the forest permeated the air in town, and Jolene didn't realize until now how much she'd missed it. Even with the windows up, it seeped through the vent, a warm, welcoming, delicious scent that meant . . . home.

The highway sloped in a gentle curve past a new McDonald's and The Store, both of which had been built since her last visit three years ago. Downtown, Sam Griedy's Hardware had gained an Ace sign, the Chinese restaurant had been repainted and was now called Golden Palace instead of Jade Palace, but other than that, Bear Flats remained frozen in time, a small Sierra community virtually untouched by the wider world around it.

She liked that.

She counted on it.

She needed it.

"Are we there yet, Mom?"

Jolene glanced at Skylar in the backseat. As always, the expression on her son's face was serious, almost solemn. He looked at her with clear, sad eyes, patiently awaiting the answer to his question, and it was all she could do not to cry. She forced herself to smile at him. "We're almost there. We're almost at Grandma's house."

She'd sworn when she'd left Bear Flats that if she ever had a child, she would never subject him or her to the type of chaotic, emotionally unstable upbringing she'd had, but history really did repeat itself, and she now found herself returning home divorced and defeated with her son in tow, her son who had gone from being a happily gurgling little infant to a grave and overly sober boy as a result of the turmoil in their household the past few years.

He'd been through far too much for an eight-year-old child.

The past six months had been especially harsh. She and Frank had been at each other's throats every moment they were together, and though she knew it wasn't good for Skylar to be around such constant hostility and told herself after each blowup that she couldn't and wouldn't allow it to happen again, she and Frank were like oil and water, and not even concern for the welfare of their son could keep the two of them from going at it.

She wondered sometimes if they hadn't both been border guards, if they'd had separate jobs working for different companies and had seen each other only morning and night the way normal couples did, whether they would have gotten along better, whether the resentments and irritations that had escalated into hatred would have retreated back into minor annoyances. But they'd both worked out of the border patrol's Yuma office, and their differences had widened into gulfs with the pressures of the job, exacerbating problems that turned out to be not so trivial after all.

Seeing the same faces over and over, throwing people back like catch-and-release fish only to capture them trying to enter the country illegally yet again, had made her more sympathetic to the plight of the immigrants, whereas Frank had become hardened against them. She remembered talking to him after September 11. (She refused to use the appellation *9/11*. What was next, calling Christmas *12/25*? Referring to the Fourth of July as *7/4*? Where was this numbers madness going to end?) She'd told him they were lucky the hijackers had entered the country through Canada. "Could you imagine the hysteria if they'd come in from Mexico?"

He'd reacted with outrage, yelling at her, telling her that there were a lot *more* criminals entering through Mexico than Canada and who knew what kind of atrocities they had planned? It was lenient attitudes like hers, he said, that were weakening America's defenses. This was a racial thing with him, she realized, just as it was with a lot of people, and it was at that moment she understood that he was not the man she'd thought he was.

Still, she'd stuck it out, trying to make it work for Skylar's sake, remaining through the increasingly rancorous arguments, answering Frank's slaps with thrown dishes, knowing deep down that it was over but not able to make the break. It was not just Frank she hated, Jolene came to realize. It was their house; it was their friends; it was Arizona; it was her job; it was the border; it was everything in her life except Skylar.

The family in the gulch had been the last straw.

She had been the one who'd found them. It had been in a remote section of the Sonora far from Organ Pipe and the drug route where Frank and a team were patrolling. She'd gone off-road to follow a trace of a track that instinct told her might lead somewhere, and, though it was against regulations, had left her vehicle without radio authorization and continued on foot when she spotted what she thought was a coyote's trail marker. It turned out it wasn't.

And then she'd found the family.

There'd been three of them—a mother, a father, a little girl—and they'd been at the bottom of a gulch, arms around each other not as though they'd been huddling together for warmth but as though they'd fallen asleep in a gentle embrace and had simply never awakened. That had obviously been some time ago, however, for the bodies were desiccated, skin parchmentlike and horrendously wrinkled over visible skulls, ragged color-faded clothes flattened out against bony frames. The mechanics of the bodies had been clearly visible, a matter-of-fact breakdown of biological processes that was neither romantic nor mysterious but merely routine and distressingly physical.

It was impossible to tell what had killed them. The heat? The cold? Starvation? Dehydration? They were a good twenty miles from the border—at a point where the crossing would have been made without benefit of road or nearby town on the Mexican side—and likely they'd run out of food before they got this far, surviving for days perhaps on desert plants and captured rodents.

She'd stood there for a long time—*too* long—staring at the dead family, trying to imagine how it must have felt for them to end their lives here in this dry, terrible place. They hadn't died alone—they'd had one another—but in a way that must have been worse, because they couldn't have perished all at once. One of them would have had to go first, and Jolene imagined that it must have been the girl. They'd probably carried her as far as they could, hoping to find a house or a road or someone to help them, maybe even praying at the last for a patrol to find them so they could

be deported and thus saved. But they'd wandered farther and farther astray, and finally she imagined the
exhausted parents, unable to carry the girl any longer,
deciding to stay and wait for rescue, then gradually
giving up as they grew weaker and weaker, as their
daughter's body started to rot in the heat.

Who had gone next? And had the last one to die
simply cuddled against the others, praying for an end
to it all?

How long ago had that been? How long had they
lain here, undiscovered, unmourned? Years, it looked
like, and Jolene wondered if the hell they'd endured
back home, wherever that was, had been worth the
risk of death to them, if they would still have made
the trip if they'd known how it would turn out.

She decided then and there to take Skylar back with
her to Bear Flats. She didn't know if it was because
this family had risked all—and lost—and the only
thing she had to do in order to escape her life was
pack a few belongings, get in a car and drive; or
whether she was tired of seeing death and suffering
and human misery day in and day out as part of her
job. Maybe it was just the weariness she felt when she
thought of all the paperwork she'd have to fill out,
and the lack of understanding and interest she'd re-
ceive from a callous, uncaring Frank. Whatever the
reason, she'd turned in her resignation that afternoon,
effective immediately, no two weeks' notice, with the
resulting complete abdication of accrued benefits.
She'd gone home, packed a suitcase of clothes each
for herself and Skylar, loaded up the back of the
Blazer with some of her more personal and precious
possessions as well as most of his books and toys,
written a quick note to Frank, then picked up her son
at school and hit the road.

Now they were here.

Jolene drove past the lumber mill with its twin black chimney stacks, corrugated-tin outbuildings, and pyramids of logs stacked next to the side of the road, then, without thinking, navigating almost by sense memory, swerved down the sloping dirt alley behind the mill, bouncing onto Second Street. A quick turn onto Fir, and they were there.

She pulled to a stop on the gravel driveway next to her mother's beat-up Impala. The place looked the same as always, only more so. The paint on the small house was not only peeling but faded, and the twin T poles holding up the clothesline in the side yard were slanting so far over that Jolene doubted a full-length towel could dry on them without dragging on the ground. The porch was a mess of dead plants in broken pots.

"We're here!" she announced cheerfully to Skylar, feigning an optimism she did not feel. She kept an eye on the ripped screen door, waiting for it to open and her mother to appear, but the door remained closed, the inside of the house dark. "Unbuckle. Let's stretch our legs."

They both unfastened their seat belts and got out of the car. The air was cooler here than in Arizona, but more humid and filled with that wonderful sawmill smell. She felt more comfortable in the mountains than in the desert, more at home. It was as though this was where she belonged, and she wondered if the feelings Skylar was experiencing were along the same lines—or if he simply felt lost and uprooted. Probably the latter, and Jolene realized that it was her responsibility to make the transition easier for him.

The transition?

Yes. They were going to stay here.

She had no intention of going back to Arizona.

The two of them walked across the crunchy gravel

to the porch, where the peeling wood creaked and groaned beneath their weight. She'd called her mother yesterday from San Diego and told her they were on their way up, though she'd declined to elaborate on the reasons. Unless her mom was in the bathroom, she had to have seen the Blazer pull into the driveway and even if she *was* in the bathroom, she had to have heard their footsteps on the creaking porch. The fact that she had not come out to greet them did not bode well. Jolene rapped on the warped frame of the screen door. "It's me, Mom!" she called.

As always, the door was unlocked, and she pulled it open and walked in. Skylar took her hand, a sign of nervousness. He'd been here three years ago for a short visit, but Jolene was not sure how well he remembered it. Glancing around at the darkened room with its drab and well-worn furniture, she couldn't help comparing it with the bright sunniness of their place in Yuma, and she tried to see the house through Skylar's eyes. He probably thought the house was sad and depressing.

It was.

"We're here, Mom!" she announced.

Her mother emerged from the kitchen, wiping her hands on a dish towel. "About time. I expected you hours ago."

No hello for her, no hug for Skylar, no smile for either of them. She'd been in the kitchen, so she *had* seen the Blazer pull in.

"Frank called," her mother said accusingly.

Skylar looked up at her nervously, and Jolene squeezed his hand, held it tight. "I've decided to—" *Leave him,* was what she wanted to say, but that was a little harsh to announce in front of Skylar, and it would initiate a conversation with her mother that she didn't want to have right now. "—take a little time off," she said.

"That's not the way Frank put it."

"Mom, can we talk about this later?"

Her mother threw the dish towel over her shoulder, turned, headed back into the kitchen. "Whatever."

This was starting off badly, and for a brief moment, Jolene thought about walking straight out to the car and driving as fast as she could as far away from here as possible. But the truth was that she had nowhere else to go. She couldn't afford to stay in hotels for more than a week or two, didn't have enough for the rent and security deposit that an apartment would require, and didn't have any friends or relatives in far-flung locales who would put her up indefinitely. It was either Yuma or her mom.

"I don't think Grandma likes me anymore," Skylar whispered, looking at the empty kitchen doorway. His hand was hot and sweaty in hers.

Damn her, Jolene thought, but she smiled for her son's sake. "Of course she does. She's just busy, is all. Come on, let's go help her out."

Jolene strode confidently forward into the kitchen, where her mother was washing dishes in the sink. "Anything Skylar can help you with?" she asked.

Thankfully, her mother turned around, smiling, and motioned the boy over. "I'll wash. You dry. How does that sound?"

Skylar gave his grandmother a brief, hesitant smile, then accepted the dish towel from her hands.

Maybe it will be all right after all, Jolene thought. *Maybe this will work out.*

"It was *hell,*" Jolene whispered fiercely. "It wasn't good for me and it wasn't good for Skylar." She glanced instinctively toward the closed door of the guest bedroom—her old room—hoping that the boy really was asleep and not just pretending so he could listen in on the conversation.

"Frank said—"

"Frank lied, Mom! How many times do I have to tell you? Jesus!"

"He just seems like a good man to me."

"He is. In a way. But we're like oil and water—we don't mix. And it was only a matter of time before someone ended up in the hospital." She glanced again toward the door, lowered her voice even more. "And I had to make sure it wasn't Skylar!"

Her mother sighed. "I just hope you know what you're doing."

"Trust me, Mom." *I can't fuck things up any more than you did*, she wanted to add, but she kept that thought to herself.

"So what are your plans? Are you going to look for a job around here?"

"I don't know. I just got here. Give me a day at least to settle in and figure things out."

"You were on the road for a day and a half. That didn't give you time to think? You didn't—"

"Jesus, Mom. Can't you just try to be supportive for once in your life?"

They were silent after that, the two of them seated on opposite sides of the living room, glaring at each other, and Jolene felt like a kid again, as though she were back in high school and her mom was clamping down on her for one of those unfathomable and unexplained reasons.

Finally she stood, pretending to yawn and stretch. "I guess I'll go to bed. It's been a long day."

"Okay."

"See you in the morning, Mom."

"Good night."

"Good night."

"I'm glad you're back," her mother said without feeling.

"Yeah," Jolene lied. "Me, too."

Four

Dennis Chen finished loading the car and looked up at the roof rack. For the umpteenth time, he checked the ropes, pulling on them to make sure he'd tied everything down tight enough. From the porch, his mother watched silently, and he sensed her disapproval even though he couldn't see her from this angle. Inside the front seat of the Tempo, his sister, Cathy, was rearranging his glove compartment in order to fit in the traveler's first aid kit she'd given him.

Dennis was twenty-three years old, and he'd never been out of the greater Philadelphia area. He knew a lot of people like that, knew men and women even older than himself who'd never ventured more than fifty miles from their birthplace, who lived their entire lives within a proscribed radius, and he could think of nothing more depressing. That was *not* going to happen to him, and it was why he had decided to make this break and to do it while he was still relatively young and unencumbered.

He wanted to travel. Even as a boy, he'd felt the pull of the open road, and though his career aspirations had varied over the years, from train engineer in grammar school to truck driver in junior high to UN ambassador in high school, they all had one element in common: travel.

This was merely the realization of a long-delayed dream.

His mom had cried when he'd told her of his plans, and even though he'd pointed out that she and his dad had traveled halfway around the world to get here, uprooting themselves from their families, their friends, their culture and even their language, she did not seem to understand the parallels. In her mind, what he was planning was a lot more foolish and dangerous.

She'd been working on him for the past month, trying to get him to cancel his trip. "Your job!" she kept telling him in Cantonese. "You can't quit your job!"

But the truth was that people quit jobs all the time, especially in his business. He'd been working for a rental-car agency for the past three years, ever since dropping out of college to his mother's great shame and embarrassment, and he'd worked his way up to manager, not through any great skill or aptitude or commitment or desire, but because he was still there. Amid a turnover rate that averaged about one employee every four months, his staying power had marked him as stable and reliable, and the owner of the franchise had promoted him up the short ladder to manager.

Managing a rental-car office had never been his career goal, however. It had been only a way to earn money while he figured out what he wanted to do with his life. And since he lived at home and had minimal expenses, he'd been able to save quite a lot over the past few years—enough to get him across country at least. If things didn't work out, he could always come back, but for now he was free, and the feeling was liberating.

He just wished his dad could be here to see this.

And to help him with the packing.

He checked the ropes again.

"Don't forget to keep your cell phone charged," Cathy said from inside the car. "And keep it *on*! You always forget to turn it on."

"I will," he promised.

She emerged from the door on the passenger side, having found room for the first aid kit. "Who knows what kind of wackos are out there? We need to be able to get in touch with you, and you need to be able to call the police."

"Don't go!" their mother cried in Cantonese. "Stay here!"

"Mom'll be okay," Cathy promised.

"Thank you," Dennis said sincerely. He and his sister never really spoke seriously, never had the sort of heart-to-hearts that siblings were probably supposed to have, but he thought now that maybe they didn't need to. They understood these things automatically, knew without saying what the other was thinking, instinctively grasped the real intent behind superficial discussions.

He was going to miss Cathy more than he'd thought.

"If you strike it rich at the Gold Mountain, we're coming to live with you," she said.

Chinese humor.

He pulled on the roof-rack ropes, just for something to do. He was finished packing, there was no real reason for him to remain, and it was already after two. It was time for him to go, but there seemed something *small* about such a departure. He was completely uprooting his life, seismically disrupting the lives of his mother and sister. Simply saying good-bye, getting into the car and driving away seemed like an anticlimactic way to recognize the event. He couldn't help thinking that his farewell should be more momentous. But he'd said good-bye to his friends yesterday, and his only family was here with him now, in front of the row house.

They were not a family that was demonstrably emotional, that went in for public displays of affection. Nevertheless, he walked over to his mom and gave her a big hug. She was stiff against him and small. He could feel the bones beneath her clothes and skin, and he realized for the first time how fragile she was.

How old.

It shocked him, and the sadness that followed the shock almost made him reconsider. Who knew how much time she had left? Was it really fair of him to abandon her like this? Was it fair to himself to squander the remaining time they had together? He let go of his mom, stepped back.

But then Cathy was hugging him, taking the initiative, and her embrace was excited, exuberant, and he knew once again that he'd made the right decision. He hugged her back tightly, with meaning, and he promised himself that if things did go well for him, he *would* send for them.

"Drive carefully," Cathy told him. "And keep your cell phone on."

"I know, I know."

His mother made him promise to call them every night at seven, no matter where he was or what he was doing, and he said he would. He was exhilarated to be setting out on his own, but at the same time it seemed good—it seemed right—to maintain the tether.

The time had come, and he got into the car, waving. Tears were rolling down Cathy's face, and to his surprise, his mother was crying as well. His own vision was blurring, so, deciding to speed things up, he started the engine, shouted out good-bye in Cantonese and with a quick wave was off.

He forced himself to concentrate on the traffic, on the route, on the specific series of steps that would get him to the interstate, purposely not thinking of his mother and his sister and what he was leaving behind.

By the time he was on Route 76, though, heading west, he was thinking about the future rather than the past, and sadness had given way to anticipation. It felt good to be on the highway, traveling, and he pushed in a mix CD that he'd made just for the occasion, old-school rock songs that dealt with travel and the open road and the lure of new places.

He had no destination, not really, but something seemed to be *calling* to him out there. He could admit it to himself now that he was alone. Yes, he wanted to travel, and yes, he was using this journey for the clichéd objective of "finding himself." But there was something else as well, something more, a purpose to this trip, though he did not yet know what it was. He'd had a dream the other night about driving down a desert road into a wall of smoke. Within the smoke, he could see eyes, hundreds of them, Chinese eyes, staring out at him, filled with a malevolence that scared him. Above the wall of smoke, as tall as the sky, rose a dark figure with a triangular head that beckoned him forward.

Dennis was not, by any stretch of the imagination, a religious person. His mom was Buddhist, as had been his dad, but he and his sister were nothing. They'd grown up amid Christians and Jews, had watched Christmas specials and hunted for Easter eggs at the park with their friends and were steeped in the Western religious traditions of American society, but the two of them had fallen through the cracks, neither fish nor fowl, and as they'd had no formal training in any religion, only this sort of peripheral exposure, nothing had ever taken. They'd never felt the need to explore any of these theories or philosophies in depth, never required an overarching theory of supernatural causation to get along in the world. They'd been perfectly happy to trust in the rational workings of a natural world without anthropomorphizing the laws of science.

But . . . .

But he had the sense now that there *was* some sort of ultimate purpose to his journey, that there *was* an unknown element pulling him on, and while that should have made him feel uncomfortable, it didn't.

It made him anxious to get out there.

Smiling, pushing his old car to seventy-five in order to keep up with the flow of traffic, he headed west.

Dennis tried to run, but the man with the bat swung hard against the back of his legs, bringing him down in a wild explosion of unimaginable agony. The man was screaming at him in English, but it seemed like a foreign language and Dennis couldn't understand a word of what his pursuer was saying. The bat came down again, this time against the small of his back, and Dennis heard something crack, *felt* something crack, and suddenly his legs no longer worked. His arms were dragging deadweight as he tried to right himself.

In the distance, he could hear a train, its lonesome whistle sounding ghostly in the moonless night. Above, crows flapped, moving back and forth, forth and back, cawing, their cries like mocking laughter.

The man slammed a booted foot down on his head, grinding cheek and forehead, ear and eye, into the hard dirt. He said something else in his nonsense English, something low and serious, something *final,* and Dennis tensed up, waiting for the end.

He awoke drenched in sweat, feeling not as though he'd escaped from a nightmare but as though he'd survived an actual attack. His muscles ached, even his bones were sore, and he got out of bed and walked over to the motel window, pushing aside the curtain and looking out. He was in some small city in western Pennsylvania—he didn't even know the name of it— and though he was well aware that his funds were finite, he'd forgone several smaller, dirtier independent motels in favor of the more expensive Holiday Inn because of cleanliness and comfort and habit. He knew he would have to change that attitude if he expected to survive for any length of time out here, but this first night, he wanted to cling to some semblance of normalcy.

The thing was, the beating he'd dreamed about had occurred right here, where the Holiday Inn was standing. Only it had been years ago, decades maybe, and the motel hadn't been there. Instead, it had been some sort of steel yard or lumberyard. Did he feel so guilty for staying at this overpriced motel that he was mentally beating himself up about it? He didn't think so. Neither did he think he'd had some sort of random nightmare. He had the feeling that there was meaning here, that he was tapping into something.

Dennis smiled slightly. He'd become awfully self-important since leaving home.

On the other side of the highway, a train went by, a freight train, and he shivered at the sound of its whistle, an echo from his dream.

It was a long way to morning, but he did not feel tired. If he hadn't already paid for the room and it hadn't been so expensive, he would've packed up his stuff right now and taken off. The idea of night driving appealed to him. But he owed it to his mom and Cathy to act responsibly, and he didn't want a cop to come across his mangled corpse on some back road after he'd fallen asleep and crashed into a tree, and then call his mom to tell her he was dead. No, he'd stay here, wait until morning, try to go back to sleep.

That was easier said than done, however, and he ended up watching the last half of an *Emmanuelle* movie on HBO before finally dozing off.

He'd been planning to get an early start in the morning, but he didn't awaken until after nine, and by the time he showered, shaved, packed and availed himself of the complimentary breakfast, it was nearly ten thirty.

He didn't leave Pennsylvania until after noon.

Five

Flagstaff, Arizona

College life was great!

Angela had never suspected it would be anything less, but NAU had exceeded her most optimistic expectations. Northern Arizona University had been on the short list of colleges offering scholarships that would give her enough money to actually attend the school, and when she'd come here with her parents to visit, she'd been very impressed with the scenic beauty of the Flagstaff area. The campus itself had been impressive as well, all red brick and vine-covered rock, its streets fronted by wrought iron gates, and it had looked to her more like an Eastern Ivy League campus than the cow town college she'd been expecting. Indeed, even after she'd seen Cal Poly, San Luis Obispo, in central California, the University of New Mexico in Albuquerque and the University of Nevada in Reno, it was NAU that had remained in her mind, and gut instinct told her that this would be a good place to attend school.

It was more than good. Her initial impressions had been correct—there was definitely a hippieish vibe to the place, and she thought that was wonderful. The competitiveness of Los Angeles, the fractious tribalism with which she'd grown up, was nowhere in evidence, and instead the mood was mellow, casual, live-and-let-live, an attitude and lifestyle that immediately made her feel comfortable.

Oh, she had a few minor quibbles. Sports seemed to be far too big a deal here, particularly for a university with no nationally ranked team, but as Chrissie had said, the winters were harsh, and since NAU had a domed stadium, attending sporting events was one of the few social options open for students during the cold months. Although Angela swore otherwise, Chrissie promised her that by the first week in December, she, too, would be gratefully attending a football game.

But she just loved her fellow Babbitt House residents. And the homesickness she'd been expecting had never materialized. She and Chrissie had bonded instantly and despite their divergent backgrounds had become, in a matter of weeks, the closest of friends. While Angela still regularly called and e-mailed her friends back home, lately it had been more out of obligation than necessity because she was as happy here as she'd ever been back in L.A. Winston and Brock were great, like her own *Queer Eye* team navigating the world of college and Arizona for her. She didn't know Drew and Lisa that well, a married couple who were both grad students and lived at the end of the upstairs hall—they pretty much kept to themselves—but Randy, who lived alone in the apartment next to theirs, and Kelli and Yurica, who had the other downstairs apartment, were all nice and were quickly becoming friends.

She'd even met someone.

His name was Brian Oakland, he was from Milwaukee, Wisconsin, and he was a junior majoring in forestry. He wasn't exactly what she thought of as her type—not that she *had* a type—but he was interesting and attractive, and the two of them had hit it off instantly. They'd been on only one date, nothing hot and heavy, so it was too early to call what they had a relationship, but the date had gone well, they'd already scheduled another, and they were spending an awful lot of time on the phone. She hadn't told her parents yet, figuring it was better to be safe than sorry. She planned to go home for Thanksgiving, and if she and Brian were still seeing each other by then, she'd tell them about him. But if they weren't . . . well, then it was better for her parents not to know anything had happened at all.

Besides, he wasn't even Catholic.

She was still trying to think of a way to break that to them.

Of course, they'd be shocked if they heard some of the discussions she and her new friends had about religion. Just last night, Winston and Brock had invited her and Chrissie over for a potluck dinner. She'd made a salad, Chrissie a Mississippi mud pie, and Winston and Brock had come up with a spectacular seafood pasta dish. Afterward, they lounged around on the overstuffed living room furniture, and Angela asked Chrissie why she thought some people made religion the bedrock of their lives while other people had no need of religion at all, why her parents, for example, thought about God constantly while Chrissie didn't even believe he existed. She always felt more comfortable talking about this subject with other people around, although she wasn't sure why. Maybe it kept things from getting too personal, gave her an easy out if the talk turned uncomfortable.

Chrissie shrugged. "Well, I think a lot of people are like children. They can't control themselves or behave in a rational, civilized manner, so they have to be threatened with punishment from Daddy in order to bring them in line. It's why so many screwups and alcoholics and drug addicts become religious. They need to think that they'll be punished after they die or else they'll just keep on doing what they're doing. They have to be *ordered* to behave."

Every time Chrissie said something like that, Angela was shocked anew. Part of her completely understood what her friend was saying and even agreed with some of it. But part of her recoiled, expecting a bolt of lightning to strike Chrissie dead at any second.

"Maybe those people really are saved. Maybe God helps them turn their lives around."

"Then why's there so much recidivism? How come God can't save all of them all the time?"

"Religion does help a lot of people," Angela said. "It gives them faith, gives them hope. . . ."

"Yeah, but I just don't believe there's an invisible man in the sky monitoring your every move and taking notes so he can punish or reward you after you die, an invisible man so petty and vain that if you don't kiss his ass every Sunday, he'll let you burn in hell for all eternity."

"Leave her alone," Winston said.

"She brought it up," Chrissie pointed out.

"I did," Angela admitted, "although I wasn't trying to start an argument or convert anyone or anything. I was just curious."

"I came from a religious family, too," Winston confided. "So I know where you're coming from."

"He just ran like hell from it when he found out that God hated him and he was going to burn forever because he loved men," Brock said, grinning.

Winston pushed him. "Infidel."

It was time to change the subject.

"So," Angela said, "tell me about the ghost."

Winston and Brock looked at each other.

"Come on! Chrissie told me this house was haunted, and she said you guys're the experts. You're the ones who've had a close encounter."

"Encounter*s*," Brock said quietly.

Winston sighed. "I know this sounds ridiculous. Believe me, I'm not some hippie-dippie, fuzzy-headed New Age touchy-feely guy—"

Brock raised an eyebrow.

"Okay, I am. But I never believed in ghosts before moving here. Didn't even have an open mind. As far as I was concerned, they were figments of gullible, overactive imaginations."

"But you believe now," Chrissie said in a low spooky voice.

"Laugh all you want, but yes, I do." He glanced at Brock. "We both do."

Brock nodded.

"The first time we heard it, we were sitting right here, in this room. Dan Hamlyn, who used to live in Kelli and Yurica's place a few semesters back, was with us. We'd just finished watching a movie. And, no, not a scary one. A comedy. *Mother,* I think, the Albert Brooks movie. I was gathering up the glasses and the popcorn bowls, Dan was getting ready to leave, and we heard *moaning* from the kitchen."

Brock's nodding became more emphatic. "Like someone was in pain, like he'd been hit in the head or something."

"Although we weren't sure it was a he. It could've been a she. It was impossible to tell."

"Scared the hell out of us, though, and all three of us hurried into the kitchen to see what it was."

Angela glanced toward the closed kitchen door. She wanted to feel frightened, but she didn't. She liked a good ghost story as well as the next person, but there was something about the telling of this tale that was too pat, that made her think it had been concocted for her benefit.

"Of course there was nothing there," Winston said. "The room was empty, and the window was closed. We searched the whole apartment, but there was no one here except us.

"The next time it happened was morning, I believe. Last winter. It was still dark out, but it wasn't that early. Six o'clock or something. I remember I was already up and eating a bagel because I had an early class."

"This time it came from the linen closet," Brock said. "And we *knew* no one could be hiding in there because it's barely big enough for a couple of sheets and our towels."

Winston chimed in. "It was like mumbling or muttering but really fast and really high-pitched. Gibberish. We couldn't make out a word of it. The creepy thing was that it didn't stop. We opened the closet door, tossed everything out on the floor, and it was still there. It wasn't coming from *behind* the closet, or above it or below it or anything. It was right there in front of us, like the ghost who was doing it was right in front of us and we couldn't see it. Scared the hell out of me, let me tell you."

"And that's it?" Angela asked.

"It's happened a couple of times since, but, yeah, that's pretty much it. I know it doesn't sound like much, and you probably think it's sound seeping in from another apartment or something, but I'm telling you, it's eerie. You can *feel* it. We hadn't even heard anything about this, but I started doing a little research and found out that this house is listed on a national registry of haunted places. Supposedly, it's the reason no one would buy the place and why they had to subdivide it into apartments. After I approached the owners with this news, the rent was dropped—on the condition that we keep our mouths shut about it. We have, pretty much, but word still leaked out, and one girl even moved because of it."

"Jen," Chrissie said.

"Yeah. Jen. She said she *saw* something in her bedroom, though I'm not sure she did. I'm pretty sure she just imagined it."

Angela smiled. "*Her* ghost is imagination. *Yours* is real, though."

"That's about the size of it."

"Well, call me the next time he—or *she*—shows up. I want to hear it."

"You don't," Winston said. "But I will."

The opportunity to do so came more quickly than any of them expected.

Angela and Chrissie returned to their own apartment soon after. It was getting late, so they flipped a coin for first shower. Angela won, and she quickly washed and changed into her pajamas. After saying good night to Chrissie, she went to bed and was asleep in a matter of minutes.

She was awakened by a knock on the bedroom door, and she had time to glance groggily at the clock on her nightstand and see that it was two fifteen before the knock came again, louder this time. She got up, pulled on her robe and opened the door a crack. Chrissie stood in the short hallway, holding her own robe closed, looking half-asleep. Behind her, through the living room, Angela could see that the front door of the apartment was open. Winston was standing in the outer hall, hair disheveled, wearing only light green drawstring pants. He saw her, and the expression on his face caused her heart to skip a beat, sent a bolt of fear through her body. She knew what he was going to say even before he said it.

"The ghost. It's down there right now. You want to hear it?"

She didn't. Not at this time of night. Despite her skepticism and the lightheartedness of their previous conversation, the idea of encountering a ghost was given weight and gravity by the hour, a seriousness it did not possess in the daytime or early evening. She was frightened, but she was the one who'd brought it up, she was the one who'd made the request, and she swallowed hard, nodded. "Are you coming?" she asked Chrissie. The other girl shook her head, and Angela could tell that despite her professions of disbelief, her friend was frightened as well.

Angela followed Winston downstairs, where several other residents were already gathered around his apartment's open front door. Most were in their sleepwear, but despite the potential for casual camaraderie, no one was talking or visiting and the expression on each face was the same. Everyone was silent, expectant, on edge.

She heard it.

The sound was muffled from here in the hallway, but it was still audible, and it was definitely coming from somewhere inside. Goose bumps popped up on her arms and legs; peach-fuzz hair on the back of her neck bristled. An unintelligible babbling, an incomprehensible alien jabber, issued from the apartment behind the open door. Winston led her past Randy, Kelli and Yurica, into the living room, into the kitchen. "Come in, everyone!" he announced. "Catch it quick before it stops!"

He was trying for a party atmosphere, attempting to keep things light and fun, but Angela could see that he was scared, and by the tense clinging way Brock held his hand, she knew that Brock felt the same. Everyone else was silent, listening, afraid to speak.

The ghost's voice was as flat as ordinary conversation yet at the same time as sharp as an audiophile CD. It was high-pitched, sounding either angry or excited, and Winston and Brock were right: it was impossible to tell if it was male or female. It seemed to be coming from the oven, and while that should have been funny, it wasn't. Although ghosts were supposed to be ephemeral, Angela had the sense that the owner of the voice had been here forever, that although the house had been built around it and furniture brought in, these were the things that were transitory, and the voice would remain long after the oven had been removed and the house torn down.

All of a sudden it stopped.

No one knew what, if anything, was being said, but the voice seemed to cut off in midsentence, and after such hyperactive gibbering the silence seemed heavy and ringing in Angela's ears.

"Show's over, folks!" Winston announced, still trying to keep the tone light. But no one was having any of it, and the residents drifted away, back to their rooms, quiet and subdued. Winston caught Angela's eye, and she understood now how shallow and cavalier she'd been earlier in the evening, how she'd completely misread the situation. She wished she'd stayed upstairs with Chrissie, that she'd immediately gone back to sleep and experienced none of this. But she *had* experienced it, and now she was afraid to even walk back up to their apartment, afraid of what she might hear in the walls on the way, afraid of what she might see in the shadows darkening the top of the steps.

Winston and Brock obviously sensed her mood because they both accompanied her upstairs, acting as bodyguards. They saw and heard nothing, however, and when the three of them reached her apartment, Chrissie opened the door. "So?" she asked.

Angela didn't know what to say.

"It was coming from the oven," Brock said.

"Did you . . . see anything?"

They all shook their heads. "Just the voice," Winston said. "As always."

Angela turned toward Winston, tried to smile. "I'd like to say thank you for a good time, but . . ."

"See you in the morning," Winston said as he and Brock turned away and started back down the stairs.

Angela walked into the apartment, Chrissie closing and locking the door behind her. "Was it scary?" Chrissie asked.

She nodded. "Yeah," she admitted. "It was." She didn't want to talk about it, didn't want to even think about it, so she forced a yawn and, wiggling her fingers good-night, retired to her room.

Where she lay in bed, unable to sleep.

Chrissie went into her room, and in the other apartments everyone else settled back down for the night, but Angela remained awake, listening for any sound in the now silent house, her body rife with gooseflesh at the recollection of that insane incomprehensible babbling. What was it? What caused it? What did it mean?

Those were all questions for which she had no answer, for which *no one* had an answer, and when she finally did fall asleep she dreamed of a black gelatinous creature with no eyes and too many teeth that lived under the Babbitt House and waited for her.

Her second date with Brian was the next night, and though she longed to tell him about the ghost, she didn't. It was too embarrassing. She knew it had happened, knew what she'd heard, but outside of the Babbitt House, in the ordinary world of cars and other people and stores and restaurants, any account of her experience would sound ridiculous.

But it was on her mind all through dinner and the movie afterward. Brian could obviously tell that something was amiss, but he didn't know her well enough to butt in, and he chose to give her some space. For that, she was grateful. She perked up enough for a make-out session in the car, and on the way home she took the initiative to ask *him* out to a free jazz concert on Friday. He seemed surprised, and she wasn't sure if that was because she was being so forward—he *was* from Wisconsin—or whether he'd simply assumed from her behavior that she wasn't interested, but he happily said yes.

Angela didn't know how Brian felt, but as far as she was concerned, they were practically boyfriend and girlfriend. Such a concept seemed quaint and maybe even a little lame in these days of the hookup, which was why she didn't mention it, but sometime, and soon, they were going to have to talk about exclusivity.

He brought her back to the Babbitt House, parking on the street in front of the open lawn. At night, set back as it was, the mansion looked scary, forbidding. There were no lights on as far as she could tell, but it was Wednesday and it wasn't that late, so she knew someone had to be home.

What if they weren't?

"Would you like to come in?" she offered, hoping the nervousness wouldn't register in her voice.

"Yeah," he said. "That'd be great."

They got out of the car, and she took his arm, grateful for the support. She didn't think of herself as some dainty little maiden who needed the protection of a big strong man, but walking into a dark haunted house all by herself wasn't exactly something she relished doing. Brian was talking easily, casually, but all of her attention was on the front of the Victorian building as they strode up the endless lawn. She thought she saw movement in the upper right window—Randy's apartment—but the window remained dark, and she didn't like that. It was probably something ordinary and innocent, but in this mood her mind turned it into something completely wrong: Randy naked and spying on her . . . a murderer who had killed Randy . . . a ghost.

They reached the front entrance. Angela withdrew her key, used it to unlock the door.

The entryway was pitch-black.

"Careful!" Winston's voice called from the darkness. He emerged from his apartment, shining a flashlight on the floor so they could see where they were walking. "The power went out. Brock's checking the circuit breakers out back."

"What happened?" Angela asked.

"We don't know. The streetlights are on and none of the other houses on the street seem to be affected, so it's probably just the old crappy wiring in this place. Maybe too many computers or microwaves were on at once."

At that second, the lights came back on, as did televisions and stereos from the various apartments. All of a sudden, the house was filled with life, and Angela let out a deep breath, her muscles relaxing. She didn't realize how tense and anxious she'd been. Brian seemed embarrassed. Kelli was coming down the hall, Chrissie down the stairs, and Winston was still standing in the doorway of his apartment, flashlight in hand.

"Maybe I should go," Brian said.

There'd be no privacy here tonight, so Angela nodded. "Yeah, it's getting late."

"I'll call you tomorrow."

In front of the crowd, she gave him an awkward kiss good night, then waved as she watched him walk across the lawn to the street. She closed the door after he got into his car.

"How did it go?" Chrissie asked.

Angela thought for a moment, then smiled. "Pretty good," she said. But through the open doorway of Winston and Brock's apartment, she could see the kitchen on the other side of the living room. She recalled that alien babble and shivered.

"Come on," she said. "Let's go upstairs. I'll tell you all about it."

Six

Jolene and Skylar walked through town, checking out the small shops, dropping in at the library, getting themselves acquainted with Bear Flats. Or, in Jolene's case, reacquainted. Her mom had wanted to watch Skylar, but as long as there was alcohol in the house, Jolene was not about to leave her son alone with his grandmother. The boy'd had a tough enough time of it already without putting him through *that*. She'd told her mother as much, and that had led to an argument, and Jolene had no doubt that the old woman was hitting the bottle right now. By the time they returned, Skylar's nice grandma would be gone, replaced with the same nasty bitter woman Jolene had grown up with.

She really did need to find somewhere else to live.

But it *was* good to be back in town.

Holding Skylar's hand, she crossed the highway to Mag's Ham Bun, where her mom had told her Leslie Finch was now manager. She and Leslie had been best friends in high school, but despite a few short phone calls and promises to get together when she came back to visit, they hadn't seen each other in . . . how long? Six years? Eight?

Jolene pushed open the heavy oak door of the restaurant and stood for a moment in the foyer while she waited for her eyes to adjust to the darkness. It was eleven o'clock, too early for the lunch crowd, and the place was nearly empty. One old man sat at the bar, nursing a beer, and what looked like a family of tourists were looking over menus in the first booth along the wall, but other than that, the restaurant appeared to be unoccupied.

"Do you want to eat here?" Jolene asked.

Skylar shrugged. "Sure."

A freestanding sign announced PLEASE SEAT YOUR-SELF, so they did, choosing a booth halfway down from the tourist family. The waitress who greeted them and passed out menus a few moments later was elderly and unfamiliar. Jolene asked her, "Does Leslie Finch work here?"

"Leslie!" the waitress called out, nearly making her jump.

Leslie Finch emerged from the short dark hallway that led to the restrooms and the kitchen, looking not like a small-town waitress but like a successful young businesswoman. Maybe it was the dim lighting, but to Jolene's eyes, Leslie appeared to be only a few years older than she had in high school. She still had the same trim figure, and though her hair was shorter and cut more stylishly, it was the same wavy brown it had been when they were teenagers. Leslie looked a hell of a lot better than she herself did, and Jolene was at once pleased and embarrassed.

"Oh, my God!" Leslie said as she approached the table. "Jo? Is that you?"

At least she was still recognizable. Jolene smiled. "Yeah. It's me."

"And is this your little guy?"

"This is Skylar." She prodded him gently with an elbow. "This is my friend Ms. Finch. Say hello."

"Hi," the boy said shyly.

"Hi, Skylar. How old are you?"

"Eight." He turned back toward Jolene. "Could I have a Coke?"

"You have milk or lemonade." She smiled at Leslie. "Are you busy? Do you have time?"

"No, I'm not, and yes, I do. Can I join you?"

"I was hoping you would. I thought we could catch up on old times."

"Or new times." Leslie beckoned over the waitress. "Do you know what you guys want to order?" she asked Jolene.

"Grilled cheese sandwich and lemonade," Skylar announced.

"Okay," Jolene told him. She smiled at Leslie. "Pick something for me. You know what's good here."

The waitress returned, they gave their orders, and Leslie informed them in a voice that brooked no argument that the meal would be on the house. "So what brings you back?" she asked as the waitress left.

Jolene did not want to go into detail, not with her son sitting here, so she looked meaningfully at Leslie, shot a sideways glance at Skylar, then looked at her friend again with an expression that she hoped the other woman would be able to read. "I'm making a few changes," she said simply.

Leslie nodded, let it lie, and Jolene could tell that her friend understood.

They were still in sync after all these years.

The conversation shifted to neutral topics: old acquaintances, the restaurant, the town. Leslie assured her as their food arrived that the character of Bear

Flats had not changed one whit in the intervening years. "Oh, it's the same as it always was. Everyone's stunningly uninformed, depressingly small-minded and bitterly jealous of . . . well, everyone else."

Jolene laughed.

"So why am I still here, right?" Leslie shook her head as she dipped a french fry in ketchup. "I ask myself that every day. Part of it's just . . . inertia. It's easier, more comfortable, the devil you know and all that. The coward's way out, I know, but you kind of get used to things the way they are, and it gets harder and harder to change. I often wish that I'd done what you did, just taken off for greener pastures and not looked back."

"It's not all it's cracked up to be."

Again, Leslie let that lie, and for that, Jolene was grateful. The two of them needed to talk later, she thought. *Really* talk. There was so much she wanted to say.

"You look like you're doing well, though," Jolene offered.

Leslie smiled. "By Bear Flats standards, yeah. And I'm not unhappy. I'm just . . . restless sometimes, you know?"

"Yeah."

"So how's your mom doing?"

Jolene shrugged. "The same."

"Are you staying with her?"

"For the moment."

"Ah, the old dynamics never change, do they?"

"Not really," she admitted.

"You could always bunk with me while you're in town. I have plenty of room."

"Lezzie Finch!" Jolene said in a tone of mock shock.

Leslie threw a napkin at her. "I can't believe you remember that!"

Both of them laughed. The frustrated boys on the varsity football team had dubbed her "Lezzie" their senior year because two of them had asked her out and she'd turned them down. It was a nickname that had spread rapidly through Bear Flats High. Jolene's own sexuality had been called into question because of her friendship with Leslie and her complete disdain for nearly everyone and everything in Bear Flats— including the boys. Not that she'd cared. One advantage of having no respect for your peers was that it removed the power of peer pressure.

"So are you back permanently," Leslie asked, "or just here for a visit?"

Jolene glanced at Skylar. "That's up in the air."

Her friend nodded.

They finished eating, going into more detail about people they'd known in high school and what had become of them. A few more patrons had come into the restaurant while they ate, but the place was by no means crowded, and Jolene asked, "Is business always this slow?"

"Lately," Leslie admitted. "That new McDonald's is killing us. It's the off-season, though. Once the mill's at full capacity and people are employed again, things'll pick up." She downed the last of her iced tea. "Why don't the two of you stop by my house? I'd love to show it to you. You're not in any hurry to get back, are you?"

"No," Jolene said. "But can you afford to take time off?" She leaned forward conspiratorially. "That waitress is already mad at you. She keeps looking over here."

Leslie laughed. "Audra? That's just the way she is.

Don't sweat it. Besides, this is a special occasion. And, conscientious worker that I am, I have enough sick and vacation time saved up to take a cruise to China. I practically live in this building. Come on, it'll just take twenty minutes or so. If there's a problem here, I have my cell. They can reach me."

Jolene nodded, smiling. "Okay. Sounds great."

Leslie went over to talk to their waitress and the other employees before heading back to her office. "I'll meet you outside!" she called out. "It'll just be a moment!"

Jolene took out three dollars for a tip and left it on the table. Their meal might be comped, but she still didn't want to stiff the waitress. Skylar used his straw to suck up the last of his lemonade, and the two of them walked outside to wait. After the dimness of the restaurant, the world seemed impossibly bright, and they were both still blinking when Leslie emerged from the building. She was wearing sunglasses, obviously an old hand at this transition thing.

"I'm just over there on Bluebird Lane, past the Presbyterian church. We could drive, but I usually like to walk. Would that be okay? I take a shortcut through the woods behind Ray's."

Jolene laughed. "Is that the path where we used to—?"

"The very one."

"With the graves?"

"Yep."

"Graves?" Skylar said worriedly. It was the first time he'd spoken since ordering his lunch.

"It's daytime," Jolene reassured him. "And we'll just be passing by. Besides, I'm here." She took his hand and squeezed it, and he squeezed back. These days, he usually considered himself too old to be holding his mom's hand, especially in public, but he did not let go as the two of them followed Leslie across the small parking lot and down the sidewalk.

The path had hardly changed. It no longer started in a vacant lot, beginning instead in the narrow empty space between two recently erected buildings, but once she was off the street, everything was familiar. Jolene could not recall the last time she'd been here, but her feet remembered the details and idiosyncrasies of the trail as though it were yesterday, automatically stepping over a half-buried boulder protruding from the hard-packed earth, skirting to the left to avoid a sticker bush around the first bend. She would have expected the trees and underbrush to have become overgrown or burned or cut down or changed in some way—and perhaps they had—but to her eye everything looked exactly the same. The old oak they'd christened the hanging tree silhouetted against the midday sun, the line of knotty pines that delineated the upper and lower halves of the town, the view of the sawmill's smokestack above the woods—everything was just as she remembered it.

Leslie in the lead, they walked through the forested area just above Bluebird Lane. Ahead, in the darkest part of the copse, Jolene could see a square of white picket fence set off from the trail on a small sunken section of ground. Within that square, she knew, were two graves with their weathered granite tombstones reading simply, *Mother* and *Daughter*. The graves had been there since before anyone in town could remember, and the rumor had always been that the unnamed mother and daughter were witches. Why else hadn't they been buried in the pioneer cemetery with everyone else? Why else were their names unmentioned on the gravestones? Generations of kids had frightened their siblings, their friends and themselves making up stories about this trail and the grave site, and Jolene and Leslie had been no different. One summer in junior high, they'd even teamed with Jimmy Payton and Cal Smyth and charged a quarter for fake haunted tours. They'd taken kids down the path, making up stories about gruesome events that they said had happened at various spots, culminating in a trip to the grave site, where Jimmy, dressed in black and wearing a mask, had jumped out from behind a tree and sent everyone running screaming up the trail the way they'd come.

The four of them had made over twenty dollars that summer.

"Want to know something freaky?" Leslie asked as they passed by the picket fence. "I've *heard* shit from there." She glanced quickly at Skylar. "Stuff, I mean. I've heard *stuff*. Sorry," she told Jolene. "I didn't—"

"It's nothing he hasn't heard from his father," Jolene said. She looked at Skylar. "But that's still a bad word, right?"

"I know, Mom."

"Okay."

"Anyway," Leslie said, "I know you're not going to believe me, but every once in a while I walk by here—and it's not even night, sometimes it's in the middle of the day like now—and I hear . . . I don't know, like, mumbling or something. Chanting. The first time, I thought it was the wind or sound carrying up from the street, some sort of aural illusion. I even thought it might be a trick, some kid's high-tech version of our haunted tour; I thought there might be a hidden speaker with a tape loop or something. But the second time, I was brave, and I walked over and . . ." She took a deep breath. "It was definitely coming from one of the graves. I couldn't tell which one. I just ran."

It was not hard for Jolene to believe. She looked to the left. Even in the daytime, the grave site exuded an aura of dread, and although she was a grown woman, she felt the same way she had as a child and as a teenager, experienced the same sense of irrational foreboding. She'd forgotten that feeling, and she wished now that they'd driven, that Skylar had not seen the grave site. She glanced down at him. As always, his expression was unreadable, serious, grave.

Grave.

"How many times have you heard things?" she asked.

"Four," Leslie admitted.

"And you still walk this way?"

"Yeah. But it's been a while since the last one. And it's not all that scary after the first few times. You kind of get used to it."

Still, they were silent until they were past the site, until the square of white pickets had been swallowed by bushes and weeds and could no longer be seen behind them.

"Who paints that fence?" Jolene asked. "Did anybody ever figure that out?"

"Good question," Leslie said. "I don't know the answer. Maybe someone does, but it's not general knowledge." She smiled. "We should set up a camera with a motion sensor on it."

"Cal always used to ask about that, remember? He thought it was some long-lost relative, a witch who lived in town disguised as a normal person."

"A witch?" Skylar said anxiously.

"Just a joke," Jolene told him. They *definitely* should not have come this way.

The path sloped down, passed through an empty field grown high with meadow grass, then ended on Bluebird Lane. Ahead down the narrow road, Jolene could see the white steeple of the Presbyterian church peeking out from between the pines.

"Almost there," Leslie said cheerily.

Her house was a small log cabin set back against the trees. In front was a vegetable garden ringed by a border of wildflowers. That surprised Jolene. Businesswoman she could see, but gardener? People changed, she realized, and though she and Leslie still had an easy rapport and seemed to have instantly fallen back into their old roles, she recognized that she no longer really knew her friend.

It was a sobering thought.

The cabin was bigger than it looked. Inside, there was a large sitting room, a decent-sized kitchen and three bedrooms. One was Leslie's room, another was her office, and the third was a guest room. "I've never used it," Leslie admitted. "In the three years since I bought this place, I've never had an overnight guest." She caught Jolene's raised eyebrow. "*That* kind. So if you two wanted to inaugurate the room, it's available."

Jolene looked over at Skylar, standing next to the window and looking out at the garden. She was going to have to make some decisions about their future . . . and pretty quickly. He was supposed to be in school right now. She'd yanked him out when she left Frank, and she hadn't even called the school to explain. They'd no doubt called to find out why he'd been absent for the past week, and she just hoped that Frank had taken care of the problem.

If she really was planning to stay in Bear Flats for any length of time, she had to get Skylar enrolled. And since it was the beginning of the school year, it would be better to do it now. It wasn't good for a third grader to miss too much class time; he'd fall behind. Besides, for a boy as shy as Skylar, each day that went by would make it harder for him to make friends and fit in.

Life was so damn complicated.

She looked around the cabin. Honestly, she would much rather be living here than with her mother, but making that transition wouldn't be easy. No matter how carefully she finessed it, her mom would end up hurt and angry, and she might even take it out on Skylar, cutting him out entirely. The boy couldn't handle another emotional loss right now.

The best thing to do would be for her to find a job and get her own place, rent an apartment.

The expression on her face must have betrayed her emotions, because Leslie walked over and put a hand on her shoulder. "Don't worry. Everything's going to be all right," she promised, smiling sympathetically.

Jolene patted her friend's hand, looking over at Skylar by the window. "I hope so," she said.

Skylar didn't like Bear Flats. There was nothing to do here. The town was boring and way too small. Plus all these trees and the fact that it was in the mountains . . .

He missed the desert.

He didn't like his grandma much either. Oh, she was nice to him and all—*most* of the time—but even when she was on her best behavior, there was something unstable about her, something unpredictable, something that reminded him of Dad.

He *didn't* miss his father. He felt guilty about that, but deep down he knew that he and his mom were better off by themselves. Only he wondered what came next, what they were going to do. Were they going to stay in this place and live here forever? Was this just a stop on their way to New York or Chicago or Los Angeles or some big city? Were they going to wait awhile and then go back home to Yuma?

He didn't know because his mom wouldn't tell him.

He hadn't exactly asked, but the way he saw it, he shouldn't have to. It was her job to explain what was going on.

And she hadn't done that.

He rolled over on the small cot, turned from his back to his side to his stomach, uncomfortable in every position. As bad as the cot was, he'd had no trouble falling asleep until tonight. Whether it was the altitude or the stress of being here, he'd been tired at the end of each day and was out like a light the second his head hit the pillow. This evening, though, he'd tossed and turned, unable to stop his brain from thinking about spooky stuff.

Those graves had really freaked him out.

Skylar flipped onto his back again, then sat up against the wall. He'd been thinking about that grave site all day long. His mom and her friend had acted like it was nothing, especially afterward, but he saw through that. They were scared of it, too. All afternoon, he'd found himself obsessing about those graves, wondering who was buried there. In a way, he wished that they'd stopped and he'd been able to get a closer look. He might not have been brave enough to do more than take a quick glance, but he still would have known what the gravestones actually looked like instead of relying on his overactive imagination. For, in his mind, there was a large stone marker and a small one, both weathered by time, the words *Mother* and *Daughter* chiseled in spooky horror-show letters. He imagined that nothing grew on top of the graves, the cursed ground bare of even a stray weed, and that wild animals instinctively avoided the site, afraid.

He tried to tell himself that the mother and daughter had probably been pioneers who'd been buried close to their cabin, but the witch theory seemed much more plausible, and he shivered as he thought about what the grave site looked like at night under the full moon.

Tick tick tick.

There was a light tapping on the window.

Heart thudding in his chest, Skylar glanced over at his mom. She was dead asleep, mouth open and snoring. Not only that, but she was way over on the other side of the room, a distance that suddenly seemed like miles.

Tick tick tick.

The tapping continued, grew louder. It could have been a windblown branch knocking lightly against the glass were it not for the fact that the noise was syncopated, a repeating rhythmic pattern no wind could have created. He'd been avoiding the window, not wanting to look at it, afraid of what he might see, but now he hazarded a glance at the drapeless pane.

A Yoda-like face peered in at him, a small wrinkled head, brown instead of green, partially illuminated by the light of the moon. The eyes shifted slowly, taking in the room, *looking* for something.

Him.

The beady eyes locked on his own, and the corners of the mouth slid upward into a malevolent smile. It was the most terrifying face he had ever seen, and his mouth went suddenly dry. He shut his eyes tightly, afraid of being hypnotized by those evil orbs, afraid of seeing the teeth inside that horrible mouth, afraid of . . . just afraid.

"Mom!" he screamed.

She awoke immediately, leaping up out of bed and instinctively rushing to his cot. He opened his eyes. He expected the face to disappear—whether monsters were real or imagined, the presence of grown-ups usually made them flee—but to his horror, the terrible creature was still there and watching them, two brown wrinkled hands placed on the window to either side of the eyes in an effort to assist the viewing.

His mom saw it, too, and she let out a loud high scream that caused his grandma to shout out from her bedroom and finally made the thing at the window pull away and disappear into the darkness of night. A second later, the lights went on and his grandma was in the room, wearing dirty pajamas, her hair wild, her face without makeup looking old and a little scary itself. "What is it?" she demanded. "What happened?"

"Someone was at the window!" his mom said, her voice breathless and still almost loud enough to be a scream.

Someone?

"It was a monster," Skylar said. His voice came out small and babyish, and he should have been embarrassed by that but wasn't.

His grandma went over to the window, looked out. She put her hands to the sides of her eyes like a reverse image of the creature. "Don't be ridiculous," she said. "It was probably just a kid from—"

"He's not being ridiculous," his mom said, and that made him feel good. Her arms tightened around him. "It was . . . I don't know *what* it was, but it didn't look human."

"Well, I don't see anything out there now." His grandma turned away from the window and faced them. Skylar saw not sympathy or understanding in her eyes but disapproval.

"Turn on the yard lights," his mom commanded. "Check."

The old woman must have heard the same seriousness in her voice that he did, because instead of refusing, as he'd expected, she left the room and walked down the hallway. A moment later, the exterior of the house was flooded with light. Holding his hand, taking him with her, his mom moved over to the window. All was black beyond the perimeter of the lights—*anything* could be out there—but the area adjacent to the house was empty. Whatever it was had fled.

The outside lights flicked off, and his grandma returned. "Nothing," she announced. He thought she sounded pleased.

His mom didn't say anything, and he didn't either. But she continued to hold his hand, and while he knew that creature might still be out there, might even be watching them from some vantage point within the trees, he no longer felt afraid.

"I'm going back to bed," his grandma said. "I'll see you in the morning. If you see any other monsters? Don't call me."

She disappeared around the corner. Skylar and his mom looked at each other and after a beat, they both burst out laughing. It was the first time he'd laughed since leaving Yuma, and even under these bizarre circumstances it felt good. Through the thin walls, he heard his grandmother's wordless sounds of disapproval—they both did—and that only made them laugh all the harder.

His mom wiped the tears from her eyes. "We're going to have to get some drapes in here," she said. It was meant as a joke, sort of, but it brought them back to the here and now, and they both stopped laughing.

Skylar looked at his cot, then over at his mom's bed. She knew what he was thinking before he even said it, and she let go of his hand and put an arm around his shoulders. "You can stay with me tonight," she told him.

He felt grateful that she hadn't made him ask—he

felt like a baby enough as it was—and he crawled into the bed first, taking the space against the wall, away from the window. She climbed in after and gave him a kiss on the forehead before turning in the opposite direction. "Good night," she said.

"Good night," he replied.

But it was a long time before either of them fell asleep.

Seven

Dennis was awakened by the train.

It shook the cheap motel like an earthquake, accompanied by a deep bass rumbling that he felt in his gut and that threatened to turn his stomach to Jell-O. It was the train's whistle that had shaken him from sleep, a loud sustained blast of air horn powerful enough to penetrate the plaster walls, cut through the static of the television he hadn't turned off and yank him from the deepest REM.

He'd seen the tracks in the daytime, of course. In fact, the highway he'd been taking had followed them for most of the afternoon. But he hadn't expected passing trains to sound so close. Or so loud.

The Midwest was weird. Especially the small towns. He'd spent all of his life in a large Eastern metropolitan area, so it was strange to him to see streets and neighborhoods where the houses had no fences, the yards no boundaries or definition. Stranger still was to see train tracks that seemed to run right through people's back lawns, tracks that were not segregated in a certain section of the city or fenced off in any way but proceeded over yards and down streets as though their builders had been completely oblivious to the community around them.

He wondered now what it was like for the people in those places. Were they awakened every night like this, jarred from sleep by trains speeding past only inches from their bedrooms? Or did they eventually adjust to the all-encompassing noise?

The train was long, but finally it passed, and Dennis lay there listening to the receding sound of its whistle. He tried for several minutes to fall back asleep but couldn't, so he flipped on the nightstand lamp, got out of bed and got a drink of warm flat Coke from the can atop the dresser. His cell phone lay next to the TV, charging, and he picked it up and looked, hoping for messages, but there were none. Earlier in the evening, when he'd called home to check in, he'd missed his mother and sister so much that he almost felt like crying. Travel was much more stressful than he'd been expecting. And much less fun. The lure and excitement of the open road had faded. Most of the time he was alone, driving through unfamiliar territory, listening to local radio stations that depressed the hell out of him. Hearing the voices of his mother and his sister made him realize what he had left behind.

But still he could not go back.

Not yet.

He did not know why, but he knew it was so.

The problem was, his money was going much faster than expected. Even with his skipping breakfasts and sometimes lunches, eating off the dollar menu at fast-food restaurants, and staying at the cheapest fleabag motels, his plan for a grand tour of the United States was destined to be over before it was finished unless something changed.

And all of his sightseeing side trips didn't help.

He toyed with the idea of stopping for a while in

some picturesque town and taking a menial job. Janitor or newspaper deliveryman or box boy. In the abstract, the idea was romantic, exciting, and when imagining such scenarios before, he'd always ended up meeting some gorgeous woman or getting involved in some type of adventure. In real life, however, he knew that he would simply be performing manual labor with sullen teenagers in a dead-end community.

He needed some way to get money, though.

Maybe he'd just buy a lottery ticket.

He sat back down on the bed and looked up. The dull yellowish glow of the lamp illuminated a water stain on the ceiling. He thought of his own room at home with its clean walls and modern furniture. It might be a long time before he had something that nice again. He sighed. Right now, even his job at the rental agency didn't seem so bad.

Still, he had that strange nagging sense that he was *supposed* to be doing this, that there was a reason for this trip. In his mind was an image from the dream that the train whistle had cut short: a walking mountain, a huge hulking creature that stood over a field filled with bloody corpses. The image frightened him but spoke to him, and was reminiscent of that triangular-headed behemoth he had dreamed of before, the one who had beckoned him down the road toward the wall of smoke.

Dennis sat there for a few moments, not sure he could fall asleep but not wanting to stay up. The rug under his bare feet felt grainy, dirty. He listened carefully for the sound of any more trains, heard nothing and, deciding to give sleep a shot, finally switched off the lamp, lay back down and closed his eyes.

This time, he had no dreams.

He felt better in the morning. For breakfast, he bought a paper cup of bitter coffee from the gas station where he filled up the car, and then he was on the road again, the dejection and discouragement of the night before little more than a memory. No matter how the day ended up, it always started well, and essential optimist that he was, he began each morning thinking that today things would be different.

This time he was right.

He was planning to drive straight through to evening. He still had half a bag of leftover Doritos that would suffice for lunch, and if he could make better time, perhaps he could buy himself a free day down the road. By noon, however, after four straight hours of nearly identical woods and rolling hills, with nothing but bad music and fire-and-brimstone sermonizers on the radio, he was ready for some sort of diversion, desperate for a distraction or amusement that would take him out of himself.

ENTER IF YOU DARE!!

The sign was impossible to miss. Bright yellow against the mellow green of the trees, its letters a shocking red, the sign was designed to attract the attention of passersby. It definitely attracted his, and Dennis looked at the cartoonish illustration of a haunted castle and the name below it: THE KEEP. His mood brightened considerably, and was boosted even more when he saw the big red arrow up ahead pointing to a small paved parking lot and a series of old wooden buildings. A plank fence in front of the buildings was painted like a castle wall, with names of the exhibits within displayed on fake windows: The Haunted Skeleton, The Petrified Tree, The Noose of Justice, The Garden of Natural Wonders.

It was a tourist trap, one of those roadside attractions he'd heard about, read about and seen in bad horror movies but had never before encountered in real life. He pulled into the parking lot, swinging into a space next to the entrance. The only other vehicle in the lot was a beat-up red pickup truck in the corner. Dennis assumed it belonged to the proprietor. He got out of the car, stretched his tired limbs, breathed deeply. The air seemed heavier and more humid than it had when he'd been in the car and moving.

The entrance to The Keep was through a gate in the fence that was open and made to look like a draw-bridge. Behind it was the largest building, and Dennis stepped inside a shabby gift shop filled with printed T-shirts, novelty knickknacks, polished-rock bookends and crappy children's toys. A tired-looking older woman with incongruous Jackie O. glasses sat on a high stool behind the cash register, working on a cross-word puzzle book. He walked up to the counter. "I'd like to see The Keep," he said.

"One dollar," she told him without looking up.

The price was definitely right. He withdrew his wal-let, took out a dollar bill and handed it to her. The woman's eyes met his for a brief second, and though he didn't think about it until later, the emotion he saw in them was fear. She pulled a purple ticket from a large roll, tore it in half and handed him the stub. "Right through there," she said, pointing. On the far wall was a painting of a castle, in the middle of it a real door.

"Thanks," he said. He walked over, pushed open the door and found himself in a darkened room. Fluo-rescent lights sputtered to life as the door closed be-hind him, and on the floor he could see several large pieces of drywall with what looked like Indian carv-ings on them. Two long tables on either side of the room were host to a variety of pots and grinding stones. But the focal point of the room was a built-in alcove covered by a clear sheet of glass. Behind the glass, propped up against the wall was a skeleton.

Dennis walked over to the alcove, peering in. He had no doubt that the skeleton was real. The bones weren't clean and bleached like the ones in movies or Halloween displays: rather the skull was cracked and yellowed, the ribs chipped and deteriorating, the legs and arms dirty and discolored. On the wall above and behind the figure were painted the words *The Haunted Skeleton,* and below that was a short description of how the man who had discovered this intact specimen in a river cave had died under mysterious circumstances, and how the succession of subsequent owners had all come to bad ends. The paragraph concluded, "Although it has been behind glass and has not been touched since entering The Keep in 1999, the proprietors will sometimes discover that the skeleton has moved on its own in the middle of the night, and more than one customer has returned to reveal that they have had nightmares about the skeleton and have seen its image in their own homes! Believe it or don't!"

Dennis smiled, kept walking.

He passed through a series of rooms in the connected buildings he'd seen from the parking lot, most of them filled with local Indian and pioneer artifacts. In the last chamber, which was larger than the others and had a much higher ceiling, there was a full-sized replica of a gallows. A worn thick-roped noose hung from the center beam, and text on a laminated board attached to the adjacent wall read, "*The Noose of Justice.* This was used to hang Niggers and Kikes in the late 1800s and early 1900s, when those outsiders threatened to disrupt forever the idyllic life created by our forebears. . . ."

Dennis looked away from the words, glancing back up at the noose. He had a queasy, unpleasant feeling in the pit of his stomach. He was shocked and offended by the blatantly racist description, and he felt more than a little uneasy when he considered how far out in the middle of nowhere he really was. He thought of that one lone pickup in the parking lot.

If he disappeared, no one would know where he was. His body might never be found.

Niggers and Kikes.

He'd left his cell phone in the car.

Dennis looked again at the description. There were a lot of militia groups in Missouri, weren't there? For all he knew, this little tourist attraction was a front for some white supremacist organization.

He suddenly felt the need to get as far away from here as possible. He considered doubling back the way he'd come, but those dark rooms filled with old artifacts and that skeleton in the alcove now seemed a lot more sinister than they had, and instead he pressed ahead and walked outside to the Garden of Natural Wonders. This property was much bigger than he'd originally thought. According to the small hand-painted signs that pointed toward three diverging paths, the Petrified Tree was off to his right, the Ancient Indian Burial Ground was straight ahead, and the Olde Faithful Geyser and exit were off to the left.

He took the path on the left.

The trail looked as though it ran along the side of the buildings back toward the entrance, but several yards in, after a short jog around a bush, the dirt path suddenly veered off in another direction, through a copse of trees behind the buildings, opening out before a small rocky rise. A series of stone steps had been carved into the side of the low ridge, and, curious, Dennis climbed them, holding on to the welded pipes that served as a railing.

What was this?

Before him was a pit filled with what looked like liquid clay, a bubbling grayish green mud that gurgled and popped as though boiling.

"It's where they used to throw them."

Dennis jumped at the sound of the voice. He whirled around to see a gnomish little man standing to the right of him.

He pretended he hadn't been startled. "Throw who?" he asked, keeping his voice calm.

"Evildoers," the old man said. "Witches, unbelievers. You know." He looked at Dennis as if he *should* know, and Dennis wanted to say, *I don't know, I don't want to know, I don't care, I only stopped here because I was tired of driving and got suckered by your sign.*

Instead, he just nodded.

Niggers and Kikes.

He turned to go.

"Did you see my noose?"

Dennis stopped, a chill caressing his spine.

"Bought it off a farmer. He had it in his barn all these years."

Dennis didn't know what to say. He forced out a noncommittal smile that he hoped was polite.

"I saw a video once of a fat guy trying to hang himself. He put the noose around his neck, then jumped off a picnic table. He weighed so much that his head popped off; his neck wasn't strong enough to support the weight underneath, you see?"

Why is the old man telling me this? Dennis wondered.

Was it because he was Chinese?

Niggers and Kikes.

He should've stayed in Pennsylvania. He should never have left.

Why had he left his damn cell phone in the car?

The gnomelike man had moved closer. *I can take*

him if I have to, Dennis thought. The old man was scrawny and his breath came out in a hard, harsh wheeze. One kick to the balls and he would be down. Then Dennis could run away. Unless, of course, the man's compatriots were waiting farther up the path.

"I was going to add a sex room to The Keep, but my old lady put her foot down. I have stories. . . . I remember one time I ate out this one skank's pussy. She'd filled it up with salsa before spreading her legs." His laugh turned into a cough. "It was like chowing down on an old fish taco."

"I have to go," Dennis said disgustedly.

The old man grabbed his arm, bony fingers digging painfully into muscle. "They're coming back," he said, and there was fear as well as fervor in his eyes. "They're rising again."

Against his will, Dennis felt a twinge of alarm.

"Who?" he forced himself to ask.

"Them."

As if on cue, a hand popped out of the muck, a spindly skeletal arm attached to a horribly wrinkled palm from which protruded five writhing clawlike fingers. It shot up from the middle of the pit, grasping at air.

"I told you!" the old man cried, and began beating down the arm with a long-handled wooden pole that looked like an extra-thick broomstick handle. Dennis hadn't seen the pole before, didn't know where it had come from—

had it been meant for him?

—and he stepped back as the old man began whaling on the spindly arm. "Fuck you!" the man said vehemently, his face turning red, his breath growing harsher and raspier. "Get back in there!"

The force with which the hand and arm were being assaulted would have shattered a normal limb, but the wrinkled skeletal appendage remained unfazed, the clawlike fingers trying to grab the attacking staff. Then the pole hit sideways, hard against the wrist, and Dennis heard something crack, saw the wizened hand flop forward, limp, even as the arm continued to stretch upward from the boiling mud.

He was reminded of his dream on the first night of his trip, where he'd been beaten by that man in the steel yard yelling crazily at him in incomprehensible English. There were echoes of that fury here, and with a shout of glee, the old man renewed his efforts, spurred on by his success, seemingly getting his second wind as he two-handedly swung the long stick like a baseball bat.

Feeling scared and more than a little sickened, Dennis hurried up the path toward the exit, the trail sloping down the small ridge and past a deadfall of old trees and brush before reaching the wooden fence separating The Keep from the parking lot. The path followed the fence past the series of buildings until it reached a previously unnoticed gate. Dennis pushed the gate open—and he was out.

The parking lot was still empty save for his car and the red pickup, and he ran across the gravel-strewn asphalt until he reached the Tempo. Pulling out his keys as he ran, he unlocked the door and gratefully got inside. Minutes later, he was back on the road, heading west, The Keep in his rearview mirror.

What *was* that arm that had popped out of the mud pit? Was it some mechanical device used to trick tourists? He didn't think so, but he didn't dare think beyond that, didn't really want to know the truth, and he pushed the image from his mind as he accelerated past the speed limit and drove as fast as he could away from The Keep.

*   *   *

The Tempo died half an hour out of Selby, a nonde-script town on the border between forest and farm-land. There was a series of bumps; then suddenly the car had no power. Dennis pushed down on the gas pedal, flooring it, but instead of accelerating, the car lost speed at an alarming rate. In a matter of seconds, he was stopped in the middle of the road. There were no other cars coming from either direction, and he hadn't seen another vehicle for the past forty-five minutes, but he moved the car to the side of the road just in case, pushing on the doorframe while trying to steer. The Tempo slid onto the dirt shoulder, and Dennis slammed the door shut.

"Damn it!"

He pulled out his wallet, found his AAA card, flipped open his cell phone and tried to call, but he was out of range. It was not until he'd walked a mile or so down the road that he was finally able to get through, and it was forty minutes after he returned to his car, his head full of *Deliverance* daymares—

Niggers and Kikes

—that a tow truck came and towed him back to the Ford dealer in Selby.

He expected to be given the runaround because he was an outsider with Pennsylvania plates, and he was not disappointed. The service manager was dressed in a blue blazer and greeted him with a used-car dealer's smile, but when Dennis pressed for a time estimate, the man's Joe Friendly routine disappeared. "We're very busy right now," he said flatly, though Dennis could see only two vehicles in the dealership's service bays. "It'll be a day or two before we can take a look at it. Depending on the problem and what you decide to do, we can have work completed maybe two days after that."

Four days!

Dennis wanted to assert his customer's rights, wanted to speak to someone higher up, the manager or owner of the dealership, but he sensed that that would only add time to the estimate, so he said nothing. He tried the polite route. "I'm just passing through and I'm in kind of a hurry, so any help you could give me would be great."

The service manager's smile was back. "We'll do what we can," he promised insincerely.

His insurance covered the price of a loaner car, but since he was from out of town and out of state, the dealership made him put the rental on his Visa card and said he could get the insurance company to reimburse him once he got back home. He drove out with a car even older and crappier than his own, and the first thing he did was hunt down a place to stay.

Selby must have gotten more through traffic than he thought because farther along the highway was an entire motel row, and after getting a rate card from each of the six motor inns, he decided to stay at the Budget Arms, the last and cheapest lodge in town.

There was a sign in the office window: HELP WANTED. Out of curiosity, he asked the clerk behind the counter what the job was while the man ran his credit card.

"Uh, kind of : . . my job." The clerk grinned sheepishly. "I'm bailing tomorrow for the Ramada Inn down the block. Why? You interested?"

Dennis shrugged noncommittally.

"Well, it's yours for the taking. The misers who own this place don't pay much, but they don't ask questions either. And they're under a deadline here." He motioned toward Dennis' loaded car. "If you're just looking for a quick buck, want to make a little gas money so you can keep on truckin', this is a good gig. Long-term, though? I wouldn't recommend it."

"Thanks," Dennis said. He finished checking in, then took the key and walked over to his room. He looked inside. Bed, TV, window air conditioner. It wasn't the best place he'd stayed . . . but it wasn't the worst either.

He unpacked the car, put his suitcases into the room, took the boxes and bags off the roof—he was becoming an old hand at this—then locked everything up and headed back to the motel office. The bell above the door jingled as he stepped inside. Before the clerk could ask what he needed, Dennis took the HELP WANTED sign from the window and carried it over to the desk. He looked at the man.

"I'll take it," he said.

Eight

Canyonlands National Park, Utah

"Jesus."

Henry glanced up at the surface of the cliff in front of him. Overnight, someone had defaced the petroglyphs that had been etched and painted onto these walls over nine centuries ago and had withstood rain and wind, heat and cold, conquering Spaniards, westward-migrating pioneers and the National Park Service. He had been here only yesterday afternoon, stationed at this very spot to answer tourists' questions, and everything had been the same as it had always been.

Now, though . . .

Now lizards had been changed into boats, spirals into squares, horses into cars. People had been crossed out and scribbled over, and geometric symbols had been obliterated entirely, leaving only indented sections of chiseled rock. He'd never seen anything like this before and had no idea how such a feat could be completed in a single night. Even with a team of vandals driving cherry pickers and wielding power tools, there was virtually no way such a massive and wholesale destruction of historically significant rock art could be accomplished.

His gaze moved from the lowest pictographs, at eye level, to the weathered etchings at the top, nearly two stories above his head. For some reason he imagined those naked Oriental twins crawling up the precipitous face of the cliff, stone implements in hand, chipping away at the ancient Indian drawings and purposefully disfiguring them, the two sisters working throughout the night, moonlight shining on their bare flesh as they scurried over the sheer stone wall.

He pressed down on the erection that was growing in his pants, grateful there was no one else here.

He needed to report this. Nothing of this nature had ever occurred in the park to his knowledge, at least not to this extent, and it was incumbent upon him to inform the superintendent and to set the wheels in motion for the investigation that would hopefully catch the perpetrators so they could not do it again. What had been lost here could never be regained, and the most important thing now was to make sure that it did not happen again.

He was about to radio in a report when he suddenly thought of another nearby site with hundreds of Anasazi petroglyphs and pictographs. It was more secluded, not on the park maps given out to visitors, but still accessible by Jeep. Quickly, he made the call to the superintendent, explaining what had happened, giving the exact location, then said that he wanted to check another site and see if it, too, had been vandalized.

"Don't touch anything," Healey warned, and Henry switched the radio off without answering. *Asshole.* Who in the fuck did he think he was talking to?

Putting the Jeep into gear, Henry drove away from the butte, then took a barely visible trail over the flat ground toward an adjacent confluence of mesas, speeding around a freestanding column of weathered sandstone into a wide box canyon. Halfway to the canyon's far side, he braked to a halt, sending up a cloud of dust that quickly overwhelmed the vehicle.

He jumped over the side and moved away from the Jeep, toward the canyon wall, waiting for the dust to clear.

He saw what he'd known he'd see.

The pictures on the rock had been transformed.

A sun with extended rays had been changed into what looked like a train track going into a tunnel. Two stylized humanoid figures were now posts on the porch of a Western building, a small forest of pine trees had been turned into a collection of sledgehammers, and a herd of wild horses were now railroad boxcars.

He caught movement out of the corner of his eye, something off to the left that darted quickly from north to south, but when he turned his head in that direction he saw nothing. Again there was movement in his peripheral vision, a furtive rush by something dark and vaguely formed, but once again when he looked directly at the spot where it should be, he saw only sand and rock. It was hot out, and sunny, but Henry suddenly felt as chilled as if it were a winter midnight.

It *was* impossible for a person or persons to have defaced the park's petroglyphs to this extent in one night.

But it might not be impossible for something else.

He whipped his head around quickly, hoping to glimpse one of those fleeing forms, catch it off guard, but there was only the canyon. He made his way back to the car, alert for any sign of movement. Leaning over the closed Jeep door, Henry turned on the two-way radio—and gibberish issued from the speaker, a harsh yet singsongy chatter that sounded like nothing he'd ever heard before and sent a rash of shivers down his body.

He pressed the TALK button. "Cote here."

No answer, only that strange gibberish, clear above the static. He realized that the walls of the canyon were too high; the radio wouldn't work in this spot.

He was cut off.

Henry Cote had done a lot of brave things in his life, from facing down an armed Viet Cong to leaping off a cliff into Wolf Canyon Lake on a drunken dare. But he was not feeling brave now, and he quickly jumped in the Jeep, fired it up and hightailed it out of the canyon, heading for paved roads and other people and the rational world.

Healey was waiting for him in the administration building behind the visitors' center. The superintendent waved Henry into his office, then shut the door behind them.

"I found more vandalism at Little—" Henry began.

"There's more than that."

The chill was back. So much for the rational world.

"Something's going on here," the superintendent said quietly.

Henry looked at him.

"I want you to keep this under your hat. I know it's going to get out because the police are involved, but it isn't just the vandalism. For one thing, Laurie Chambers is missing. She's been gone nearly two days. I haven't told anyone, and I waited a day just to make sure myself—you know how she is; she could've just gone out on an overnight and forgot about the time— but she hasn't checked in and . . . and no Jeeps have been checked out of the pool. Her truck's still at her cabin."

"Jesus," Henry said, sitting down. "Laurie?"

"I know."

"She knows this country like the back of her hand."

"There's more."

Henry steeled himself.

"This is the part I don't want to get out. You understand me? I wouldn't even be telling you if you hadn't found what you had out there." He took a deep breath. "There's a dead body. A woman. She's not Laurie, too small, but she's someone, and I found her here in the building, in the workroom. I haven't told Pedley or Jill or Raul or anyone. The police are on their way, but I told them to keep things quiet. I don't want to alarm anyone unnecessarily."

"I understand why you don't want the *public* to know," Henry said. A decade or so back, there'd been a serial killer on the loose near Yosemite, and attendance had fallen precipitously, jeopardizing several park projects. Canyonlands was much more primitive, much more remote and much less popular than Yosemite. "But why not tell us? What's the point?"

"I need time to figure out what to say. I don't want to get everyone all . . . panicked."

"No one's going to panic. Who do you think you're dealing with here?"

"Nevertheless, keep it to yourself until I say so, got it? I'll decide when the time is right."

From down the road leading into the park came the whine of sirens.

Henry stood, and despite the circumstances it was all he could do not to smile. "Good luck with that," he said.

The body had been beaten into unrecognizability.

Along with the other rangers on duty, Henry peeked around the corner of the doorframe into the workroom. He'd imagined the dead woman's body lying naked on one of the long worktables next to the scattered tools and artifacts like a corpse ready to be autopsied. So it was a surprise to see it slumped on the floor next to one of the bookcases in faded jeans and a torn bloodstained T-shirt, her head a pulpy red mess dripping on the dark bruised skin of her neck. A forensics team was examining the body, inspecting it with gloved fingers, touching it with metal calipers, photographing and videotaping it from various angles.

Her, he had to remind himself. She was a *her,* not an *it.*

The woman did not appear to be a park employee or anyone he recognized, and quick conversations with the other lookiloos confirmed that they were just as much in the dark as he was. Speculation was rife that one of their own had murdered the woman—who else could have gotten into the building at night?—but Henry did not believe it for a second, and he knew from their earlier conversation that the superintendent didn't either. No, this was of a piece with the vandalism out there, and he could easily imagine those naked twins beating the woman to death with the same primitive tools with which they defaced the rock art, then carrying her body back here.

He shifted his legs slightly, pressing them together, trying to keep down his erection.

Despite the day's heat, the night was chill, and, unable to sleep, Henry walked onto the small porch of his cabin, staring out at the desert, half expecting to see two female figures sauntering sexily toward him. He thought about the defaced cliffs. He wanted to believe that the vandalism was random, pointless, but he kept coming back to those twins. Somewhere deep down, he knew the two were connected, and he could not help wondering if the revised artwork was meant

as a message, was a way for
something
to tell him . . . tell him . . . tell him what? He didn't
know, had not even the faintest clue, and as much as anything else, it was the incomprehensibility of it all that
gnawed at him, that kept his brain spinning and unable
to sleep.

Henry glanced toward the other cabins, saw nothing
but darkness. A porch light had been turned on at
Laurie Chambers' place—Why? Was it supposed to
act as some sort of homing beacon, drawing her
back?—but other than that, the cabins appeared de-
serted. Ironic, he thought, that the one cabin that appeared to be occupied was the dead woman's.

Dead woman's?

She's only missing, he told himself, but he thought
about the bloody pulpy face of the body in the workroom
and knew in his gut that Laurie had been murdered, too.

A meteor streaked across the starry southern sky, visible for a fraction of a second in his peripheral vision,
and he was reminded of those shadows in the box canyon, those brief glimpses of darting black forms that
he'd been given and that even in broad daylight had
scared the living hell out of him. Were they still there
now? he wondered. If so, what were they doing? He
had the sudden desire to drive out to the canyon and
see for himself. It was stupid, he knew; it was wrong; it
violated every rule and every scrap of common sense he
had, but he wanted to see the rock art at night, to look
for those mysterious dark forms and see if they were
once again defacing ancient cliff drawings.

Must be that Indian blood in his veins.

He didn't hesitate, didn't try and talk himself out
of it, but immediately went back inside the cabin, got
his keys and closed the front door. Before he could
change his mind, he was in the Jeep and off.

But of course he was not about to change his mind. The desire to be out there in the canyons, to see for himself what went on at night, was strong within him, a drive, almost a need, and though he didn't understand it, he accepted it.

Henry knew the trails of the park like the back of his cock, and once off the pavement he sped over eroded sandstone and hard-packed dirt as easily as if he'd been navigating city streets on a bright sunny day. There were numerous other cliffs and rocks containing petroglyphs, but instinct led him back to the box canyon, and once again he arrived in a cloud of dust. He braked to a stop and waited until the dust had settled before he got out of the Jeep. He'd brought several flashlights and a high-powered hand-held halogen, and he trained the powerful search beam on the cliff directly before him. The light played across the dark rock wall, illuminating the train track going into a tunnel, the collection of sledgehammers, but not showing anything new. He shone the light around the canyon, but it revealed nothing and served only to make the surrounding darkness blacker, so he shut it off, waiting for his eyes to adjust.

The world was silent, and that seemed strange. He could hear the snickering of his shoes on the sand, the ticking of the Jeep's engine cooling down, but that was it. Ordinarily, the cries of nocturnal animals from owls to coyotes sounded in these canyons, but tonight all was still, and Henry found that extremely disconcerting.

He wished he'd brought his shotgun.

But he knew a gun wouldn't do any good against what was out here.

He stood next to the Jeep.

Waited.

Watched.

And then he saw them. Shadows on the canyon

floor, two shadows moving in tandem across the moonlit sand, and Henry's heart accelerated from its usual laconic tom-tom to the rat-a-tat-tat of a high-powered assault rifle. They were not hiding as they had been earlier in the day, not confining themselves to the edges of his vision, but sliding directly toward him in full view, defiant, proud, threatening. He realized as they moved closer that they were upright. Not only were the shadows autonomous, unattached to any concrete form or object; they were not, as he had originally thought, projected onto the ground. That was an optical illusion fostered by distance. They were flat and one-dimensional, but they stood like people, feet to the sand, head in the air, and though they glided rather than walked, they were human figures.

He was frightened but excited, and made no effort to escape. The shadows reached him, began slowly and sensuously swirling about his body. He saw silhouetted nipples, outlines of perfect vaginal clefts. He was aroused as he had never been before, and he reached down, half-hypnotized, and unfastened his jeans, pulling down his briefs, freeing himself, letting the pants fall around his ankles. The shadows bent before him, appeared to be kissing his quivering erection, and although there was no sensation of touch and he could feel nothing, the sight was too much for him, and he began spurting, thrusting uselessly into the air as his seed spilled onto the sand below.

The shadows rushed over to where the thick drops congealed on the ground, and began licking them up.

The semen disappeared.

It was impossible, it made no sense, but Henry did not question it, was not even surprised. His penis had finished, was now starting to shrink, but he took it in his hand and milked a few last drops, watching as the semen fell onto the sand and the twins' shadows gobbled it up.

Were the shadows more solid now, less ephemeral? He thought so, but he could not be sure.

The dark flat figures continued to swirl about him, and there was a hunger evident in their movements, a craving he sensed and felt and that frightened him to the core.

He turned and fled.

It was an instinctive reaction and a stupid one. He'd been close by the Jeep and the only place to go was away from it, but that meant he was abandoning his only hope of getting out of the canyon and back to the real world. It didn't make any difference, though. The shadows refused to follow him, and when he looked back, he saw them retreating the way they'd come, looking like two predators on the prowl.

Where were they going now?

The seductive sensuality they'd exhibited around him was gone, and once again their purposeful glide seemed menacing, predacious. He waited until their dark forms had blended with the blackness of the canyon before he ran back to the Jeep, jumping in and driving out of there as fast as he could go.

What had happened? What had he done? He was filled with the unshakable certainty that he had helped them, had given them strength. Whatever occurred from here on in, he was part of it; he was involved. He thought of Laurie, of the dead woman in the workroom. In his mind Henry saw once again the sickening spectacle of the shadows hungrily devouring his semen. He felt tired, drained, frustrated, scared and, most of all, used. And as the Jeep bumped over the rounded sandstone he had to blink back tears so he could see the way back to the road.

Nine

The Keep, Missouri

It was long after midnight, but Hank Gifford lay awake, his eyes on an infomercial promoting some type of kitchen gadget, his mind on the mud pits out back. Next to him, Arlene snored loudly in her sleep, drooling on the edge of his pillow. He would have pushed her back to her own side of the bed, but that might wake her up, and the last thing he wanted to do was listen to her meaningless talk in the middle of the night.

The mud pits had him worried because he wasn't there to watch them. It was unavoidable. He couldn't monitor the situation twenty-four hours a day. *But what if one of them got out when he wasn't looking, when he was asleep?* He imagined a spindly shriveled form slinking along the trails of the garden, sneaking into the museum, working its way up to the house.

Of course, if he saw one of them out, he'd shoot it and stuff it. That would be a great addition to The Keep.

Except . . . what if he didn't see it? What if he was asleep when it got into the house? What if he awoke with the sulfur smell of the pits in his nostrils to see a skeletal figure climbing atop Arlene, ripping her face off and turning toward him with a terrible grin of malicious glee?

That's what worried him; that's what kept him up.

Hank picked up the remote control from the nightstand and pressed the MUTE button, listening. The house was silent. Good. He turned the sound back up a little. He was tempted to go out and check on the mud pits, but while he'd gone there with his flashlight at night many times before, he was afraid to do so now.

They're rising again.

He'd been telling that to the customers, and it was true. He didn't know how he knew it, but he did. They *were* rising, all of the heathens and unbelievers who had been fed to the pits. He had no idea how many of them were down there, their bodies sunk in the muck—no records had been kept of such things—but his daddy had told him all those years ago that every last one of them had been taken care of by the men of the towns, that after the purges none had been left in this part of Missouri.

That could mean ten.

It could mean a hundred.

He'd always known they would rise again. His daddy had told him that, too. One of the infidels had apparently sworn it with his last breath—at least that's how the story went—and the men of the towns had believed him. Even as good Christians they'd recognized the truth behind the heathen curse, and—

The bedroom's south wall exploded as though hit with a battering ram.

Arlene awoke screaming, and Hank scrambled out from under the blanket, off the bed. The right leg of his pajama bottom got stuck on the stray wire that stuck out from the side of the box springs, but he pulled hard, ripping the material, and continued his frantic escape. *They're out,* he thought wildly. *They're attacking.* Debris was flying all about; dust was everywhere. A piece of brick zoomed by his head, smashing the mirror on the dresser. He hazarded a look back, beheld a gigantic black form larger than the house. It wasn't *them,* he saw. It was a train. Even through the cloud of dust, he could make out the headlight on the front of the locomotive, the slanting grille that protruded through the hole in their wall. Only . . .

Only it wasn't a train. Not really. It was . . .

Something else.

But he didn't have time to think about that. The house was collapsing around his ears, and Arlene had been pinned to the bed by a fallen beam. The end of the rabbeted board lay embedded in her back, and blood gushed from her mouth onto the pillow—

his pillow

—each time she tried to cry out. He knew he should try to help her, but he turned without pause and attempted to run out of the room, away from the big black form that looked like a train but was not a train. The wall in front of him dropped, the doorway disappearing in a hail of plaster and wood as structural support gave way, and he staggered backward only to be slammed from behind by something that was at once hard and soft, something sticky and mushy but backed by a substance as hard as steel. He was knocked sideways to the floor as the bed fell atop him, Arlene's crushed and bloody body mashing hard against his own, her lifeless lips dripping into his ear. For a brief second, behind her, above her, in back of the broken bed, he could see the massive object that looked like a locomotive.

There was a noise, a roar, as of a hundred people screaming in unbearable agony.

And then there was death.

Ten

Flagstaff, Arizona

Angela had high hopes for date number four.

The third date had gone well. The jazz concert had been pretty nice, even though the music was more her parents' speed than hers. Brian had obviously felt the same way, because he suggested they skip out at intermission, and they ended up walking along the sidewalks of the campus at night, talking about their pasts, their futures, their visions of the world. The evening was chill, fall beginning to creep in after sunset even though summer still ruled the day, but that only made them pull closer and gave a pleasant edge to the otherwise tranquil stroll. They'd ended up at his dorm, doing what people usually did at the conclusion of a successful date.

This time they decided to try a rock concert.

The auditorium was packed. They arrived early, but still the parking lot was jammed, the lines were long, and inside there was standing room only. The buzz was all about the band, none of the usual small talk by friends and couples, and Angela eavesdropped on the closest conversation, a gaggle of high school girls who couldn't seem to decide who was cuter: the guys in Hoobastank or the members of Lightyear, the band playing here tonight. Ordinarily, that would have been the death knell for Angela's interest in the group, but on the other side of her, two older male music majors were speaking admiringly in measured tones about the band as well.

"This should be interesting," she shouted. The preconcert music had suddenly cranked up several decibels.

"What?" Brian shouted back.

"I said, 'This should be interesting'!"

He nodded. "They're really good!"

The lights dimmed.

Even though Lightyear was from the Phoenix area, what locals referred to as "the Valley," the band members were still Arizonans, and the crowd treated them like conquering hometown heroes. A huge roar greeted the musicians as they took to the stage, and though Angela had gone to a lot of concerts and a lot of clubs back in Los Angeles, she had never experienced a reaction like this. She, too, got caught up in the excitement, and as the band slammed into its first song, she felt the way she had the first time she'd seen Pearl Jam: as if she were in the presence of greatness.

The concert was amazing. She was an old hand at this stuff, jaded as only an L.A. native could be, but after the show she wanted to hit the table at the back of the hall and buy the group's CD. These guys were definitely going places. The lines were too big, though, and she wasn't sure she had enough money with her, so she decided to pick one up tomorrow at Hastings. If they didn't have any CDs in stock, she'd order one.

Brian was silent on the way back home. She expected him to stop off somewhere—a coffeehouse so they could talk, even a lovers' lane so they could make out—but he drove her directly back to Babbitt House. Despite the good vibes left over from the concert, and even before he said a word, she had a queasy sensation in the pit of her stomach, a bad feeling.

"I don't think this is working."

The car was pulling to a stop in front of the lawn, and his eyes were still on the road, not on her.

Where was this coming from? She thought things were going great. Not just tonight but overall. They had fun together, they never seemed to run out of conversation, and physically . . . well, they were both obviously into each other. She'd even e-mailed her friends in L.A. about him because it looked like this was going to last awhile.

And now it wasn't "working"?

When had this happened?

She looked at him and found that although she was surprised, she was not *surprised*. That bad feeling had been trying to tell her something and on some level she'd understood.

Angela cleared her throat. "Why?" she asked, not trusting herself to say more. There was a sudden distance between them, they were no longer a *we* or an *us* but two separate people, and she was now asking the question of a stranger.

The car had stopped, but he remained looking out the front window, would still not turn to face her. "I just . . . I don't know. Sometimes you can tell, you know, if things are working out or not. . . ."

Why hadn't he said anything about this before? He'd obviously been thinking about it for a while because nothing had happened tonight that could have possibly resulted in a change of heart. She grew angry as she recalled their light conversation at dinner, the easy good time they'd had before the start of the concert. He'd been lying the whole time, putting on an act, and she hated him for it. Why had he gone out with her tonight? Why hadn't he canceled? Because he already had the tickets, wanted to see the show and thought it was too late to line up anyone else? She was suddenly sure that was the case.

She said nothing, let him hang there.

"I don't know," he said. "I haven't met someone else, if that's what you're thinking. It's just that I thought . . . well, maybe I *should* meet someone else. I mean, I like you and all, and we had some fun, but neither of us thought there was any real future in this relationship, did we?"

She had. She stupidly had, and it was all she could do right now not to cry like a baby.

He looked at her, finally, and the expression on his face implored her to agree with him, begged her not to cause a scene.

"Fine," she said. It was all she *could* say, and though she wished she had some witty rejoinder or were mature enough to behave as though none of this bothered her, she was not that composed or sophisticated, and she was just grateful that she didn't trip over the curb or slam her skirt in the car door as she exited the vehicle.

"Do you want me to—" he began.

"No," she said without turning around, not knowing what she was turning down and not caring. She didn't want anything from him at this point. She continued walking toward the house, willing him to leave, waiting to hear the sound of his car, and was grateful when she finally heard him pull away and head up the street.

She stopped walking, breathed.

What the hell had just happened?

It wasn't any big deal. She knew that intellectually. She'd gone on a couple of dates, and it hadn't worked out. It had happened before and would no doubt happen again. The thing was, she'd invested herself this time; she'd really liked this guy, and she'd thought it had a serious chance of working out.

No. That wasn't it.

What really bothered her, what left her feeling emotionally beaten up, was the fact that she hadn't seen this coming. Before, she'd always had a good bead on the romantic reality of every relationship or potential relationship in which she'd been involved. She'd been able to read the emotional truth of any situation, and the fact that she'd been so tone-deaf this time shook her to the core.

And, bottom line, it always hurt to be rejected.

She continued up the lawn, reached the front door. Chrissie was going to be out, on a date of her own, and Angela was glad. She didn't want her roommate home right now. She wasn't up to facing people or answering questions; she just wanted to crawl into bed and watch TV and be by herself. Tomorrow they could dissect what had happened. Maybe morning would give her some perspective.

She took out her key, opened the door—

And Winston and Brock were waiting for her in the foyer.

"We saw what went down." Winston said sympathetically. "We happened to be—"

"Spying," Brock finished for him. "And we could tell from your body language what was happening."

"When you stopped on the lawn after he drove away? My heart broke."

"We're so sorry."

Angela didn't know whether to be grateful or annoyed. She was a little bit of both, but she was thankful to have such caring friends, and though it was a clichéd Lifetime channel sentiment, she realized that knowing Winston and Brock were there for her made it easier to deal with the rejection. She declined their offer to come into their apartment and commiserate, though. "I'd rather be alone," she told them.

"Understood," Winston said. "Understood."

"Thank you."

"But a word of advice?"

"Hit me."

"When life gives you lemons—" Winston began.

"—throw them at your enemies." Brock smiled. "Aim for the eyes. Do as much damage as possible."

"Exactly. Take whatever you're given and use it as a weapon."

Laughing, she threw her arms around them. "I love you guys."

"We love you, too," Winston told her.

She felt better as she walked up the stairs, but she was still glad that she didn't run into anyone else, and when Chrissie arrived home early, gave a small knock on her door and asked if she was awake, Angela remained silent in the dark.

There was a traffic jam on the way to school the next morning. The highway was clear, but getting to it took her nearly twenty minutes—even though it was only four blocks away. Despite the series of one-way streets in the old downtown district, traffic usually flowed well here, and when Angela looked east and saw that *all* of the southbound roads were jammed, even the one coming from the Snowbowl and the Grand Canyon, she knew that there was something seriously wrong.

She didn't know what it was, though, until she reached the campus and arrived late to her first class, Cultural Anthropology. The room was abuzz with the news, and even the instructor had deviated from his planned topic to discuss the day's events.

A tunnel had been discovered under the street.

A tunnel crammed with corpses.

All of the information was secondhand, but it appeared as though the corpses were old, perhaps mummified. If so, this was a significant archaeological find, and the professor said he was planning to make arrangements for the class to view the site once the police were through, perhaps as early as this afternoon. "Keep an eye on the department bulletin board. I'll post on the Web site, but since a lot of you probably have classes in this building throughout the day, it might be easier for you to just stop by. I want to stress that this is entirely voluntary and won't affect your grade. In fact, it's not even going to be extra credit. This is strictly for those who have a special interest in local prehistory, an opportunity for you to be in on the ground floor, as it were, of what could be a major discovery in the field."

He started rhapsodizing about the possibilities of what they might come across. "As you know, there are several notable archaeological sites in the Flagstaff area, most prominently Wupatki and Walnut Canyon. But the unearthing of what may be a tomb in downtown Flagstaff, an area not previously known to house *any* significant dwellings or artifacts, by people who did not typically inter their dead in this manner, could prove to be important and consequential. We have the potential to learn more about how these people lived and died from this single discovery than from any prior dig."

Angela raised her hand. "Who found it?" she asked.

"From what I've been told, city workers were digging a trench under State Street for the new expanded sewer system when they came across a hard rock slab that turned out to be the roof of the tunnel."

The remainder of the class period was spent on a series of digressions regarding the burial customs of local tribes and the Anasazi. "Are you going?" a guy who sat several seats away from her asked as Angela made her way out into the corridor with the rest of the students. She looked around in surprise to make sure he was talking to her and not someone else. The two of them had never said a word to each other before. She did not even know his name.

"Uh, yeah," she said.

"Me, too. See you there, huh?" He smiled and waved as he started toward the elevator on the opposite end of the corridor.

She watched him go. This morning, after she'd told Chrissie about Brian, as they'd grabbed their hurried respective breakfasts, her roommate had said nonchalantly, "It's probably for the best. You're too young to be tied down. Have some fun first." She'd been surprised and hurt by the comment, had thought her friend was not taking her feelings seriously. But now she thought Chrissie might be right.

She turned in the opposite direction and took the stairway down to her next class.

It was clear by early afternoon that the bodies were not that old, that not only were they not from some ancient Indian tribe, but they probably weren't even pioneers. Still, Dr. Welkes intended to lead his classes on a tour of the underground chamber to view the bodies, and the mystery remained. Who were these people and why were so many of them crammed into a short tunnel under State Street? For the police had discovered that the tunnel began beneath an old hotel that was in the process of being renovated, and ended a few yards away in the basement of what had been a department store and was now a series of boutique shops. Both buildings had been constructed in the late 1800s, placing the date of death sometime around the turn of the last century.

But why were there so many corpses? Police

counted thirty-three in that confined space. The professor and his graduate assistants had already scoured Flagstaff newspapers from that time period and found no mention of any unusual burials or mass deaths, no sudden surge of missing persons. Waiting in front of the professor's office at the appointed time, one of the grad assistants speculated that the deaths had been from disease and the tunnel had been used as some sort of quarantine area.

"At this point, that's as valid a theory as any other," Dr. Welkes said. He looked at his watch. "It's about that time. Shall we go?"

There were around twenty of them gathered in the hall, and they picked up their books and backpacks, following the professor toward the stairs. Angela looked around for the nameless guy who'd spoken to her after class. She was disappointed he hadn't shown, but that was more than made up for by the excitement of seeing what one wit was calling "the tunnel of death."

There was a tap on her shoulder. It was Brenda, a girl who sat behind her in Dr. Welkes' class and who was also in her American Lit class. "Angela, could I carpool with you?" she asked. "I live on campus and I don't have a car."

"Sure," Angela told her.

"If any of you have flashlights, bring them!" the professor announced as he started down the stairs. "It's going to be dark down there!"

Two more people ended up carpooling with her, and hers was the first vehicle behind the professor's Jeep. He led them to a designated parking area behind the closed hotel. A policeman was waiting for them, and when all of the students had parked their cars and assembled on the sidewalk, the officer led them under the yellow crime scene ribbon into the hotel.

If this had been an amusement park ride, it could not have been designed any better. The lobby of the hotel, in the early stages of renovation, was devoid of furniture, and the ceiling and floor were composed of dark stripped wood. Tattered sections of old wallpaper hung against dirty white walls, and the out-of-service elevator was visible as a broken metal box through the open double doors. The hotel looked for all intents and purposes like a haunted building, and the lack of electric illumination combined with dim fractured sunlight seeping through the dusty front windows only emphasized the resemblance.

The students had been talkative and enthusiastic on the way over, even while waiting on the sidewalk for everyone to arrive, but the atmosphere of this place was deadly, and ever since entering, they had all been silent, cowed.

Afraid.

Angela didn't know about anyone else, but she *was* afraid, and she wasn't quite sure why. She thought of that terrible mumbling in Winston and Brock's apartment, and maybe that was part of it, but it seemed to her that what frightened her was more than a resemblance to something that had happened before. This was something new, even if along the same lines, and her dread was amplified by not knowing what was to come.

One girl from Dr. Welkes' advanced course stopped in the middle of the lobby, her face chalky, and said she'd changed her mind: she didn't want to see the corpses; she'd wait for them outside. Angela knew how she felt, and part of her wanted to flee as well, but her curiosity was stronger than her fear, and as the other girl turned and exited, she followed the policeman, the professor and her classmates through a service door and into a stairwell.

"Lights on!" Dr. Welkes called, and those who had flashlights turned them on. The policeman had a strong, powerful beam that illuminated a large swath of the area before them, but here in the back of the crowd it was dark, and Angela was glad her dad had made her pack an emergency flashlight in the trunk. Brenda had nothing with her and so she stuck close by.

They started down.

At the bottom, moving single file, they passed two industrial washing machines with adjacent dryers and a massive furnace, half-disassembled, before reaching more crime scene tape. The officer held up the yellow ribbon as they ducked underneath it. Beyond was a janitor's closet and, at the back of that, an ancient metal door that had been recently pried open. Crumbling and irregularly broken brick around the exposed doorjamb testified to the fact that prior to this it had been sealed shut for many years.

The policeman's powerful beam shone into the darkness.

And they saw the bodies.

One by one, they walked into the tunnel. The corpses were farther down, not near the entrance but a few yards in, beneath the street rather than below the hotel. Even from her vantage point near the end of the line, Angela could see them, however, and she wished she'd turned around with the other girl and waited outside. It seemed suddenly hard to breathe, and her hand on the flashlight was sticky with sweat.

The bodies were unmoved; the police had left them exactly as they had been found, huddled along the sides of the tunnel, crammed into impossible positions, shoved against each other. Sunken eye sockets were granted life by moving flashlights, and though these weren't mummies, they looked like they were. Clothes had rotted into colorless rags and the skin beneath was horribly wrinkled, stuck fast to bone, all trace of fat and muscle long gone. Every one of them, no matter the pose or placement, appeared to be smiling, that familiar skull's rictus grinning into the passing beams.

Angela didn't want to be here. She was not claustrophobic—or had not been until now—but she was filled suddenly with a desire to escape from this passage. It was more powerful than an urge or impulse, more like an increasingly desperate need, and with each step she took into the tunnel it grew stronger until finally she stopped, unable to go any farther. Behind her, Brenda said, "What's wrong?" Ahead, at the front of the line, Dr. Welkes was speculating about the identity of these dead people.

And a hand reached out to grab her.

A corpse hand.

Then she was screaming, and then everyone was screaming. The bodies were alive, moving, and people were scrambling over each other, pushing each other aside to rush back out of the tunnel the way they'd come. Angela heard the professor's cry of surprise and the policeman's roar of bewilderment behind her as the beam of her flashlight hit an undersized corpse that was rocking back and forth on its haunches, bobbing its insanely grinning head at her. She tried to leap over it but was pushed by someone in back of her. She stumbled over the rocking body and went sprawling, landing atop another skeletal form making its way grimly across the floor toward the open doorway. She felt skin the texture of sandpaper, smelled the scent of foul dust in her nostrils. For a brief second, her lips touched hair—dead brittle hair—then she jumped up, knocking into another student before finally reaching the open area near the tunnel's entrance and bolting out into the janitor's closet.

Like the others in front of her, she did not stop

there but dashed into the basement and up the stairs to the lobby. Instinct was telling her to continue outside, onto the street, but the others had stopped near the door, and she immediately understood why. Embarrassment. Here in the dark dismantled lobby, the horror of what they'd experienced was still fresh, real, but on the other side of those doors, they would have to explain their fear and panic, would have to notify anonymous passersby that there were mummies or zombies under the street, that the dead bodies that had been discovered were alive.

And none of them were willing to do that.

Besides, who was to say whether it had really happened or whether they'd simply scared themselves and imagined it all?

She was. She could still feel the sharp pressure on the skin of her arm where the corpse's bony fingers had grabbed her.

Brenda was sobbing, as were several of the other students, both male and female. Dr. Welkes and the police officer had finally run up, so everyone was accounted for; everyone had made it out alive.

"Jesus!" the policeman kept shouting, his voice too loud in the empty lobby. "Jesus!"

He was the one Angela felt sorry for. He was going to have to write this up, put it in a report, explain what had happened to a group of skeptical cops, who would then have to release the information to the newspaper and the public. And she had no doubt that the bodies in the tunnel would be still once again, that whatever team came out to investigate would find nothing unusual or out of the ordinary, no sign of animation amongst the decaying corpses. That was the way these things always worked.

They stood there in various states of denial or emotional recovery, looking at each other. Angela expected someone to take charge, thought the policeman or the professor would tell them what to do, but both men seemed lost in their own thoughts as they repeated, "Jesus! Jesus!" and muttered incoherent words, respectively.

So they didn't talk about what had happened, didn't try and find another cop or fireman or public-safety worker to verify what was down there, made no effort even to get together later and discuss what they'd seen. They simply ended up wandering aimlessly out the front doors onto the sidewalk where the fortunate girl from the advanced class waited for them, completely unaware of the horror that had transpired beneath her feet.

Angela drove Brenda and the other two students who'd carpooled with her back to school, none of them speaking, then drove immediately home—where she told everyone in Babbitt House what had happened. Randy wasn't in, but the others were, and Angela gathered them in the first-floor foyer, in front of Winston and Brock's apartment, and described in detail what she'd seen. The cone of silence that had existed with her fellow anthropology students had shattered, and now she couldn't seem to stop talking, telling and retelling specific scenes over and over again as her friends and roommate plied her with questions. None of them seemed to doubt her, and she found that surprising. If she'd heard such a story from one of them, she would not have believed a word of it.

Of course, they'd all heard the ghost the other night, too.

Come to think of it, maybe she *would* have believed it.

It was Chrissie who finally put a stop to the show and dragged her upstairs to their apartment. Angela didn't realize until they were behind closed doors, until she gratefully sank into the couch, how bone tired she was. It was as if all of a sudden everything caught up with her, and her body, which had been running on adrenaline, finally succumbed to the stress of the day and collapsed in on itself. She stared numbly at the television while Chrissie turned it on.

"Do you think it'll be on the news?" her roommate asked.

"I don't know," Angela admitted. "It just happened. And I didn't see any news cameras there. But maybe word's leaked out by now."

Chrissie, too, accepted without question that what Angela said had actually occurred, and she thought that for someone who claimed not to believe in "ghosts or gods or anything supernatural," Chrissie seemed oddly uncritical. She wondered if her friend was changing her mind.

Angela was so exhausted and stressed-out she could have sat there for the rest of the evening, unmoving, unthinking, but she felt dirty—soiled and contaminated by her contact with those carcasses—and what she wanted more than anything else was a hot shower to wash off whatever freakish germs had attached themselves to her, to scrub her skin totally clean. She'd sat down only a few moments before, but she got up again, quickly, as though staying on the couch even a second longer might infect it with some incurable disease. "I'm going to take a shower," she announced. "Could you burn my clothes in the incinerator for me?"

"We don't have—" Chrissie began, then laughed. "Oh. Joking."

She *was* joking—but not really. She honestly didn't care whether she saw the clothes she was wearing ever again, and she knew it would be a long time and a lot of hard washes before she put any of them on.

Angela went into the bathroom, turned on the water

to warm it up, then took off her clothes, dumping them on the floor rather than in the hamper. There was a black spot on her skin where the corpse had first grabbed her. It was not a bruise but looked more like mold or rot. She saw it first in the mirror, then examined it more closely by sitting on the toilet and holding that section of arm as close to her eyes as possible. The mark was not in the shape of fingers or a hand, as might be expected, but was instead an amorphous blob that resembled an amoeba. She touched it, picked at it with a fingernail, but, though the spot somewhat resembled paint or ink, she could not scrape any of it off her skin. In the shower, she used a loofah and Comet cleanser, scrubbing as hard as she could, but again was unable to remove the stain or even lighten the blackness. The skin around it grew red and raw, but the mark remained.

She was worried and scared. She thought she should tell Chrissie, thought she should go to the emergency room at the hospital, but instead, irrationally, decided to sleep, telling herself that it would be all right in the morning, that everything would be fine. Angela finished showering, put on her pajamas, dashed into her bedroom and locked the door before climbing into bed and getting under the covers. "Good night!" she called out to Chrissie.

"Angela!"

"Good night!"

"Are you—"

"I'm tired! I'm going to bed! We'll talk about it in the morning!"

In the morning, the black spot on her skin was gone, but dark mold grew on each of the four corners of her top sheet in identical amoeba-like blobs. It seemed thicker than it had when it was on her skin, hairier and somehow more malevolent. Disgusted, frightened,

Angela kicked the covers off and dashed away from the bed. She quickly slipped on her robe, unlocked the door and called Chrissie, who came running into the room, obviously hearing the fear in her voice.

"What is it?" Chrissie demanded, but she saw even before she finished the sentence. Her eyes widened at the sight of the sheet's black corners. "Oh, my God!"

"Don't touch it!" Angela shouted.

But she was too late. The sheet was lying half on and half off the bed, tangled up with the comforter, and Chrissie reached for the corner closest to the edge. Her finger poked the black mold, then jerked away instantly. A look of revulsion transformed her face, and Chrissie backed toward the door as though she were being menaced by a slow-moving knife-wielding maniac.

"It was on my skin last night," Angela said. "The black stuff. I should've told you, I should've gone to the hospital, I should've . . . I don't know. What do you think it is? It looks like some kind of mold. Should we take the sheet in to—"

"Bitch!" Chrissie shouted. And slammed the door.

What the hell? Angela hurried after her roommate, opening the door and following her into the sitting room. "Chrissie?"

Her friend turned, and the expression on her face was angry, threatening.

Black, she thought. *They call that kind of look black.*

She stared at Chrissie's pointing finger, looking for mold, but the skin was clear.

"Stay away from me, you stupid brown bitch," Chrissie ordered, and there was real venom in her voice. She shoved her way past a stunned Angela and returned to her own room.

The door closed.

Locked.

Eleven

Bear Flats, California

The kitchen smelled of bacon, eggs . . . and booze.

Jolene's jaw clenched, the muscles under her ear hurting in that tight tense way she remembered from childhood. Her mother was sitting in her usual spot at the breakfast table, dipping toast into the last bit of yolk on her plate, smiling and humming softly to herself. Jolene remembered this from her childhood as well, the "good" time, as she'd always thought of it. This was her mom at her peak, not drunk enough to be abusive, not sober enough to be self-pitying, with just enough of a buzz on to make her feel calm, content, at ease. If her mother could have stayed this way throughout the day, perhaps life at home wouldn't have been so bad, but this stage was merely a respite between the desperate highs and lows, and although it was the best stage in the cycle, it was also the shortest.

"Hurry up and eat your breakfast," Jolene told Skylar. "We have a busy day."

The boy sat down silently at the table while Jolene got him a plate of bacon. He was still a little shy and nervous around his grandmother, and although Jolene pretended not to notice, she did.

And was grateful.

She didn't want him feeling too comfortable with her, getting too close. He would only end up being hurt.

"Here," she said, setting the plate down. "Orange juice or milk?"

"Milk," Skylar told her.

She was finally going to try and enroll him in third grade at Bear Flats Elementary this morning. It was strange to realize he would be attending the same school she'd gone to when she was his age. He was dreading the prospect because it meant that this was not just a vacation or hiatus but a permanent move, and she had mixed feelings for much the same reason.

If they really *were* going to relocate here, maybe it was time for her to start thinking seriously about finding a job.

Her mother must have read her mind. "You know," she said helpfully, "if you want to make yourself useful, Anna May Carter let out that she needs some help down at the historical society. Theo Frye up and bailed on her after all these years, and the new museum's set to open in a few months. I'm not sure how much it pays, but it's work."

Jolene had heard about the new museum. It was the talk of the town, although God knew why. It's not as if Bear Flats was a big tourist destination or a site of historical significance. In the real world, moving the museum from its small storefront downtown to the old Williams residence was as insignificant as the renovation of a Taco Bell bathroom in Tucson. But here in Bear Flats, residents were excited that the history of their community would finally be displayed in a venue more appropriately impressive.

As embarrassed as she was to admit it, Jolene, too, felt a sense of pride knowing that the town's historical artifacts would be housed in the former residence of its lone millionaire. She must be more of a yokel than she thought.

"Thanks, Mom," she said. "I'll check it out."

After breakfast, she and Skylar drove to the school. She'd been hoping and half expecting to get him in today—which was why they'd gone so early—but the principal informed her that there were forms to sign and process, and that Skylar could not start class until the transcripts from his previous school had been sent, faxed or e-mailed over. It would be another day or two at least.

In the school parking lot, she called Leslie from her cell phone. "Hey, it's me, Jolene."

"Jo!"

"I was wondering if you could do me a favor: watch Skylar for me while I meet with Anna May Carter for an hour or so."

"Sure. No problem." There was a pause. "Anna May?"

"My mother says she needs someone to help with the museum's move now that Theo Frye's gone. I think my mom talked to her about me."

"I'm sure I can find you something better than that."

"I don't know if I want anything better," Jolene admitted. "This sounds like a temp job or at least a job I wouldn't feel guilty about quitting, and I need to just sort some things out in my mind before I make any long-term commitments. I promise, though: if I decide to stay and look for permanent employment, you'll be the first person I'll hit up for a job."

Leslie laughed. "It's a deal."

Leslie wasn't working until three, so Jolene dropped Skylar off at her house. She felt guilty for doing so. The boy was obviously uncomfortable—even under the best of circumstances he had difficulty adjusting to new surroundings—but she couldn't very well take him on what was essentially a job interview, as casual as it might be. And he would definitely be better off with Leslie than with her mother. Jolene told him to be good, promised to be back as soon as possible and left quickly, before Skylar said something that would make her reconsider.

It would be good for him to get away from her, she told herself. It would be good for him to get to know Leslie.

As it happened, Anna May needed help right away and had a grant from the county that would allow her to pay nearly twice minimum wage for the estimated two-month transition period. "It's a part-time job," the old lady said, "but you won't find a higher-paying one anywhere in town. Or one that's so rich with interesting information. You'll earn and learn, I like to say."

The two of them met in the old museum, next to the Hallmark store on Main, and Jolene said that she would be willing to start today if she could get off in time to pick up her son before three.

"No problem," Anna May promised. "We're very flexible around here." She patted Jolene's shoulder. "Besides, I know you're a good hard worker. And your mama told me about what a difficult time you're having."

Jolene forced herself to say nothing. If her mother had been blabbing about her situation all over town, there were undoubtedly a dozen different versions of events all currently circulating.

"Let's go out to the Williams place. I've been boxing things up here since seven, and I think it's time to take some of them over. Besides, I can show you what our plans are for the future, and you can help me with a few things I haven't been able to do on my own."

"This sounds like mostly physical labor," Jolene said. "Are you sure you wouldn't be better off just hiring some high school boy?"

Anna May laughed. "No. I want someone who understands the importance of what we're doing. Someone smart I can talk to. Besides, between the two of us, we can lift almost anything that needs to be lifted. If not, there's always George and his dolly. He can be here in a heartbeat."

Jolene was still not sure she'd be any better at this than a muscle-bound teenager, but she didn't say any more, and after they'd loaded eight of the ten packed boxes into the historical society's van and she'd called Leslie to tell her the revised schedule, Anna May drove the two of them to the Williams house.

It was as nice as Jolene remembered it. Chester Williams had died over five years ago, but someone had obviously been keeping the place up. The landscaped flowers were in full bloom, the windows spotlessly clean.

"I'll bet you're happy to have gotten this home," Jolene offered.

"Oh, it's wonderful!" Anna May said enthusiastically. "The Williams estate not only donated the house but everything in it! Combined with our existing archives, plus extra donations, we'll be able to turn this into an authentic eighteen-eighties residence and remake the grounds into a sustainable homestead with native plants. That'll take a while, of course. For now, we're just going to relocate our museum, but our goal is to eventually turn this into a destination-worthy learning experience."

Jolene found herself smiling. And not in a cynical or superior way. She was genuinely caught up in the other woman's enthusiasm and despite her initial dismissive attitude found herself thinking that the Bear

Flats museum really *could* be the crown jewel of the county. She imagined school kids from all of the other mountain communities coming here for field trips, families visiting on weekends.

Anna May unlocked the house's front door, and the two of them carried in the boxes, placing them in the center of the front room. Couches, chairs, a bureau and a coffee table had been shoved against the far wall, and the middle of the room was filled with boxes from previous trips. "We'll get these sorted once everything's moved over," Anna May said. "Right now, I'm just trying to figure where everything's going to go."

Jolene peered down the hallway toward the kitchen.

"Do you want to look around? Go ahead. I'm just going to look through a few of these closets and see if there's anything that can be thrown out. We're thinking of having a rummage sale to raise money."

Jolene walked through the dining room, the family room, a formal parlor and a study, then checked out the bedrooms upstairs. Like the exterior of the building, the rooms of the house were in perfect shape. It looked like a museum already. By the time she walked back downstairs, Anna May was in the pantry off the kitchen.

Jolene opened a narrow door on the opposite side of the kitchen and saw a series of steps leading down. She flipped a switch next to the door and a light went on.

Anna May emerged from the pantry carrying a notebook.

"What's down here?" Jolene asked, gesturing.

"Like I said, I haven't had time to go over everything in detail. That's one of the reasons I need someone. I'm still going through the closets, but why don't you look around and see what you can find? If you come across anything interesting, call me. Or, if you want, you can start cataloging the items downstairs. Just grab that other notebook on the counter that says *Inventory* and continue on with the next number in sequence. It's pretty simple to figure out. All you have to do is copy the other examples and put one of those little orange stickers on each item you write down."

Jolene picked up the notebook and a pen, and walked down the steps to the basement. It was chilly and damp, but that was not what made her shiver as she passed beneath the floor of the kitchen. No, it was the *feeling* of the place, the emotional rather than physical atmosphere. Maybe she'd been conditioned by too many movies, but the vibe here was that of a haunted house, and she found herself wondering exactly where and how Chester Williams had died. Beneath her foot, a stair creaked. Ahead, the far corner of the basement lay in shadow, illumination from the single bare bulb unable to reach that section of the room.

She reached the bottom of the steps and looked around. She'd been expecting a massive storehouse of covered furniture and arcane treasures from Williams' storied travels. Instead she found herself in a medium-sized space only slightly larger than her mother's living room, with a low bare wood ceiling, a dirty wooden floor, a workbench with tools along the west wall and a few leftover household items scattered around the open area in the middle.

Maybe it had been cleaned out before being donated to the historical society.

No. If that were the case, the basement wouldn't have been so dusty.

Most likely, this was an area of the house that simply hadn't been used for years, perhaps decades.

She walked slowly through the dark room, still feeling the strange sense of cold dread that had come over her as she'd descended the stairs. Up ahead, near the south wall, she could see a square outline on the floor.

Was that a trapdoor?

Jolene moved closer, pushed aside a wicker basket. Yes. The light here was dim, but that was definitely a recessed handle lying flush with the wood.

Was there a basement beneath the basement?

If there was, it had not been entered in quite some time. The floor here was covered by a coating of dust even thicker than that in the center of the room. Jolene heard Anna May's footsteps above her. She glanced up at the cobweb-covered ceiling, then looked down at the floor, wondering what was beneath it. She'd never heard of a double basement before and couldn't imagine what the reason for its existence might be, but whatever it was, she had the feeling it was not wholesome.

Wholesome?

What kind of word was that?

She didn't know, but it fit.

Jolene bent down, touched the handle of the trapdoor and jerked her hand away the second her fingers touched the cold metal, her heart pounding. She wasn't brave enough to open it herself, wasn't sure she even had the right to, so she called up to Anna May, and when she didn't get an answer she bounded back up the stairs to the sunlight and the real world. It felt as though she'd emerged from Dracula's dungeon. Windows had never been so welcome. Anna May was indeed in a hallway closet that appeared to be right over that section of the basement, and Jolene explained to the older woman what she had found.

Anna May's face lit up. "Oh, this is exciting! A

secret cellar! This is the kind of find I live for." She
put down her notebook on a closet shelf and followed
Jolene back through the kitchen.

"Do you have a flashlight or something?" Jolene
asked. "The basement itself is pretty dark and I'm not
sure there's any light . . . down there."

"I'll be right back!" Anna May ran out to the van
and returned a few moments later with two flashlights.
"A good historian is always prepared," she said as she
handed one to Jolene.

The two of them descended the stairs.

Once again, Jolene experienced a profound uneasi-
ness upon entering the basement, and as she led Anna
May to the trapdoor, goose bumps accompanied what
appeared to her to be a significant drop in temperature. They were prepared to work hard and pull together on the small handle in order to open the door,
but it must have had some type of spring hinge because it came up fairly easily, revealing a primitive
ladder bolted to the edge of the opening and going
down six feet or so to a hard dirt floor. They shone
their lights into the darkness and saw what appeared
to be a bookcase in the center of an otherwise empty
chamber. There seemed to be no books on the shelves,
only a series of small unidentifiable items.

Jolene had even more trepidation about going into
this lower cellar than she'd had about entering the
basement they were in. She was not just wary of the
room; she was afraid of it. But Anna May had already
pushed her flashlight into the waistband of her pants
and had started down the ladder, and the only thing
Jolene could do was follow.

The air smelled dirty and old, like someone had
gone to the bathroom down here a long, long time
ago.

Anna May stood in front of the bookcase. "What's

this?" she asked, puzzled. She picked up a rounded brown leathery object and its identical twin.

They were ears.

Jolene shone her flashlight beam. On the shelf next to the ears were several fingers and what could only have been a penis. Hanging on hooks from the ceiling at an angle, not visible from above, were scalps: long black braids and ponytails that must have been Indian.

"Oh, my!" Anna May exclaimed, and the utterance was so incongruous that Jolene almost laughed.

Almost.

But the sight was so gruesome that it killed all thoughts of humor, overwhelming everything with its inexplicable horror. Neither of them said anything more but simply shone their lights on the other shelves, illuminating more ears and fingers, toes and genitals, a hand, a foot, even what looked like a black shrunken heart. Why were these here? Had Chester Williams saved these body parts as souvenirs?

From what? A war? Or had he been some sort of serial killer, hoarding portions of his victims in this concealed cellar?

She'd had a gut feeling when she'd first seen the trapdoor that nothing good could be behind a room so secret, buried so deep in the earth, and she'd been right.

"What *is* this?" she asked.

She meant all of it—the subbasement, the shelves, the scalps—but Anna May assumed that she meant the specific object she was prodding with her finger, and she turned guilelessly around. "I think it's a dick."

Again, Jolene thought, under other circumstances, she might have laughed.

But not here.

Not now.

"Look at this," Anna May said excitedly. She was

crouching down and shining her beam on the bottom shelf of the bookcase. Reaching out, she drew forth an object that was instantly recognizable. A book of some sort, a bound volume with a filigreed cover.

Anna May opened the book to the first page, began turning subsequent pages slowly while Jolene shone her light on it. "It's a diary!" she said. "It's Chester Williams' diary!" She turned to the last page. "No. It can't be. It starts in 1874 and stops in 1876. He wasn't even born yet. The name on the overleaf is *Chester Williams,* though. . . . It must have been his father's! Or grandfather's!" She looked up at Jolene with a triumphant smile on her face. "Didn't I tell you this was fascinating work?"

Jolene tried to smile back, but she was more frightened than fascinated, and for some reason she kept thinking of that terrible face she and Skylar had seen in their bedroom window. The brown wrinkled head would fit perfectly on one of these shelves next to the fingers and toes.

"Let's go back up," she said. "It's getting a little stuffy down here, and I have allergies."

"Fascinating," Anna May murmured, looking at the book.

"I have an idea. Why don't we switch? You stay down here and do inventory, and I'll go upstairs."

"No, no. We'll both go back up. There's a lot I still need to show you. But I'm definitely coming down here later. There's so much food for thought." She looked around the small dark room. "What do you suppose this was? And why are all of these body parts here?"

"I don't know," Jolene said honestly.

And she didn't want to know.

*   *   *

Skylar sat on a couch in front of the TV, flipping channels while Ms. Finch sat on another couch, flipping the pages of a magazine. His mom's friend was nice and all, but it was obvious she had no kids and didn't know what to do now that she'd been suckered into babysitting one. He felt sorry for her in a way, and for the first time he was glad that he'd be starting school soon. At least around other kids his own age he'd be able to relax and be himself and not worry so much about the adults around him.

He still didn't want to be here, though.

Last night, he'd had a dream that his dad had come to Bear Flats to kidnap him and take him back to Yuma. It was more of a nightmare than a dream, because he didn't want to go with his dad, and he could tell from the look in his old man's eyes that there was some serious craziness in store once the two of them were alone. But he did want to go back to Yuma, and that part of the dream was pretty cool.

If only his *dad* had taken off, and he and his mom had stayed in Arizona.

The phone rang, and Ms. Finch jumped up to get it like a person grateful to finally have something to do—which made Skylar feel even worse. She took the call in another room, so he wasn't able to eavesdrop, but she was back almost immediately.

"I'm sorry," Ms. Finch said, "but that was the restaurant. They need me. I have to go in for ten or fifteen minutes."

"Can I stay here?" Skylar asked.

"No. Not by yourself. But I'll make it quick. And you can have fries and a Coke while I work things out. How does that sound?"

"Can we walk instead of drive?" He couldn't believe what he was saying even as his mouth formed the words. The last thing he wanted to do was pass by that haunted grave site . . . yet that was exactly what he was asking Ms. Finch to do.

"Sure," she told him. "Just let me put on my shoes."

Why had he suggested a stupid thing like that?

Because he'd been thinking about those graves—

Mother Daughter

—ever since they'd passed by them the other day.

And he wanted to see them again.

It was true. The grave site had never been far from his mind, and though just the idea of it frightened him, he was also intrigued by it. He supposed that was why he'd asked to walk by the spot.

Ms. Finch changed from sandals to her tennis shoes and grabbed her purse, and the two of them were out the door. They walked down the road, past the church, then turned into the woods and started up the trail. The path seemed darker this time, spookier, although that might have been because he now knew what lay ahead. Ms. Finch didn't seem to notice, though, and they talked on the way. The conversation was easy, casual, and he thought that maybe she wasn't as desperate to get rid of him as he'd thought she was. She told him about his mom as they walked, what she'd been like as a kid, and although it was weird to think about, it was also kind of nice. His mom didn't talk much about the past, he realized. He wondered why.

They reached the part where the trees grew bigger, thicker, closer together, and there, in the darkest part, exactly as he remembered, was the square of white picket fence. It was off to the side of the trail, and it was just as creepy as he remembered. He suddenly wished they hadn't walked, and at that moment he wanted nothing more than to hurry by and not look back. But, as before, his mouth betrayed him, and he blurted out, "Can I look at it?"

Why had he said that?

Ms. Finch hesitated.

"Just for a second," he promised.

She nodded. "Okay."

"Did you really hear voices?" he asked as they walked over the sunken ground to the fence.

"Yes," she said. "I did."

They didn't say anything after that, and when he peeked over the pickets and saw the gravestones, they looked just as he'd expected them to look: gray and weathered, the words *Mother* and *Daughter* etched onto the granite in fancy old-fashioned script.

"Come on," Ms. Finch said. "Let's go." There was a hint of urgency in her voice, and he wanted to believe that it was because she had to get to the restaurant, but he didn't think that was it.

They turned away—

And heard mumbling.

Chills coursed down his body, as fluid as water poured on him from above. The source of the sound was unclear, but the mumbling grew in volume, and he had no doubt that it was coming from beneath the ground. They were words, sentences, but not like any he had ever heard before, a superfast jumble of high-pitched syllables with no apparent pauses.

He thought of that evil face at the window with its beady eyes and malevolent grin.

This was the language of that terrible visage.

"Go!" Ms. Finch ordered, pulling his arm. He offered no resistance but allowed himself to be led away, and the two of them hurried over the sunken ground back to the trail, the babbling growing ever louder behind them.

"What is it?" he asked as they rushed up the path. "Do you think it's real?" He knew it was real, but he wanted to hear from her that it wasn't, wanted the reassurance of an adult telling him that there no monsters, no boogeymen, that there was nothing to worry about.

"It's the same thing I heard before," she told him, and though she wasn't quite as frightened as he was, the fear was still there.

They did not slow down until they reached the buildings and the street.

He wanted to tell Ms. Finch about that face at the bedroom window, wanted her to know that whatever was out in the woods by those graves had reached out to him and his mom after they'd passed by here the last time. But she was striding briskly down the sidewalk toward Mag's Ham Bun, and he definitely got the impression that she did *not* want to talk about this, a suspicion that was confirmed when she said with false cheer, "Hot today, isn't it? I'll bet that Coke sounds good."

"Yeah," he said. But he wasn't thinking about hot days or cool drinks. He was thinking of that creepy babble coming from those graves, and his skin prickled with the memory of it.

Mother Daughter

He thought of that horrible face he and his mom had seen.

And he wondered what they'd see at the window tonight.

Twelve

"I'm telling you, no trains have been hijacked. No unauthorized engines are on any tracks anywhere on the grid or have been for the past week."

"I saw it in Colorado, just past Grand Junction. If I hadn't diverted myself onto a siding, I would've been killed and you and the company would've been out a hell of a lot of money."

"I know what you said. I read the report."

"Then?"

"Then what?" Holman scratched his balding head. "Look, Tom, I don't know what happened. Maybe you were tired. Maybe you imagined it, maybe . . . maybe it was an optical illusion of some sort. The only thing I'm certain of is that you didn't encounter a rogue engine on that route."

"Or a ghost engine?"

"Now you're just being an asshole."

"I saw it, Pete. From far off, around a curve. It wasn't some quick glimpse of a vague shape. It was a black locomotive. I watched it speed toward me, and it made me take sixteen off on a siding. When it got close, its lights practically blinded me. I saw it!"

Sure you did, Holman wanted to say, but he remained silent. He glanced out the window. In the desert sky, the clouds looked like a herd of miniature tyrannosauruses jumping over a hurdle to attack an oversized dachshund.

This life did things to a man. Holman didn't know if it was the rootlessness or the loneliness or the fact that they had to live with that endless repetitive rhythm hour after hour, day after day, but whatever the reason, railroaders were far more likely to be hypochondriacs, paranoiacs and conspiracy theorists than your average man on the street.

At least in his experience.

And Tom Miller was exhibit A.

The engineer left his office frustrated and angry, and Holman sighed as he swiveled in his seat and looked out again at the sky. Hell, he was getting squirrelly himself. He'd been in the freight yard office for going on three years now, and he spent more time watching clouds than he did trains. It was the randomness of the clouds that appealed to him, the amorphous ever-changing shapes he enjoyed watching. The herd of miniature tyrannosauruses he'd seen a few minutes back had coalesced into a segmented snake; the giant dachshund was now a sinking *Titanic*.

Trains never did that. Boxcars were always boxcars, flatcars always flatcars, and, like he was a child, it was only the occasional anachronistic caboose that brightened up his day and gave him any joy at all.

"There!" Tom shouted from the outer office. "There! I told you, you son of a bitch! I told you!"

Holman went out to see what the commotion was and found the engineer sitting in front of the computer, logged on to an amateur site, one maintained by train fanatics who used digital webcams to record specific sections of track in order to capture the scheduled passing of passengers and freights.

This time, they'd caught something else.

Holman stared in shock at the image on-screen.

It was indeed a black locomotive but one unlike any he had ever seen. It was racing down a section of track that the streaming crawl identified as east central Colorado, past a train on a siding that could have been Tom's, could have been someone else's. The strange thing was: the engine had no markings, no detail, not even a recognizable design. It was as if a child's drawing of a locomotive had been granted three-dimensionality and been brought to life. There was about it the same sort of simplistic relationship to reality.

Only . . .

Only there was a malevolence to it as well, and a sense of wild fury. The engine looked sinister in its bulky blocky blackness, and the way it sped past that stationary freight on the siding, the speed with which it passed and the sheer volume of smoke that poured out at that moment, bespoke a tremendous anger. Holman had no doubt that if the other train *had* been on the same track, the locomotive would have smashed right through it and continued on unscathed.

Tom hit a key on the computer and the mystery train repeated its approach and passing.

"I told you!"

"What is it?" Holman wondered, and realized he'd been speaking aloud only when everyone else in the office chimed in with "I don't know" and "You got me" and "I've never seen anything like *that* before."

Ghost engine, Tom had said. He hadn't been joking, and Holman now understood why. Since his father's day there'd been tales of ghost trains, retellings of the Flying Dutchman story transferred to the rails, knockoffs of other myths concocted by bored conductors or imagined by tired engineers on late-night runs.

Neither he nor anyone he'd ever met had believed any of them, but he thought now of the adage that behind every legend was a grain of truth.

He watched the dark engine speed past the webcam.

Or more than a grain.

"What do you think now?" a triumphant Tom demanded.

"I believe you," Holman said simply.

That seemed to throw him. "Then, uh, what do you think it is?"

"I have no idea. But it didn't register on any of our sensors and didn't show up on the grid."

"A ghost engine?" Tom said. The triumph was gone from his voice.

"Maybe so," Holman admitted. "Maybe so."

Thirteen

Selby, Missouri

Luke, the previous desk clerk, had been right. This job just flat-out sucked.

Dennis sat behind the counter, reading a Barry Welch paperback about a coven of witches in a Utah time-share community, glancing up every so often to see if anyone on the highway was even *considering* turning in to the motel parking lot. There'd been no one checking in or out all morning, and the only human contact he'd had was when the grotesquely overweight man in 110 had come in to complain that the ice from the ice machine melted too fast.

Dennis had promised to inform the owner.

He hadn't told his mom or his sister that he was working here. They thought he was still tooling around the countryside, exploring the wonders of this great land. If they found out he was spending his days behind a ratty counter in a fleabag motel in Selby, Missouri, humoring psychotic behemoths, they'd demand his return faster than he could say "I'm fine," his mom with an insufferable I-told-you-so attitude, Cathy with a sense of politely masked disappointment that would be even harder for him to face.

Two more weeks and he was out, he decided. By

that time, he should have enough money to coast all the way to the coast.

He turned back to his novel.

"She's a stupid old witch and a crazy old bitch! She's a stupid old witch and a crazy old bitch!"

Dennis' head snapped up at the sound of the children's singsong voices.

"She's a stupid old witch and a crazy old bitch! She's a stupid old witch and a crazy old bitch!"

He knew that chant. He'd forgotten about it until now, but when he was a little kid, a group of neighborhood boys had said that to his mother when they saw her on the street. Cathy had been too young to know what was going on, but he had been mortally embarrassed, and it was not until his father, home from work, had caught the boys at it, lectured them and threatened to tell their parents that the taunts had finally stopped.

The kids now were also shouting the refrain at an elderly Chinese woman as she walked along the sidewalk in front of the motel, and Dennis experienced a weird feeling of déjà vu. He was the adult now, in a position to stop those kids the way his father had done, and he checked to make sure the register was locked, then ran out from behind the counter, out of the office and onto the sidewalk.

"Stop that right now!" he ordered. "Leave that woman alone!"

The old lady hurried off as the kids turned toward him. There were three of them—two skinny dirty boys wearing cutoffs and T-shirts, and one belligerent fat boy in jeans and torn Hawaiian shirt—and they faced him with sullen resentment. "Who are you?" one of the skinny kids demanded.

"It's none of your business."

"Was that your mama?" The fat kid laughed derisively.

"Go home!" he ordered. "Get out of here!"

"No!" they all shouted.

"Now!"

"Chink!" the fat boy yelled at him, picking up a piece of gravel from the sidewalk and throwing it.

He ran at the kid, but the punk stood his ground, and it was only after Dennis yelled, "I'm going to kick your fucking ass!" in the most threatening voice he could manage that the little shit finally took off, his friends following.

Dennis slowed, stopped, as the boys dashed around the corner. What the hell was wrong with kids these days? Even in small towns in the middle of nowhere, they seemed to have lost their fear of adults. When he was little, even the wimpiest grown-up was someone to be feared and respected. Now it took direct threats to coax even a halfhearted response out of them.

He started back toward the motel office. *Chink.* He almost laughed. Had he ever heard that word in real life before? He'd read it in old books, but that was about it. The word never even showed up in movies, as far as he knew.

Social progress apparently came very slowly to the hinterlands.

Niggers and Kikes.

He flashed back to the "Noose of Justice" at The Keep, and the smile on his lips faded. Suddenly the child's anachronistic racism didn't seem so benign. There was a history of intolerance here, he realized, an entire culture he'd never been exposed to on the East Coast, and more than ever before, he felt like a stranger in a strange land.

He walked back into the office, went back behind

the counter, picked up his book and waited for customers who didn't come.

That night, he dreamed of a world that had to be hell. Under a blazing red sky, on an endless expanse of burning sand, he was being herded with hundreds of other young men by tall black creatures on horseback. To his eye, the creatures resembled elongated Abraham Lincolns, but against the red sky they were only silhouettes, no details of their features visible. Around him, the other young men cried and wailed, gnashing their teeth, and he knew with certainty that they were all going to die.

For that, he was grateful. They all were. Anything was better than this existence, and as the fiery red sky turned black, a dark hulking mass loomed out of the nothingness behind them, and a shadow fell that was cool and welcome and familiar.

The shadow of death.

In the morning, Dennis awoke late. This was his day off, and he planned to spend it exploring Selby. He was acquainted with the town in a broad, general, touristy sort of way. He knew where the fast-food restaurants were, the grocery store, the gas stations, the major cross streets. But beyond that, Selby was a blur of indistinguishable homes to him, and he thought it would be a good idea to get to know the community in which he was living, even if he was here only temporarily.

He could have driven, but the town was small and instead he decided to walk. He followed the sidewalk, then turned off Main Street onto Crescent Avenue, where an elementary school segued into a park and then into a junior high school.

There was something familiar about this town. No,

not familiar. Welcome. No, not welcome, exactly. Comfortable. No, not that either . . .

He didn't know what the feeling was, couldn't describe it. His mother believed in reincarnation and probably would have said that he'd been here before in a previous life. There was some of that flavor to the experience, although he didn't really believe in reincarnation, and once again he had the feeling that he was caught up in something bigger than himself, that there was a *reason* for him to have embarked on this journey—and a reason he was here in Selby right now.

He followed Crescent to its end. A row of tall trees, their upper branches swaying ominously in a wind that had not made it down to the ground, lined the cross street at which Crescent terminated, and instead of turning left or right on the other street, Dennis continued walking forward. Something led him through the trees, where he found, not the forest he'd been expecting, but what appeared to be the beginnings of a new housing development. There *were* trees at the edges of the open space before him, but they'd been cut down and bulldozed into deadfalls, and the dusty acreage ahead had been completely sheared of all vegetation.

He paused for a moment to take it all in, then pressed on, walking through deep-tread truck tracks, past color-coded stakes, until he reached the far opposite end of the nascent subdivision. This was the line to which the wilderness had been pushed back, and he climbed over a pile of debris, then passed between trees and overgrown bushes, until he came to the purpose of his journey, the reason he had been led here.

It was a graveyard.

At least he assumed it was. But there were none of the ritual accoutrements usually associated with cemeteries. No tombstones, no crosses, no mowed grass, no clearly delineated grave sites. There were only occasional irregular mounds within the unmarked open space, and a few intermittent boulders that could have been randomly deposited rocks but appeared to him to have been deliberately placed. Dennis stood at the periphery of the small clearing. An effort had been made to hide this burial ground, to make it appear to be nothing more than an ordinary plot of land, and he wondered why.

The nearby elms were still swaying to a wind he could not feel, and the morning sun had not yet risen over the tops of the trees, keeping the graveyard in slightly darkened semishadow. It was creepy and he wanted to leave, but he stood his ground, sure that he was supposed to learn something here, to take something from this.

What was it with all this mystical crap lately? There was absolutely no objective reason for him to think that he was *meant* to do anything. Yet he did. Deeply. And he had no idea why. He would have ascribed it to the fact that he'd been alone and on his own for the past few weeks, but the belief had been with him since the beginning of his trip, was, in some strange way, the *reason* for the trip.

He thought of that mountain monster in his dream, that giant behind the wall of smoke.

He was afraid to move forward, he realized, afraid to actually step into the graveyard. To do so would be blasphemous. He knew it instinctively. He felt it in his bones.

Bones.

Whose bones were here? Dennis wondered, looking over the untamed plot of land. And why had so much effort gone into hiding this little cemetery? He forced himself to walk into the shadowed clearing, bracing himself for a psychic assault that never came. He stepped gingerly over one of the disguised mounds, stopped and bent down in front of a crooked rock protruding from the earth. Was there writing on the speckled gray surface? He squinted, looked closer. If there had been, the characters had long since been weathered away, because he saw nothing save the natural roughness of stone, the generic pores and cracks that made it look like every other rock around town.

He had a sudden urge to dig down under one of the mounds, to see what was under there.

He had a sneaking suspicion it would not be human.

The trees stopped moving, the high wind dying, and the sun emerged from above the elms, a crescent sliver of light like the crack of a door opening onto the shadowed ground below. Dennis stood. He had missed his chance. Whatever he was supposed to have learned or taken from this place had not been imparted to him. That window was closed.

He walked slowly back the way he had come, wondering whether the hidden graveyard was scheduled to be razed and graded. Despite all of the work going on around it, the small plot of land and its barrier of trees and bushes had remained untouched until now, and Dennis found that ominous. It was as though a protective force field had been set up around the site to keep destruction at bay.

On the other side of the bulldozed brush, workmen had arrived and were starting up tractors and Caterpillars. No one stopped or questioned him as he made his way across the cleared ground to the road, and he continued his exploration of the town, walking up and down residential streets, discovering a topless bar in Selby's industrial district, buying a Coke at a mom-and-pop grocery store located next to a boarded-up dairy. Selby was bigger than he'd expected and more varied than it appeared from the highway, but no matter where he went or what he saw, the makeshift cemetery remained on his mind, a nagging image that refused to be dislodged from his brain.

Still, he was determined to learn about his temporary home if for no other reason than to talk about it with Cathy at some later date when they could both look back on this experience and laugh. So after a quick Jack in the Box lunch, he got in his car and drove in the opposite direction of the new development and the hidden graveyard, passing a cluttered hodgepodge of thrift stores, auto dealers, beauty salons and churches.

Selby's lone radio station was an automated country channel that seemed to play the same songs in the same order on a continuous twenty-four-hour loop. The motel owner kept it on in the office all day and all night, and if Dennis had to hear Tim McGraw one more time, he was going to break that damn radio and throw it through the fucking window.

He sorted through the CDs in his car, wishing he'd brought along more. It was strange how his musical requirements had changed on this trip. The recent rock CDs and downloads he'd listened to endlessly in his bedroom back home had quickly lost their luster, and the music he craved was quirkier, more individualist fare. One CD he wished he had now was a self-titled release by Brigit's Well, a classically trained Celtic duo. He'd bought it at an Irish festival a few years back, after hearing the two women perform, and though he'd listened to it only sporadically since, the haunting tunes had stayed with him, and at odd times he found himself thinking about the music.

Like now.

The buildings thinned out. He passed a lumberyard;

the fenced lots and downscale offices of plumbers, roofers, construction companies and tree trimmers; and a sprawling junkyard filled with endless rows of cars, bikes and other wheeled vehicles, before the city was replaced with farmland.

A nice place to visit, he thought.

But he wouldn't want to live here.

It was still early afternoon when he returned to the hotel. He tried calling some of his friends back in Pennsylvania, but none of them answered, and after leaving voice mail messages, he dialed his mom's number. Cathy was still at school—he'd call her after dinner—but it was still nice to talk to someone from the real world, even if it was only his mother.

He spent the remainder of the afternoon watching reruns of old comedies on TV, losing himself in the mass media of the larger culture in order to keep from thinking about the smallness of the town in which, for the moment, he lived.

He was scheduled to work at five in the morning, the beginning of a thirteen-hour shift, but he could not sleep, and sometime after midnight Dennis found himself walking down the sidewalk carrying a flashlight. He tried to pretend he was simply out for a stroll, attempting to tire himself out so he'd be able to sleep, but the truth was that he had a specific destination. And he knew exactly what it was.

The graveyard.

Bulldozers and heavy equipment had been hard at work during the day on the land adjacent to the street, but as before, the forest beyond the deadfall was untouched, and the hidden cemetery was exactly the same as it had been earlier this morning.

Protected

He could not help wondering about the site's improbable survival, and the thought sent a chill down his spine.

The mounds looked different at night, more uniform, less random, darkness smoothing out the distinctions, making the place look more like a regular graveyard. There were shadows here now, shadows created by the moonlight that had no obvious source and that moved stealthily around the edges of the clearing even in the total absence of wind.

Only . . .

Only one of the shadows was not a shadow at all. It was a man, an old man, who came limping in from between the trees at the opposite end of the graveyard and knelt down before one of the not-so-randomly positioned rocks. He was carrying what looked like a black cloth bag, the kind magicians sometimes used in the service of a trick, and as Dennis hid behind a tree, holding his breath and hoping he would not be seen, the man withdrew a live chicken from the bag. Grasping the clucking, thrashing animal by the neck, he slit its throat with a knife that suddenly appeared in his hand, and as the animal spasmed its last, he held the wound open wide, letting the blood fall onto the protruding rock. The man was whispering something, a chant perhaps, but Dennis could not make out any of the words.

What was this? Some sort of Santeria ritual? It seemed unlikely here in the white-bread bowels of the Midwest, but he could think of no other explanation for the bizarre rite he was witnessing.

The kneeling man placed a finger on the rock, in the blood, then touched it to his forehead and bowed deeply.

Dennis could not see the old man's face—for all he knew, the man *was* Hispanic and a Santeria practitioner—but he was glad of that. Something told him he didn't *want* to see the features of that shadowed face.

Maybe it wasn't Santeria but Satanism.

The idea did not seem as far-fetched as it should have, and Dennis tried not to make any noise as the man crammed the dead broken chicken back in the black bag. If push came to shove and a fight broke out, he had no doubt that he could physically take the old guy . . . but he was not sure that was all that was at work here.

The man stood and spoke out loud two words that could have been Spanish but sounded like *"bo sau"*— "revenge" in Cantonese—then hobbled off the way he had come. A darkness descended over the graveyard upon his exit, and Dennis realized that for the few moments the man had been there, the moon had shone its light directly onto the spot where he'd been kneeling.

Dennis crept out from behind the tree and stepped into the clearing, walking carefully around the suddenly uniform mounds, shining his flashlight on the ground until he reached the blood-soaked rock. The small standing stone was wet and shiny, and where the blood had spilled on the adjacent ground there were two jet-black stains in the shape of Chinese characters. He wished now that he had allowed his mom to teach him to read and write Chinese the way she'd wanted to. But it was too late for that now, and the best he could do was commit the characters to memory and try to find out later what they meant.

Bo sau.

Revenge.

He wanted to touch the bloody characters but was afraid to do so. There was an aura of malignancy about the shapes, a sense that whatever venom they possessed could be imparted to anyone who touched them, and Dennis backed fearfully away, wondering what exactly the old man had done. He had never been so frightened in his life, and though he continued to think he'd been meant to see this, he still did not know why. For the first time, it occurred to him that whatever had led him here, whatever had compelled him to take this trip, might not be so benign.

He turned back the way he'd come, vowing never to return to this spot.

This *spot*? Hell, there was no reason for him to stay in this *town*. He'd earned enough cash to get him to Colorado at the very least, maybe all the way to California if he skipped a few meals and spent a couple of nights in his car. He could go back to the motel right now, pack up his stuff, catch a few winks, then, in the morning, collect what he was owed from the owner and be off. If need be, he could get another crappy job in another podunk town and stay there for a week or so to pick up some extra cash.

But he was not going to remain in Selby another day.

That settled it. Feeling better, feeling lighter, as though a great burden had been lifted, Dennis made his way past the deadfall, over the graded land of the soon-to-be subdivision and back onto the sidewalk.

Ten minutes later, he was sorting through his belongings and filling up suitcases, thinking about what he'd need before he hit the road.

If only he'd packed his Brigit's Well CD . . .

Fourteen

Flagstaff, Arizona

In her dream, Angela was living in a tent in the woods with an ugly little monkey that was her baby. She was hiding but from whom or what she did not know, and that made her feel even more tense and anxious than if she had known the identity of her pursuer. She peeked out from between the flaps of her tent to make sure no one was near the camp, listened for a moment to ensure that she heard no unfamiliar noises in the surrounding woods, then quickly emerged, baby in one hand, pail in the other, to get water from the creek a few yards down the hill.

The baby chittered in her arms, showing its fangs.

There was no sign of anyone about, no indication that another person was anywhere near the woods, but something felt off, something felt wrong, and she wished she had waited to get the water.

It was too late to turn back now, though. She was already out and halfway there, so she might as well go through with it. She sprinted between a tree and a manzanita bush—or came as close to sprinting as she could with her arms full—and saw the creek just ahead. Reaching it, she knelt down, scooped up a bucket of the fresh clear water—

And a shadow fell upon her.

She looked up, startled, heart pounding crazily.

It was Chrissie, but it was not Chrissie. She was a man instead of a woman, and she was standing on the opposite side of the creek dressed in some sort of gray uniform that looked familiar but that Angela could not quite place. There was a striped hat and overalls . . .

An engineer.

The man who was Chrissie was a train engineer.

With a vicious snarl, the man stepped into the water, drew from behind his back a lantern and swung it at Angela's head. Angela put up her hands to ward off the blow, but her baby was in her hands, and the metal edge of the lantern struck the monkey full in the face, causing it to cry out once, shrilly, before a splatter of blood erupted from the back of its shattered skull, spraying all over Angela. The drops that landed in her open mouth tasted salty, sickening.

Then Angela was running over train tracks, over soft ground covered with dry leaves, over hard dirt roads, toward town, never looking back, knowing she was being chased but afraid to see how close her pursuer was getting.

Once in town, she ducked into a shop. She'd never seen the shop before, but she knew its layout perfectly and ran through a doorway hung with beaded curtains, down a narrow flight of steps and into—

The tunnel.

It was crammed not with dead bodies but with living people, and they were all hiding there, the same way she was. She knew instantly that it was the engineer from whom they were seeking sanctuary.

Footsteps sounded on the floor above their heads. The slow deliberate knocking of boots on wood.

Engineer's boots.

Around her, women started sobbing; men whimpered; a child cried. Angela tried to push her way through the densely packed crowd, wanting to get as far away from the entrance as possible, knowing that this time the engineer would ignore all of the others, that this time he had come for her. But the wall of bodies held fast, no one willing to give up space or pass his or her advantage to Angela.

The boot steps started down the stairs.

Someone screamed, and then the man who was Chrissie was standing in the doorway, larger than life, bloody lantern in his hand. He looked in on them and laughed, a deep echoing basso profundo, but made no effort to enter the tunnel. Instead, he withdrew, and seconds later the door was shut.

Sealed.

And as the boot steps retreated up the stairs, and in the darkness the air became thicker, warmer, harder to breathe, she knew with a certainty that went all the way to the core of her being that they were going to die.

Angela awoke gasping, as though she really had been trapped in that airless tunnel and had just now escaped. She was in her own room, in her own bed, and through the wall she could hear Chrissie opening and closing the drawers of her dresser.

It sounded like boot steps on stairs.

Angela shivered and remained in bed. Whether because of her dream or that last encounter with her roommate, she was afraid to face Chrissie, and she remained safely in bed, hiding, until she heard the sound of the shower, whereupon she quickly kicked off the blanket and jumped up.

Instinctively, she looked down at her bed. She'd thrown out the moldy sheets and the clothes she'd been wearing when the corpse had grabbed her—she'd tied everything up in a Hefty garbage sack and tossed the whole thing in a Dumpster in back of a gas station on her way to school yesterday—but the mold on her bed was back, and this time it covered a much larger area. Beneath the strange thick hairiness, the bottom half of her sheet resembled skin, human skin that had been pulled tight enough to reveal the capillaries within. She backed away, disgusted but unable to take her eyes off the sight. She'd been sleeping on that. With horror, she recalled that her feet under the blanket had felt warm and comfortable, as though resting on velvet, and she nearly gagged when she thought of her toes touching that terrible corpse-spawned mold.

What was going on here? What kind of alternate universe had she entered?

She quickly glanced down at her bare feet, at the legs of her pajama bottoms, grateful to see that there were no black spots, no mold, nothing out of the ordinary. Inwardly, she breathed a sigh of relief, but she knew that she'd be checking on herself every ten minutes for the rest of the day just to make sure there was no sign of unusual growth on her skin.

Should she go to the student health center and get herself examined? Probably. She'd almost done so twenty times yesterday, deciding against it only out of fear of what she might learn. Which was no doubt what she'd end up doing today.

There was a clunk in the pipes as someone in another apartment turned on a faucet. Angela listened. The shower was still on but would not be for long. An ardent environmentalist, Chrissie took short showers in order to conserve water, and Angela wanted to be out of the Babbitt House before her roommate emerged from the bathroom. She slipped on a pair of jeans and a T-shirt, slid into some sandals, tied her hair back with a scrunchie, grabbed her books and purse and sped out of the bedroom, through the sitting room and into the hall.

Where she didn't breathe a whole lot easier.

The second-floor hallway was empty, but the atmosphere was heavy, oppressive, what she imagined it must feel like to be in a haunted house. She was hoping that her own perceptions were simply skewed, that there'd been no objectively verifiable change to the house itself. But after what she'd experienced, she could not be sure that that was true, and she knew she wouldn't be able to relax until she was outside and in the open air.

She thought of the mold on her bed, the sheet that looked like skin.

Angela hurried downstairs, grateful not to run into anyone. On the first floor, she passed by the open entrance to Winston and Brock's apartment. Neither of them was visible, but through the doorway, she saw a large black spot on their usually immaculate white couch. She sped past, feeling cold, her chest tight as she held her breath.

"Angela!"

She heard Winston calling from behind her, and though she didn't want to, she stopped, turned around. He was coming out of the apartment, and he moved next to her, arms outstretched.

"Chrissie told us what happened," he said sympathetically. She was focused on a stain that darkened Winston's collar: black mold. She glanced up at his face and saw his look of concern slide into a sly gleeful grin. "Serves you right, you stupid brown bitch!"

From inside the doorway came the sound of Brock's derisive laughter.

Stupid brown bitch.

Those were the same exact words Chrissie had used. She ran out the front door, onto the lawn, tears stinging her eyes. There was silence behind her, but in her mind she heard everyone in the building laughing, saw all of them lined up at the windows, pointing at her, the tips of their fingers covered with black mold.

Her hands were shaking as she withdrew the key chain from her purse, her fingers fumbling as she tried to find the right one. Not wanting to encounter Chrissie, she'd come home late last night after hiding in the university library until it closed, so her usual parking spot had been taken and she'd been forced to park up the street. Fortunately. She did not want to be anywhere near Babbitt House right now.

She got in, took off. She was crying as she drove down the street and circled back toward the highway, and she was still crying when she finally made it through the center of town to school.

Being in Dr. Welkes' class was weird.

Half of the students weren't there, and most of those who had shown up were like zombies or drug addicts: glassy-eyed and staring, movements lethargic and skin pale. The professor himself seemed out of it. He attempted to continue on as though nothing had happened, and though he'd no doubt given this same lecture on the Anasazi many, many times, he stumbled over his words, got lost in his thoughts, let sentences trail off with no resolution. It was as if they'd all been damaged or affected by their experience in some deep indefinable way and were no longer able to function in the normal world.

She felt the same way herself.

She wondered if the cop did, too.

Angela realized that she had no idea if news had leaked out to the general population, if the policeman had filed a report, if a journalist covering the police beat had picked up on it, if there were stories in the newspaper or segments on the TV news. She'd been living in her own hermetically sealed environment, and since no one from the outside had contacted her, she did not know what was going on in the real world.

The class seemed to last forever, and when Dr. Welkes dismissed them early, there was a rush to escape from the room. Angela had chosen a seat near the door today and as a result was one of the first people out. Not wanting to see, talk to or be with her fellow students, she hurried to the far end of the corridor and took the stairs down instead of the elevator.

Her next class was political science, but she decided to skip it, and having nowhere else to go, she found herself in front of Edna Wong's desk in the university's housing office, sobbing as she described Chrissie's sudden shift in attitude and the racist echoes of Winston's unprovoked attack.

The housing administrator was sympathetic, understanding, all of the things Angela had expected her to be, but unless she was mistaken, there was something else present as well, a *knowledge* of what had transpired, an awareness of events that went beyond what Angela had told her.

Edna leaned forward. "I'm not supposed to ask this, so this is off the record and I'm going to deny I ever said it." She shot a quick glance toward the closed door. "Are they all white? Your roommates?"

Puzzled, Angela nodded. "Yes."

"I thought so."

"Do you think that has something to do with it?"

"Maybe, maybe not," the old woman answered cryptically. "It's too early to know."

"Too early?" This was getting stranger by the second.

The housing administrator did not directly respond

but appeared to change the subject. She, it seemed, had heard about the fateful field trip to the recently discovered tunnel, and she asked Angela to explain what had happened in her own words. "Be honest," she said. "Tell me everything, no matter how unbelievable it sounds."

So she did, even telling the old lady about the corpse hand grabbing her and the subsequent spreading of the black mold.

Edna expressed no surprise, simply nodded.

Suddenly, Angela was not sure she wanted to be here.

"What is your ethnic background? You are Hispanic, correct?"

Angela nodded, blushing, though there was no reason for her to be embarrassed.

"Interesting," Edna said. Then she smiled brightly and put a hand on Angela's. The tears and despair were gone now, replaced by wariness and curiosity. This wasn't going at all the way she'd thought it would. "We don't have any housing available at the moment, dear, but even if we did, I'd ask you not to leave for a week or so anyway. I'd like you to . . . keep an eye on the situation. Do you think you could do that for me? You're my first priority if housing becomes available, and believe me, I'll keep my eye out for you and let you know if anything comes up, but until then if you could monitor what goes on, without subjecting yourself to any uncomfortable situations . . ." The housing administrator's voice trailed off.

Angela nodded, though the thought of returning to Babbitt House created knots in her stomach. In her mind, she saw black mold spreading from apartment to apartment as each of the residents waited in the hall to call her a stupid brown bitch.

The nod turned into a shake. "No," she said, and it felt weird putting her foot down like this with someone so much older than she, someone in a position of authority. "I can't."

Edna smiled sympathetically. "I understand, dear. I understand completely. And I would never make you do something that you didn't feel confident about." She swiveled in her seat, punched a key on her computer. "What I can do is try to arrange a swap. It's been a few weeks—there are bound to be complaints in here, people who don't get along with their roommates. Maybe I can find one who'll be willing to switch with you."

Angela felt even weirder about that. She couldn't justify putting someone else into her situation. After all, the mold was still there, spreading, infecting people.

She was living in a goddamn science fiction story.

"Shouldn't we . . . call somebody?" she suggested. "Something's going on there. Maybe the police are already working on it—I don't know—but there have to be some professors here, microbiologists or something, who would be interested in studying my bedsheets, who might be able to do something about it."

"They can't do anything," Edna said, and the certainty in her voice once again made Angela think that the old woman knew more than she was telling. She felt cold, and thought that perhaps she ought not to have been as open as she had been.

The housing administrator's phone rang, and Angela took the opportunity to leave. "I have to go," she said, standing, grabbing her books.

"Wait a moment," Edna said.

But Angela didn't wait. She gave a quick wave, then was out the door and hurrying down the corridor. She strode past the front desk and out of the housing office, grateful to be out in the open air. Back in California, it was still summer, but here in Flagstaff the air was tart and tangy, something she found refreshing.

She needed to call her parents, e-mail her friends back in California. She needed some grounding. Part of her was thinking it might be time to just pull up stakes and head home, forfeit her scholarship money, find a part-time job for the next three months, then transfer to East Los Angeles Community College for the spring semester. But she'd worked too long and too hard to get where she was, and she'd never been a quitter. Just getting out of her neighborhood and going off to college had been a battle—a battle most of her peers had lost—and she wasn't about to let a few horror-show special effects send her scurrying back to the safety of the familiar.

Was this the way people in monster movies rationalized their behavior? Was this why they always acted so stupidly?

She wasn't acting stupidly, Angela told herself. She was being brave.

Outside of the building, she saw the student who had asked whether she was going on the field trip to the tunnel, the one who hadn't shown up. He'd been in class today, but she'd been distracted and hadn't paid much attention to him. Although now that she thought about it, he was one of the few who hadn't seemed dazed or scared or completely out of it. He and the other students who hadn't come.

"Hey!" he called, catching sight of her. "Wait up!"

She did. Out of curiosity more than anything else.

"What was with that class today?" he asked as he reached her.

She looked at him. She still didn't know his name, and she doubted that he knew hers. There was something irritating about his assumed intimacy, yet at the same time she was grateful for it, thankful to have human contact that was not . . . weird.

"I'm sorry," she said. "I don't believe I know your name."

He grinned. "Derek," he said. "Derek Scott. And you're . . . ?"

"Angela Ramos."

"So, Angela, what was with that class today?"

He was still smiling, which meant that he was curious but not worried, and she wasn't sure how much to tell him. She was acutely conscious of how crazy the whole thing sounded.

He gave her an in. "Is it because of all those bodies? I heard someone freaked out down there and there was a stampede."

So that was the story going around?

"I wish I'd gone."

"Why didn't you?" she asked.

"Something came up." As though worried she might take that to mean girlfriend trouble, he added quickly, "I had to pick up my brother from school. My mom's car broke down."

So he was interested. And local.

That emboldened her.

"You're lucky you didn't go," she said. She looked at Derek, took a deep breath and told him everything. She wasn't sure he'd believe *any* of it, let alone *all* of it, but she needed to get it out. Derek's reaction was a far cry from Edna Wong's subdued acknowledgment. He didn't ask any questions while she spoke, but the look on his face said it all. He *did* believe it, and her story not only shocked but frightened him.

When she got to the part about the black mold on her bed and how Chrissie had touched it and undergone an instant personality change, Derek stopped her. "What did you do with the sheet and blanket? Did you take it in somewhere and have it analyzed?"

"I was going to," Angela admitted, "but I . . . threw it all away."

"What!"

It had been a stupid move then and seemed even stupider now. She had no idea why she'd done such a thing, and the only reason she could come up with was that she'd been contaminated, too, just like Chrissie. The black stuff had been on her arm originally, and even though she'd scrubbed it off and it hadn't come back, maybe some trace memory remained and caused her to protect the mold rather than try to eradicate it.

Where was that bedding now? she wondered. Had the mold broken free of the garbage sack? Was it even now spreading around the city? A feeling of panic gripped her.

"It was on my sheet again this morning," she told Derek. "Even worse. Unless someone's been in my room, it's still there."

"We have to tell someone." She could hear the fear in his voice and it both terrified and reassured her. At last someone was having a normal reaction to what was going on. "I have an Intro to Microbiology class. The instructor might know what to do. If not, he'll probably know who does. Come on!"

Derek grabbed her hand and practically pulled her down the sidewalk through the light crowd of students.

Finally, she thought. And the two of them hurried across campus toward the science building.

Fifteen

Arlington National Cemetery, Virginia

Josh McFadden gulped the cold dregs from his cup while he tried to decide what to do, finishing off the vile liquid more so he would have something with which to occupy himself than from any real desire for coffee.

The *last* thing he needed right now was more caffeine.

He was jittery enough as it was.

Josh stood in the doorway of his office looking out at the rolling lawn, Technicolor green in the fresh light of the new day. Where identical rows of white headstones, a man-made monument to order, a blatant refutation of the chaos of war, should have stood, disorder and confusion had reasserted themselves. Sometime during the night, the memorial park had been vandalized. Someone—or a group of someones—had dug up what appeared at first glance to be a considerable number of graves, disinterring the bodies. These corpses, in various states of decomposition, were not just strewn about the grounds but had been thrown deliberately over the white gravestones, their dark irregular shapes marring the perfect symmetry of the cemetery.

In the center of the park, cutting a jagged swath through the aligned rows of identical stone markers, digging deep into the grass and exposing the black soil underneath, were tracks from twin sets of narrow wheels, a heavy vehicle that had left destruction in its wake. From here, it looked like a bulldozer had smashed through the east gate and driven on a vaguely slanted course toward the older section of the cemetery.

No.

Not a bulldozer.

A train.

Josh didn't know how he knew it, but that seemed right. He wasn't an expert or anything, but the ruts in the ground looked like those that would be made by an engine that had gone off its tracks.

The thing was, the train seemed to have simply disappeared once it reached a certain point. Either that or it had retreated so perfectly, backtracking along the same path so precisely, that no evidence of its withdrawal was visible.

There was something eerie about that, eerie and unfathomable, and rather than think about it, Josh was spurred to action, going into the office and calling Tank, his supervisor. Let that overmuscled asshole earn his paycheck and deal with the problem. It was about time he did some work around here.

Meanwhile, Josh was the one alone in the graveyard.

Even though the train was gone and it was daytime.

He didn't think that made much difference, and he'd locked himself in the office, phone in hand, ready at a second's notice to dial 911, until the cavalry arrived.

The entire cemetery was soon overrun with Pentagon types, soldiers, FBI agents and even a few ordinary cops who wanted in on the action but were quickly turned away. Everyone had a job to do and everyone did it, and both Josh and Washington Carter, his job-share partner, were quizzed by an endless stream of investigators, asked the same questions over and over again until their brains were numb. Certainly no one suspected either of them of anything, but water flowed downhill, and Josh knew that the two of them would get the blame for what happened. He might as well start sending out résumés right now.

What he couldn't understand—what *no one* could understand—was how such destruction could have occurred without anyone hearing it. The fences and gates were also wired to the hilt with the most elaborate and up-to-date security systems known to man, yet none of the alarms had been triggered when that behemoth had crashed through the barrier into the cemetery.

It wasn't until later, much later, after all of the information on the affected graves had been recorded, that they learned that every one of the disinterred bodies had been a Civil War veteran.

There was probably a reason for that, Josh thought. It probably meant something.

But neither he nor anyone else could figure out what.

Sixteen

Canyonlands National Park, Utah

Henry stood on the sand, looking out over the water. He was naked but unashamed. Proud, in fact, though he realized why only when his penis started to grow and he felt one tongue licking his balls, another sliding up and down the crack of his ass. He looked down to see the twins slavishly working on his nether regions, and as a family floated by in a sailboat, he hoped they could see these two gorgeous babes who so desperately desired *him*.

The old Henry wanted to tell the woman behind him that she was licking the spot where he shit, that she might even get some kind of disease from it, but the new Henry reveled in this forbidden debauchery, and he experienced a strange triumphant sense of pleasure from the submissiveness of the Asian twin in back of him.

The one licking his scrotum began moving her head slightly as her tongue flicked faster against his testicles. The underside of his erect penis rubbed against the silky smooth hair on top of her head, the sensation building to a fever pitch, and then he was coming, then he was spurting, what felt like a cup, a quart, a gallon of sperm pumping into her straight black hair.

It didn't drip onto her ears or bare back but was absorbed into the hair, and as he watched, the blackness began to grow. It was no longer hair but a shadow of hair, of a head, of a body, of a person, a shadow that expanded to cover the sand, the water and finally the sky before engulfing him as well.

Henry awoke with his underwear off and his penis stuck to his hairy stomach with dried crusted semen.

He tried to sit up, but it was painful and felt like the skin was being ripped from his cock. He examined the organ, trying to determine the best way to liberate it, before finally wetting his palm with spit, rubbing his penis and gradually working it free.

Grimacing, he sat up. The events of the dream (*nightmare*?) had been fantastic, but the location was real. Of that he was sure. Although he couldn't place it, Henry knew he'd seen that spot before. He glanced up at the photo of Sarah by the beach but knew that wasn't the place. The truth was, he was not even sure it was the ocean, at least not in a traditional sense. Yes, the water extended as far as the eye could see, but the waves were microscopic, barely up to his ankle. That could have meant that the whole thing was some type of symbol or metaphor for something else, but he didn't think so. He was sure he'd actually been to that site, though the harder he tried to recall it, the more knowledge of it seemed to slip away.

He found his underwear balled up at the foot of the bed. He had no idea how his briefs had gotten there or how they'd gotten off his body. He *hoped* he'd done it himself in his sleep, but he couldn't be sure and that worried him.

Henry went into the small bathroom, tossed his underwear in the hamper and took a long shower, scrubbing his skin until everything was gone, then letting the hot water hit his back until it began to run out. He got dressed, made and ate breakfast, then paced around the inside of his cabin, glancing out occasionally at the overcast sky. It was his day off again, and the superintendent had made it clear that until further notice, all rangers and park employees not on duty were to remain in their cabins. Henry understood that this was a precautionary measure, that a lot of strange, unexplained, *dangerous* things were going on out there . . . but the thought of staying indoors all day still made him stir-crazy.

He glanced over at his bookshelf. Next to "the Canon"—the collected works of Edward Abbey and Wallace Stegner—were a handful of books from his past, along with a few newer volumes lent to him by friends that he hadn't gotten around to reading. He chose one of these and settled down on the couch. *Half Asleep in Frog Pajamas.* He'd been a big Tom Robbins fan back in the days when books had meant something to him, when fiction and literature had provided him with a road map for life, and he was looking forward to visit once again with an old trusted friend. But he was put off by the author photo on the dust flap. This was Tom Robbins? His heart sank as he looked at the black-and-white shot. Gone was the happy hairy hippie with the wide, open smile pictured on the back of *Still Life with Woodpecker* or even the grinning New Age loon from *Skinny Legs and All.* In his place was a sober pretentious yuppie wearing the expression of someone too preoccupied with himself to give anyone else the time of day.

Henry put the book down without reading a single word of it. He was getting to be an old fuck. Music made him sad now, too, songs he hadn't heard for a long time filling him with an almost unbearable melancholy. Just last night, he'd heard an old John Prine song carried on the wind from someone else's cabin,

and all of a sudden he'd started crying. Of course, he'd
been half drunk, so that might have had something to
do with it, but still . . .

He'd been drunk a lot lately. It was the only way he
seemed to be able to deal with what was happening.

They'd found Laurie Chambers yesterday in a ra-
vine in the Maze. Or, rather, a hiker had found her.
He'd called it in on his cell phone, and a helicopter
had had to retrieve her body. She'd been mauled and
half-eaten, most likely by predatory animals after the
fact, and authorities were still waiting for an autopsy
to determine the cause of death.

Henry already knew the cause of death.

The twins.

Laurie had been found in a remote environmentally
sensitive area, but all about her the cliff walls had
been defaced, the sandstone carved and etched with
nonsensical drawings: top hats and train tracks, horses,
guns and suns. What did it mean? Henry wondered.
What was the point of it all? For there *was* a point,
and it *did* mean something. Of that he was sure.

He felt the way he had as a teenager in algebra
class, where, try as he might, he simply could not grasp
the concepts his teacher was trying to impart to him;
no matter how much he studied, understanding remained frustratingly out of reach.

A shadow passed over the sun, bathing the room
in darkness.

Shadow? Sun?

It was heavily overcast and had been since he'd
awakened.

Henry got up from the couch, walked to the window. The dark translucent object that had been shad-
ing the already filtered sunlight moved away from the
glass onto the narrow porch, standing free. It was, as
perhaps he should have known, a shadow of human

size, the silhouette of a naked woman. One of the
twins? From the other window in the kitchenette, another human shadow detached itself. This one, to his
surprise, was that of a man.

He turned around. The entire cabin, he saw now,
was aswarm with shadows, both inside and out. On
the porch, a small crowd of swirling shapes seemed to
be circling the building, jostling for position as they
circumnavigated his home. In the bathroom, the small
frosted window appeared to be winking at him as a
shadow near the sink bopped back and forth in front
of it. In the kitchenette, the form of a man wavered
near the refrigerator.

What the hell was going on?

He was not as scared as he could have been or
perhaps should have been, and that was good. Rather
than standing there frozen in place, he opened the
front door and strode out on the porch, ready to do
battle. The caravan of shadows passed over him,
around him, *through* him for all he knew, but he felt
nothing. "Get out of here!" he ordered. He lashed
out at the moving band, hoping to scatter them, but
the shadows continued on, unwilling or unable to
stop.

Henry looked out at the desert leading up to his
door.

And saw the twins.

They were darker than the other shadows, more
substantial, almost three-dimensional, and they were
standing in the same spot they had been in his first
dream of them.

He was starting to get scared now, but he stepped
off the porch and walked toward them anyway. As he
did so, the other shadows fled his cabin, dispersing
into the air, into the ground, until only the sisters were

left. It was as if the others had come to the house to get his attention, to direct his focus toward the twins.

There were no features visible on those black blank faces, but he knew they were watching him nevertheless, and they waited until he was within spitting distance before they glided across the sand away from him. To his surprise, they headed not back into the desert but toward the other rangers' cabins.

He wanted to shout at them, wanted to tell them to stay away, wanted to keep them from his friends and coworkers, but he was afraid to speak up. Besides, he knew it wouldn't do any good. He had no control over them.

He wondered if he really wanted to protect the other rangers—or if he simply wanted to keep the twins to himself.

He realized that he already had the beginnings of an erection.

He followed the flowing shadows to Ray Daniels' cabin, where alarm bells went off instantly in his brain. The cabin's shades were drawn, but the front door was wide open—and Ray *never* left his front door open. The two forms blended with the darkness of the interior, disappearing from sight, and Henry slowed his pace, an instinct for self-preservation warning him not to rush in. Hoping the twins would reemerge, he waited a moment, squinting into the gloom, trying to see any sign of movement, but within the dark doorway all remained still.

And silent.

The hair on Henry's arms prickled. There was no noise, not even the sound of birdsong or lizardscuttle.

Just like in the canyon.

He wanted to run away. Something bad was in that cabin, and there was no way this situation could turn out okay. But he steeled himself for the worst and forced himself to put one foot in front of the other. "Ray!" he called out. "Ray! You home?"

Silence.

Henry took a deep breath, walked up the single step to the porch and poked his head inside the cabin. "Ra—" His voice died as he saw his friend's body.

Ray was lying nude on the floor, what was left of his face gnawed to the bone, the terror in his intact eyes in direct contrast with the death's-head grin of his exposed lower skull. In the ranger's clutching right hand was a corner of the Navajo throw rug he'd bought last year at Third Mesa. His left hand was a stump, fingers nowhere in sight, a puddle of blood pooled around it.

Henry was sickened. But not surprised.

He looked to the left, catching movement out of the corner of his eye. A thin line of light issued from beneath an improperly closed blind in the kitchen, offering faint illumination that revealed two dark figures seated at the breakfast table.

The twins.

They were seated across from each other and though no sound issued from their shadow lips, they were laughing, rocking slightly in their chairs, their bodies jiggling with mirth.

Once again, he had the feeling he was supposed to glean something from this, that he was being given a message or warning, that something was trying to impart information, but he had no clue what it could be.

Confused, scared, but above all angry, Henry strode over to the closest window and pulled the shade nearest him. It rolled up with a loud snap and light poured into the cabin. He moved to the next one, pulled it open. And the next one. And the next one. By the time he looked over at the breakfast table to see the reaction of the twins, they were gone.

Good, he thought, satisfied.

He looked out of the cabin's windows toward the flat expanse of desert to the west. And froze.

In the middle of the sand stood a train.

The sight was more threatening and far more frightening than that simple description made it sound. For the train was bathed in darkness, not merely black, but suffused with an aura of dread that could be sensed even from here. This was no shadow or slightly more substantial shade; it was a concrete presence in the desert. There was an antique steam engine with accompanying tender, four passenger cars and a caboose. He could see a yucca that had been squashed under one of the engine's metal wheels, could see the odd murky heat waves shimmering around its irregular surface. How it had gotten there and where it had come from—

hell

—he would not venture to guess, but there was no doubt that it had arrived.

He remembered a story his father had told him about seeing a ghost once on a train in Nebraska. His dad had been riding the rails looking for work, using the freights, as so many migrants had at that time, to get him from seasonal fruit picking in California to corn harvesting in the Midwest. It was night, of course, and he'd lost his lone fellow traveler back in Wyoming when the man had hopped off at his hometown. The night air was cold, and Henry's father was huddled in a corner of the boxcar, wrapped in a stolen horse blanket. It was practically pitch-black, with only a thin sliver of moonlight showing from a crack in the closed door. And then . . .

It wasn't.

There was strange luminescence in the opposite corner. Not the radiance of an electric light or a gas flame but a vague gray glow that gradually brightened into a sickly green. For a brief moment, his father said, he'd seen the form of a man, an Indian warrior, and though the ephemeral figure was fierce in its appearance, he had felt no fear. The ghost disappeared, not fading away, but blinking out of existence, though a remnant of that gray glow remained for several moments longer. They were passing through an area where the railroad had been built through Indian territory, and his father assumed it was his own native ancestry that had allowed him this glimpse of a spirit long departed.

Henry thought of that now, looking at the train in the sand. He watched for a few more seconds out the window, then exited through Ray's back door to get a better view. Other rangers, he saw, were walking out of their cabins, too, having also noticed the phantom locomotive. The train was no hallucination; it was really there—not that he'd needed any proof—but he was still a little surprised that other people could see it. Jill was on duty, as was her husband, Chris, but Stuart, Pedley, Raul and Murdoch were all converging on the well-worn trail that linked the park service housing units.

He joined them. Although the dark train was still more than a mile off, everyone stopped at the edge of the path, afraid to move closer. The feeling of dread emanating from those motionless black cars was powerful even this far away, and Henry remained alert, on edge, ready to bolt should even a puff of steam emerge from the smokestack.

"Slow train to the coast," Stuart whispered next to him.

Henry remembered the euphemism. They'd used it in the army to refer to someone who'd died. There was one kid in basic training who had keeled over while running, been taken to the infirmary and never returned, and when asked for details about what had happened, the DI had said simply, "He took the slow train to the coast." That was Henry's first exposure to the phrase, but like everyone else in his unit, he'd used it excessively over the next three years, eight months and twenty-eight days. It had been decades since he'd heard, said or even thought of the term, though, and the image conjured by Stuart's whisper frightened him even more.

Slow train to the coast.

The coast.

He thought of his dream, the vast expanse of water, and that linguistic connection, tenuous as it might be, caused his skin to ripple with gooseflesh. Again he sensed meaning and purpose just beyond his reach.

All of them were quiet, those who dared speak whispering like Stuart. The train waited—*like a lion,* Henry thought—and the rangers waited, too, wondering what was going to happen next, whether the train was going to speed away, disappear into thin air, turn and crash into them and their cabins . . . or sit there forever until one of them grew brave enough to approach it and investigate.

He looked from Stuart to Pedley to Raul to Murdoch, then turned back toward the train.

Why was it here? What was its purpose?

Were the twins on it?

The desire to learn the answer to that question was almost enough to get him to walk across the sand to find out.

Almost.

There was the blast of a steam whistle, one short

quick burst that made them jump as one. There were noises in that sound that should not have been present in the whistle of a train, subliminal tones he could neither hear nor identify but that for some reason made Henry think of multitudes screaming. He was about to run away, following an instinctive desire to flee back into a cabin so he wouldn't be out in the open, when the black train took off, not starting slowly and picking up steam, but departing instantly at full speed, like accelerated film footage. In seconds, it was past the dunes and gone from sight.

"What in fuck's name was that?" Raul breathed.

"Yeah," Stuart said.

"Ray's dead," Henry told them numbly.

"A train?" the superintendent said skeptically. He looked around at the faces of the rangers before him and obviously did not see what he'd hoped to see. Henry looked around, too. There was no embarrassment or hesitancy on the features of his coworkers, only grim determination and barely concealed fear.

Hope disappeared from Healey's face. He sat down resignedly on one of Ray's chairs. "Tell me what happened."

All eyes turned toward Henry. He was now the point man for all of this mumbo jumbo. He'd found Ray's body, and though he hadn't said anything about the twins, they all knew by now that he was the one who'd discovered the vandalized rock art. Which apparently granted him some sort of authority.

Sighing, Henry explained in a matter-of-fact, step-by-step manner exactly what had happened. He left out the part about the shadows in his cabin and following the shades of the Oriental babes over to Ray's, but in order to keep the story as emotionally true as possible, he described his uneasy feelings and the certainty he'd felt while looking at Ray's cabin that something terrible had happened inside.

Then he talked about the train.

They'd all seen that, so he held nothing back, describing that black locomotive in all of its hellish glory, explaining how even from far away he'd sensed its dark power. The others nodded as he spoke. He saw the fear on their faces, recognized it, felt it again himself.

"I guess what we're saying," he told Healey, "is that we need some assurances that something will be done to protect us. We're out there every day while you're safely in your office—"

"My office isn't that safe," the superintendent pointed out.

"All the more reason for us to come up with . . . some sort of plan." Henry realized he was floundering. He had no place left to go.

"There's something out there," Stuart said. "And I don't want to meet it face-to-face."

Henry glanced out the open door. The state police had left only a few minutes prior, taking with them signed statements from the witnesses and, under plastic, Ray's body. It was the same forensics team that had come out to examine the still-unidentified woman and Laurie Chambers, and one investigator had joked that they ought to set up a satellite station here at Canyonlands, though no one had laughed. Henry thought now that the remark had hit too close to home. They were all on edge, *waiting* for someone else to die, and he wondered if any of the other rangers were thinking of quitting or, at the very least, transferring to another park. He certainly was.

No. That wasn't true. He was thinking about leaving Canyonlands in an objective, disassociated way, but he was not actually considering it.

Because of the twins.

There was a stirring between his legs, and he tried to think of something gross so he wouldn't get an erection: run-over squirrels, squished bugs, dog shit.

He suddenly realized that everyone was looking at him again. He'd zoned out and had no idea what turn the dialogue had taken. It seemed as though someone had asked a question and was waiting for his response. His gaze settled on Healey. "I'm sorry," he said, shaking his head to indicate his distracted state. "What?"

"I said," the superintendent repeated with exaggerated patience, "what do you think we can do to alleviate this problem?"

His mind ran down a host of options: restricting access to sections of the park, always working in teams of three, hiring a shaman. . . .

He thought of the twins.

Henry looked around the room at his fellow employees. "I don't know," he admitted. "I don't think there's anything we *can* do."

Seventeen

"I can't believe it," Leslie said.

Jolene leaned back on her friend's couch, sipped her wine. "Believe it."

"But I don't understand why you haven't gone back. I mean, this is amazing stuff here. Aren't you the least bit curious?"

Jolene sighed. How could she explain to her friend the utter *wrongness* of that cellar, the horrible fear she'd felt while down there, the terrifying nightmares she'd been having ever since? She couldn't, she realized. Those were feelings too profound for words, sensations that could not be translated into language. "No," she lied. "I'm not curious."

They were silent for a moment, both of them sipping their drinks.

"A penis?" Leslie said finally. "Really?"

Jolene nodded.

"So you think Chester or one of the other Williamses was some kind of serial killer?"

"I guess," Jolene said.

But that wasn't what she really thought, was it? That wasn't the reason she hadn't gone back. The truth was that her fear ran far deeper than that, was far more primal. It was the childhood fear of ghosts and monsters and the vast unfathomable unknown, and it was connected to the face she and Skylar had seen through the window at night. And the graves.

"Do you think I could see it?"

"The penis?" she said, stalling.

"The house. Everything."

Jolene shook her head.

"Come on!" Leslie prodded. "What's gotten into you?"

"Nothing."

"Why? Do you think Anna May would be against it?"

"No," Jolene admitted. "One thing I'll say for Anna May is that her commitment to history is pretty pure. She's not planning to hush this up to save reputations or protect the family because they donated the house. She's keeping quiet until she finds out everything she can and gets an accurate picture, but she intends to go public with all this and tell everyone."

"A house of horror brings in a lot more tourists than a dusty old museum."

"It's not even that. She genuinely thinks all information should be available no matter how gruesome or damaging or embarrassing it might be. I kind of admire her for that."

"Information deserves to be free. Isn't that the computer hackers' code or something?"

"I don't know." Jolene thought for a moment, finished her drink, then sighed. "I guess I can take you over there if you want. I do feel kind of bad for bailing on poor Anna May. I should at least apologize. She's called my mom's house about a dozen times over the past week, and I've been ducking her."

"Really?"

"Yeah."

"Now, *about* your mom's house . . . ," Leslie said.

Jolene groaned. "One problem at a time, please."

Leslie laughed.

Maybe it wouldn't be so bad, Jolene thought. Maybe she'd built up the cellar experience in her mind so much that it had been blown way out of proportion and she was obsessing over something that wasn't nearly as horrific as she believed it to be.

She hoped.

They drove over to the Williams place in Jolene's car. Anna May's Oldsmobile was parked in the circular driveway, and Jolene pulled to a stop behind it, tapping lightly on the horn to announce their presence. Maybe the old woman wasn't as skittish as she was, but Jolene knew that if she were working in this house and someone surprised her by showing up without warning, she'd probably have a heart attack. The place was spooky. Even if she hadn't seen what she'd seen, she'd be creeped-out by the building. Especially on a day like today, where the sun was hidden behind a dark bank of threatening clouds, and the entire town lay under a gloomy shadow.

By the time they got out of the car, Anna May was on the porch. She was smiling widely, and for that, Jolene was thankful. At least the old woman wasn't angry with her. Although that also ratcheted up her guilt another notch. How could she have been so thoughtless as to abandon Anna May without an explanation?

She wasn't thoughtless, Jolene told herself. She was scared.

She found herself wondering if the reason Anna May was working alone was because the other members of the historical society had been frightened away, too.

"Mrs. Carter!" Leslie called. She bounced up the

porch steps and gave the old woman a hug. "Haven't seen you in a while."

"I've been busy," Anna May said. "As you can see."

Indeed, the interior of the house was filled with boxes, papers and pictures that had been brought over from the old museum. The Williams family's furniture had been temporarily pushed against the wall along with other donated pieces. Jolene glanced over at Leslie, who shot her a "What do we say now?" look. Neither of them knew how to bring up the questions they really wanted to ask.

They needn't have worried. Anna May was eager to describe her most recent discoveries. In all her years of researching the history of Bear Flats and Pinetop County, she said, she had never run into such a treasure trove of bizarre and fascinating findings.

"This house," Anna May said, marveling, "is a twelve-year-old boy's dream. There's a secret passage from one bedroom to another; there are double attics and, of course, that hidden cellar. It's like a house built for the underground railroad." Her eyes took on an excited gleam. "Although when you read the diary, you'll find that Chester Williams—the *first* Chester Williams—was definitely not the kind of man who would have been involved with that."

Jolene shivered.

"I'll let you read it after I'm finished," Anna May said. "It's . . ." She shook her head. "I can't even describe it. But there are big revelations in there. *Major* revelations."

"What happens?" Leslie asked. "Can't you even give us a hint?"

The old woman grinned. "Murder!" she whispered excitedly.

A file folder filled with papers slid from the slanted

top of a box onto the floor, and all three of them jumped at the sound. Leslie laughed. "We're a brave bunch, aren't we?"

It was the opening Jolene needed. "How *have* you been able to work here all by yourself?" she asked Anna May. Her voice dropped. "Especially after what we found."

"I don't know," the old woman mused, seriously considering the question. "It is very . . . spooky, I must admit. But it's so exciting that I suppose I forget and lose myself in the adventure of it all." She smiled broadly. "Do you want to see what I found this morning?"

"I don't know," Jolene said honestly. "Do I?"

"We do!" Leslie announced for both of them.

Anna May led them along a pathway between the stacked boxes to the parlor. She picked up something from atop an antique table that at first glance looked like the corpse of a baby tied up with string. "I found this in a closet behind one of the closets." She held up the object and for the first time they could see it clearly. It was a marionette. Made from glued-together body parts, mummified pieces of nose and toes wrapped in motley and attached by gutstring to cross-hatched sticks, the figure grinned at her, small white teeth, like the teeth of children, embedded in its upward-angled mouth.

Jolene's blood ran cold. The face of the marionette looked like the face that had peered in at her and Skylar through the window, down to the brown parchment skin, and she turned away from it, hoping the other two couldn't see the trembling in her hands. "I have to pick up my son from school," she said.

"You have forty-five minutes," Leslie told her. "The school's two minutes away."

"It *is* scary," Anna May admitted, putting the marionette back down on the table. "A lot of the items I've come across have been. And that diary . . ." She shook her head. "I assume that's why you didn't come back after that first day?" she asked Jolene. "You got scared off?"

"I'm sorry," Jolene said. "Really. I meant to call you, and I feel so bad that I didn't, but . . ."

"Don't worry about it." The old lady smiled. "Theo was frightened away, too. I don't blame either of you. I guess I just get so . . . carried away with finding out new things, I just don't think about everything else around it. History's my life. I love it. The good, the bad and the ugly."

"The older generation's made of sterner stuff," Leslie jokingly offered.

"I think you're right," Jolene said seriously.

"Oh, pshaw," Anna May said, smiling.

Jolene wasn't sure she'd ever heard anyone actually say "pshaw" before.

"So what is it with all this?" Leslie asked. "Do you think Chester Williams' father or grandfather or whatever really was a serial killer? And why did the rest of the family keep all this stuff? You'd think they'd throw it away. I mean, I can see keeping quiet about an old relative and not wanting anyone to know you had a murderer in the family, but to hold on to these body parts as family heirlooms or something?" She shook her head. "We're talking *Texas Chainsaw Massacre* here. The Williamses had to be one seriously disturbed brood."

There was a thump from the floor above. "Hold on a moment," Anna May said. She moved quickly back between the boxes and up the stairs. "I'll be right back!" she called. Her footsteps stomped up the stairs.

"What do you think that was?" Jolene asked. Her

first irrational thought was that Anna May had found something alive in some secret room in the house.

Or something *not* alive.

"Sounds like something fell," Leslie said simply.

Yes. That had to be it. Her friend was undoubtedly right. But as they walked slowly about the parlor, looking at artifacts and photographs, Jolene was acutely aware that she could hear no noise coming from upstairs, that aside from the sounds of their own movement, the house was silent.

Leslie tentatively touched the marionette. "God, that thing's creepy."

"Everything here is."

"Remember when we were kids, how old-man Williams seemed like such a tight ass? One of those upper-crust stiffs too good to associate with the likes of normal people? Who would've guessed he was sitting here with body parts in his mansion?"

Jolene nodded, feeling cold. "And his wife was dead by then, so he was all alone in here with these secret rooms and his hidden cellar and souvenirs from his family's kills. What do you think he did at night? I saw no TV; there aren't a lot of books. Maybe he just sat here and made things like *that*." She pointed to the marionette.

"It just goes to show: you never know what's going on behind other people's closed doors."

Jolene looked up at the ceiling. There was still no noise from upstairs, and the definition of "I'll be right back" had been stretched well beyond its limit. Something was wrong.

There was another thump on the ceiling above them, this one louder than the first. Much louder.

It sounded like a body falling to the floor.

"Anna May?" Jolene called.

No answer.

She and Leslie shared a quick glance; then the two of them were rushing between the boxes and up the stairs, pausing only for a second at the head of the hallway before pushing open doors and peeking into rooms.

"Oh, God!" Leslie screamed.

Jolene hurried across the hall to where her friend was staggering away from an open door. Even before she got there, she could see Anna May's brutally beaten body, could see the mushy mass of red that had been her face, the indented cavity that had been her chest, the spreading puddle of blood on the floor. But it was not until she was actually in the doorway that she could see the slashes across the old woman's legs, slashes so deep that the white of bone showed through the red of flesh. It was from these gashes that the bulk of the blood was flowing, and there still appeared to be the remnants of a rhythm to the outpouring of thick crimson, the dying throb of a pulse. She had to have been killed only seconds before.

Fingers dug deep and suddenly into Jolene's arm, and for a brief flash of an instant she thought she was about to be slaughtered as well, but it was Leslie. "Who did it?" her friend demanded, looking up and down the hallway. "Where are they?"

That's what she wanted to know, too. There was no one in the bedroom. No killer, either human or animal. But on the walls of the room was what appeared to be a creeping black mold. The consistency of the substance seemed more shadow than fungus, as though the mold was in the process of evolving or, more accurately, as though it was in that place, in that space, but on another plane or in another dimension and was trying to break through.

No, Jolene thought. That wasn't right. It was more like a scene from the past was being overlaid on the present and they were seeing the ghosts of things that once were.

Anna May's bloody body was no ghost, however, and she and Leslie backed away from the door, both of them still looking furtively around the hall as though expecting some sort of phantom to jump out from another doorway at any time. "Let's get out of here," Jolene said. "We'll call the police, let them figure out what happened."

Leslie was already starting to regain some of her composure, and as the two of them hurried back down the stairs, she whipped out her cell phone and called 911. "Anna May Carter's been murdered!" she shouted. "We're at the Williams mansion! . . . I don't know! It's on Fistler! . . . They'll know where it is—just tell them to get over here fast! . . . Leslie Finch." They were downstairs by now and making their way through the maze toward the front door. "No, we don't want to wait! . . . Okay, we'll wait in the car, but if we see anything, we're out of here!" They ran outside as Leslie finished talking to the dispatcher. She turned toward Jolene as they sprinted across the asphalt toward the car. "They want us to wait here. I told them we'll stay in the car. The phone's still on, in case something happens, so don't say anything you don't want recorded for posterity."

Already they could hear sirens, and for once the sound had a soothing effect on her. Jolene opened the driver's door and jumped in, the image of Anna May's brutally murdered body front and center in her mind, overriding everything else. Suddenly the bodies of the family she'd found in the gulch seemed nice, comforting, almost pleasant.

"She didn't scream," Leslie said as Jolene automatically locked all of the car's doors. "She didn't make a sound."

Jolene hadn't thought of that, but it was true, and in a way that was the oddest thing of all. The reaction to pain was instinctive. Even if she'd died almost instantly, Anna May should have cried out at the first blow. And why hadn't they heard the footsteps of her murderer?

Because he was a ghost.

She didn't want to go there, didn't want to think about that.

It had been less than three minutes since Leslie's call, but the first police car was already arriving. Even for a town this small, that was damned impressive. Two other cars followed, skidding to stops in the circular driveway, a total of six officers emerging with guns drawn.

Thank God, Jolene thought.

One officer, obviously the man in charge, motioned for them to remain in the car, then led four of the others into the house. One remained near the first patrol car, pistol drawn and at the ready should mayhem spill out into the driveway. She and Leslie were silent, waiting, listening, and they sat like that for what seemed like an hour but was probably only ten minutes or so. She hoped this wasn't going to take forever, because she had to pick up Skylar from school pretty soon. If the police had to interview them and take statements, she'd probably have to call her mom and tell her to pick up the boy.

She didn't want her mom picking him up.

Two policemen emerged from the house with stunned looks on their faces. One was holstering his gun; the other had already put his weapon away and was numbly carrying a *Yu-Gi-Oh!* backpack.

Skylar's backpack.

Jolene's heart lurched in her chest and it was suddenly difficult to breathe. She unlocked and opened the car door in one impossibly perfect motion and was running toward the front of the house before Leslie could even get out a surprised, "What's the matter?" She flew past the startled cops and dashed inside the house calling her son's name at the top of her lungs, the rational and suddenly subservient part of her brain telling her this was a stupid move, that there were three rattled cops at a murder scene, that she was likely to get herself accidentally shot.

"Skylar!" she screamed. "Skylar!"

There was some sort of answer—not her son's voice but the deeper baritone of one of the policemen—and it seemed to come from downstairs.

The cellar.

She should have known. She was terrified to go back there again, frightened to the bone by the very idea, but her fear for her son was far greater and she was not going to let anything or anyone stop her. She sped through the messy maze into the kitchen, then took the steps to the basement two at a time. As she'd feared, as she'd known, the trapdoor to the secret cellar was open and two of the policemen were looking down at it.

"Skylar!" she screamed, and the two men turned slowly toward her. The blank expressions on their faces sent a searing bolt of pure terror straight through her, and like a wild animal she shoved the men aside and looked into the cellar.

Where Skylar was naked, rocking back and forth on the dirt floor in his own excrement, laughing to himself like a person who had gone completely insane.

"Hey."

The voice came from right next to him, and Skylar

jumped, whirling around, but the school hallway was empty, no one in front, no one in back, the doors to all of the classrooms closed. He desperately had to pee, but he was suddenly afraid to even walk down to the end of the hall, let alone go alone into the boys' bathroom. He wondered, if he returned to class, whether he'd be able to hold it until recess.

No way.

Luckily, the door to another class opened a little ways up ahead, and a girl walked out carrying a hall pass just like his. She strode purposefully toward the restrooms, and he followed, feeling braver now that his courage was being shown up by a girl. He'd almost caught up to her by the time they'd reached the bathrooms, and he pushed open the door marked BOYS while the GIRLS door was still swinging.

The lights were off—part of the efforts by the school to save money on electricity—but the high, frosted window and double skylight were not enough to fully illuminate the tall space, and though it was a sunny day, in here it felt overcast. The gray tiled room was empty, and, frightened, he quickly sped over to the closest urinal, pulling down his zipper as he walked, in a hurry to get out of here.

"Hey."

Skylar jumped, almost peeing on his shoe. It was the same voice, and it echoed between the tiles, the added reverberation making it sound not only strange but sinister. It had followed him here, and his heart was pounding in his chest like a jackhammer. He tried to finish quickly before it came again, and planned to run out of the bathroom even if he wasn't fully zipped and haul back to class and the safety of other people.

"Hey."

He'd peed enough. He could make it to recess. He

stopped, shoved his penis back into his pants and turned without flushing.

"Hey. Hey. Hey. Hey. Heyhey. Heyheyheyhey . . ."

The voice sped up, became higher. Other words were added, words he didn't understand, and in seconds it was the voice from the grave.

Mother Daughter

A shadow passed over the skylight, over the window. The bathroom was thrown into darkness, and Skylar started screaming. "Help! Help!"

The alien language now sounded like laughter.

He was afraid to run, afraid to move. He was no longer alone in the restroom—of that he was sure—and the only thing he could do was keep calling for help and hope a teacher or a janitor heard his cries and came to rescue him.

Suddenly there *was* a light, although where it came from he could not say. It illuminated an area between himself and the door, and Skylar saw a small figure dancing on the tiled floor, held up by strings. His breath was coming in short harsh gasps that hurt his throat. It was a puppet, a brown ugly-looking thing with a hideous grinning face that reminded him of something he had seen before. The puppet seemed to be growing, getting bigger, but he realized that was because it was moving closer to him, the mysterious light accompanying it as it danced crazily.

Skylar had stopped screaming. He didn't know when, didn't know why, but when he tried to yell again for help, he couldn't. His voice had disappeared. The only sound that came out was a parched croak.

But he shouldn't have to keep yelling. Someone should be here by now. Hadn't anyone heard him call? He'd been screaming at the top of his lungs.

The puppet drew closer.

Skylar backed up until he was against the metal wall of the first stall and could move no more. There was a shadow behind the light now. He could see an outline of the figure that was working the puppet. The light remained in place, the puppet moved out of it, and the controlling figure stepped into the breach.

It was the old man he and his mom had seen that night at the bedroom window, and he realized now why the puppet's terrible face had looked so familiar. It was a smaller version of this one.

"Skylar," the man said with a strange accent.

It knew his name!

"Hey."

"No," was all he could get out.

"I have so much to show you," the old man said, and Skylar started whimpering.

The figure grinned at him.

And took his hand.

Eighteen

Flagstaff, Arizona

According to the tests, there was nothing there.

That was flat-out impossible.

Angela and Derek listened to Dr. Mathewson's exasperated description of the analyses performed on the black mold.

"I know it's *there*," the professor said. "I can see it. We all can see it. But when examined microscopically, analyzed spectrographically or tested for chemical interaction with various solutions, it's as if it doesn't even exist. It's as though we're looking at"—he moved his fingers in a wispy motion above his head—"air."

Angela had no idea how such a thing could be true. But she believed it. As far as she was concerned, there'd been more magic than science involved here since the beginning. That still didn't tell them what they were dealing with, and she knew the lack of hard facts frustrated both the professor and Derek. She was frustrated, too, but for different reasons. She didn't necessarily require a rational explanation for all that was going on, but she still wanted to know what was happening and why.

Part of her felt guilty, as though she'd brought it

on herself, as though this was some sort of cosmic punishment being meted out to her.

That was her parents' influence. And the church's.

She'd spent the previous night at Derek's house. At first, she'd declined his offer, worried about what his family might think, but he drove her there, introduced her, and gave his mom a thumbnail sketch of what was going on, and his mother insisted that Angela sleep in the guest room.

"Thank you," she said gratefully. "It's only for tonight. I promise."

"For as long as it takes to get your situation sorted out," his mother said.

"Derek has a girlfriend!" his brother, Steve, called in a singsong voice. "Derek has a girlfriend!"

"Shut up," Derek told him.

"Derek has a girlfriend!"

"He's my *half* brother," Derek told Angela, motioning toward a mantel where photographs of the family were displayed. She saw pictures of Mrs. Yount with two different husbands.

"Mom!" Steve whined.

"Derek!" his mother warned.

It felt good to be in a family environment once again. It had been nice to be on her own and in the adult universe, too, but when things got rough, having a family around made it much easier to face the world.

She'd used up nearly all of her anytime minutes calling her own family and her friends back in California, and they probably thought she was having some type of nervous breakdown. No doubt as a result of living away from home for the first time. She'd told them everything, and they believed none of it. Why would they? The story was ludicrous. She'd moved into a haunted house with a bunch of colorful characters; then she'd been grabbed by a living corpse in a tunnel full of corpses and after that, black mold had started growing on her sheets, black mold that her roommate touched and that turned her and everyone else in the apartment building into racist assholes? It sounded like the plot of a grade-Z horror movie.

Besides, her family and friends were too far away to help anyway.

At least Derek had turned out to be a stand-up guy.

She glanced over at him, talking to the professor. The two of them were looking over a series of printouts. She was not sure Derek understood any more of it than she did, but at least he was in there; at least he was trying.

Dr. Mathewson dropped the papers in defeat.

"So what now?" Derek asked.

The professor shook his head. "I'm going to speak to my colleagues here, confer with others at universities that have better and more sophisticated equipment, contact the CDC and . . . keep on trying. We'll nail it eventually, but I'm afraid I have nothing to offer you at this time."

"Thanks anyway," Angela said. "For trying."

"Thank *you*," he told them. "This is a real challenge. At the very least, I'll get a paper out of it."

Once outside, Derek looked around at the stone buildings of the university. "There are a lot of smart minds hard at work behind those walls. You'd think we could find one that could crack this for us or at least come up with a usable theory."

"Right now, I just want to go back and get my stuff while everyone else is at school." They'd both decided to skip classes and take off work for the day, and Derek had agreed to help her load up everything of hers from Babbitt House and temporarily store it in his garage until she could find a new place to live.

"All right, then," he told her. "Let's go."

If, before, the ornate facade and rolling lawn of the Victorian residence had seemed charmingly bohemian for an apartment building, those features now seemed scary and threatening. The gingerbread on the structure gave it the appearance of a haunted house, and the vast lawn separated it from the rest of the street, keeping it isolated. Her clothes were in there, her PC, assorted books and CDs, but she was tempted to leave everything and give up her rights to it just to get away from this place. She did not want to go back in that building.

Derek had already started up the walk, however, and he turned around. "Come on. Let's get this over with."

He was right, and she hurried to catch up with him. *Stupid brown bitch.*

She hoped Chrissie was not going to be here. Or Winston.

The front door was locked. Angela withdrew her key ring from her purse and was sorting through the keys to find the one for the front door when a water balloon burst on the cement of the walkway next to Derek's feet. The air was filled with the tart, sickening stench of urine. "Not by the hair on my chinny chin chin!" Randy yelled from above. Angela heard his window slam shut.

At precisely that instant, as though choreographed, Kelli and Yurica stuck their heads out of the window next to the front door—their living room window— and yelled in unison: "Go back to Mexico, slut!" Giggling, they ducked back inside.

"This place is a goddamn loony bin," Derek said.

"It's the mold," Angela told him. She paused. "At least I think it is." She opened the front door.

Derek cringed, ready to duck at the first sign of anything coming at them, but there was nothing. "Do

you think this is happening to Dr. Welkes? And everyone else who went down in that tunnel?"

"I don't know," Angela admitted, and they
walked inside.

Ordinarily, at this time of day, Babbitt House was
empty and quiet save for one or two residents who
might be home studying and perhaps listening to
music. Now, however, it seemed that everyone was
home, and though she couldn't see them behind the
closed doors or through the walls, she could sense
them there, listening, watching, waiting.

And there was . . .

Something else.

A noise.

It had started off as a low hum, barely audible as
they walked through the front door. Within seconds,
however, mumbling was coming not only from Winston and Brock's apartment but from all of the apartments, like surround sound. It was the same
unintelligible chattering she'd heard before—

the ghost

—and it seemed to freak out even Derek. "What
the hell is *that*?" he asked, his voice shaky.

"It's a ghost," Angela admitted. "This place is
haunted."

"Is that from the mold, too?"

"No. It's in addition to the mold."

"Jesus Christ," Derek breathed.

The babbling took on a more frantic tone.

"Let's hurry up," Angela said, "and get out of
here."

The two of them dashed up the stairs. She half expected blood or dark water to start oozing from the
walls, the whole building to begin tumbling down, but
they made it to the top without incident.

At the far end of the hallway stood Drew and Lisa,

both of them dressed only in underwear, standing stock-still, like statues. That alien voice was still babbling, the sound issuing from all around them as though speakers were hidden in every wall, and what might have been a comic tableau under other circumstances was transformed into a disturbing scene of unfathomable horror.

They had to do this quickly.

Angela strode to the closed door of her apartment, trying the knob. It was locked. She knocked loudly. "Chrissie?" She was hoping against hope that her roommate was not in, and the lack of an answer briefly let her think that she'd be able to remove her belongings unimpeded. But the moment she put her key in the lock, turned it and tried to open the door, she met resistance. Her fleeting sense of relief dissipated. She pushed harder, trying to force open the door, but Chrissie was leaning on it from the other side. "Bitch!" Chrissie screamed. "Brown fucking beaner bitch!"

Derek touched her arm. "Come on," he said. "Let's go. Let's get out of here. Let the police handle it."

"No!" Angela insisted, more angry now than scared. "Those are my things, and I'm taking them with me."

"Bitch!" Chrissie screamed.

"Fuck you!" Angela yelled back. She retreated a step, then shoved her shoulder against the door like she'd seen cops do in movies. Derek's hand closed over hers on the knob, and then the two of them were pressing their combined weight against the door. Gradually, it gave way before them, Chrissie's strength no match for theirs.

The door flew open.

Angela sucked in her breath. Next to her, Derek did the same. Mold had grown throughout the apartment, creeping over everything. The couch was completely black, as were the television and kitchen counter. Inky tendrils climbed up the walls like tree branches, exploding into a galaxy of jet stars on the ceiling. The floor was covered with a dark carpet of fungus.

And the smell . . .

The two of them moved no farther than the doorway. Chrissie was naked and screaming at them, her skin milky and untouched by the terrible infestation, her eyes wild with rage, but it was not she that prevented them from going inside. It was the overwhelming transformation of the apartment itself. Angela barely recognized the place. It looked like a bat cave. And she knew with certainty that her bedroom had to be even worse. That was where the mold had started, and there was no way it had escaped unscathed. No doubt all of her belongings had succumbed to this creeping corpse-spawned blight.

She and Derek backed out and closed the door just as Chrissie rushed them, arms extended, hands clawed, shrieking. "You ugly brown—" There was a hard thump as she hit the door.

"Let's get out of here," Derek said.

Angela nodded. Down the hall, Drew and Lisa were still frozen like statues.

Although they were closer now.

She and Derek hurried down the stairs. Winston and Brock were in the entryway, standing before the now-open door of their apartment, from whence that crazy jabbering was issuing at earsplitting levels. The last time she'd been allowed a glimpse into their living quarters, she'd thought she'd seen a black spot on the couch. Now the black was everywhere, not as comprehensive or concentrated as it was upstairs . . . but still bad.

She was afraid they might have problems with her two former friends, thought she and Derek might have to fight their way out of the house, but she'd obviously seen too many movies because no such confrontation occurred. Winston and Brock glared at them and called her names like "beaner" and "brown bitch" that echoed Chrissie's words exactly, but she and Derek made it outside without further incident and ran over the lawn toward the street and the safety of the car.

"Holy shit!" Derek exclaimed after they'd gotten in and locked the doors behind them. "That was intense!"

Angela was too tired to do anything but nod. She felt drained and at the same time keyed up. Her knotted stomach was cramping, and she hoped she wouldn't vomit. Hazarding a glance back at Babbitt House, she saw identical black shapes in every one of the windows facing the street. It had to be mold . . . but the shapes looked like shadows or silhouettes of people, and out of the corner of her eye she thought she saw one of them move. She quickly turned away. "Come on," she said. "Drive. Fast."

Derek started the car, pulled away from the curb, heading up the street toward the hulking mountains that towered over the city. "Where?" he asked.

"It all started in that tunnel," she said, "with that . . . zombie. Let's go to the police station, find the policeman, see what he knows. He was there. He saw what really happened."

"What's his name?"

"I don't know, but it should be easy to find out."

Her cell phone rang, and Angela took it out of her purse, surprised. She peered at the small screen, but the number was blocked so she couldn't see who it was. She pressed the button to answer. "Hello?"

It was Edna Wong.

She wanted to talk.

*　　*　　*

They met in a little downtown health food restaurant called Mountain Oasis. There was no privacy, but these were the off-hours and the only other patron was a gray-bearded Karl Marx look-alike who was eating soup while he read an impressively thick book through depressingly thick eyeglasses.

Angela and Derek were already in the neighborhood and arrived ten minutes before Edna, who had to fight the traffic from NAU. The old woman walked through the doorway just as their decaf iced teas were being refilled, and Angela waved her over. She and Derek had been sitting at the table in virtual silence, trying to decompress, to absorb what had happened, unable to talk yet about what they'd seen.

They were seated opposite each other, and Edna took a chair from an adjoining table and sat down facing both of them. "You want to know about the tunnel," she said without preamble.

"Yes," Angela told her. Derek nodded.

"Okay, then." The housing administrator took a deep breath. "I only know rumors. Maybe they're true, maybe not. Maybe they're just stories. But I'll tell you what I heard.

"When I was a little girl, Flagstaff was an almost completely white city. Oh, you'd see Indians in town from time to time, but it wasn't like today. The state's Hispanic population all seemed to live down by Tucson and never ventured above Phoenix, and I'd never even seen anyone who was African-American. As far as I knew, there were only three Asian families in town, including mine.

"The thing was, it had not always been this way. At one time, in the early 1900s, after the railroad came in, after they'd built the station, there were quite a few Chinese families living here, doing the work no one else wanted to do." She smiled ruefully. "Coolie labor. But there was as much anti-immigrant sentiment then as there is today, more probably, and a lot of locals were resentful, claiming that the Chinese were taking jobs away from white Arizonans."

The waitress stopped by, pad in hand, and Edna smiled at her. "Just water, please."

"Sure thing," the girl said cheerfully.

"I'll leave a big tip," Edna promised.

The waitress laughed. "Don't worry about it."

"Anyway," Edna continued, "there were some beatings and a few scattered attacks. Tarring and feathering. An attempted lynching. Flagstaff was still considered the wild frontier back then, and lawlessness and vigilantism were not unknown in these parts. Some people could see the writing on the wall, and a few of the local businesses who relied heavily on cheap Chinese labor created 'safe rooms' just in case." She paused. "And tunnels."

"Is that—?" Angela began.

Edna nodded. "Yes. At least, that's what I was told. Eventually, there were riots, anti-Chinese riots. Stores and businesses that hired Chinese workers were looted; rooming houses and shacks where they boarded were burned. There was thousands of dollars' worth of damage, dozens of injuries, and several people died. None of them were Chinese, though. This part's documented. You can look it up in newspaper articles from that time in the university library. I have."

The waitress brought her water, and Edna thanked the girl, taking a long sip. "The Chinese workers and their families all seemed to have disappeared. No one knew what had happened to them. Eventually, after things had calmed down, a few were found working at the hotel or at the mill. Supposedly they'd hidden in the secret rooms and the tunnels while all the chaos was going on above. But many of the families never returned, and the story passed down to me was that later, maybe at night when it was safe, they'd left the city. The rumor was that they'd ridden the rails east."

Angela suddenly understood. "But they didn't leave," she said, stunned. "They never left the tunnel. They died in there. That's what we saw."

Edna nodded soberly. "But there were *tunnels*," she said. "Plural. At least that's what I heard. So . . ." She trailed off.

"So there could be more," Derek said.

"Yes."

He looked down at the floor. "There could be bodies under us right now."

"They were supposed to be somewhere in this downtown district," Edna agreed.

Angela suddenly felt a lot less secure. With all of the gangs and violence and big-city problems of Los Angeles, she thought she'd be living a peaceful bucolic little life here in northern Arizona. She never could have imagined something like this. "But—" Her voice came out thin and cracked, and she cleared her throat. "But they were moving," she said. "At least some of them were. That one hand grabbed me. And what's that black mold? We tried to have it tested, but it doesn't even show up. It's not there. So it has to be some kind of magic or something. Is there some sort of curse on those tunnels and the people who died there? Or is it . . .? I don't know. *What* is it?"

"That I can't tell you," Edna said. "All I know is that the tunnels were supposed to be part of an underground railroad for Chinese immigrants to protect them from vigilante mobs. Beyond that, I'm as much in the dark as you. But I thought knowing about the history might help you somehow or at least give you a place to start."

"Thank you," Angela said. But she wasn't sure it did help.

Edna thought for a moment, then sighed. "Well, maybe there is something else. I don't know. But I'll tell you anyway." She took another long sip of water. "When I was a little girl, my uncle came to visit us from Missouri. He was very tall for someone who was Chinese, very charismatic. He had some kind of glamorous job, although I don't remember what it was. Anyway, he stayed for about a week and it was wonderful. But one day, my parents were out somewhere and my uncle asked me to show him where my grandfather was buried. It wasn't in a real cemetery, since Chinese weren't allowed to be buried with Caucasians at that time. It was a makeshift cemetery out on the north end of town that was shared with other outcasts. Indians had their own burial grounds, but the rest of us, the other minority groups—and there were only a handful of families all total—made do with this little plot in the forest, a little clearing of unowned land.

"My uncle bought a chicken first and put it in this black bag. I thought that was very odd. I kept asking him what he was going to do with it. I was fascinated, really. But he wouldn't say. Then when I showed him my grandfather's grave, he knelt down before it and started doing some kind of . . . *ritual* is the only word to describe it. He started whispering some sort of chant—I knew some of the words but not all of them—then he took out the chicken and slit its throat. He let the blood drip on the grave, then put his finger in it. He wrote some Chinese characters on the gravestone—I couldn't read yet, so I don't know what he wrote—then he put some blood on his forehead, stood up and bowed. Two words I remember he did say were *'bo sau.'* Revenge. He gave me a lecture and told me my mother and father should be doing this, too. We all should. But I got scared and started crying, and then he picked me up and then we left.

"When I told my mother about it, I remember she seemed scared. I think she even shivered, although that may just be my memory. But what she said was, 'He's trying to raise the dead.' That was enough to scare me, and it's all we ever said about it. My uncle left the next day, and I never knew if that was why, if my parents kicked him out or he stormed off, but he never came back to visit.

"I know my parents were never involved in any such thing, and I've never heard of anything else like it since. But my uncle said *all* good Chinese should perform that ritual, and I've thought about that over the years, wondered if there were others. Now I'm wondering if it's not connected to those bodies in the tunnel."

They were silent, no one sure of what to say after that. Angela's head was spinning.

"More iced tea?" the waitress asked cheerily, stopping by.

They acquiesced, fooled around for a few moments putting sugar in their glasses, squeezing lemon, stirring. Edna sipped her water.

Trying to raise the dead

It had to be related.

Derek began updating Edna on the most recent events, including their aborted sojourn into Babbitt House, and the old woman, shocked and frightened, said they had to call the police. And tell the county health authorities. "This could be the beginning of an epidemic," she said.

Neither of them had thought of it that way, and they both realized Edna was right.

"*You* don't know anything about this mold or fungus or whatever it is, do you?" Angela asked.

Edna shook her head. "I'm sorry, no. I've told you everything I know that could possibly help. This I've never heard of."

Angela thought about the riots. Mob violence spread through crowds much like a disease or virus, infecting ordinarily rational people. Maybe this black mold had been around back then, too. Maybe it had sparked the anti-Chinese sentiment that had led to these horrible consequences. Maybe Flagstaff had been built on ground saturated with this toxic spore, and unearthing the tunnel had once again released it into the general population.

She agreed with Edna that the authorities needed to be notified, but she had no confidence that the people sent out to investigate wouldn't be affected, too. She glanced suspiciously over at Derek. Had *he* been contaminated? He hadn't actually touched the mold. And he looked okay. But . . .

Perhaps the best thing to do would be to cut her losses and speed back to California as quickly as a Greyhound bus could carry her.

A cell tone rang out at the table, and all of them checked their phones. It was Edna's, and she looked down at the text message. "I have to go," she said. "Problems at the office. As always." She smiled kindly, touching Angela's arm. "I'm so sorry, dear. This just hasn't been your semester, has it?"

Angela smiled back. "That's the understatement of the year."

The housing administrator took out two dollars from her purse and placed the bills under the salt shaker. "If you need me, you know where to find me."

"Thank you," Angela said.

"Thanks," Derek echoed.

Edna hurried off, and the two of them looked at each other. "What now?" Derek asked. "Police station?"

Angela quickly finished the last of her iced tea. "Yeah," she said. "Let's go."

Nineteen

Greg Rossiter stared glumly out the window of his office at the cubicles of junior FBI agents, all of whom wanted his job.

His old office had had a window that looked outside. At the city. At the sky.

He pulled the shades, hiding the outer office from view. Ever since *The X-Files* had gone off the air, his stock had gone down in the bureau. Sad but true. No matter that he had successfully investigated over fifty cases in the last five years and had worked on two high-profile incidents featuring objective, verifiable supernatural phenomena—the presence of that fucking TV show had granted him more legitimacy than any closed case could. Now he was on the outs, considered passé, a relic from another era.

Just like Fox Mulder had been.

Goddamn, he hated that program.

Rossiter paced restlessly around the room before returning to his desk. Everything was focused on counterterrorism these days. That, too, had knocked his career off track. Not that he didn't understand, but, shit, there were other domestic threats as well, other crimes, other dangers that deserved the bureau's full attention.

Like vampires.

It was strange how dispassionate he was about the paranormal phenomena he had encountered. Uncovering the existence of these monsters hadn't turned him into a paranoid Chicken Little but had left him surprisingly unaffected. His job was still just a job to him, not a crusade, not a lifestyle, and instead of spending every waking moment worried about the infiltration of the supernatural, he was more concerned with how such things affected his career trajectory. He wasn't sure if that was good or bad.

The door opened, and his assistant poked her head into the room. "Sir?"

He looked up, scowling. "What is it?"

"The director wants to see you."

The director? Rossiter stood, straightened his tie, made sure his shirt was tucked in properly. "Where? In his office?"

"Yes. Now."

A lot of agents, he knew, would be quaking in their boots at the very thought of such a summons, but he thrived on opportunities like these, knew how to work them to his advantage. They were openings, not challenges, and if he played his cards right, he could use this brief meeting to jump-start his stalled career.

But what did the director want to see him about? That was the only variable here.

It didn't matter. Even a dressing-down could be spun into gold if the spinner knew what he was doing.

And he did.

Rossiter looked at his ghostly reflection in the window to check his hair, then strode purposefully out of his office, past the cubicles of the junior agents, down the outside corridor to the bank of elevators. Once inside the elevator, he stared straight ahead, a neutral expression on his face, acutely conscious of the fact that he was being observed.

He was expecting others to be present at the meeting—his immediate supervisor perhaps, other agents with whom he'd worked—but he was unprepared for the level of high-powered attendees that greeted him, and though he tried not to let it show, the sight of the White House chief of staff, the national-security adviser and the head of the Secret Service all seated in a semicircle in front of the director's desk left him feeling overwhelmed and slightly intimidated. Still, he acted as if this happened every day, as though he were used to such company, and he took the remaining empty chair and sat down quietly, waiting to be told why he was here.

"Agent Rossiter," the director said curtly. "There's been an incident in Manhattan, and as you're reported to have some experience with unusual or ostensibly unexplainable occurrences, I've decided to bring you in on the case."

"Thank you, sir."

"Put simply, Grant's Tomb has been defiled. We've blocked off Riverside Drive to keep the public away, and the area around the building itself has been cordoned off. Bomb scare's the cover story. As you doubtlessly know, the sepulchre is guarded at all times, as well as being monitored by our best surveillance equipment, so theoretically such a thing should not be able to occur. In fact, we have no idea how it *did* occur, and this colossal security failure is what we've been discussing for the past forty-five minutes." He glanced disapprovingly around the room, and Rossiter was amused to note that the other men looked chastened. "To state the facts, President Grant's body has been removed from its final resting place and . . . butchered. The desecration was conducted with such ferocity that it would be easy to conclude that it was perpetrated by a wild animal, although obviously it would require a human to disinter the corpse. The purposeful dismantling of the body, however, and the distribution of the parts, imply that the entire operation was human in origin. In addition, the tomb's walls have been defaced with childish drawings.

"His wife's corpse remains untouched."

There was silence in the room. Rossiter was not sure what to say. "Are there photos yet?" he asked.

"Yes. And streaming video that you can access, as well as a written report by the answering officer."

"I'll need to see the site for myself. I'll need to talk to on-duty personnel. I'll get over there right away and—"

"After." The director cleared his throat, looked around the room. "The president wants to see you first."

The president!

The situation was progressing from good to great.

Still, Rossiter was cautious. "May I ask what this is concerning?"

The chief of staff frowned at him. "At this point, everything is on a need-to-know basis. All you need to know right now is that you are to report immediately to the president in the company of Director Horn."

"Yes, sir," Rossiter answered.

The director frowned again, although whether it was at the chief of staff or himself Rossiter could not say. The director handed Rossiter a manila file folder, emphasizing that despite the high profile and public visibility of the crime scene, he was to do his utmost to ensure that word of what had occurred did not leak out to the press. "The last thing we need is publicity. Particularly right now."

That seemed to be a cue for the others to stand and take their leave. None of the men offered so much as a good-bye. They simply filed out of the room. The director stood up, pressing an intercom button on his desk. "Have a car ready," he ordered. Rossiter couldn't hear the response—he was not sure the director had even waited for one. He knew only that Horn was striding purposefully toward a nearly hidden side door in the office, making a single brusque motion indicating that Rossiter was to accompany him.

They took a private elevator to the first floor, where they got into a black town car with darkened windows. The director remained silent on the short trip through the D.C. streets, and Rossiter followed his example. There were questions he wanted to ask: Did the bureau believe that the tomb desecration had a supernatural cause? Was that why he had been called in? Were any connections suspected between this and the disinterring of Civil War dead at Arlington? But he sensed that this was a time to remain quiet, and he did.

The car passed through the White House gate and rolled smoothly by the guard shack without stopping. The residence, he noticed through the smoked glass, was partially hidden behind scaffolding and a gigantic billowing sheet of bright red tarp.

"Christo's new project?" he joked.

The quip was met with flat silence.

"They're making a few cosmetic repairs to the building. Touch-ups." They were the first words the director had spoken since leaving his office.

Rossiter said nothing, kept his eyes open and his mouth shut. He'd been in D.C. now for well over a dozen years, through three administrations, and he had never seen anything like this. He had no idea what sort of lunatic impulse had made him joke about the appearance of the White House; he'd merely been fishing for information about this obviously extraordinary sight, and he'd stupidly thought a stab at camaraderie would yield results. He should have known better.

One step back.

So much for the career rehabilitation.

The car stopped on the side of the White House opposite the construction. The door was opened for them by a uniformed marine. They stepped out from the backseat and were immediately ushered into one of the building's side entrances. Rossiter had been to the White House only once before, as part of a formal ceremony, and had entered through the front along with everyone else. This private entrance was new to him, but he remained passive, stoic, acting as though this sort of thing happened to him all the time.

They were led through a narrow winding corridor that did not seem to intersect any rooms, hallways or public spaces, and emerged in the antechamber of the Oval Office, where the chief of staff and the head of the Secret Service were already waiting, having beaten them there. Two other men were standing in the room as well, but the national-security adviser was missing. Rossiter had no idea what this could be about, but it had to be big.

The door to the Oval Office opened, and the president emerged. He looked taller than he did on TV, more presidential, and although Rossiter hadn't voted for him, he could see now why a majority of the country had. At the moment, the president was striding purposefully toward them with his shirtsleeves rolled up and his tie loosened. It may have been an affectation, but it got across the point that the man was busy and here to work, and Rossiter found himself standing more stiffly at attention.

"Gentlemen," he said by way of greeting. His eyes locked on Rossiter's. "You're Agent Rossiter?"

"Yes, sir."

"Follow me. I have something to show you."

All seven of them, the president in the lead, strode down a tall wide hallway to a closed door guarded by military personnel. One of the uniformed men opened the door, and they stepped inside a large gallery that looked as though it hadn't been redecorated since Abraham Lincoln's day.

Only . . .

Only the far end of the room was discreetly covered by a thick navy blue curtain that stretched from floor to ceiling and completely covered everything in back of it. The curtain was so jarringly out of place and so hastily put together that it was clear it did not belong and was not intended for use in some ceremony or celebration. Before Rossiter could even think about the possibilities implied by the drapery, the president led them behind it.

And stopped.

Where a wall had once been, there was now a gaping hole surrounded by rubble. Beyond the missing section of room, Rossiter could see a series of other galleries with shattered walls and that fluttering red tarp outside at the far end. The entire east wing of the White House looked as though it had been crashed into by a gigantic wrecking ball or massive vehicle of some sort. *A train,* he thought, looking at the shape of the opening and the scarred floor. Throughout all of the affected rooms, military personnel were bustling about, although whether they were searching for the perpetrators or clues or were merely trying to secure the area, Rossiter could not say.

The others had apparently seen the destruction already, but though presumably Horn had been told of it and knew what to expect, the FBI director still seemed shocked, and his normally unflappable demeanor was nowhere in evidence. "My God."

Rossiter remained unmoving and impassive, hoping the contrast would be self-evident.

The chief of staff cleared his throat. "The president believes that a train crashed into the White House and caused this damage."

"It *was* a train," the president insisted. "I didn't see it, but I heard it. And we *all* felt it." He looked around the room as though daring anyone to disagree. "It may have been invisible, but it was there, and it crashed through the east wing, whistle blowing, steam engine at full power. . . . Did I mention that it was a steam engine? Well, it was." For the first time, the president seemed distracted, unfocused. "I happened to be in the briefing room over there"—he pointed through the gaping wall—"along with most of the cabinet. We saw the impact. We saw the train crash through the walls, even though we couldn't see the train, and we saw the people scrambling out of the way, saw the desks and furniture smashed and shoved aside. Amazingly, only one man died. But that man was Jordan Mayhew. A Secret Service agent. My *daughter's* Secret Service agent." His eyes met Rossiter's. "I need to know what happened here. I'm told you're the man for the job, that you have some experience with this sort of occurrence."

"Well, yes, Mr. President, but—"

"No buts. Find out what this thing is, whether it's a ghost train or some sort of invisible weapon or stealth bomb or death ray. As silly as this sounds, I'm betting on ghost train. I'm a stubborn man, but I'm not a stupid man, and while my worldview has never encompassed the supernatural, I know what I heard; I know what I saw. We all do. Examine whatever's necessary in here. Interview anyone you need. I'm giving you unfettered access to my staff. But I want you on this ASAP."

"Yes, sir."

"You heard about what happened at Arlington, I assume?"

"Yes," Rossiter answered. "But I'm not on that case, and I don't really—"

"You're on it now." The president glared at the director. "I want Agent Rossiter in charge of anything that could be even tangentially connected to this, with the authority to coordinate any unexplained unsolved cases that he deems pertinent to his investigation. I don't care about your ordinary chain of command— I want it suspended until this is solved. Do I make myself clear?"

"Yes, sir, Mr. President."

It was all Rossiter could do not to smile. In one quick trip to the White House, his fortunes had completely reversed themselves and instead of languishing forgotten in the bowels of the FBI building, he was being given special assignments and unprecedented authority by the president of the United States. His career was not only back on track, it was further along than he had ever expected it to be.

Assuming he got results.

The pressure was on him now. He had been granted the opportunity of a lifetime, but it was up to him what he did with it. If he fucked this up, he'd be lucky to be scrubbing toilets.

The president focused his gaze on Rossiter. "That was a ghost train, too. At Arlington. No one's ever going to admit that publicly, and everyone's afraid to admit it even to me, but we know that's the case, and obviously these two are connected. What I want to know is, why is this happening, what's causing it, and can we expect more such attacks in the future?"

"I'll find out," Rossiter said confidently.

"I want daily reports."

"We'll set up a morning briefing," the chief of staff said. "But right now, Mr. President—"

"I know, I know." He nodded at Rossiter. "Stay as long as you need, be as thorough as you can, do whatever you need to do, but solve this."

"Yes, sir."

The others left, leaving Rossiter alone with Horn. The director was scowling, and Rossiter didn't want to piss him off any more than he doubtlessly was already, but he needed to get to work and fast. "Do you think I could have a few agents to help me with legwork?"

"You're the boss," the director said sarcastically.

Great.

"I'm going to oversee the situation here, talk to some of these military investigators, see what I can come up with on my own. After that, I want to take a look at Grant's Tomb."

"Be very careful," Horn said. "You're balanced over quicksand here."

It sounded like a warning rather than a threat, and Rossiter decided to take it that way. "I will, sir. And thanks."

Defiled?

That was putting it mildly.

He had seen the photos and the video on his laptop on the way over, so Rossiter had been expecting severe damage, but he was still taken aback by the savagery of the desecration. It seemed not only much more immediate in person but much more extensive.

True, Grant's wife had been left alone, but the sar-
cophagus of the president had been smashed open,
and the body inside thrown onto the stone floor and
ripped apart, arms and legs dispersed to the four corners of the tomb, the formally dressed torso beaten as
though it were an old rug. Small fragments were all
that remained of the skull, and where the head should
have been, there were only oddly shaped pieces of
leathery skin and muscle, resting with clumps of wiry
hair and teeth on a bed of fine crumbling powder next
to the shattered bronze busts that had been positioned
around the interior of the crypt.

The marble walls of the oversized room had been
defaced but not with spray paint or marking pens or
any of the usual suspects. No, this graffiti had been
chiseled onto the stone, and on the pendentives below
the dome, the perpetrators had carved serial pictures
of a single train.

Rossiter focused on those four images. There were
other carved pictures as well—people, mountains, abstract shapes—but it was the train that interested him
because he had the feeling the artist was trying to
impart a message with it, that the pictures were meant
to tell them something about what was going on.

He just couldn't figure out what the hell it was.

The carvings were detailed, though. He had to give
the perp that. He only hoped they were detailed
enough, because one of the first things he intended to
do was transmit photos to someone who knew trains,
with the hope that if the make and model of the vehicle could be identified, they might learn something
about the perpetrator or even the locomotives that
had crashed into the cemetery and the White House.

A long shot, he knew, but with no prints or physical
evidence so far, they didn't have much else to go on.

Already, in his mind, he was lining up intelligence

sources for information about ghost trains, poltergeist phenomena and even military PK experiments. While he was at it, he needed to consult with experts on American literature and folktales to see if there were any regional stories about invisible locomotives. Sometimes legends were grown from a grain of truth.

One of the older members of the forensics team, a bald, fat guy whose name Rossiter had already forgotten, stood up and looked at him with an expression somewhere between awe and horror on his face. "Can you believe that that used to be the president of the United States?" he said, motioning toward the fragments of skull on the floor. "That was General Grant? All these years, he's been lying here intact and now, poof, he's gone. We're witnessing history. This is the end of an era."

Rossiter eyed him coldly. "Yeah," he said. "Now get back to work."

Twenty

"BRIGIT'S WELL."

It was the name on the blackboard marquee outside the coffeehouse that caused Dennis to stop in Milner. And stay. The speed limit through the center of town was twenty-five miles an hour, and he'd slowed to that as he passed by the local shops and businesses. The first stoplight turned yellow as he approached, and assuming this was a speed trap and a cop was hiding nearby for the express purpose of ticketing drivers with out-of-state plates, Dennis stopped. As he waited, he looked to his right and saw the coffeehouse with its freestanding blackboard.

And he turned right at the corner and pulled into the first open parking space he found.

He'd arrived in town on Monday and Brigit's Well wasn't scheduled to play until Saturday night, but he'd been acting on gut instinct this whole trip, spurred by the undoubtedly false premise that there was a reason behind his journey, that he was being led across country for a specific purpose—and if anything was a sign, this was it.

Also, he had to admit, he was excited to hear Brigit's Well again. Finding the duo out here in the middle of nowhere was like seeing an old friend amid a gathering of strangers, and there was something comforting about that. He wondered if they had a new CD out. He hoped so, although even if they didn't, he'd buy another copy of the old one again, for traveling music.

Just the thought cheered him up, and while Milner was not exactly the garden spot of the Western world, he was happy to be here.

While he told himself that he was driving aimlessly across country, seeing America, California had always been his unspoken destination. He and Cathy had always wanted to see Los Angeles, and from the outset his vague plans for the future had always involved finding a job and starting a new life in Southern California. Yet for some reason, as he'd crossed from Missouri to Nebraska, he'd moved north instead of south, heading not toward Oklahoma, Texas, New Mexico and Arizona but through Nebraska into Wyoming.

Until he'd landed here.

The strange and unbelievably realistic dreams he'd been having ever since leaving home had intensified as soon as he'd started heading north, and for a while he'd been afraid to fall asleep at night. If he hadn't been even more afraid of drugs, he would have bought some No-Doz or other over-the-counter medication to ward off sleep, but instead he simply toughed it out. Certain cities seemed to be flash points, where the nightmares came hard and heavy. In Kearney, Nebraska, he'd been tormented by visions of bloody skeletons working hard on some unseen project, swinging hammers in the bright morning sun while he lay gutshot behind them on the sand, trying to hold in his spilling intestines with his fingers. In Brubeck, Wyoming, he dreamed he was floating paralyzed down a river while on the shore cowboys with long knives cut up piles of stacked bodies, saving noses and ears for souvenirs, stringing them on long leather cords that hung from their belts. He wondered if he got out a map of the United States, put marks on all of the places where he'd had these terrible dreams and then connected the dots, whether some type of recognizable shape or pattern would be formed.

In all of the dreams, behind the events, not causing them but watching them, was that giant spirit, the one he'd seen in back of the smoke at the end of the road, beckoning him. He spotted it in the sky, above the trees, above the mountains. Sometimes its head was triangular, sometimes oval, sometimes square. Sometimes it was made of fur, sometimes rock, sometimes bark. But it was always there, and Dennis had the feeling that it was trying to communicate with him, trying to tell him something, though he had no idea what.

He probably could have stayed in Milner for the week without unduly straining his wallet, but there wasn't much to do here and he'd gotten in the habit of working. Since he'd be hanging around town anyway, Dennis thought he might as well see if he could make some extra cash. He found a temp job delivering newspapers for the local daily, the *Milner Sentinel,* an old-fashioned publication that was delivered in the late afternoon rather than the early morning. The regular guy was on vacation for a week, so it was his job to pick up the bundled papers from the printer and then drop them off at the homes of the individual paper-boys, who then delivered them to subscribers. He had to be at the printer's by two thirty each afternoon, and he generally finished dropping off the last bundle around four.

For his efforts, he got fifteen bucks a day—which just about covered his meals in Milner, if not the motel.

Although the city was too small to have a real Chinatown, there was a Chinese restaurant and an adjacent Chinese-owned gas station, and Dennis ended up spending a lot of his spare time hanging around there, chatting with the owners and the workers. He got to know them only because most of the other people in town—the white people—had been so universally unfriendly. He hated to think it was a racial thing, not in this day and age, but after that incident with the kid in front of the motel in Selby—

Chink!

—and after visiting The Keep, he could not help wondering if this entire section of the country was hostile to minorities, particularly to people of Asian descent.

This was what it must have felt like to be a black man in the South in the early 1960s, he thought.

Last night, he'd gone to eat at the restaurant and Carl Fong, the twenty-something son of the gas station's owner, had invited him over to his table. The crowd had grown to five by the end of the meal, and when Carl said they were going to cruise around for a while and asked Dennis if he wanted to join them, he said yes.

These were not the kind of people with whom he would ordinarily hang—were what his sister mockingly called "yellow trash"—but still, it was fun to find himself crammed in the backseat of an old Jeep Cherokee, speeding up and down the quiet streets of the town, racing a flat-topped farm boy down Main Street, yelling come-ons to a gaggle of drunken middle-aged women stumbling out of a bar without their husbands. It was an eye-opener, in a way, because growing up in a large metropolitan area, he'd always had friends from a wide variety of backgrounds. Aside from his family, he had never hung out exclusively with people who were Chinese. But here in Milner he had no choice, and it was kind of weird to have everything filtered through that lens.

Like himself, Carl and his friends seemed caught between worlds, neither fully Chinese nor fully American, neither Buddhist nor Christian, but having grown up in a closed community where they were social as well as cultural outcasts, they had a harder edge to their outlook, a more cynical and aggressive attitude than he was used to.

After buying a twelve-pack at a liquor store near the edge of town, they drove out by the river and parked.

"You ever think that serial killers are, like, doing God's work?" Carl asked, taking a swig of Bud.

The others laughed.

"No, I'm serious. All these religious guys always want one thing: to get to heaven. It's the focus of their fucking lives. Everything they do is so they can get there. Maybe God sent these killers to do his bidding and help them out, send them on their way."

The laughter was a little more tentative. It was hard to tell sometimes whether Carl was joking with his outrageous statements or whether deep down he really believed some of the crap he spewed. As the outsider Dennis didn't feel qualified to comment at all. He figured it was his job just to listen.

Jack Chu tossed his empty beer can toward the water, clearing his throat. "I had a dream about that last night. Kind of."

A dream? Dennis focused his attention on the younger boy.

"It wasn't here—it was someplace else. And it wasn't now. It was a long time ago. I was this foreman guy. We were supposed to be building something, but my job was to kill the men who didn't work. There was this one dude taking a break, drinking out of this canteen? I smacked his head with a hammer. This other guy was taking a piss and I shot him. Two other guys were talking, and I shot them, too."

Carl Fong laughed. "Sounds like a good dream."

Uneasy chuckles.

Dennis was hoping some of the others had had weird dreams as well, and he wanted to open up and relate the stories of his own nightmares, but the conversation was already moving on to sex and he lost his chance.

Later, in his motel room, he was still wired and not sleepy, so he turned on *Letterman* and picked up the copy of the afternoon's newspaper that he'd saved for himself. The top story was about a graveyard that had been unearthed by construction workers while excavating an undeveloped plot of land for The Store. A tractor and backhoe had simultaneously shattered two rotted pine coffins and brought to light the decomposing remains of the interred men. Judging by the shreds of decayed clothing, jewelry and symbolic money that had been buried with the bodies, it appeared to have been a Chinese cemetery, a disused and previously unknown burial ground from a forgotten past.

Dennis thought of the hidden graveyard he had discovered back in Selby, remembered the man he had seen perform some sort of ritual at the grave site, the words he had spoken that sounded like *"bo sau."*

Revenge.

Coincidence?

There were no coincidences.

He had a tough time sleeping after that, and he brought the paper with him to the gas station the next morning. It was news to Carl Fong and his friends that there'd been a previous Chinese community in Milner, one large enough to require its own cemetery, and they immediately asked their parents and some of the older residents whether they knew anything about it. Everyone expressed surprise and admitted that they'd never heard of such a community before. Of course, the history of the Chinese in America was spotty at best. Records had not been kept on members of society who lived on the margins, who were ostracized by the mainstream, and out of shame, families had not passed down information on failure and rejection, instead emphasizing only positive success stories—of which there were very few in the early days. Listening to Carl's parents and some of the other old-timers talk, Dennis understood why his mom had been so fearful about his making this trip. For years, throughout the United States, Chinese immigrants had been illicitly sold as slaves, beaten and robbed by thugs, their murders never investigated by an uncaring justice system. Word of the harshness of life in America had spread to China, and before coming here, most émigrés had known what to expect, had been duly warned that with new opportunities came great risk. Even in California, where the Chinese community in San Francisco had grown fast and early, spreading throughout the northern half of the state to provide an entire support system for the miners of the gold rush, it had been illegal for anyone of Chinese ancestry to own property. Up through the twentieth century! In fact, it was *because* of the Chinese community's growing economic clout and burgeoning population that such laws were passed—white America had been afraid of being taken over by the yellow peril.

He'd assumed his mother had been simply overcautious, fearful of a land and country she still did not fully understand. But perhaps she knew more than she was telling.

He called his mother just before lunch and wanted

to talk to her about this, but their conversations had become so generic and superficial that he had no idea how to bring it up. As always, they ended up discussing the minutiae of her day, and as always, she ended up begging him to come home.

After finishing his route and delivering newspaper bundles to the paperboys, Dennis swung by the site where The Store was to be built and got out of the car to see if he could check out the cemetery. But there was a fence around the lot, workmen all around, and numerous NO TRESPASSING signs posted, so he simply stood on the sidewalk watching, not even trying to get in. He remained there for a while trying to get a feel for the place, hoping he'd pick up on some of the same strange vibes that had overtaken him at the hidden graveyard in Selby, but there was nothing. When a belligerent construction worker wearing a head scarf and wielding a shovel finally demanded, "What are you staring at?" Dennis decided that it was time to go.

He stayed in his motel room that night, declining to accompany Carl and his friends on their nighttime rounds. It was fun to do once, to take a vacation from his reality and sample someone else's world. But it was depressing as well, because he knew that if he had been born here instead of in Pennsylvania, this would be his lifestyle, too. He was only a visitor. This was how they lived.

He watched the last half of *Robocop,* then called his sister, feeling sad. He told her about the Chinese cemetery, and her response was a matter-of-fact, "I'll bet that Store's going to be haunted."

He laughed. "Maybe," he said. There was a pause. "But . . ."

"But what?"

He didn't know what to tell her because he didn't know what he was thinking, didn't know what he felt.

There was just a vague unease about dreams and graveyards and the history of the Chinese in America that didn't quite make sense.

The conversation concluded awkwardly, and Dennis clicked off feeling worse than he had felt before he'd called.

At least he had Brigit's Well to look forward to. Although just thinking about going to a coffeehouse to see a female duo play Celtic music made him feel like the biggest banana on the planet, especially when he realized that it was the sole reason he had stayed over in this town.

He wished Cathy were here.

She was a banana, too.

Carl and his friends were much more hard-core. He doubted they would be caught dead listening to Brigit's Well.

After a night's sleep filled with terrible nightmares that he could not for the life of him remember, Dennis ate breakfast at Waffle House, spending the morning at the park writing down the events of the last few days in a spiral notebook he'd bought at Walgreens. He'd decided to keep a journal of his travels, and though he'd only just started, he figured he'd go back and fill in the blanks as time allowed. For lunch he went over to the Golden Phoenix.

"I *saw* it," Jack Chu said from his post at the cash register as Dennis walked in.

Carl and the others were seated around the first table, laughing. "Yeah, right," Victor Yee taunted.

Dennis picked up a menu. "What?" he said.

"I saw a black train engine last night."

If this was a joke, he didn't get it. "Aren't most engines black?"

"No! This one wasn't even on the tracks. It was *next* to the tracks! In the field behind my house."

"Did your mom or dad or anyone else see it?" Carl asked.

"No, but—"

"You dreamed it."

"No, I didn't!" He turned toward Dennis. "I think it was a ghost train."

The others were laughing even harder, but Dennis didn't laugh at all. There was something in Jack's face that made him realize the boy was totally serious, and there was something about the image of a ghostly black train in an open field that pulled at him, that dovetailed with the graveyards and the nightmares and everything else he'd encountered on this trip. He could even see the massive engine in his mind, and he wondered if it had appeared in one of the dreams from last night that he'd forgotten.

Over egg rolls and chow fun, they discussed Jack's ghost train. As the conversation went on, as the need to make each other laugh abated and the desire to rag on the youngest member of their group was sated, Carl and his friends conceded that Jack really did seem to believe he'd seen something strange. It was Bobby Lam who suggested that they stake out the field tonight at the same time Jack claimed to have spotted the train. "We'll see if it comes back."

"And if not," Carl said, "we'll drink beer."

They all laughed.

Dennis decided to go with them. He didn't really think anything would show up, not two nights in a row, not with all of them waiting there, but there was still a chance, and as he was flying by the seat of his pants on this trip, allowing himself to be overtaken by events, he figured it would be a good idea.

But two hours in, with both six-packs consumed and every topic of conversation having seemingly run its course, he was not so sure. It was after midnight, and his motel room, bed and television were sounding pretty good to him right now. He looked back toward Jack's house, then across the empty field. What was he doing out here? If his friends back in Pennsylvania could see him now, they'd be laughing their asses off. Cathy would give him a lecture and say he'd been corrupted by the ignorant yahoos who populated the hinterlands. Even his mom, superstitious as she was, would think he was wasting his time on nonsense.

He was about to suggest that they give it up when . . .

Something changed.

They all felt it. A shift in the air. A drop in temperature. The faint whiff of foul-smelling smoke. On the hood of the car, Carl and Bobby sat up, and Jack ran around from where he'd been leaning on the trunk, breathing heavily. Victor, who was taking a piss by a tree off to the right, hurried back, still zipping up.

It was coming.

Dennis heard it from far off, not a *chug-chug-chug* like a normal train, but more of a w*hooosh,* like wind or water heard at a great distance. They were all swiveling their heads in various directions, trying to determine from where it would appear. Would it come up from the ground or down from the sky? Would it crash into one of the houses or just pass through it ghostlike? Would it come in on the real rails and then veer off?

It simply appeared. Not in place, but at the edge of the field, in motion, heading not toward them or Jack's house but toward the line of windbreak poplars to the west. The locomotive was indeed black, with a tender behind it and an old-fashioned passenger car behind that. After those three, the train grew more indistinct. Dennis had the impression that more cars were coupled to the train, but the night was dark, the rear of the railroad blurry, and it was impossible to tell what was there and what wasn't. Even the three visible sections did not seem to have the heft of reality, and though they weren't exactly transparent, they were, in some indefinable way, ephemeral.

The train stopped.

And passengers got on.

They were ghost passengers, but he could still see them clearly in the moonlight, shambling out from between the close-growing poplars, climbing up the step on the side of the passenger car, grabbing the assistance bar and pulling themselves in through the open door. *The people whose graves have been disinterred,* Dennis thought, and he knew that was right the second it occurred to him. He saw baggy shirts and coolie hats, pigtails and sandaled feet.

They were leaving Milner, going someplace better.

Something in the scene spoke to him on a deep level he didn't even know existed. He was not frightened, as he probably should have been, but, rather, moved, touched by the knowledge that after untold decades these souls were free. He saw a woman go up the steps to the passenger car, holding the hand of a little girl. With each person who climbed onto the train, the black locomotive became a little less evanescent, a little more substantial.

The whooshing noise had stopped when the train did, but there was another sound now, a more organic sound that seemed to be coming from the smokestack and that reminded him of music. He stood still, listening, and thought he had never heard anything so wonderful: so peaceful and comforting and welcoming. There were no words, not even a tune, just strange swirling tones, but to him it sounded like an invitation, and before he knew it he was walking forward, toward the train.

This was why he'd driven across country, why he'd come on this trip.

"Hey!" Carl said. "What the fuck are you doing?"

He was vaguely cognizant of the fact that Carl was talking to him, but he didn't answer, kept walking across the rough grass of the field, his attention focused on the black railroad cars in front of him. He wasn't dead, wasn't a ghost, so he probably wouldn't even be able to get on the train, but he knew he had to try. This was his purpose. This was why he was here.

"Stop!" "Get back here!" "Don't!"

They were all yelling at him now, but the call of the train was even stronger and he continued on. No one tried to stop him, and he realized that it was because they were afraid to get any closer.

Why wasn't he afraid?

He didn't know.

The smoke smell was strong, the temperature somewhere around freezing and falling with each step, but neither of those elements deterred him, and he forged ahead until he was standing before the passenger car. The others had all gotten aboard; there was no one waiting in line. Through the windows he could see nothing, no faces, no silhouettes, only impenetrable darkness.

He had a moment of hesitation.

Then he thought of the woman holding the hand of the little girl, heard in his ears and felt in his mind the soothing voice of the railroad and grabbed hold of the metal bar to pull himself up the steps.

Only the bar wasn't metal.

"Dennis!" Jack yelled from somewhere far behind him.

And he was on the train.

Twenty-one

Bear Flats, California

Jolene, sitting in Leslie's living room, slammed the leather-bound diary shut with trembling fingers.

Was it really bound with *leather*?

She had the sudden urge to drop the book and wash her hands, her arms, her entire body, but she forced herself to remain as she was. She was just being paranoid—although it was hard *not* to be paranoid after what she'd seen, after what she'd read. Surreptitiously, she looked down at the cover of the diary to see if she could spot veins, hair, fingerprints.

Skylar lay asleep on the couch next to her, his fingers clutching her blouse and holding on to the material tightly, as though he was afraid to let go. Across the room, her mother, completely sober, sat unmoving in her chair, the expression on her blanched face not exactly concerned and caring, but definitely less self-absorbed than Jolene had ever seen it. Leslie stood in the kitchen doorway, leaning on the frame, a drink in her hand. The sound of ice cubes clinking in the glass was loud in the stillness. She was trembling, too. "I thought you were going to read it out loud," she said.

Jolene took a deep breath. She looked down at her

son, brushing a wisp of hair from his forehead to calm herself down.

"They want revenge," Skylar had told her after he'd been brought to the hospital and sedated, after a doctor had confirmed that no bones were broken and he had not been sexually assaulted. She wasn't sure he understood the concept of "revenge," wasn't even sure he knew who "they" were. But she was sure of one thing: this was why he'd been abducted; this was why he'd been released.

To relay this message.

They want revenge.

But who had taken him? And how had he ended up in the cellar?

That, she still didn't know.

Despite the circumstances, the police, in all of their literal-mindedness, had not seen any harm in allowing Jolene to take the diary out of the Williams house, and she had done so hoping it would provide some clues. But after reading one random page, she'd been so horrified that she'd shut the book, refusing to read more.

"I don't want to read it aloud," she said. "Skylar might wake up. He might hear it."

Leslie's voice was uncharacteristically solemn. "Is it that bad?"

Jolene nodded. The page she'd read, near the back of the diary, had described a man who had been killed and gutted for no reason other than he'd trespassed on the Williams land. The man's innards had been fed to hogs, and the hands and feet had been hung out to dry with the beef jerky in order to make chew toys for the hounds. There had not been much graphic detail, at least not by today's slasher-movie standards, but there'd been an obvious joy in the telling, in the remembering of what was clearly a satisfying event,

and the tone had turned her stomach. She thought of
her last sight of Anna May, an image that would remain burned forever in her mind, the old woman's
body beaten and slashed, a spreading puddle of blood
on the floor.

They want revenge.

"Let me read it," Leslie said, walking over.

"It's all yours." Jolene handed her the diary, once
again experiencing an instinctive desire to wash her
hands or at least wipe them on her pants. Leslie sat
down on the floor in front of her, opened the elabo-
rately bound book and started quickly skimming
pages.

Jolene looked across the room at her mother, who
met her glance with a small apologetic smile, then
turned her gaze down at her son. Asleep, he seemed
smaller than he did when awake, and it broke her
heart to see a furrowed brow where there should have
been only smooth skin and an angelic expression. She
touched his fist, which was still holding tightly to her
blouse, and could feel the tension in his muscles. Life
had been tough enough for the little guy already. Now
this. Could he ever hope to emerge unscathed?

Counseling, the doctor had told her, and while that
carried its own stigma, it was probably the only way
through this.

"Jesus," Leslie breathed. She glanced quickly over
to make sure Skylar was still asleep.

"What is it?" Jolene said tiredly. "Hit me."

"I know who's in those graves," Leslie said. "The
ones on the path." She looked up from the diary.

There were goose bumps on Jolene's arms.

"It's a Chinese woman and her half-and-half daughter. They were discovered living with a miner up in
Hells Canyon and Chester Williams gleefully rallied
the town and had all three of them lynched. I gather

it happened quite a while before the other events in this diary, when he was younger, but it seems to have been some kind of turning point in his life because he doesn't just mention it; he goes into detail. 'I pulled the rope hard and the girl flew up into the tree,' he writes. 'We laughed as her legs continued to dance.' " Leslie turned the page. "After that, the man was buried in the cemetery, the one by the golf course, and the mother and daughter, not being Christians, were buried out in the woods, where the path is now."

Jolene shivered.

The family in the gulch

Yes. That's exactly what it reminded her of. Strangers in a strange land who, looking for a better life, found only death. She wondered who had been hanged first, the woman or the girl. She hoped the woman had gone first. As a mother, she could think of no fate so horrible as being forced to watch one's child killed. Unconsciously, her arm snaked around Skylar's shoulders, held him tight.

Leslie was looking at her, face pale. "He cut off their thumbs after they were dead, and kept them. It says here that all these years later, he still liked to take them out and look at them."

Jolene glanced over at her mom, expecting some sort of reaction, but there was nothing. Her mom had actually known the most recent Chester Williams, this man's grandson. She would have expected her mom to have some sort of emotional response to these revelations.

"There were more than two thumbs in that basement," Leslie said.

Jolene thought of what her son had said—

They want revenge

—and for the first time thought she might know who "they" were.

"Those two weren't the only ones," Jolene said softly. "There were more."

Leslie nodded. "I'll keep reading."

He dreamed of the face from the window, that brown wrinkled head and those horrible grinning teeth. Only the face wasn't at the window. It was directly above his, looking at him from inches away, and Skylar realized from the gentle side-to-side movement of the head and the corresponding sway of his own prone form that the man was carrying him.

Except it wasn't a man.

It had been at one time, but that was long, long ago. The thing that held him now, that had taken him from the bathroom at school and was now bringing him somewhere else, was a corpse but more than a corpse, a monster of some kind, though not one that Skylar recognized or could identify.

And he was not himself. He was a puppet. He had somehow been transformed into a marionette, and the corpse thing was transporting him through some sort of tunnel deep underground to . . . where?

He didn't know, was afraid to even wonder.

"I have so much to show you," the monster said sibilantly, and though he was speaking an unfamiliar language, Skylar understood him perfectly. The monster jerked on his strings, and Skylar was pulled into a sitting position in the crook of skeletal arms. He saw, in hollows within the surrounding dirt, a little boy who'd had his head, hands and feet chopped off, a man and woman who'd been buried alive, an old man who'd been strangled, a teenage girl who'd been cut in half.

They all appeared to be relatives of the monster carrying him. Skylar saw similarities in the cast of features, in the color of skin.

"They want revenge," the thing whispered in his ear, and at that, the severed head of an old hag opened its opaque white eyes and shrieked.

Skylar awoke clutching his mom's midsection. More than a dream, what he had experienced was a memory, a re-creation of actual events. His heart was pounding, but he hadn't awakened crying or screaming, and for that, he was grateful. Ms. Finch was here and his grandma was, too, and he didn't want to embarrass himself in front of them.

Although, looking around, he could tell instantly that they were just as scared as he was. Maybe more. They'd been talking about something while he'd been asleep, something spooky, and while he was curious about it, he didn't really want to know.

He let go of his mom, sat up.

"Are you okay, hon?" she asked.

He nodded, not trusting himself to speak. He had never been less okay in his life. Even being back with his dad would be a picnic compared with this.

Why did the monster let me go? he wondered.

He had no idea. He'd sensed the creature's rage and hate, knew that behind that terrible grin was a furious evil that wanted nothing more than to tear him limb from limb and laugh as the blood flowed. He was one of those the monster wanted to take revenge *against.* But it had held back for some strange reason he did not understand, and he realized that it was not the one calling the shots. It was as much a puppet as he himself was. There was another force *behind* the monster, an entity far more powerful that was using it to communicate with him. He had the feeling that it had something to do with all of those dead bodies he'd been shown, although how or why he couldn't figure out.

He looked at his mom. "Are we staying here to-night?" he asked.

"Yes," she said but did not elaborate. He was sure it was because of that face at the window, and he was glad not to be going back to his grandma's.

The old lady stood up. "I'll take him to bed," she said. "I'm tired myself. We can both get a little shut-eye."

He didn't want to sleep with his grandma—he wanted to sleep with his mom—but he didn't say any-thing as his mom said, "Okay." She gave him a big kiss and a long hug, and he squeezed her back, grate-ful that she was here. "Night night," she told him.

He pulled away. "Night night."

He followed his grandma to the bedroom door but would not go in until she'd turned on the light. Out in the front room, his mom and Ms. Finch were talk-ing. He hummed a song as he kicked off his shoes and crawled into bed, not wanting to hear what they said, not wanting to know what they were discussing. He gave his grandma a cursory "Good night," then rolled over and plugged his ears as he tried to fall asleep.

He hoped he would not dream.

There *were* more.

A lot more.

Leslie had barely made a dent in the diary by the time Skylar awoke just before midnight, but already she'd encountered more murders than the Manson family could have dreamed of. The language was ar-cane and formal, the setting far enough in the past to be emotionally distant, but still the horror came through, and the trivialization of death that usually accompanied history was nowhere in evidence. Even through the filters, she knew this Chester Williams had been an evil, psychotic son of a bitch.

He had stabbed men and shot them, hanged children and flayed women, eviscerated the corpses of those he had killed, and all, apparently, with the tacit knowledge and blessing of the community.

Leslie felt sickened, as much by the dispassionate tone of Williams' writing as by the horrific events his words described.

The strange thing was, his victims were *all* Chinese. Or seemed to be. References were made to other earlier killings, to wars and to a great project that took many lives and that Chester Williams was apparently instrumental in getting off the ground, but those were beyond the scope of this diary, and Leslie wondered if there was an earlier journal or perhaps a series of them still hidden in the Williams mansion.

All of the murders he wrote about, however, were of Chinese people. He seemed to have some special sort of hatred toward them, and while prejudice was probably fairly common back then, the extent of his animosity was definitely extreme.

Leslie looked at the book in her hands. She still had three-fourths of the diary to go. What was going to happen in the later years?

Major revelations, Anna May had said. *Murder!*

She hadn't been lying.

Leslie explained to Jolene about the killings, speaking quietly so as not to disturb Skylar and his grandmother.

"I wish Anna May was here," Jolene sighed. "She might be able to put this in context."

"Your mom might know—"

She waved Leslie away. "Don't even."

"Anyway, what context? Let's be honest. The guy was a psycho. Period."

"And his son after him, and his son after him."

"If Anna May had really known anything, she

would have been a little more cautious, you know what I'm saying? But you saw her. She was like a kid in a candy store. She had no clue anything would or *could* happen to her."

"What I want to know is who—or *what*—kidnapped Skylar. It's like it was all . . . planned, you know? That's the scary part. He was probably abducted when I was on my way to see you, before we'd even *thought* about going to see Anna May, and he was probably locked up down there in the cellar when we were just starting to talk about heading over there. It dropped him off so I could find him. It knew what we were going to do before we did it."

"Maybe we weren't meant to find him. Not us specifically."

"That's the thing," Jolene said. "I think we were."

"Why?"

"I don't know."

Leslie thought for a moment. "I'll bet those voices from the graves were speaking Chinese."

"But what were they saying?" Jolene ran an exasperated hand through her hair. Her voice was still low so her mother and son could not hear, but there was an intensity there that Leslie had not seen before. "I feel like we're on the *Titanic* or something here and we can just see this little bitty piece of ice, but there's this big giant iceberg underneath it and it's going to rip our boat to shreds."

It was an apt metaphor and Leslie realized that it perfectly captured the way she felt, too. "But what can we do?"

"Sit tight and wait for it to hit."

"Or read as much as we can and prepare ourselves." Leslie moved onto the couch, scooted close to Jolene and opened the diary so they could both read.

Twenty-two

Canyonlands National Park, Utah

Henry left the burning burger in the frying pan on the stove and stood dumbly in front of the television. It was the end of the *NBC Nightly News,* the segment that usually featured a semihumorous puff piece in order to make the transition between the horror of world events and the glitzy superficiality of the following entertainment program a little less jarring. Today, however, it was one of those Robert Ripley–ish stories about bizarre human behavior and unexplainable events. He'd missed the first part of the piece, but a shot of Salt Lake City had captured his attention, and he'd tuned in, growing increasingly rapt as the story unfolded.

Apparently, Indian men from all over the country were making a pilgrimage to Utah. By plane, by train, by car, by bike, by foot, they were riding, driving, rolling and walking to the Beehive State from their various reservations. If there was a reason for this migration or a specific destination, the participants weren't telling, and the few men that the reporter tried to interview either refused to answer questions or claimed that they didn't know why they were participating in this lemminglike journey. According to the reporter, several wives in several states had filed police reports, unaware of this mass migration, knowing only that their spouses had apparently gone missing.

Gone missing.

When had the smoothly flowing "disappeared" changed into the awkward and grammatically suspect "gone missing?" Could a person really "*go* missing"? Henry had his doubts.

The piece ended with a promise that NBC news would keep viewers informed of this story as it continued to unfold.

Smelling the burning burger, Henry hurried back to the kitchenette and moved the frying pan to a cold section of the stove. He took a bun out of the package. Something about the bizarre pilgrimage seemed naggingly familiar to him—or, more correctly, seemed as though it *should* be familiar to him—and while he saw no real similarities, he was reminded of the strange events that had been happening at the park lately. Healey said there were rumblings of spooky occurrences at a few of the other national parks, though nothing as documented and definitely nothing of this magnitude. Perhaps there was some sort of curse affecting the whole nation, the psychic equivalent of a massive storm that covered vast geographic areas.

Indian blood talking again.

But *did* he have Indian blood and *was* it talking? For he felt no compulsion to start on a mysterious sojourn, to hop in his Jeep and take off down the highway or tie on his tennis shoes and start walking the roads.

Of course, he was already here in Utah, the travelers' ostensible destination.

He got ketchup out of the refrigerator, and mustard. Too lazy to slice onions and tomatoes, he plopped the burned patty on the bun, doused it with condiments

and stood eating it over the counter. He glanced out
the kitchen window, tilting his head to see sideways,
looking at the spot where the train had been. There'd
been wind, as usual, before they'd made it out into
the desert to investigate, but not enough to erase the
deep grooves that had been carved in the sand and
stretched in a straight line toward the horizon.

Whatever the train had been, it was not merely a
shade or phantom. It was corporeal; it existed in the
physical world.

But what did it mean? What did any of it mean?

According to the news piece, some of the Indians
were traveling to Utah by train. Was that the reason
the train had appeared? He didn't think so. There
might be a connection, but if there was, it was something much more subtle and complicated, something
he probably couldn't even grasp.

And it involved death.

Henry glanced at the television, where the news was
over and cameras were recording the arrival of well-
dressed stars at a Hollywood gala. He wished he were
there . . . or in Chicago . . . or New York . . . anyplace
where there were a lot of people and so many electric
lights that a permanent bubble of illumination kept
the darkness of the natural world at bay. He smiled
ironically, looking up at Sarah's photograph on the
wall. He'd come around to her point of view after all.

Something passed in front of the television.

He jumped, startled, swiveling his head to look all
around the cabin, but nothing was there. Only his
furniture—

And a thick fuzzy shadow in the corner by the
fireplace.

He sucked in his breath. The shadow moved, separated into two thinner shadows like a single-celled or-
ganism dividing in half. He recognized the two halves

immediately. They were naked, they were female, and they were moving slowly toward him across the cabin.

The twins.

"No," Henry whispered.

But he had no willpower, and he pulled down his pants, and the shadows swirled around his growing organ, touching it but not touching it, until he was thrusting in the air and spurting onto his own tile floor.

And the shadows licked it up.

And grew darker.

He spent all the next day in the visitors' center, doing busywork. Everyone did. Ranger talks had been canceled, trails closed, and the backcountry declared off-limits to both hikers and off-roaders, who were to be redirected to Arches. All of their outdoor duties had been suspended until further notice. Healey was taking no chances, and Henry actually admired the superintendent for that. For all intents and purposes, Canyonlands was shut down, and it couldn't be easy on Healey with park officials from Washington breathing down his neck and demanding rational explanations that just weren't there.

They were all on edge, short-tempered with each other and frightened by every stray creak in the building's wooden floor. They were like soldiers under siege, trapped in a fort in hostile territory, and though Moab was only a few miles away, with gas stations and stores, fast-food restaurants and motels, it felt to him as though they were out in the wilderness, far, far away from civilization.

After work, to let off steam, he *did* drive into Moab, meeting Ector at the Boy Howdy for beers. But his friend was churlish and untalkative, the atmosphere in the normally laid-back bar seemed tense, as though a fight might break out at any second, and he ended up leaving after only about twenty minutes. On his way back through town, he glanced at the Chinese and Japanese restaurants, and shivered at the shadows thrown by the bonsai-shaped foliage and the orange setting sun.

Back at his cabin, he felt as though he were going stir-crazy. He'd always been comfortable here in Canyonlands. Ever since he'd started working at the park, he'd felt at home amid the stark beauty of the land, happy within the confines of his little cabin. But now he felt restless and ill at ease, and for the first time he wished he had a bigger place.

He made himself a ham sandwich, watched the news, got tired of TV and turned on his stereo, tried to read a book, couldn't concentrate, turned on the TV again.

The lights went out.

It was dark now, night. He felt his way over to the supply cabinet where he kept his emergency gear and pulled out a battery-powered lantern that he immediately switched on and placed atop the coffee table. In the odd glow of the fluorescent light, he found candles, and he went about setting them up at prearranged points around the room, lighting them. The cabin wasn't fully illuminated, but at least he could see.

Why was there a blackout, though, and was just his place affected or all of them? He glanced out the window but could see no lights on in any of the other cabins. Taking out a flashlight, he made his way over to the phone, intending to call Stuart and find out what was going down, but the phone was dead, too.

That set off alarm bells.

A knock on the door made him jump. He immediately thought of the twins, saw in his mind's eye Ray's bloody body on the floor of his cabin. He remained in place, unmoving, hardly daring to breathe, hoping whatever was out there would give up and go away.

The knocking came again.

"Who is it?" he called, looking around for his rifle. His heart was hammering in his chest, not just because of who—or what—might be on the other side of his door, but because he shouldn't have to *look* for his rifle. It should have been resting in the same spot in the back of his broom closet that it always was.

Only it wasn't.

It had been taken.

The knocking continued.

"What?" he yelled, frustrated. He looked under his bed, tried his clothes closet, checked behind the couch. Nothing. He still had his ax by the fireplace, and he picked it up, hefted it in his hand and, before he could change his mind, opened the door, stepping back in case he needed room to swing.

A group of four Indians stood on his doorstep.

He frowned. Behind them, he could see a pickup truck on the road, lights on, engine still idling, man in the driver's seat. He didn't know why he hadn't heard the noise from inside the cabin. "Yes?" he said cautiously.

"We're here to pick you up," said the Indian on the left, an older gentleman with a bandanna and a ponytail.

He should have been confused. And he was. But he also should have been frightened. And he wasn't. He stepped onto the porch and the Indians nodded.

"Let's go," Ponytail said.

"Where?" Henry asked, realizing with something like amazement that if the answer was right, he would accompany them.

"To the Point."

The answer was right.

Twenty-three

Jarrett, Nevada

"Children! Children! Stay away from there! Brian, get back!"

Bees crawled over the outside of the kindergarten classroom dozens thick, individual insects falling onto the ground below like drops of water melting from an icicle. Miss Iris had never seen anything like it. She'd already called the custodian, who was on his way over to take care of the problem, but the kids were fascinated by the bees, and though Ashley Curtis had already been stung, the teacher was having a hard time keeping the other kids away.

Just as frightening was the black mold that was growing on the wall next to the bee swarm, just below the eave of the building.

Neither the bees nor the mold had been there an hour ago.

"Back in the room!" she ordered. "Everyone back inside!"

"But it's recess!" Joel complained.

"We'll have recess *after* Mr. Gehring takes care of the bees. But if you don't listen to me and go back inside right now, there won't be any recess at all."

That got them. There was moaning and whining,

but they dutifully filed back into the classroom and took their places on the learning rug. A train went by on the tracks next to the school, rattling the windows as it always did, and though most of the kids were used to it by now, some of the boys still craned their necks to see over the desks. Miss Iris sat down in her chair, picked up *Chicka Chicka Boom Boom* and started reading. The children joined in, chanting the parts they knew, and soon the missed recess was forgotten.

"It's done!" the custodian announced a while later, poking his head in the door.

"Thank you, Mr. Gehring," Miss Iris said, and the class repeated it in unison: "Thank you, Mr. Gehring!"

"I've roped off that area of the playground, so you kids stay away from there, you understand? There might still be poison."

"I'll make sure they do," Miss Iris promised.

She read the children another story, then had them go to the art tables and draw pictures of their families for the upcoming back-to-school night. Afterward, she allowed them to go outside for recess. "Remember what Mr. Gehring said," she told them as she led the line of students out the door to the playground. "There's still poison on the wall and it can make you very sick. So stay behind the rope, okay?"

"Okay!" they responded.

Miss Iris dismissed them and went to look at the spot where the bees had swarmed, but instead of running off to play on the swings and slides, the children accompanied her, being careful to stay far away from the yellow rope. The bees were gone, but the black mold remained on the side of the building and it had grown in the last forty minutes. It was no longer merely an amorphous shape but now looked like a profile of George Washington's head. It resembled one of their art projects, the silhouettes they cut out of black paper.

Miss Iris' heart skipped a beat. This was no accidental resemblance. The face on the wall was too perfectly formed, too specific for that. Its shape was deliberate, although that made no logical sense whatsoever.

And the bees were coming back.

They heard the insects before they saw them, a buzzing that started out faintly, like an alarm clock beeping someplace far away, growing louder, until by the time they saw the fuzzy dark cloud swooping down between the trees toward the school building, the noise sounded to Miss Iris like two vibrators shoved up against her ears.

"Back inside!" she ordered, but her voice was lost in the din and before she could recalibrate the volume and say it again, the bees—hundreds of them, maybe thousands—had flown straight to the wall despite the residue of poison, swarming over the mold, conforming precisely to its contours, their teeming mass taking on the appearance of a three-dimensional George Washington. They were moving constantly, wings beating, legs working, bodies twitching, and the combined motion gave the appearance of a face that was alive.

And talking.

The children, who'd been hitting each other and squealing and jockeying for position, were standing still now, as though listening intently to something, and Miss Iris noticed that the noise of the bees had altered appreciably. The sound was no longer merely buzzing but buzzing with rhythm, tone, color. Buzzing that sounded eerily like a voice. When combined with the movement of the face, it appeared as though George Washington was speaking.

She couldn't make out what was being said, but the

children seemed to hear something, and they listened carefully, even the squirmiest ones. Before she could order them inside, they were running as one away from the wall and toward the center of the playground. "Class!" she called, starting after them. She assumed they were rushing out to play, though the uniformity of their movements worried her, but it was clear almost instantly that they were following orders, not running for fun.

The first kids reached the playground equipment—

And began smashing their faces into the metal poles of the monkey bars and the support posts of the swings.

"Oh, my God!" she screamed. She rushed after them. "Stop! Brian! Joel!"

Other kids had reached the equipment and were slamming their jaws down on the monkey bars, biting the sides of the slides. Blood was everywhere, gushing from eighteen small mouths, dripping down dresses and shirts, falling on the asphalt. Eerily, the children did not cry out, made no sound, but attacked themselves and bled in silence.

Lisa Johnson spit out her remaining teeth, yanking one from the right side with her fingers, then picked up a handful of wood chips from the play area and bit into it.

Joey Higgins took two small sticks and placed them in the holes where his top two front teeth had been.

Others began doing the same, putting sticks and wood chips into their mouths, shoving the small pieces hard into their bleeding gums, smiling crazily at each other, and she realized with a sickening lurch of her stomach what they were doing.

They were making wooden teeth.

Back on the wall, George Washington appeared to be laughing uproariously, his uninhibited guffaw the sound of bees buzzing, and though Miss Iris considered herself something of a tough customer, her eyelids fluttered, the world went black, and she fell to the ground in a faint.

She awoke moments later, screaming, when Ashley Curtis began knocking her teeth out with a rock.

Twenty-four

Flagstaff, Arizona

"This seems wrong," Angela said as Derek found a parking space in the south lot and pulled into it.

"I know," he said. "But real life's still going on. We have classes, we have jobs, and if we don't show up, we'll flunk and get fired."

She smiled. "That's the part they don't show you in movies. Usually, everyone drops everything and fights the monster or solves the mystery and once the problem's solved you assume they're going to live happily ever after. They don't show the part where they get fired from their job and can't pay rent and end up being evicted and homeless."

"We're still going to fight the monster and solve the mystery. We just have to do it after work and after class."

Angela was suddenly serious again. "What do you think's happening at Babbitt House?" In her mind, she saw the Victorian house covered with black mold that was starting to spread to adjacent homes.

"I don't know."

"I want to go by there later."

"Angela . . ."

"We'll just drive past. That's it. You speed by, and I'll look out the window."

"We'll see." He looked at his watch. "Right now, I need to get my ass to work and you need to go to class. We'll meet in the quad at eleven, then go see Dr. Mathewson and find out if he's had any luck."

"He would've called us if he had," she pointed out.

"Maybe something'll happen this morning. Never can tell."

They waved, heading in opposite directions, and Angela started off toward class. It had been awkward saying good-bye, she thought. They'd spent almost every second of the last few days together, and though there was nothing romantic between them, there was still an intimacy, and it seemed as though parting should involve a hug, a touch, something that would acknowledge the closeness.

Attending Algebra and then English Composition was decidedly strange. After the surreal chaos of the past several days, to sit in an ordinary classroom, surrounded by students dutifully taking notes, listening to an instructor lecture on an academic topic, felt very peculiar. Several times, particularly during the math class, she found herself looking at the exposed section of arm where the corpse had grabbed her as she searched for signs of anything amiss, trying to detect stray black spots of mold that might still be on her skin.

Chrissie had a music appreciation class right now, and Angela wondered if her roommate—*former* roommate—was there or had given up going to school entirely and was spending all of her time in a decaying Babbitt House, looking at the moldy black walls, ranting and raving about Mexicans and growing crazier by the minute.

Something in that train of thought seemed important to her, as though it might hold the key to part of this mystery or at least might shed some further light on what was happening, but though the connection was on the tip of her brain, it could not make the leap to consciousness and the more she tried to pin it down, the farther away it seemed to slip.

Angela listened to the lectures and took notes, but though she knew Derek was right, that real life went on and after all this insanity was over they would have to resume their ordinary existence, the information she copied into her notebook seemed trivial and unimportant. And no matter how hard she tried, she couldn't make it seem anything less than frivolous in a brave new world filled with living corpses and alien mold.

The English class got out early, and Angela rode with the herd down the stairs, out of the Humanities Building and into the quad, where a crowd of people seemed to be milling about the far end, others from the periphery and from just-released classes joining the throng. Was it a concert, a rally, a speech? She started across the open space to see for herself, but as she drew closer her gait slowed. The mood here seemed not festive or intellectually engaged but angry and emotionally charged. She held back even as others ran forward, rushing toward the center of the action. Someone unseen was yelling words she could not make out, inciting the crowd, and at every lull in his speech, a roar of approval would issue from those in the front.

There was a huge cheer as a dancing woman seemed to levitate above the crowd, and for a brief moment Angela thought it was part of some magic show. Then she saw that the woman was not rising in the air and dancing; she was being hoisted by a rope tied around her neck. Her body thrashed about as the tightening rope was pulled over the limb of a pine tree.

It was Edna Wong.

Angela gasped audibly and nearly fell over. Nearby students turned to look at her, and on their faces she saw mingled expressions of disgust and satisfaction.

Edna was kicking her feet crazily, trying to gain purchase, though she was already more than ten feet in the air. Her fingers clutched at the noose around her neck, and the wild expression on her face was one of terror and incomprehension. Angela had never seen anything so awful, and she screamed at the top of her lungs, a cry from the depths of her soul, pushing her way through the assembled students toward the front of the crowd, shoving a cheering blond girl to the ground in a desperate instinctive effort to save the old woman.

Edna was jerking spasmodically, arms flailing, legs kicking out and back like those of a cancan girl, no longer making even a token effort to save herself. The crowd laughed as urine and excrement dropped from under the housing administrator's legs, her bladder voiding, her bowels evacuating as she died.

"No!" Angela cried.

"That'll teach you, you slant-eyed slut!" someone shouted in a thick New York accent. Angela saw a skinny student with a huge halo of hair tying the end of the rope to the trunk of the pine tree. She recognized him from her first day here. He'd walked by the housing office while she'd been waiting in line.

The throng cheered.

Now that she was in the midst of it, she saw black fuzzy patches on girls' blouses and on boys' pants, dark mold growing on arms and necks and cheeks. It was like being at a zombie rally, and while she was scared, she was more angry, and she started screaming at the people around her. "What are you doing? Murderers!"

A goateed guy next to her turned, his face contorted with hate, his hands balled into fists. "You stay out of it, you stupid brown bitch!"

Derek socked him in the stomach.

She didn't know where he had come from or how he had found her, but she was grateful he was here. Before the goateed guy could get up off the ground or the people around him could come to his assistance, Derek grabbed her hand and they were running, shoving their way through the crowd, elbowing people aside, making their way toward the parking lot and safety.

What had happened? How had it started? Where were the campus police? Angela's mind raced, bogged down with the impossible logistics of such a lynching, but no matter how she imagined the scenario, she could not seem to make the pieces fit. She and Derek broke free of the crowd and dashed between the two science buildings, circling back around on the outer sidewalk to. the south parking lot. They were both completely out of breath from running, and with no one pursuing them, they slowed to a tired shuffle as they passed between the cars to Derek's Hyundai.

"It was Edna Wong," Angela said numbly. "They—"

"I know. I saw."

"So what do we do now?"

"Tell the police."

"And if they don't do anything . . . ?"

It was a very real possibility, and discouraged, disheartened and demoralized, neither of them said another word until they were in the car and out of the parking lot, heading up the highway past Bookmans.

Before them, above the city, rose the majestic San Francisco Peaks, and in every direction the deep blue sky was as big as it was purported to be in Montana, but Angela still felt trapped and claustrophobic, as though she were in a room with walls closing in on her. This was the last straw. She could not stay here anymore. She needed to go back to Los Angeles, although at the moment even that teeming metropolis did not seem safe. It would be only a matter of time before Flagstaff was taken over. And then the rest of Arizona. And then California.

But at least it would take a while to get that far. And maybe, in the meantime, Dr. Mathewson or someone else would figure out a solution and it would all be over.

Unless she was a carrier.

Maybe that's what had happened. Maybe she was the cause of it all. Maybe she was spreading the mold.

No, she refused to let herself think that way.

But she couldn't help it. She imagined her friends turning on her, calling her a stupid brown bitch, saw in her mind's eye her mother's kitchen and her father's workroom overrun with fuzzy black mold.

For the first time, she understood the utter hopelessness felt by people who considered suicide.

They went under the train tracks and around the curve. Humphreys Street was blocked off for some reason, so Derek continued on to the next stoplight and turned left, intending to take Aspen to the police station.

"Stop the car!" Angela screamed. "Oh, my God!"

Derek slammed on the brakes, and the Hyundai slid a few inches to the right as it stopped in the middle of the street.

The car was stopped half a block in front of the hotel where she'd gone with Dr. Welkes' class.

And *they* were coming out of it.

The corpses from the tunnel.

Crawling, limping, sliding, pulling themselves forward with skeletal arms, broken legs dragging uselessly behind them, they emerged into the sunlight. It was a vision from a nightmare, all the more horrifying and unbelievable because it was happening in the middle of the day while smartly dressed women and business-suited men walked down the sidewalk from their offices to the restaurants where they intended to eat lunch.

"Jesus Christ," Derek said, throwing the car into reverse and backing up on the one-way street.

Angela kept her eyes focused on the scene through the front windshield, even as it began to recede. She saw men and women turn and run away the second they saw the skeletal figures moving across the sidewalk and onto the street, saw cars come to screeching halts, saw curious people emerge from stores and restaurants to find out for themselves what was happening.

A tall mummified man dressed in rotted rags shambled across the street like something out of an old horror movie.

Someone must have called the police, because sirens suddenly sounded, growing instantly louder, and Derek backed the car into an open space at the corner of the block just as four patrol cars, lights flashing, sped by. She wanted to see what they were going to do—*Try and capture the corpses? Start blasting away with their guns?*—but Edna was dead and swinging from a tree in the center of campus, murdered by a gang of crazed students, and that had to be their priority. Derek must have faced the same dilemma because he looked at her quizzically, as though wondering which was to go. She said, "Edna," and he nodded, taking the car around the corner and going up to the next street so he could drive straight to the police station.

The place was a madhouse. Two police cars and two motorcycles rolled past them, lights and sirens on, as the Hyundai tried to pull into the small visitors' lot, and they had to jockey for a space with four other civilian vehicles whose drivers all seemed desperate to report something.

"I think those cops were heading south," Derek said. "Toward the school."

"We'll find out."

The only parking space left was a handicapped spot, and Derek pulled right in, parking between the blue lines. "Limp," he suggested drily.

They got out and hurried through the front door into the station's lobby, where at least a dozen men and women, although mostly men, were lined up in front of the counter and noisily declaiming their reasons for being here to all who would listen. One couple, incongruously young, looked like they could be college students, and Angela wondered if they, too, were here to report the lynching.

Lynching.

She never thought that was a word she'd be using outside of a historical context. She tried not to think about the look of agony and abject terror on Edna's face as the doomed woman tried to claw at the noose around her neck.

She wondered if Chrissie had been in that crowd somewhere. And Winston and Brock.

She hoped not.

A blue-uniformed officer emerged from a side door and stood before the front counter, hands raised. "Ladies and gentlemen! If you are here to report the incident on Aspen, we already know about it and have officers on the scene. The situation is under control.

If you are here to report on the incidents at NAU or Flag High, we are aware of those, too, and our men are on it."

Incidents?

Angela looked at the young couple. The girl was now sobbing on the boy's shoulders. They weren't college students, she realized. They were high school students.

What had happened at the high school?

She was not sure she wanted to know.

Nearly all of the people, with visible relief, were heading outside, but Angela, holding tightly to Derek's hand, remained and moved to the front of the room. The officer behind the counter looked at them as they approached. "Yes?"

"We were at NAU and then we were on Aspen Avenue, so we saw both . . . incidents," she said. "But I just thought you should know that they're both probably connected. There's this mold that—"

"Oh, that was you who reported that," he said, eyebrows raised in surprise. "Thank you. We were already operating on that assumption with Aspen. Obviously. The officers at the high school and college are aware of it, too. Just in case it's a factor. I don't know if Sergeant Sandidge ever got back to you, but we quarantined the apartment house on State Street and called in the CDC, which apparently one of the NAU professors had already done. I assume you talked to him?"

They both nodded.

"Well, someone from Atlanta should be here today. Possibly someone from the FBI. We're on this."

"Thank God," Angela breathed. Already she felt better.

There were still two men standing in front of the counter, one talking to the uniformed female cadet at the desk, another waiting to talk to Angela's officer. "Excuse me," he said. "We're a little overwhelmed right now. Unless there's anything else . . . ?"

"No," Derek said. "Thanks for your time."

The two of them went outside, where the visitors' lot was quickly emptying. The Hyundai did not have a ticket for parking in the handicapped spot—cops definitely had higher priorities right now—and they got in, Derek starting the engine. "Let's see where they are," Angela said.

She did not even have to explain what she meant. "I was thinking the same thing," Derek said. He turned onto Aspen, planning to head back the way they'd come, but several streets ahead they could see red and blue flashing lights and striped barricades cordoning off the block containing the hotel, so he drove down to the highway, intending to come at it from another angle. There was a traffic jam on the old Route 66, however, cars and trucks completely stationary in front of them, and Derek pulled into a Wells Fargo parking lot and backtracked to an alley, driving between the old buildings toward the hotel.

There were neither sawhorses nor police cars blocking the alley on any of the side streets, and they crossed Beaver and Leroux without interference before hanging a left on the street in front of the barricades. They could have continued down the alley, entering the hotel parking lot the back way, but obviously the sight of those animated corpses had frightened Derek as much as her and he did not want to get too close to them.

Thank God.

But . . . where were they?

And what had happened to the police? And the people?

Derek slowed the car as they passed by the barricades. The lights of the patrol cars were on and flashing, but it appeared at first as though the cops had run away or disappeared. Then Angela saw them, along with the onlookers who had come out from the various stores, offices and restaurants. They were lying on the ground, their faces covered with black mold that had started to creep onto the asphalt and cement beneath their dead bodies.

"No," she said, shaking her head. Her voice was small and frightened. "No. No . . ."

"Where did they go?" Derek asked. His voice was louder but just as scared. He stopped the car for a moment, so they could look, but nothing was moving on the street or sidewalk. There were only the bodies of the policemen and the onlookers dead on the ground.

And then a desiccated corpse jumped out from the open hotel door and landed on all fours, its head swiveling around like that of a demented lion searching out prey. Angela screamed, but the windows were up and the creature couldn't hear her. If it even *could* hear. Naked and brown, it was so dry and emaciated that even its sex could not be determined, and its ears either had been cut off or had shrunk so small that they could not be seen. The corpse jumped again, this time into the street, hopping over the blackening body of a policeman, then past a dead woman in a red dress, then down a walkway between a frozen-yogurt shop and a travel agency.

"Follow it!" Angela ordered. She was terrified, but from some inner reserve came a strength of purpose that trumped her fear. There was no one alive here but them. If they didn't track this creature, the monsters would get away and no one would know where they were.

Monsters.

It was amazing how quickly such a childish word

had become part of her lexicon, how fast her mind had adapted to a world in which there *were* monsters.

She could see that Derek wanted to argue, that he didn't want to go, but she shouted at him again to follow the escaping corpse, and with squealing tires he swung the car around and rolled down the street parallel to the track that the mummified body had taken. They looked between buildings, down the alley, between more buildings, down a street, until they finally saw the rotted carcass jumping out from behind a soap boutique. Even from this far away, the sight was terrifying and disturbing.

"I think it's headed for the highway," Derek said, speeding up. There was still a massive traffic jam ahead of them, but he stopped only for a second at the corner, then turned left, going east on a westbound lane.

Angela cringed instinctively, and one car heading toward them honked as it switched lanes and passed by on the right, but there were remarkably few vehicles on the road, and Angela saw that it was because a multicar collision had blocked the westbound highway about a mile up ahead.

At about the same spot where the eastbound traffic jam started.

She didn't like that.

Derek slowed the Hyundai and stopped, and only a few yards in front of them the corpse leaped out, jumping across the highway between the cars and toward the adjacent railroad tracks. It was impossible to see where it went after that, so Derek quickly shifted the transmission to park, got out of the car and climbed onto the hood so he could see over the other vehicles. He hopped down almost immediately and got back in. "It's heading down the tracks, not over them."

He put the car in gear and continued eastward. A few other drivers had broken ranks and were driving on the wrong side of the highway as well, but Derek remained in the left lane in an attempt to avoid them as much as possible.

"Where do you think the other—?" Angela began.

And then she saw it.

A black train on the tracks.

How could they have not noticed it immediately upon entering the highway? Not only were the engine and its dark cars large and clearly visible above the line of vehicles on the road, but they were decidedly unusual, though not for a reason that was readily ascertainable.

Maybe the train hadn't been there before.

That was a definite possibility. Indeed, there was an air of otherworldliness about the train, a phantom aspect. The locomotive and its railroad cars seemed strangely fuzzy and indistinct, as though made from a material not familiar to the human eye.

They reached the end of the traffic jam, another multivehicle collision, and it was instantly apparent that both accidents had occurred this close together so as to provide the corpses from the tunnel a safe corridor they could use to cross the highway.

There seemed to be a lot more of them now than there had been in that one underground passage. Edna Wong had said there were other hidden sites around Flagstaff that had been built to provide sanctuary, and Angela wondered if they were emptying out, too, if the train had arrived for them as well, some undetectable whistle from the locomotive calling them forth. For although many of the ambulatory dead were undoubtedly on the train already, she could see others atop the gravel embankment, the decaying twisted bodies making their freakish way toward open doorways in the black cars. It had been a sunny day, but clouds now blocked the sun, and though the clouds were white, they still cast a dark shadow over the city below. The corpses' tattered remnants of clothing fluttered in the slight breeze.

Down the tracks, the mummified figure they'd seen hopping out of the hotel leaped into sight.

"We have to follow the train," Angela said. She knew instinctively that if they were ever to find any answers, if they were going to get to the bottom of all that had been happening lately, they had to see this through. The dead were leaving for a reason, and where they were going might tell her what she needed to know. "How much gas do you have?"

"Half a tank."

"Fill up fast." She looked down the highway for an open station.

"I have to get my mom and my brother. I can't leave them here. Not with everything that's going on."

Angela understood—and agreed—but they would have to do it fast or they might lose the train. There was no telling when it might leave.

Derek was already speeding around the crash and the gaping spectators who'd been the victims of it; he intended to cross the tracks at the next intersection and circle back around to his neighborhood. Angela took out her cell phone, dialing 911, and as he zigzagged through the back roads of Flagstaff, she told the dispatcher about the dead police and the fleeing corpses. She didn't expect to be believed, but they'd find out the truth when they sent someone out to investigate. She wasn't sure how many other officers the Flagstaff Police Department had, but if they needed to take cops off another case, she hoped it would be from the high school and not from NAU. Edna deserved at least that much respect.

They drove fast, took shortcuts, wasted no time, but it was still fifteen minutes before they returned. Although Derek's mom had a rough understanding of some of what was going on, he decided on the way over to tell his family nothing of today's events. The truth would take too long to explain. He'd simply ask them to get into the car because there was something he wanted to show them. He hoped aloud that his brother, Steve, was home, that they wouldn't have to hunt him down at school or at some friend's house, but they got lucky on that count and he was just arriving home from a minimum day, being dropped off by a friend's mom, when they pulled up in the driveway.

There was no packing or gathering of possessions. Having driven to Derek's house, they picked up his mom and brother and drove back.

But as Angela had known, as she'd feared, the train was gone by the time they returned, although black smoke still hovered in the air above the tracks. No police, fire trucks or ambulances had responded to the accidents, and Good Samaritans were helping two crash victims who appeared to be injured. Everyone else was kind of milling around in a daze, looks of stunned incomprehension on their faces.

There'd been no talking in the car, but Angela could tell that Derek's mother had been getting more and more suspicious, and now she said, "What's going on here? What did you bring us out to see?"

Derek didn't answer but stopped the car and jumped out, leaving his door open. "Where did it go?" he demanded of the people closest by. "The train? North or east?"

The smoke smelled foul. *Brimstone,* Angela thought. *From hell.*

"I think it forked off toward Page!" someone shouted.

"Follow the smoke!" another man suggested.

That was a good idea, Angela thought. Derek obviously thought so, too, because he was back in the car seconds later and driving toward Flagstaff Mall.

"What is going on?" Derek's mom demanded. "Where are you taking us?"

"North," he said.

Twenty-five

Washington, D.C.

Rossiter stared out at the cubicles in front of his office, trying to digest what he'd learned.

On the desk was a volume of the unexpurgated memoirs of Ulysses S. Grant. He'd known, of course, that presidents' memoirs and diaries were sanitized, their words edited and bowdlerized for public consumption, ostensibly for reasons of "national security," but he'd been surprised to learn that he'd needed top top secret clearance in order to view a manuscript so old. What in God's name, he'd wondered, could possibly be in there?

He'd found out quickly enough. The drunken old bastard had written down far more than he should have, had spilled the beans about a brutal massacre that had occurred in the Utah territory in which scores of innocent civilians had been killed by U.S. troops for no apparent reason. The president had gotten involved after the fact, directing the cover-up like a military operation, a tactic so successful that no mention of it had ever been made anywhere by anyone involved—except here. But Grant was maddeningly vague about the location of the slaughter or the ostensible reason it had occurred.

Ordinarily, the cover-up was worse than the crime. But in this case, that was obviously not so.

"I most regret the incidents in emulation," Grant wrote.

> *I have no means of knowing how news of the Massacre could have reached the ears of others, but it is plain to me that it has. My emissaries tell me that it is impossible to judge how many have been killed in these like-minded attacks, and though the victims be heathens and infidels, killing without cause is ever wrong.*

Heathens and infidels.

It was the only clue Rossiter had as to the identity of the victims, and since vast sections of the nation were at that time uninhabited by Christians or Europeans, particularly in the West, it didn't exactly narrow down the field.

He was not one to scoff at curses and ghosts and retribution from beyond the grave, not after what he'd seen, not after Wolf Canyon. And he could understand why Grant might be targeted, why his tomb might be desecrated and his body defiled. It tied in as well with all those Civil War dead who'd been disinterred and tossed about Arlington National Cemetery. Even the White House might be fair game for vindictive spirits out to avenge a massacre.

But how did that relate to the other unexplained incidents that were happening all over the country?

The latest was at Mount Rushmore, where twin lines had been carved on the faces of the presidents, as though a giant with a switchblade had slashed twice across the stone.

Or a train had driven sideways across the mountain. For that was the first thing he thought when he saw the photos: *train tracks*. Although since that was all he'd been thinking about for the past three days, such an interpretation was probably to be expected.

Grant's head wasn't carved on Rushmore, though. So what was the connection?

And what *was* the significance of trains in all this?

Everything was confusing; nothing quite fit together. He was already taking heat from all the president's men for not putting this mystery to rest. The leader of the free world needed to be able to focus on a whole range of important issues that were coming to a head, the chief of staff said. But instead he was obsessing over the attack on the White House to the virtual exclusion of everything else.

As well he should, Rossiter thought.

He pressed a key on his desktop PC and the image of a train, generated from data extracted from damage to the White House and analyses of shatter patterns, appeared on-screen. The president was right. Whatever had crashed through the building may have been invisible, but it was definitely a locomotive. Rossiter pressed another key and the angle shifted, offering a three-dimensional view of the CGI train. He'd contacted railroad experts from all over the country, hoping someone would be able to identify the engine, assuming they would recognize it as one that had been in use during Grant's tenure, between 1869 and 1877. But either the computer model was flawed or the information it had been fed was contradictory, because *no one* recognized it. The picture looked like a typical train to him, but he was assured by a whole host of scholars and railroad professionals that it did not resemble any known locomotive.

Rossiter found that troubling.

The press had been successfully kept away from Arlington and Grant's Tomb, and were buying the cover story about the White House, but reporters were all over Mount Rushmore, and it was probably only a matter of time before the lid blew off everything and he found himself hip-deep in dog shit.

News was starting to come in from a variety of sources, and he had a whole team of agents sifting through information both new and old, trying to find connections and correlations. A lot of it was useless and had no bearing on anything, but some of it was pertinent to the investigation and he wanted to make sure nothing was overlooked. There was, for example, a report that some sort of phantom train had appeared in Zion, Canyonlands or one of those other Utah national parks. *That* was something that called for further investigation.

It had to be something that bore a grudge against the United States, he thought, because it was targeting not just relics from the Civil War era but buildings and land owned collectively by everyone in the country, like national parks. Whatever it was, it was not after a specific person or place; it was attacking the most potent symbols of the entire nation—

The screen on his monitor suddenly turned red, the picture disappearing, and a loud shrill beeping issued from the speakers.

There'd been an attack on the White House.

The instant his brain recognized the thought and realized what was happening, a live camera shot of the White House appeared. He felt as though he'd been punched in the gut. A huge gaping hole, almost as high as the building itself, had been punched in the structure, nearly cleaving it in half, and chunks of debris from the sides of the opening continued to be knocked out and thrown forward as if some great invisible force was tunneling through the building.

A train.

He knew it without question.

The White House was the most heavily secured and monitored building on the planet, so at the click of a mouse he could access literally dozens of hidden cameras located in each and every office, gallery, library and bedroom. But this situation was a first—nothing even remotely comparable had ever happened before—and without consulting a two-hundred-page instruction manual, he did not know how to call up the views from specific rooms, so Rossiter palmed his mouse and hurriedly clicked from one camera to another, scrolling through the progressive scenes, trying to catch up to the train. A program designed by some computer whiz specifically for a situation like this sorted the shots by order of incident, so the first section of the building hit was followed by the next affected area and the next and the next, allowing him to chart the progress of the intruder.

Rossiter clicked as fast as he could. All of this was being recorded, but he was watching it in real time and he did not want to miss a second of it as it happened, wanted to see exactly what occurred when it occurred. A microphone from somewhere in the White House captured ambient sound that did not quite match the scenes on his monitor, loud crashes and screaming that were a second or two off and made the video appear dubbed, like a foreign film.

He found the head of the invisible train. It was moving much more slowly than he expected, and he assumed that was because it was pulling to a stop. It crashed through a small office, shattering furniture and light fixtures, people leaping away in front of its unseen mass. One man tripped over a chair and was gruesomely crushed, his body folding in the middle and then splitting open as wheels with the weight of a locomotive behind them cut him in half, blood not merely gushing but shooting out and splattering all over the walls of the room.

There was no way this could be hushed up or hidden. Photos of the White House were going to be on the front page of every newspaper all over the world, video running 24-7 on CNN, Fox and every other news channel on the planet.

But that wasn't his concern. There were teams of people to deal with the press and control the spin. He needed to focus on the facts, not the fallout.

Even as he thought that, though, he couldn't help reflecting that after this there would be universal interest in potential threats from paranormal phenomena and a sudden urgent need for experts in the field, for people who had the ability and the knowledge to combat psychic and supernatural threats.

Like him.

The government and its machine would try to tone down that aspect or eliminate it entirely, might even go so far as to claim that a bomb blast from some terrorist organization was responsible for the damage to the White House. Looking at the video in front of him, such an idea seemed ludicrous, but the American people had been misled before and today's press corps were not nearly as diligent in their sleuthing as their brethren forty years ago had been. They were more likely than not to accept the party line, particularly if the White House handed out "exclusive" photo ops and interviews, passing them out to the various media outlets.

The administration might still pull it off.

Or not. And his career would go into hyperdrive.

Assuming he solved this case.

He pushed all thoughts of public perception and the press from his mind and clicked through real-time shots of each affected room of the White House, looking for the president. If he'd been injured or killed, all bets were off. It would be an entirely different game then.

But there he was as the invisible train began to come to a stop in the Oval Office, taking out one entire wall so the room looked more like a horseshoe than an oval. The president was standing on top of his desk, face red and contorted with rage, screaming what looked to be orders, although the sound of his voice could not be heard through the chaotic noise issuing from the speakers. If this video or a still from it ever made it out of the bureau into the real world, Rossiter thought, the president would look like a complete madman and his political career would go down in flames.

An agent less scrupulous than himself might leak exactly that, once all the furor died down in a few months.

The president was knocked off his desk and fell backward, bouncing off his chair onto the ground, as the train finally came to a complete stop. The rug was torn and bunched up, chairs had been tossed aside and shattered, but the desk had only been pushed a little and was still intact. From behind it, the president rose to his feet. Marine guards and a phalanx of Secret Service agents rushed into the office, followed by the chief of staff, to whom Rossiter grudgingly gave a few points for showing unexpected bravery. They all made sure the president was unharmed, then, against his angry protestations, surrounded him with a human shield.

Everyone seemed to be holding their breath, waiting to see if anything emerged from the invisible train. Ghosts, perhaps. Rossiter was holding his breath as well, and as the minutes passed and nothing happened he grew more and more anxious.

One of the marines stepped forward, bayonet extended, and tentatively tried to touch the unseen engine.

But the weapon passed through open air.

The train was gone.

Twenty-six

In the Passenger Car

The train was moving, traveling, though Dennis couldn't feel it. There was no swaying, no rocking, no sense of motion. Neither the engine nor any of the other cars made a sound. He knew they were on their way to someplace, even if he didn't know where.

He walked through the passenger car, not surprised to find that every seat seemed to be filled. The faces he passed were all Chinese and were all pale and ghostlike. It was what he'd expected, but it was unnerving nonetheless. No one seemed to be looking at him—no one seemed to be looking at *anything;* they just stared blankly ahead—but he knew they were aware of his presence, and he was acutely self-conscious as he walked past them down the aisle. They envied him his life, and though their faces remained passive, he could sense the resentment rolling off them in waves.

He reached the end of the passenger car and pulled open the metal sliding door to the connecting corridor. Again there was no sound, no movement, and he felt off-balance passing from one car to the next through such a calm, even space.

He slid open the door on the opposite side of the

connector. This car was empty. He could have any seat he wished, and he chose one in the center so that he'd be able to see or hear someone approaching him from either direction.

Dennis looked around. Aside from the ghostly passengers in the other car, he might have been on an Amtrak to New York.

No, that wasn't quite true. For outside the windows was a world filled with darkness. And though the floor was now solid beneath his feet, and the doors and seats he'd touched seemed perfectly normal, he could still sense in his fingers, like a tactile memory, the strange, sickeningly organic feel of the handle he'd used to pull himself onto the train and those first few seconds of disgusting springiness beneath his shoes as he'd entered the other passenger car.

Where were they going? he wondered again. This—
ghost
—train followed no tracks, so theoretically they could be headed anywhere.

The door at the front of the car opened, the one through which he'd entered, and a lone man approached slowly down the aisle. He, too, was Chinese, but he seemed different from the other passengers, more modern in appearance, though he wore strange homemade clothes unlike anything Dennis had ever seen before. His manner was muted and subdued—
dead—like the others', but there was an intelligence animating his expression. Or, more accurately, an awareness. And he stood before Dennis and bowed before sitting down next to him.

Dennis moved next to the window. The air from outside felt cold.

"Mr. Chen," the man said. It was a statement, not a question.

He *had* been summoned. He *had* been led here. The man knew his name.

"Yes?" Dennis replied. The fear revealed itself in his trembling voice.

His ghostly companion began talking, and Dennis listened as other voices filled his head, as the blackness beyond the window brightened.

And began to show him things.

Bear Flats, California

After devouring the diary (a somewhat inappropriate description since at one point Chester Williams had actually *eaten* the flesh of one of his victims), Jolene and Leslie asked Ned Tanner, the police chief, whether they could remove some personal effects from the Williams place. It was a crime scene, he told them at first, but after further entreaties, he admitted that investigators had learned just about all they were going to from the site. So with an officer accompanying them, the two women returned to the mansion on what was probably a wild-goose chase, looking for additional diaries that might shed some light on what they'd discovered so far.

Only it wasn't a wild-goose chase.

In the secret cellar where Skylar had been found, Jolene found another marionette made from stitched body parts lying atop two oversized leather-bound books that looked like family Bibles but that, she realized almost instantly, were diaries. Neither the diaries nor the marionette had been there before. She was sure of it. And a quick glance at Leslie's face confirmed her suspicions.

It was as if someone—
something

—had wanted them to find the books, had known they were coming and specifically placed the journals where they might easily be discovered.

"This is it," she said for benefit of the policeman accompanying them.

"Yeah," Leslie added. "Anna May wanted us to go through these, but we were so shaken up after what happened that we just forgot all about them."

The journals were heavy, so they each took one, declining the policeman's offer of assistance. Leslie lifted off the puppet first, and she grimaced as she did so, though she held it only by the strings and did not touch the object itself.

Skylar and his grandmother were still at Leslie's house. Jolene was afraid for them to go back home—

it knew where they lived

—and until she knew for certain that everyone was safe and out of danger, they were staying together. She'd even briefly considered letting Skylar go back with his father temporarily, calling Frank and asking him to drive over and pick up his son. But that was only a passing thought, a momentary lapse, because she knew that not only would such a move be emotionally devastating to Skylar, particularly in his current state; it would make it much more difficult for her to take her son back afterward. She knew what Frank was capable of doing.

No, all four of them were staying at Leslie's until further notice, and that was where she and her friend brought the journals. They told neither her mother nor Skylar what they had—it was safer for them not to know—and though they were both dying to know what was in these earlier diaries, they waited until night, until her mother and her son were asleep, before opening the leather covers.

They took turns reading.

Highway 6, Utah

Driving through the darkness, the Indian men told Henry that they had found out about him from a Papago shaman in Phoenix. He didn't know any Papago shaman in Phoenix, Henry informed them, but his protestations were halfhearted. There was nothing ordinary connected with any of this, and it would be hypocritical for him to pretend that he recognized only normal channels of communication.

"I'm not sure if I'm even one one-millionth Papago," he admitted. "That was just a rumor my old man told me when I was a kid. Probably a lie."

A short heavyset man with a flattop turned to look at him. "They've come after you," he stated matter-of-factly. "Just like me. The shadows. They drained you."

Henry thought of the twins, remembered spurting semen all over the tile of his kitchenette while the shadows lapped it up, recalled the way he had felt spent and used afterward. "What's going on?" he asked suspiciously.

And they told him what they knew, what had been passed down to them from their fathers, what they had discovered in visions and dreams.

Why they were going to the Point.

Twenty-seven

November 1866

Chester Williams sat in Harrison's office glaring at the railroad president. "They cannot be allowed to work side by side with real people!"

Harrison took the cigar out of his mouth and pointed its lit end at Williams. "I'm telling you, they get the job done. They do it in half the time for half the money, and they're willing to do work that the micks won't do for *any* amount. If we expect to finish our tracks on time, we need Chinks, and a lot of them. Who gives a shit if they're heathens?"

Williams leaned forward, his face red. "I do!"

"Well, I'm afraid that's not good enough. I appreciate everything you've done to help this project along, but I will not allow you to dictate the terms of employment for my company. We need those Chinamen and I'm hiring even more. Another shipment came in on the *Dora Lee* two days ago and they're on their way over from San Francisco even as we speak."

"You can't do that!"

Harrison slammed his fist down on the desk, causing a stack of papers to topple over. "No man tells me what I can and cannot do with my own company!" he bellowed. "No man!"

Williams knew at that moment that he had lost the argument. Facts would have no sway with the railroad owner now. Even appeals to morality and common decency would fall on deaf ears. The man felt he had been insulted, and in truth, he had. Williams harbored no respect toward someone who would hire a Chink, and if he had known it would come to this, he never would have used his pull with the Senate or invested any of his own money in this venture—no matter how noble its goal or how necessary its completion to the future of the nation.

Williams stood, put on his hat and gave a formal half bow that he knew Harrison would find insufferable. "Good day to you, sir!" He strode out of the office without looking back, angry beyond words at the way the meeting had gone. He had accomplished nothing, had in fact set his own cause back and hardened Harrison against his objective.

Was there anything he could do at this point to stop the calamity to come? There had to be. He could not in good conscience allow the railroads to employ hundreds of the yellow devils, a step that, once taken, would further erode the moral boundaries of society and lead the country ever closer to the gradual acceptance of these heathens. That was an evil he could not countenance, and it was incumbent upon him to do all that he could to forestall such an event.

An idea was forming in the back of his mind, one that he was not quite ready to recognize but that he thought might prove advantageous in the future.

On the sidewalk, outside of the United Pacific building, he paused for a moment, looking up at the cloudy sky, already feeling a little bit better. He took a deep breath, then reached into his jacket pocket and pulled on his gloves.

It was starting to get cold.

*   *   *

Williams stood over his wife's grave.

And spit on it.

It had been five years since he had killed the harlot, since he had taken advantage of his husbandly prerogative and strangled her until her filthy tongue had been hanging swollen from between her dead lips, and not a day had gone by since that he did not rejoice in her demise. She'd died hard. The way she should have.

But first she'd watched him kill her lover, Chin Lee.

Even now his blood pressure rose as he recalled how he had discovered them—*in his own house!*—mocking him, humiliating him, cuckolding him. She had to have known he'd come home, had to have heard him enter the house and walk through the parlor, then the kitchen, then the hallway, calling her name. But either she'd been so in thrall to her passion, or more likely in his view, she had wanted him to discover her, and she had continued with her unnatural coupling even as he burst into the room.

She'd been on her bed, completely naked in a way he'd never seen her before, legs spread wide, while the Chinese servant lapped at her sex like a dog. He had never spied anything so disgusting, had never even heard of something so utterly perverse and depraved, and the animalistic cries that issued from her lips as well as the expression of passionate gratification on her sweaty face made him sick to his stomach. The Chinaman was naked, too, and when Alice saw Williams standing apoplectic in the doorway, and knew that she had been discovered in her sin, she had grabbed her lover by the shoulders, pulled him up and taken him inside her, gasping as his engorged organ pierced her ready opening.

It was a direct taunt, a deliberate slap at his manhood, and if he had not been wearing his sword, things might have turned out differently. But the sword was drawn instantly and with anger, pulling easily from its oiled sheath, and Williams had sliced it across the Chink's brown back, satisfaction welling within him even as blood flowed from the cut and the coward tried to scramble off the bed to safety, screaming wildly.

This time, Williams had thrust rather than sliced, and the long blade slid easily and deeply into the servant's side. The screams were cut off, replaced with a gasping gurgle. He pulled the blade free, casually wiping it on the mattress, feeling like a man who had just crushed a particularly loathsome insect. Alice was screaming by now, her exposed stomach and breasts covered in Chinese blood, and he looked at her, watching her face as he delivered the fatal blow to the twitching, dying thing on the floor, shoving the sword through the center of the Chink's chest and leaving it there.

Then he'd turned to his wife.

Her cries had turned to whimpers, and she was hunched up against the headboard as if to protect herself, her wanton legs now seemingly glued together. But he was in the mood for justice, not mercy, and he'd strangled her with his bare hands, pressing his thumbs against her windpipe while she thrashed beneath him in an obscene echo of her earlier passion. By the time she started to claw at his arms, she had no strength left and was too weak to do any real damage. Her face turned red, then blue; her eyes bulged; her tongue protruded as she tried in vain to breathe.

And then she'd died.

He had allowed others to clean up the mess, not deigning to dirty his hands any further, although he had directed them in their efforts and made sure that his orders were followed to the letter.

Williams looked around at the other graves, content that the monument to his deceased wife was still the finest, largest and most elaborate in the cemetery. The servant was not buried here, of course. He was not buried anywhere. His body had been taken into the woods south of town and left there. The blood and the organs had attracted animals, and he had been eaten. His bones, no doubt, were rotting there even now, under exposure to the elements.

Williams smiled to himself with satisfaction.

But the smile faded as he heard the whistle of the mail train passing through the center of the city. It made him think of Jeb Harrison. The railroad president might think he knew business, but he definitely didn't know the Chinese, and if Williams was sure of one thing, it was that before the project's completion he would regret having hired those slant-eyed sons of bitches. They might seem like hard workers now, but down the line, when it was important, when they were really needed, the Chinks would not be there or would fail to do what was required of them and something would go horribly wrong. He knew it in his gut. You just couldn't trust the heathen Chinee.

Besides, this was an American railroad and should be built by Americans.

Even if they were micks.

The train whistle grew faint as it moved farther away, and Williams gave Alice's grave one last look. The half-formed notion he'd had earlier, the one that had been lurking at the back of his mind ever since, had been given additional consideration, had been thought through a little more. There was meat on those bones now, and he had no doubt that once he fleshed out the details, his idea would prove to be a most propitious one.

But for now he would just stay out of Harrison's way.

And wait.

March 1867

"WhooooWooooWooooWooooWooooo!"

They heard the war whoops before the hooves this time, which meant that the Sioux had been close and the horses were starting from a camp nearby rather than galloping over the plains. Johnny Fowles and the other three hired guns drew their weapons, readied their backup, then checked to make sure the rest of the railroad camp were doing what they were supposed to be doing. Those with rifles were taking up position near the other men who were busy securing supplies. The Chinese huddled together in their section of camp, looking confused the way they always did, and Johnny felt angry. They were like children, the Chinese, dumb children who didn't seem to be able to learn, and their complete inaction in the face of these attacks put everyone at risk.

It was cheaper to replace Chinese than food or wood or rails, and if it appeared that people or supplies were in danger, Johnny's orders were to sacrifice the Chinese first. But that was pretty damn hard when the Chinks remained as far as possible from the fighting, expecting to be protected like they were little princes and princesses.

"WhooooWooooWooooWooooWooooo!"

The attackers were almost here, and though Johnny, Tibbits and Duncan were in position and ready, Maxwell, the other gun, was still fiddling with his ammunition.

"Damn it!" Johnny swore.

"I can't send a message!" Peterson yelled from the telegraph table. "I think they cut the lines!"

And then the Indians were topping the rise, looking like ghosts in the massive cloud of dust that accompanied their galloping horses. Both the Sioux and the Cheyenne had started attacking railroad workers on a regular basis, and by far he preferred fighting Cheyenne. They had the bigger reputation as warriors, but they fought cleaner, more straightforwardly. They were easier to outfox. Sioux, on the other hand, were crafty. Rather than engage in a battle head-on, they would create diversions, try to outflank and outmaneuver, arrive in waves. He was always waiting for the other shoe to drop when he fought the Sioux and that kept his focus split, made him a less effective fighter, which perhaps was the intention all along.

Johnny sighted and shot, gratified to hear the weapons of the other hired guns sound almost simultaneously. Four dark figures in the front of the dust cloud went down, then two more, then three more—

Then the attackers were upon them and he could not keep track. All was chaos, and the only thing he could do was lie low and shoot at whatever was on horseback. Rifle fire was going off in all directions, and screams of agony mixed in with the war whoops the Sioux used to intimidate their enemies. He couldn't tell who was who or what was what, but when the front of the fighting moved past him and he was forced to turn around and pick off successful intruders rather than repel an attempted assault, he saw that the telegraph table was no more and the cook's tent was down. He thought he saw Buster Thornton, one of the construction foremen, fall to a bullet and go under the hooves of a horse. He, Tibbits, Duncan and Maxwell were all still in action and unharmed, and the four of them fired away, dropping Sioux warriors right and left, scores of other railroad workers also joining in and killing the natives.

Amazingly, impossibly, the Chinese stood in their section of camp completely untouched, watching what went on as if from within a protective shell. They remained stupidly in place, while everyone else valiantly tried to fight back against the aggressors.

Finally, as always, the Sioux retreated. They always seemed to know the point at which the damage they inflicted would be greater than the losses they suffered, and they invariably quit before the equation shifted. He fired after the fleeing horses and was gratified when one last warrior went down, his horse continuing on riderless.

The fight was over—for now—but it soon became apparent that they'd suffered more losses this time than ever before. Three men were dead, over a dozen were seriously injured, and quite a few were walking around telling anyone who would listen that they were quitting, that no amount of money was worth risking slaughter. A fire had been started at the north end of camp and two tents were ablaze, but now the Chinese were finally getting involved, relaying buckets of water from the creek, and it would be only a matter of minutes before the flames were out.

The goal of the Sioux had been to stop or at least forestall the building of the railroad, and at that they'd been partially successful. The tool wagon had been overturned and quite a few of the implements were either stolen or broken. You had to admire that on some level. Remaining so concentrated that even amid the chaos, in an extremely limited amount of time, the Indians had been able to wage such a specific and successful attack was indeed impressive.

"Fowles!"

Johnny looked over to see Duncan walking toward

him grinning, pistol holstered, two rifles over his
shoulder. "Ten!" he crowed. "All kills!"

Johnny nodded tiredly, acknowledging the other
gunman but not deigning to answer. The man was a
braggart and without a doubt the most self-centered
person he had ever met. Even with all of the disaster
surrounding him, Duncan could see only how he was
personally affected. And, characteristically, he believed he came out of it a hero.

Someone had already ordered the Chinese to gather
the fallen Sioux, and the small pigtailed men were
moving in pairs to pick up the deceased and take them
to the tracks, where Maxwell and some of the lower
hammer-swinging brutes would cut them open and
leave them for the buzzards. Johnny walked past the
dead and dying bodies. He would never admit it to
another living soul, but deep down a part of him sym-
pathized with the Indians. This had been their land
for God knows how long, and now strangers were
building a railway line right through the middle of
it. He would have fought back, too, if he'd been in
their situation.

A hand clapped him on the back, and Johnny spun
around, nearly drawing his pistol, but it was only Tibbits, and he relaxed a little, drawing a deep breath.

"It's over," the hired gun said. "Relax. I just came
to commiserate."

"Sorry. I'm still there."

"I know." Tibbits, with his sad eyes, always looked
like he was carrying the weight of the world on his
shoulders, and for all Johnny knew, he was. The two
of them never talked about the past—or the future—
only the present, but despite the man's protestations
to the contrary, Johnny always got the feeling that
Tibbits didn't really like killing, that he wished he'd
gone into some other line of work.

As opposed to Duncan.

The younger man came between them, throwing a muscled arm around the shoulders of each. "Can either of you beat my ten?"

Johnny shook his head. The truth was, he'd never been a man to keep track. It was not something of which he was proud; it was merely what he did.

Tibbits sighed heavily. "I don't rightly know."

Duncan chuckled conspiratorially. "Well, we know Maxwell ain't even going to come close." The chuckle turned into a manic laugh that set Johnny's teeth on edge.

"Chinks weren't much help," Tibbits noted, choosing to ignore Duncan.

Johnny nodded. "Gets under my craw sometimes."

"Good workers, though," Tibbits said.

He watched two of them pass by, carrying a gutshot Sioux toward the tracks. "Yeah," he said. "I guess they are."

Another Indian raid.

Harrison was so angry and frustrated he felt like hitting the wall. This time, they hadn't attacked the crew or the camp but had damaged the rails two days east of line's end. It had been a surprisingly primitive assault, conducted not with modern weapons or stolen explosives but with rocks and sheer manpower that had been used to seriously damage the tracks. A supply train headed west toward Wyoming had been derailed, all four cars overturned. Though the engineer and the other four men on board had escaped thanks to a bevy of pack animals that had been on their way to the workers' camp to replace those lost in recent attacks, by the time agents of the railroad returned to survey the damage, the cars had all been burned and adjacent tracks piled high with debris.

Now he had to get a crew to repair the damage before another supply train could be sent to the workers—which would delay construction for at least a week.

Assuming he could *find* workers willing to brave the threat of attacks.

He could always ship some Chinese over there. They did anything they were ordered to do. And for pennies on the dollar. The Chinks were so happy to be in America they were willing to take on any shit job that was thrown at them.

Harrison stared out his office window at the rail yard. What about that, though? There was no way he could finish this project on time without the Chinese. Six thousand of them were on his payroll right this moment. He didn't regret for a second hiring them on, but a lot of them were coming over now, and thanks to railroad work, they were dispersing across the country. He hated to admit it, but maybe that blowhard Chester Williams was right; maybe there was some sort of reason, some long-term goal. America was a big country and still largely unsettled. They'd had to kick out the British, the French and the Spanish to get where they were today, and they were still trying to put down these Indians. Maybe the Chinese were thinking ahead, planning for the future, hoping to get a piece of the pie and settle a large portion of the land themselves.

He hated to think he was contributing to that.

But what could he do about it? He owned a railroad company. It was his job to keep the trains moving, not decide who was to settle where.

Still, this was his country, and he didn't want to see it ruined. As obnoxious as Williams was, the man might have a point. The next time he was in Washington, Harrison decided, he'd bring it up with people

who might have some ideas on the subject, who might
have some answers, who might be able to do something about it.

July 1867

O'Hearn stood above the navvy, kicking him as hard
as he could while the Chink tried to scramble away.
"When I say now, I mean now!" he shouted, emphasizing each word with a boot to the backside. He had
no idea if the worker understood what he was saying
or even if he'd understood the original order, but it
felt good to get his frustration out this way, and he
continued kicking even after the man had become
unconscious.

The translator, as usual, was sick and useless, sweat-
ing with a fever in one of the Chinese tents. O'Hearn
didn't think he'd ever seen a more womanly man. The
son of a bitch was probably a eunuch. Didn't they do
that kind of thing over there in China?

The peculiar thing was, the other Chinese seemed
to never get sick. Either that or they just didn't show
it. His men had had the dysentery and assorted stomach ailments for half the season. But those Chinks just
kept on toiling day after day, unchanged and unfazed,
like machines. It was probably because they'd brought
all their own food with them, with all of those weird
herbs and shit. They even boiled their water before
drinking it. If that food they cooked hadn't been so
goddamn disgusting, he would have asked them to
cook for the whole camp, but he wasn't about to subject his men to that heathen slop.

Besides, if regular people ate that food, they might
get poisoned.

Or the Chinese might poison them on purpose.

They made him mad sometimes with their passivity,

and on those occasions he found himself wanting to just beat the living tar out of them—which he often did. But that didn't seem to make any difference. Even with bruised and bloodied faces, they still stared at him blankly through those slanty eyes, and it made him want to beat them all the more. Every so often, though, he thought he saw something else behind the submissiveness, an inner hidden fire, a desire for revenge, and he thought that maybe the Chinks *would* like to poison all the rest of them.

Or maybe it was just his imagination.

The one he'd just kicked into unconsciousness lay unmoving on the ground, and his companions stood by watching impassively. O'Hearn motioned angrily for them to pick him up and take him away, and four of them did so, looking at him all the while with those unreadable eyes, their fellows standing behind them motionless. Some of them had to have wives back home, he thought. He wondered, if he fucked their wives in front of them, whether that would get a reaction out of the passive sons of bitches.

It had been a long time since he'd had a woman, and even an Indian one or a Chinese one sounded good at this point. The railroad had promised to provide women when they were recruiting workers, but they'd gone back on their promise, and the men were getting restless. It wasn't right to live like this; it wasn't natural. They weren't priests.

Nearby, he heard the crack of a whip as one of the hands tried to make a recalcitrant horse team pull a load of ties to the track. That gave him an idea. Maybe tonight, for the men's amusement, he could arrange a little wager. To cheer them up. He could take out the Chinese translator, tie him to a post and whip him. The men could place bets on how long the Chink would last before passing out.

They were going to be in this pass for the better part of a week, so there wouldn't be much variety in the work. Besides, everyone knew their jobs by now. They needed the translator only under special circumstances. If he was out of commission for a few days, it shouldn't pose a hardship.

It might even teach the translator to be a little bit more of a man in the future.

O'Hearn grinned.

And the men always liked a little sport.

March 1868

Although he still kept the house in Chicago, as well as an apartment in New York, for the past five years, Chester Williams' primary residence had been in the small town of Bear Flats, California. It was near there that he had made his fortune in gold, and it was there that he had made his home, using California's finest builders to construct a house he had designed with one of New York's top architects. He felt at home here, and in this backwater village, away from the prying eyes of his peers and the gossiping mouths of their wives, he had set up a virtual fiefdom, a community in which the constabulary existed to do his bidding and the other homeowners lived in fear of his wrath. Several of the local businesses had been set up specifically to serve his needs—he was the only customer of the bookbinder, for instance, and if it had not been for him, there would be no haberdasher in town—and not only did he notice the deference the locals showed to him; he expected it.

It had been known for quite some time that Crazy Merle, the miner who lived up in Hells Canyon foolishly insisting that there was an undiscovered vein of gold running through Dodge Mountain, had taken on a Chinese wife after killing her husband in a drunken rage back in Colima. He and the woman had even had a half-breed kid a while back, and though no one had bothered them until now—afraid that Merle might shoot them on their way up the canyon, more than likely—Williams decided that that had to change. It was an abomination, a man consorting with a Chinese, and after returning from his most recent meeting with Harrison, he decided that such behavior would no longer be tolerated in Bear Flats.

Williams sent his *new* servant, Eton (an Englishman, no more of the darker peoples for him), to fetch Lane McGrath, the sheriff, and twenty minutes later the old man was in his study, looking warily about. This was the first time anyone from the town had been allowed within his private domain—meetings usually took place outdoors—and Lane was understandably uneasy. He knew this was something important.

Williams dragged it out, amused by the sheriff's discomfort. "Would you like something to drink, Mr. McGrath?"

"No, sir," the sheriff answered.

"I think I'll have a brandy. I always find that brandy soothes my nerves. Are you sure you wouldn't like to join me?"

"Uh, sure. I mean, thank you, Mr. Williams."

Williams smiled, poured the drinks, then sat down in the smoking chair opposite Lane's. He took a slow, deliberate sip of his brandy. "I asked you here because I would like to discuss a situation that I believe has become intolerable. I am speaking, of course, of the miner in Hells Canyon. Merle, I believe, is his name. People call him Crazy Merle."

"Yes. I'm aware of Merle."

"Are you also aware that he consorts with a Chinese woman, against the laws of California and the laws of nature?" He leaned forward. "They have a half-breed child, an abomination under God, and they are flouting their sin right under our very noses!"

Lane was obviously at a loss. "Merle's crazy but he don't cause no trouble. At least not that I'm aware of," the sheriff added quickly. "He mostly keeps to himself and we don't hardly see him except when he comes down for supplies every few months."

"That is not the point I'm making, Mr. McGrath."

The sheriff was silent.

"It is no longer tolerable to me that this evil and depravity exist in our fair corner of the world. We are abetting this wickedness by allowing it to continue and pretending we do not know what is going on."

"You want me to evict Merle?" Lane asked, starting to catch on. "From his own legal claim?"

"I want more than that," Williams said.

And smiled.

They went up Hells Canyon on horseback and on foot, the sheriff and his two deputies in the lead, Williams marching right behind, rifle in hand. A goodly portion of the town tromped behind them as they made their way up the winding road, and Williams was gratified to see such a response. There'd been nothing but support yesterday at the town meeting, but talk was easier than action, and sometimes what people said they'd do and what they did were two different things.

The miner could have shot at them from his cabin, but the throng was dozens strong and even Merle wasn't that crazy. Besides, the sheriff announced their arrival at the head of the canyon by shouting out, "Merle! We need to talk!" as though this were some sort of mobile town meeting and they'd all come this far just to palaver.

The crazy bastard fell for the lie.

He wasn't stupid enough to meet them unarmed, but with one blow to the head from the butt of his Winchester, Lane knocked the miner to the ground while one of his deputies took the man's weapon. There was no sign of the Chinese woman or the daughter, but Williams and a host of townspeople searched in and around the cabin until the two were discovered huddled in a corner of the small mine that Merle had dug out of the cliffside.

When all three of them were subdued, Williams stood on the front porch of the cabin and explained the situation, speaking loudly enough for even those in the rear to hear.

He sentenced the Chinese to death.

Merle put up a fight, so crazy now that he seemed to think he was actually in love with the woman. He kicked backward, then thrust himself forward and broke free of the sheriff's grip. His rifle had been confiscated and was well beyond his reach in the hands of Cole Blackman, the grocer, but Merle was quick and wiry and scrambled away from Lane, grabbing rocks from the ground and throwing them as hard as he could at everyone around him.

Lane shot him in the leg, bringing him down.

Then things happened fast.

Claude, the haberdasher, brought forth a rope and, with the help of Jacob and two other men, dragged Merle to a dead tree and strung him up.

Williams hanged the girl himself, putting the noose around her neck as she whimpered and cried. The woman was screeching in that obnoxious babble those people called a language, and he roared that someone needed to shut her up. Little Erskine, the deputy sheriff, drew back his hand and hit her hard across the mouth. Blood gushed out from her split lips and broken teeth, but the screaming didn't stop until the deputy punched her in the stomach. Williams looked into the little girl's dark slanted eyes, saw her tears—then pulled the rope hard, jerking her into the air. She danced above them, looking for all the world like a music hall performer. Everyone was pointing and laughing, and Williams laughed, too.

Then they hanged the woman. She kicked and fought, and he noticed beneath her dress that she wore no undergarments, that her sex was open and exposed for all to see. A wave of disgust passed over him. He was reminded of Alice and how she'd opened herself to their servant, allowed him to lick her down there like an animal, and when the woman finally died, he felt no small degree of satisfaction, laughing with the others as she pissed herself.

The outing had been a rousing success. Not only had they rid the county of a madman, a Chink and a half-breed, but he had finally instilled in his fellow townspeople the importance of keeping more Chinese from coming to America and getting rid of the ones who were already here. They were not only evil; they were devious. They'd taken jobs building the railroad that should have gone to American workers, and they had even insinuated themselves into marriages with American men. Crazy Merle might have been a step above feeb, but his devotion to that Chink wife was absolute, and it was only a matter of time before the foreigners set their sights on society's other outcasts and then, in good time, regular people.

They had to be stopped now.

His assessment was met with universal agreement.

It was impossible to extrapolate from this one incident that people in other towns in other parts of the country would feel the same way, would come to see the light if they were only exposed to the truth, but he thought it was worth a try, and though winter was not quite over and travel conditions were still harsh, he had to do what he knew in his heart was right. And necessary.

He headed east.

Williams traveled from California to Kansas, finding receptive audiences in each town he visited along the way. He stayed away from the big cities with their modern ideas and wrongheaded notions. He went instead to God-fearing communities where decency still held sway, and was rewarded with crowds that seemed to grow larger as his journey progressed, as though news of his message had preceded him.

As perhaps it had.

As he *hoped* it had.

He found a particularly warm welcome in rural Missouri, where anti-Chinese sentiment already ran high. He had not expected to find many Chinee so far from the Pacific Ocean, but in Selby and its environs there were apparently several Chink families living in bunkhouses on the bad side of town, the adults working in laundries and restaurants, the children running wild, and the fact that they had already migrated this far inland made him realize the urgency of his mission. It was in Selby that he met a man named Orren Gifford, an angry young buck with the gift of gab who was a carpenter by trade but was passing himself off as a preacher because the pay was better and the work was easier. He and Gifford led the townspeople in a rally where, in one night, they succeeded in getting the timid town fathers to pass a resolution barring Chinks, kikes, niggers and wops from Selby. Not only were they not allowed to own land or marry; they could not work here or even stay overnight. Jimmy Johnson, the normally milquetoast mayor, ended up in front of the crowd next to Gifford, yelling at the top of his lungs, "Any one of 'em who sets foot in our fair town will end up tarred and feathered and riding out on a rail!"

The crowd ate it up.

The next morning, Gifford took Willimas outside of town to a series of mud pits. It had been rumored for years that Indians had once used the pits for healing baths, like they did at some of those fancy health spas out West, but the boiling mud was far too hot for a person to sit in, and when a local farmer's boy had fallen in a few seasons back, walking with his dad on the way to town, he'd died instantly. By the time the farmer found a big enough branch to fish him out with and a boulder to balance the branch over, the flesh had been stripped from the boy's bones. The kid looked like he'd been in a fire, and the sight was so bad that even his own mama hadn't been allowed to see him.

The mud in the pits gurgled and bubbled, some of it brown, some of it gray, some of it white.

"Lot of deer carcasses been thrown in there," Gifford said. "Elk, too. So's they wouldn't attract the buzzards. I imagine a fair number of local boys have tossed other things in as well." He looked meaningfully over at Williams. "Not a one of them has ever bubbled to the surface."

He let that sink in.

"I'd bet there's room in them pits for a lot more."

Williams smiled. "I'll bet there is," he said.

After stopping in Kentucky and Virginia, he continued on to Washington, D.C., where he found, to his surprise, that Harrison had already been speaking in private to some of the congressmen whom Williams had intended to approach about the Chinese problem.

Apparently, the railroad president had learned a few hard lessons lately and had come to see the error of his ways.

Just as Williams had predicted.

Nothing had been decided, nothing was set in stone, and as was always the case with politicians, no one was willing to commit to a specific course of action. Still, the general consensus seemed to be that once the railroad was finished, something had to be done, and that was probably the best that could be hoped for.

For now.

May 10, 1869

It was a day of celebration for America, and Harrison wished he could be everywhere at once. Parades were planned for Chicago and New York City, where hundreds of people were expected to line the streets to commemorate this historic occasion. In cities all along the route, picnics and festivities to rival Independence Day would be occurring, and in Sacramento and Omaha, the two ends of the line, even greater galas were scheduled.

But on this important day, his place was here, at Promontory Point, where the lines would finally be joined.

Despite having had to blast through the Sierra Nevada and navigate some of the most dangerous and unforgiving terrain known to man, the Central Pacific had finished its half of the railway first, on April 30. They'd been waiting for the past week and a half for the Union and United Pacific workers to hurry and finish their portion. Harrison attributed it to the fact that the Central Pacific had more Chinese. If there was anything those Chinks knew, it was dynamite, and their expertise with explosives had helped the line through many a rough patch.

Although Harrison found that worrying as well. Thousands of soon-to-be unemployed foreigners with extensive knowledge of explosives was not a situation he found comforting.

He looked over the heads of Doc Durant and Leland Stanford to see Chester Williams deep in conversation with one of the generals who had come West with a regiment of men and was now standing near the Union locomotive with assorted other dignitaries. He still didn't trust that man. There'd been rumors in Washington that he'd been trying to secretly negotiate backroom deals involving the railroads, but nothing seemed to have come of it. He was glad of that. The last thing he wanted was to be in business again with that blowhard. Harrison took his wife's arm and turned away, not wanting to catch Williams' eye accidentally and have the man come over to him.

The president hadn't come. He'd expected as much, but General Grant's absence was still disappointing, and even the sheer number of other officials who'd made the trip out here to the middle of nowhere could not offset the loss of the president.

It was getting hard to hear, and he assumed that meant that the ceremony would be starting soon. Three bands seemed to be playing at once, and because there were enough people here for twenty band concerts, the sound was cacophonous. Someone somewhere let out a whoop and fired a shot in the air, and Harrison knew that once that golden spike was driven into the rail, the air would be filled with celebratory gunfire.

A boy came to get him and bring him to the spot where the last rails were to be laid. Coins had been tossed and it had been decided that Stanford and

Durant were to do the honors, but all of the partners needed to be present for pictures. Flashbulbs started going off the moment he approached the tracks.

The official ceremony began, and the last two rails were laid, Chinese workers carrying one, Irish workmen the other. Bands played, the crowd cheered, and photos were taken from every which angle as the steel rails were put in place. Poses were struck, more photos were shot, and a half hour later, Stanford and Durant finally drove in the golden spike.

Americans could now ride the rails from coast to coast.

It was indeed a glorious day, and Harrison imagined he could almost hear the people celebrating all over this great nation. There would be fireworks tonight. And drinking. And, for the single men, carousing. It would be a party to remember, and appropriately so, for the project that had been completed here today would change the face of transportation—and the face of America—forever.

Still, despite the congratulations from friends, enemies and peers, despite the constant flash of cameras and the hearty praise from unknown society gentlemen, he found himself glancing over at Chester Williams, who stood by himself, an unnerving smile on his broad florid face as he stared across the tracks at the tent encampment of the Chinese.

Williams was up to something. He was sure of it. The man had some sort of plan, some sort of scheme he was hatching. Harrison was curious—who wouldn't be?—but the more he looked at that unsettling grin, the more he decided that it was probably best not to know.

The crowds were gone, the trains departed, and only the workers, the militia and a few straggling souls were left behind. The soldiers were supposed to have left, too, and some of them had, but a hefty number remained.

Because Williams had paid them to do so.

Despite his contacts, despite his power and influence, his attempt to make headway with those politicians in Washington had come to naught. They'd been too afraid to act, some citing moral qualms, others bringing up constitutional concerns, others simply admitting that unless their brethren went along, they would not sponsor such legislation. He had tried to play upon their antagonism with the president, but that hadn't worked either, so he'd gone straight to the source and hired members of the U.S. Army to do the dirty work. He knew already that the boys in uniform were underpaid. He knew as well that some of the younger ones who had yet to see action, having come along after the end of the war, relished the idea of killing some enemies.

It was a match made in heaven.

The deed could be done only after the public was gone, though, after the press had left. This "operation," as the general called it, had to be performed with the utmost secrecy.

Williams had had the translator tell the Chinks that because they had done such a wonderful job building the railroad, there was another job in the offing, one that paid twice as much. Many of them still left, going back to their families in San Francisco or even back to China, unhappy with the life of a navvy and unwilling to take on such a burden again. Others had departed with the Irish crews and the other workers, dispersing eastward.

They could be taken care of another day.

But a lot of them stayed, and Williams estimated there were at least two hundred in the east camp and significantly more in the west camp. Quite a few of these were slaves, men who had been brought, bought and beaten into submission. Others believed the lie and were willing to remain behind an extra few days for the chance at earning more money and forging a better life.

They struck at dawn.

Most of the Chinks were asleep in their tents, and when the cavalry came galloping through, ripping apart the canvas with swords and bayonets, they ran screaming out onto the field, where other soldiers rounded them up like cattle and herded them away from the tracks. Williams watched it all from his post atop a hillock, using a spyglass the general had lent him, and he smiled with delight as the soldiers beat and kicked the men, whipping them when they got out of line as they drove the heathens northward. Clearly it paid to hire professionals.

He followed behind as they headed away from the camp, as the soldiers gathered the Chinese together in the center of the plain and began circling around. He wasn't sure how large the militia was, but their horses kicked up enough dust to blur the rising sun, and soldiers encircled the hundreds of workers with only a few feet between each.

At the general's command, rifles were raised.

And fired.

The noise was deafening, and smoke from the rifles joined the dust in the air to create a haze as deep as fog that temporarily obscured everything. Several Chinks bolted from between the horses, figuring they had a better chance outside the circle on the open plain, but they were quickly shot down. A few small figures attempted to crawl away, and in the dust and chaos a couple actually got pretty far, but eventually they, too, were hunted down and killed.

The slaughter was not quick. An hour later, the soldiers were still reloading and firing, although by that time most of them had come down from their horses and were walking over broken bodies to stalk wily bands of survivors. The smell was overpowering, a sickening stench that not only made Williams gag but had several of the younger soldiers vomiting onto the chaparral. Emulating some of the older, more experienced fighters, he pulled his shirt higher, buttoning it over his mouth and nose so the cloth acted like a filter. He smelled dirt and his own sweat, but it was vastly preferable to the disgusting scent of blood and death.

Some time later, the general came to him and said the deed was done: the Chinese were no more. He invited Williams to come with him and tour the battlefield.

He went in with his knife.

And helped finish off the ones who were still moving.

Summer 1869

It was a new day.

After their success at Promontory Point, Williams followed the line east. He heard through friends that the righteous slaughter of the heathen Chinee had been kept quiet, that the president himself had arranged for the site to be cleaned up and the bodies burned, and had decreed that no one was to know what had happened in Utah. Williams took a grim satisfaction in knowing that his adversaries were so highly placed, but what the president said did not affect him. He did not have to abide by any presidential order. He was Chester Williams, man of means, and he would still be so when Ulysses S. Grant was once again a retired drunken general.

And while the newspapers might be persuaded not to report what had happened, he himself was bound by no such constrictions. He could say whatever he wanted.

And did.

His words incited a riot in the ordinarily peaceful town of Spellman, Wyoming, encouraging citizens to ignore the namby-pamby police chief and take matters into their own hands when the chief declared that the Chinese family living in a tent by the Baptist church was entitled to full protection under the law. The townspeople stormed the jail, locking the chief and two policemen in a cell; broke the windows of a grocer who had sold fruit to the Chinks; smashed the printing press and equipment in the newspaper office; and, finally, set the Chinks' tent on fire. The family attempted to escape, the mother carrying a baby and the father pushing two other children out in front of him, but they were beaten back with sticks and rakes, brooms and pitchforks, forced to return to the fiery tent. When they tried to dash out the other side, where flames had already destroyed the canvas, they were again beaten. This time, the baby, its clothing already burning, was knocked out of the mother's hands and flew onto the hard ground, where it remained still and lifeless. The mother refused to be deterred by the blows rained upon her, attempting with single-minded determination to reach the body of her infant even as a hoe cracked open her head. The rest of the family were battered as they endeavored to escape the growing flames, and one by one they fell.

In Stanton, Nebraska, three Chinese men were brought bound before Williams almost as soon as he'd entered the town. They'd stayed behind after the railroad crew had passed through, and had been captured over a month ago, kept in captivity in the mayor's basement until someone could decide what to do with them. Williams toured the basement and noted with approval the leg-irons, the tin of drinking water, the filthy straw. The men were animals and had been treated as such. He followed the mayor back upstairs and looked over the emaciated Chinks. He could see collarbones and ribs, joints in the legs and arms. The oversized heads with their sunken cheeks, long teeth and narrow eyes looked positively inhuman.

"String them up," he said.

He watched with satisfaction as the three strangled to death in the air.

His journey was long, and on the way he began taking souvenirs: ears, noses, fingers, toes. The Indians did that, he was told, to frighten their enemies and savor their victories, and some of the veterans of the Indian wars with whom he came into contact had adopted the practice as well. It was in the town of Sycamore that he first took knife to flesh and sliced off an ear, and the exhilaration he felt when he sawed through the gristle was unlike anything he had ever experienced before. Later, traveling, knowing that the ear was wrapped in a leather bag carried with his personal effects, he was filled with a sense of power. He felt better, stronger, more successful than he ever had, than all of his money could make him, and he began to think it was because of this talisman, this ear. He knew the thought was superstitious, but it felt true to him nevertheless, and he decided he needed to collect even more talismans in order to amplify this euphoric sensation.

He returned to Selby, Missouri.

It was here that he'd been headed all along. Although left unspoken, this had always been his ultimate destination, and he'd been savoring the prospect of returning, even going so far as to draw it out, taking side trips to other locales merely for the sake of prolonging the delicious sense of anticipation.

Orren Gifford greeted him like a long-lost brother. The carpenter-cum-preacher had not heard of the events at Promontory Point, but Williams filled him in, and the eyes of the other man gleamed. "We chased out six Chink families from Selby, tarred and feathered five men since you was here. But there's still twenty or so living in the woods, on the outskirts. I count at least fifty head in the other towns in the county: Waterbury, Cottonville and North Newsom." He grinned. "The pits are still waiting."

They rode by night, a posse of nearly a hundred men, bearing torches and weapons, hunting Chinee. Some were burned; some were shot; some were dragged by the horses through rough ground until dead. Those were the ones who had put up a fight, the ones who might have caused trouble. But the rest were captured and brought along, and well over two dozen stood bound, bruised and battered in front of the mud pits the next morning.

In the bright light of day, some of the men were clearly having second thoughts. They were brave under the anonymity of night, but when it came time to stand up and be counted, they did not have the courage of their convictions. It was up to Gifford and himself to set the example, and they threw the first one into the mud pit themselves. With the preacher at his side, Williams grabbed a scrawny young man by his queue and pulled him to the ground; then the two of them picked him up and swung him into the boiling earth. There was a split-second scream of unbearable agony, then silence as the body sank into the thick white mud.

One of the brutally beaten fellows awaiting his fate

began chanting something very loudly in Chinese. There was a cadence to it that seemed unlike their normal babble, a rhythm that sounded almost poetic, like a nursery rhyme. Others chimed in at what had to be specific cues, for they spoke in unison, and it occurred to Williams that the heathens believed this was some sort of prayer. Or spell. It was nonsense, though, and he moved forward and grabbed that man and, again with Gifford's help, dragged him to the edge of one of the pits.

The Chink looked at him. There was fear in those slanted eyes, but beneath that was calm and a knowledge, a certainty, that frightened him. Williams turned his head away, looking instead at the bubbling mud. The infidel had been chanting the entire time, the others still chiming in, but now the doomed man stopped. His English was broken and heavily accented but still understandable: "We come back. How long it take. Get your children and their children—"

Williams had heard enough, and he threw the bound man into the pit. Only Gifford didn't know he was going to do so and continued to hold the Chink's feet, so only his head and shoulders dropped to earth and fell into the mud. He should have been screaming, crying out in terrible agony, but in the last few seconds before his face was eaten away, the man said clearly, "Be back."

Then Gifford tossed in his feet and the whole body rolled into the mud and disappeared.

It had been a curse. And though he was a Christian and had no truck with any pagan religions, he believed it. Deep down, where it counted, he thought the curse was real.

They all did.

As cowardly as it might be, he was glad at that second that he did not live in Selby, that he did not live anywhere in Missouri. Once this was over, he would never be back. Gifford, the other townspeople and their kin would remain here and have to deal with this, but he would be long gone.

Everyone was silent.

Williams kept on as though nothing out of the ordinary had happened, as though anyone who believed in the sort of mumbo jumbo spouted by the dying man was a rube and an imbecile. He grabbed another Chinee on his own, a small woman, and pulled her to the edge of another pit, kicking her in. He glanced over at Gifford, who still stood there flummoxed. "What are you waiting for? Get to work!"

The preacher did. They all did, and within the hour all of the Chinese had been fed to the pits, where their flesh burned off and their bones mingled with the mud. By the end of it, the mood was festive, as though everyone had forgotten all about the curse, and Williams smiled as he watched the last heathen exterminated, four burly white men dropping in a thin screaming boy.

This, by God, was America.

Twenty-eight

St. George, Utah

They lost the train's tracks, no pun intended, somewhere around Page, but despite the pleas from
Derek's mom and brother, they did not turn back.
Instead they continued on into Utah until, sometime
after nightfall, they reached St. George. It was a
small town in the southwest corner of the state, and
the only motel with a vacancy was a small mom-and-
pop place that, despite the beautiful flower patch out
front and the quaint name of Jacaranda Country Inn,
reminded Angela of the Bates Motel.

They were all tired, none of them had any ideas,
and for dinner they found a pizza place, eating in
silence beneath a too-loud television tuned to ESPN.

Angela felt discouraged, but she was not completely disappointed that they'd lost the train. For
beneath her determination was fear, and the truth
was that she'd had no idea what they would do if
they successfully trailed the locomotive to its even-
tual destination.

She felt better out here on the road. The horror
was still there, but away from Flagstaff, outside the
confines of the city, it did not seem quite so oppres-

sive. Nor quite so bleak. For most of the day they'd
been traveling through vast expanses of nothingness,
past Lake Powell and the Vermilion Cliffs, past tan
sand and tan buttes where no plant grew. She found
it hard to believe that the mold could make it through
here. Or past here.

If it weren't for that train . . .

After dinner, they walked back to the motel. From
within the houses they passed, Angela heard the
canned laughter of sitcoms, the nursery-rhyme
chanting of rap music, the crying of babies, the lec-
turing of parents, all of the ordinary sounds of every-
day life, and she envied those people their ignorance
and their bliss. There was nothing she would like
more than to be able to go back to a time when her
biggest worries were how well her Friday night date
would go and whether she would get an A or a B
on a test.

She wondered what was happening at Babbitt
House right now.

She hoped the cops had raided the place and locked
everyone up under quarantine.

That wasn't fair. The Chrissie who'd called her a
stupid brown bitch was not the Chrissie she'd been
living with since the beginning of the semester. That
was the mold talking. And as easy as it might be to
take her cue from science fiction movies and assume
that the mold brought out and amplified her roommate's true deep-seated feelings, Angela knew in her
heart that wasn't the case. The black fungus had *im-
posed* those ideas on Chrissie and the others, had
made them that way.

But why hadn't she been affected? She was the one
the corpse had grabbed.

She had no answers, only questions.

Back in the motel room, they turned on the television. Derek and his brother, Steve, were sharing one queen-sized bed, while she and Derek's mother took the other. No one except Steve cared what they watched, so they let him flip around until he found a local independent station showing reruns of *The Simpsons* and *King of the Hill*. Derek's mother went in the bathroom to take a shower, and Angela dozed off for a while.

When she awoke, the lights were off and the news was on. Only Derek was still awake, and he put a finger to his lips, telling her not to make any noise.

On the Salt Lake City newscast, the top story was a massive gathering of Native Americans who had assembled in the northern portion of the state and had come from all over the country for no apparent reason, or at least no reason they were willing to divulge to television reporters.

A handsome man with a microphone stood on railroad tracks before a jam-packed crowd that had to number in the thousands. "Promontory Point was the spot where the Central Pacific and the combined Union and United Pacific railways met to form the transcontinental railroad in 1869, and where the golden spike that joined the two was driven in by Leland Stanford and Thomas Durant. Why so many people have been caught off guard here is that there is no anniversary involving events at this location, and there do not appear to be any speakers or performers or any other reason for this historic gathering. So as of this moment, what's happening here at Promontory Point remains a mystery. We will keep you informed as events continue to unfold."

Derek turned down the sound with the remote control. "Correct me if I'm wrong, but Chinese workers helped build that railroad, didn't they?" he said, speaking softly.

He was right. She didn't know why that was important; she just knew that it was.

Promontory Point.

"That's it," Angela said. "That's where we're going."

Twenty-nine

Promontory Point, Utah

"Holy shit," Henry said.

It looked like a Native American Woodstock. For as far as the eye could see, people and tents, campers and pickup trucks, were packed like sardines across the open land. The air was filled with a thousand separate sounds that coalesced into a single ebb-and-flow hum. His companions made no effort to join the throng, to find its center and purpose; they simply parked the pickup on the edge of the gathering and started to set up camp. This consisted of placing a rusty hibachi next to the truck, grabbing cans of beer out of the cooler and spreading out sleeping bags on the dusty ground.

They talked to no one.

They didn't have to.

He understood why they were here, knew now the story behind it, but there was still something of a disconnect. He felt as though he were *watching* himself do things rather than doing them. According to Wes and the other Papagos who had picked him up, there was a purpose to their pilgrimage, yet none of them seemed at all focused. Rather, they were on autopilot, following some predetermined plan rather than making conscious decisions.

Henry didn't like that.

They sat around, talked of nothing, drank, exchanged occasional greetings with other men from other tribes.

Night fell.

And with darkness came the shadows.

There were women *and* men, as well as figures so vague they were impossible to identify, and they came up from the ground, down from the sky, in from the plain. He should have known they would be here, but he had not expected it and it did not appear that many of the others had either. The shades moved seductively, enticingly, their purpose explicit, and Henry noticed that they were more solid than before, more dense and real. He was seized by the terrifying notion that despite what Wes and the others believed, the Indians had all been lured here for this purpose. They had been tricked into congregating in one area—in *this* area—so they could be assaulted, used and drained.

He looked about him at the approaching figures. There were gradations of darkness now, areas that suggested eyes, nose and mouth, pubic hair and nipples. There was, in addition, the promise of something more, the suggestion that if allowed to finish what they had started, these forms would become real, would gain flesh and substance and provide the complete pleasure they could only simulate now.

Most of the men weren't responding, were trying to chase the shades away, and even those who did succumb seemed to be fighting it, desperately attempting to keep their clothes on, to stop themselves from interacting with the spirits. Henry was thankful for that. And relieved. Surrounded by those like himself, their moral support granting him a strength he did not possess when alone, he found that he was not aroused by the twins when they came to seduce him. Once again, he was able to see the female body for what it really was: a collection of nerve endings and orifices with grotesque physiological functions. And while the twins did not exactly *have* bodies, the idea was enough to dampen his already wan libido.

As strange as it might seem to someone else, it felt good to be himself again.

One of the Chinese twins—they were Chinese; he knew that now—sidled next to him, running her left hand slowly over her voluptuous breasts even as her right hand reached out. The other sister stood in front of him, rubbing herself between her legs, her body undulating in time with the movements of her hand.

He was not aroused in the slightest.

And, as before, he could sense under the surface sensuality an anger, a seething rage hidden beneath the sexual behavior.

Henry looked up at the bed of the pickup where Wes and Milton were trying to shoo away the full shadows of two slight boyish-looking teenage girls.

"It is our life force," Wes explained. "That is why the dead crave our seed. It gives them what they do not have."

To Henry's right, one older man had succumbed and was masturbating furiously, pants around his ankles. As he reached his climax, a horde of shadows flew about him, attempting to ingest his semen. Henry's twins fled there as well, and he watched in fascination as their forms seemed to change, became more like the rounded buxom matron seducing the elderly man before they merged into one figure identical to the man's seductress.

From here and there, throughout the crowd, came

cries of anguish or remorse, grunts of pleasure, but gradually those noises were supplanted by the rhythms of conversation, by the sounds of radios, tape decks and CD players being cranked up as men turned away from the shadows, ignoring them in favor of the mundane trivialities of ordinary existence. This continued for the better part of an hour, the shadows growing ever more frantic and desperate in their attempts at seduction until finally, as one, they departed, not retreating the way they had come but fading away, blending into the night. They made no noise—they never did—but from the earth itself came a strange rumbling sound, a howl of frustration muffled by layers of dirt, and it was then Henry knew for certain that they had been thwarted in their efforts. He felt good, proud of himself and the others around him.

"Thank God," Wes breathed, brushing back his hair.

They looked at each other, and Henry thought that they would talk about what had just happened, finally have a heart-to-heart about why they were here and what they were going to do and . . . everything.

But they didn't. Either of them. They fiddled with their sleeping bags, they got cans of beer out of the ice chest with Milton, Antonio and Jack, and all of them stood or sat there silently as the night deepened around them.

And they waited for the train.

Thirty

Promontory Point.

Rossiter watched the DVD of spliced-together stories from four network newscasts and six local stations that Agent Saldana had quickly burned and brought to him. *Pathetic,* he was thinking as a bland man with blond hair reported from the site. With all of its massive intelligence-gathering capabilities, the FBI was relying for information on Cal Perkins, third-string feature reporter for one of Salt Lake City's independent television stations?

So much for the conspiracy theorists who imagined the FBI as a monolithic well-oiled machine with unlimited resources that was secretly and effectively compiling information on every individual in the United States—although this did give ammunition to the other side, those critics who saw the FBI as a bunch of ineffectual know-nothings who falsified evidence to justify incompetent investigatory work and who couldn't solve a crime if it bit them on the ass.

Shit.

They just couldn't win.

Rossiter forced himself to smile at the junior agent.

"Good work, Saldana. You're thinking out of the box. I like that."

"Thank you, sir." The agent beamed as he walked back to his desk.

Rossiter had been honing his interpersonal, organizational and leadership skills over the past several days. It was still too early to know for certain, but he had the feeling that a promotion might be in the offing after this. Smiling while offering encouragement and words of praise did not come naturally to him, but putting on a happy face was a small price to pay if it meant moving up the ladder.

Although with all of the speculation in the press about the physical damage to the White House and the president's questionable decision to stonewall rather than deal honestly and publicly with the situation, the pressure was on. If he didn't wrap this up and quickly, his ass was out.

He replayed the DVD, watched it again. He had no idea why all of those men from all of those tribes were gathering at Promontory Point—no outsiders did, and the men who were there weren't talking—but the fact that that was where the two sides of the transcontinental railroad had met meant that it was an important site in the history of trains.

And though Lincoln had signed the Pacific Railroad Act, the railway had actually been completed during Grant's tenure.

Trains.

Everything was coming together.

Sort of.

He sifted through printouts of other reports that had been gathered for him, incidents that might be related, might not. One group in particular stood out. In several states for the past month or two there'd been sightings of mysterious black trains speeding by on disused rails or even on Amtrak routes. Concurrently, in quite a few of those towns, ghosts had been heard, mysterious disembodied voices in homes or stores or, in one instance, a gas station restroom. They were always described as speaking gibberish, some incomprehensible babble that one churchgoing woman in Missouri said sounded like "a gay man speaking in tongues."

Only yesterday, in Bear Flats, California, a police officer had come across just such an incident in a house where a gruesome murder had recently occurred. He'd had the presence of mind to record it on his cell phone, and the recording had buzzed instantly around the Internet, catching the ear of Ron Banks, one of the agents on Rossiter's team. Banks had conducted a follow-up interview, filing a report, and Rossiter looked over the printout now. He'd glanced at it less than half an hour ago, just before Saldana had brought in the DVD, but something about it nagged at him, and he read through Banks' summary again.

Chester Williams.

That's what it was. The name Chester Williams rang a bell, although he'd been so overloaded with reading and bogged down with research since being assigned to this case that he couldn't remember where he'd read or heard the name before. He circled it on the page so he'd remember when he came back to it.

He hadn't had a chance to actually hear the recording of voices that the police officer had made, so Rossiter went over to his computer and called it up. The sound was muffled and crackly at first, with ambient noise from the officer's breathing and footsteps that was louder than anything else, but gradually the voices came to the fore. Two of them: a man and a woman.

The ghosts were speaking Cantonese.

He recognized the language instantly. It had been over ten years since he'd made a name for himself in Rio Verde, Arizona, but those few weeks had been etched upon his consciousness with a razor, and one of the things he remembered clearly was the unique cadence of Cantonese. He had no idea what they were saying, but he knew what language they were speaking.

A lot of Chinese had worked on building the transcontinental railroad.

Again, everything seemed to be tied together. If he could just figure out the connections . . .

He decided to call the Wings. The family had been very helpful to him in Rio Verde—the grandmother had been a veritable sourcebook of arcane lore—and maybe they could assist him here as well.

Very helpful? *Assist him*? Who was he kidding? He'd merely been tagging along on that venture. If it hadn't been for the grandmother, his bones would probably be bleaching in the desert right now—along with those of the entire population of the town. He owed his career to the Wings.

He made a few phone calls.

The Wings, it turned out, had flown away. Their restaurant was closed, and the family no longer lived in town. Rio Verde itself was thriving. There were two new gated communities, both with man-made lakes, one with a golf course, and the rebuilt downtown featured all sorts of trendy eateries and boutiques. The dude ranch was long gone, but in its place was a resort and spa that catered to wealthy Phoenicians. With the influx of new money, though, must have come a new attitude, one that rendered obsolete the old-fashioned Chinese restaurant of the sort the Wings had owned.

Or maybe they'd just wanted to get out of town after everything that had happened.

He expected that sack-of-shit police chief to be a little more help than he turned out to be, but either the man knew nothing, or more likely, he wasn't willing to divulge what he knew, and after a short conversation Rossiter hung up the phone angry.

He would just have to track the family down. He had all of the resources of the bureau at his disposal, and not only could he learn their various addresses fairly quickly, but he could probably download satellite photos of their houses. Indeed, in a matter of minutes he learned that Sue Wing was an English teacher at a Chinese school in Irvine, California. Her parents and brother lived in Tucson.

The grandmother had died.

Rossiter was sorry to hear that. And not just because it put a roadblock in his path. As hard as it was to believe, time had softened him, and over the years he had come to not only respect the old woman but admire her knowledge, skill and bravery. In the back of his mind, he supposed, he'd always assumed she would be around, a source of information he could consult whenever need be. It was something of a shock to learn that she was gone.

He decided to call Sue Wing. She was the one he had dealt with, his go-between with the rest of the family, and it was she who seemed to have been the closest to her grandmother and the most interested in supernatural phenomena. Besides, her parents barely spoke English. And her brother had been too young when it happened; it was doubtful he would know much.

Her number appeared on his screen, and he dialed it, clearing his throat so as to sound as professional and unthreatening as possible. She picked up on the second ring. "Hello?"

"Sue Wing?" he said.

"Yes?" came the tentative voice on the other end of the line.

"This is Agent Rossiter from the FBI—"

The line went dead.

He immediately called back, but the line was now busy. He tried once more, just in case, but he knew she had taken the phone off the hook. He felt a flash of anger and was tempted to call one of his old asshole comrades from the Phoenix field office who was now working in Southern California and have him haul her in for questioning, but he quelled that impulse.

What would the girl know, anyway? The grandmother was the expert. With her gone, his chances of learning anything worthwhile dropped to nearly nothing.

Besides, he couldn't allow himself to be distracted. Time was of the essence, and he couldn't afford to fuck things up.

Rossiter glanced down at the printout next to his computer, saw the circled name.

Chester Williams.

He'd almost forgotten about that, and though he still couldn't remember where he'd come across the name before, it would be easy enough to track down. He called up another screen and typed in "Williams, Chester," and an entire page of distilled information appeared. Now he knew why the name was familiar. Williams had been an investor in the United Pacific Railroad. He had been influential at the beginning of the drive to build the transcontinental railroad, but his involvement had faded as time went on. He'd spent his final years in Bear Flats, California . . . where he'd formed an organization called the ACL, the Anti-Chinese League, which had spread across the country and at its peak had over two hundred chapters and featured among its supporters a wide array of politicians.

That was one coincidence too many.

Rossiter pressed a button on his speakerphone. "Agent Saldana," he said. "Come in here, please." He'd intended to say "*Get* in here," without the "please," but at the last second he'd softened it. He was getting pretty good at this if he did say so himself.

A moment later, there was a knock at the door and his assistant let in Saldana. Rossiter stood. "I need you to lead a team of four men to the town of Bear Flats, California. A police officer reported hearing ghostly voices speaking Chinese and recorded an incident on his cell phone. This occurred in a house where an unexplained murder recently took place, a house built by railroad tycoon Chester Williams. I'll message over everything I have. I suggest you print it out *and* bring a laptop."

The agent seemed surprised instead of flattered. *Wrong response,* Rossiter thought, but he kept his expression neutral.

"I assumed I would be going to—"

Rossiter cut him off. "*I'll* be leading the team at Promontory Point. I want you to lead the second team—"

"But I thought—"

"Or not." Rossiter turned away dismissively and pressed the button on his speakerphone.

"No!" Saldana practically shouted. "I'm sorry! Thank you, sir. I will be happy to go to Bear Flats."

"Step on it, then. I want you there tonight. And I expect hourly reports once you're in town."

"Yes, sir."

Rossiter looked at the unmoving young man. "I said I would send you everything I have. Is there anything else?"

"No, sir."

"Then what are you standing there for? Get moving!"

Saldana practically tripped over his own feet attempting to flee the office, and Rossiter smiled. Being nice had its place . . . but there was nothing like good old-fashioned fear to light a fire under someone's ass.

He glanced at the clock. Time was wasting. He wanted Saldana in Bear Flats tonight, and he wanted to be at Promontory Point with his own team by midnight. He doubted they would make it, but he sure as hell was going to try. He went over a list of agents in his mind, trying to decide not only who would be the most thorough, knowledgeable and self-motivated— but also who would be the least annoying on the flight over.

Successful FBI work sometimes required more than merely brains and ability.

He pushed the button on his speakerphone. "Hanson," he said. "Singh, Worthington, Munoz . . ."

Thirty-one

Bear Flats, California

Jolene looked down at the faces of her mother and her son. Both appeared more peaceful in sleep than they ever did awake, and she wished they could always be this way. Skylar shifted position, one arm flopping above his head, and her heart went out to the boy. Although he was strong, although he coped, adapted and survived, her greatest wish was that she could make his life easy, that she could spare him these hardships and give him the kind of carefree childhood he deserved.

She reached out and touched his cheek. It was soft, almost as delicate as it had been when he was a baby. A fierce protectiveness rose within her. If anyone or anything ever attempted to harm one hair on his head, she would kill them.

Her mother shifted in her sleep, muttered something unintelligible, then sank again into deep slumber.

Her mom had been doing very well. She'd found a small liqueur bottle in Leslie's cabinet yesterday that she'd polished off, but that had been it, and when they'd all gone to the store this morning, she hadn't even gone down the liquor aisle. Jolene was proud of her, and she wished she knew how to tell that to her mother without sounding patronizing.

She straightened, massaging her stiff neck with one hand, and glanced around Leslie's living room. Her friend was at work. She had been great through all of this, and though Jolene had not seen her in years, had not even bothered to keep in touch, the two of them had picked up exactly where they'd left off. It was as though she'd never moved away. Once best friends, always best friends, Jolene thought, and the sentiment brought her close to tears. She hadn't had a friend since to whom she'd been anywhere near as close. Part of it was due to the demands of being an adult. With work and family and the responsibilities of life, there just wasn't the free time to hang out together that there had been in high school. But part of it was also the mysterious chemistry that had brought them together in the first place, that had led them to bond over their shared disdain for jocks and cheerleaders in the back of Mrs. Wilson's social studies class. They'd been kindred spirits back then, instantly attuned, and connections formed at that pivotal age were always much stronger than those created later.

She or Leslie or both of them might move away in the future, but Jolene knew that they would not lose touch this time. They were bound together, friends forever.

Her throat felt dry, and she made her way to the kitchen to get a drink of water. Although the drapes were drawn, Jolene avoided looking at the windows. Leslie's curtains were frilly and sheer, and she was afraid of what she might see. Outside these walls, normal life went on for everyone else in town, but more and more she felt trapped within the house, barricaded against evil forces she could not hope to fight against. She knew that wasn't healthy, knew it was fostering

an attitude of fear and paranoia, but she *was* afraid.
For her son as much as herself. And after reading
those diaries and seeing what she'd seen, she knew
that there *were* evil forces.

Evil was not an abstract concept or metaphoric construct. It was real. And it lived.

They want revenge.

She wished Leslie would hurry up and come home.

Jolene walked back out to the living room, turning
on the television but keeping the sound low. *Jerry
Maguire* was on. She'd seen that movie with Frank.
Before Skylar was born. Although the film itself still
seemed recent, that period of her life felt like a long,
long time ago, and thinking about it now made her
sad.

She turned off the television.

There was the sound of movement from within the
bedroom. It was probably nothing, but she couldn't
afford to ignore it. She walked over to the bedroom
doorway to check.

And Skylar awoke screaming.

In his dream, Skylar was himself, but he was also a
marionette. His strings were being worked by the ancient Chinese man who'd spied on him and his mom
through the window and who'd kidnapped him in the
school bathroom. The wrinkled face grinned down at
him as knotted fingers tilted and twirled the strings to
make him dance. He didn't want to dance—he wanted
to run—but his own will and muscles were no match
for the overpowering force of the strings.

Suddenly there was another puppet approaching
him. It was being controlled by a scowling bearded
white man in an old-fashioned suit and hat. This marionette was made from the body of a mummified child,
and its eyes and mouth were sewn shut with black

suture that gave its face the appearance of a shrunken head. The strings made its skeletal arms and withered legs move up and down in a grotesque approximation of walking. Skylar's instinctive reaction was to run, and he tried to do just that, but the old Chinese man holding his strings started cackling and forced him to approach the other puppet with arms outstretched, as though inviting a hug.

Skylar wanted to scream but couldn't. He had no voice.

All of a sudden, there was a knife in his right hand, and with a hard, painful yank, the string attached to that arm made it thrust forward. Within seconds, he was jabbing at the other puppet, stabbing the mummified child in its shriveled stomach, in its bony chest. No blood emerged from the slices and tears in the dried skin, only puffs of dust, but despite the furious machinations of the bearded puppeteer, the marionette began to slow down, like a toy whose battery was dying. Another hard yank on the string connected to his right arm, and Skylar was stabbing the puppet in the face. Sutures ripped open, and opaque eyes glared out at him. The toothless mouth screamed silently.

Then he was being hoisted into the air, his feet scrambling up the collapsing skull of the marionette, his hands grasping the strings attached to the mummified child and climbing to the top, where he leaped upon the bearded man's hands.

His Chinese controller was laughing loudly now, no longer cackles but full-out guffaws. The bearded man at first let out a grunt of surprise, but Skylar sliced the muscle of his arm and then he was crying out in pain and fear, cries that turned to whimpers as Skylar moved up to his shoulder and began stabbing his neck and cheek and ear, the blood spurting out and covering him in a spray of crimson.

He could not see, and he fought against the strings with all of the strength he had, just so he could wipe the blood from his eyes. The straining paid off and he finally overcame all resistance. He used the backs of both hands to wipe off his eyes—

And he was back in that cellar, lying naked on the hard dirt ground. Only he was not alone. The same bearded white man was unwrapping a piece of folded wet linen on a wooden workbench. He was not dressed in suit and hat this time but was clothed only in his underwear, which was stained red with blood, some of it dried, most of it not. There was blood on his skin as well, and when Skylar sat up, he saw that the man was withdrawing from the dirty wet linen a human hand. The stump of the wrist was ragged, as though the hand had been yanked off an arm rather than cut, and in the middle of the red was a circle of white bone.

Chester Williams, he thought. *The man's name is Chester Williams.* The old Chinese man had told him that. He remembered it from last time.

Williams picked up a long knife from the workbench and lovingly used it to sever a finger from the hand. A thin trickle of blood dribbled out.

Skylar gagged, throwing up on the ground next to him, and that captured Williams' attention. The bearded man turned around, and Skylar saw with horror that he had an erection.

He pointed to Skylar with the dripping knife. "Don't worry, sweetums. You're next."

And then Skylar was in a dark place that didn't seem like anyplace at all. He couldn't tell if his feet were on the ground or if he was floating in some limitless space, because there was no resistance against the soles of his shoes or any other part of his body. He put his hands out in front of him and tried to walk, but the darkness was so complete that he had no idea if he was moving forward or remaining in place or spinning in the open air. He sensed that he was not alone—although he was not sure of it until he heard the voice speak to him.

"Skylar."

It was not the same voice as before, the voice of the Chinese man, the puppeteer. There was something inhuman about it and vaguely snakelike, especially in the way it drew out the sibilance of his name.

He did not answer, tried to make himself small, tried to hide, though for all he knew the entity could see in the dark and was watching him right now.

"Destroy the house. It is the key."

Images accompanied the words. But more than images. Understanding. He *understood* what he was seeing, comprehended the *reasons* behind it.

And what he saw was the mansion where he had been taken, the one with the secret cellar that he knew now to be the Williams place. Chester Williams had been a bad man, an evil man, and much of that evil had been brought to the house. He'd heard his mom and his grandma and Ms. Finch talking about Chester Williams and his diaries when they thought he was asleep, and he remembered seeing the scalps and toes and other severed body parts when he'd been brought into that hidden cellar, but that was only part of it. Chester Williams had done much, much worse within those walls, and though Skylar saw some of it, he knew he was being shielded from the worst atrocities, and for that he was grateful.

And still the house stood, its secrets protected through the generations by Chester Williams' son and then his grandson, not just a monument to the barbarity of the man but a living repository of his evil deeds. Williams himself was still there somehow, not as a ghost, not exactly, but woven into the fabric of the building itself: the walls, the floor, the ceiling. It was the house that was keeping his presence alive, and it was the house that served as the focus of hatred for all the victims of his hideous crimes. They had been waiting for a long time, in a place as dark as this, for the chance to strike back at the man who had rallied mobs against them, who had tortured them and had them killed, and now they had a mob of their own, an army of the murdered, who had finally been able to connect with each other and now had the means to exact revenge not only on Williams but on the society that had condoned his actions.

"Destroy the house," the voice repeated, and Skylar understood that this would help stop the old Chinese man and his brethren by taking away the focus of their anger. It was the anger that drove them, that had kept their spirits alive all these years. Without it, they had no purpose, no meaning, and would undoubtedly dissipate, fading away into wherever it was that the dead normally went.

A muscle in his arm twitched at the memory of the string that had controlled him.

"Why me?" Skylar asked.

The answer was not clear. There were more images: his mother in her border patrol uniform discovering a family of corpses in a ditch in the desert; a group of huddled Chinese workers from long ago, dead in a tunnel, looking very similar to the family in the ditch; Skylar himself playing with Carlos, his best friend back in Yuma; Skylar again, walking by the mother-daughter grave site. There was a message he was supposed to take from that, but he had no idea what it was. *"You were chosen,"* the voice said, but he didn't really know what that meant, and he wondered if what it really came down to was that he'd been in the right place at the right time.

Or the wrong place at the wrong time.

"Who . . . who are you?" Skylar asked the disembodied voice.

There was a lightening of the darkness as the entity showed itself.

And Skylar awoke screaming.

Jolene held her son tightly. Her mother had awakened as well, shocked instantly out of sleep by Skylar's primal piercing cry, and Jolene was both heartened and surprised to see that the expression on her mom's face was one of ferocious protectiveness. She did not know this woman. This was not the mother with whom she had grown up—although it *was* the mother she had always wanted—and for the first time she was filled with the hope that her son might finally have the grandmother he deserved and that she herself might eventually be able to forge a real relationship with her mom.

If they made it out of this alive.

Skylar's screams had turned to sobs, and she murmured generic reassurances in his ear. "It's all right. . . . It's okay. . . . Mommy's here. . . ."

There was a knock at the front door. She assumed at first that it was Leslie, home from work, but the knock came again. Leslie wouldn't knock. She had a key. "Who is it?" Jolene called out, heart pounding. She passed Skylar to her mother and went into the living room, looking around for the carving knife she'd been keeping close by, just in case.

"Agent Anthony Saldana. FBI."

That was the last response in the world she had

expected to hear, and it came so far out of left field that she was too stunned to respond.

"Are you Jolene Connor?" the man asked.

"Yes," she answered through the closed door. She looked back at her mother, who was staring with wide frightened eyes. Skylar had stopped crying and was wiping the tears from his face, his gaze focused and alert.

"May I speak with you?"

"Go right ahead."

"I need to talk to you about your experience in the Williams house. I interviewed Chief Tanner about an hour ago and just finished talking to your friend Leslie Finch, who told me where to find you." There was a pause. "Would you open the door, please?"

The voice belonged to someone used to being obeyed, and she was not sure if that was a request or an order. She was still suspicious and didn't want to let anyone in, but with trembling hands she turned the dead bolt and opened the door a crack, peeking out from beneath the chain lock. The gray-suited man on the front porch was holding out a sheathed badge and ID card. In the drive behind him, another man was waiting in a black car. She thought of bringing up the fact that until recently she'd been a border patrol agent and so was a fellow alumnus of federal law enforcement, but she didn't think it would carry much weight.

"Open the door, please," the agent said.

Jolene obeyed, although she remained standing in the doorway, refusing to invite him in.

"I understand that you were in the house when Anna May Carter was killed and that your son was found in the basement hysterical and in a state of undress. Is this true?"

Jolene nodded.

Saldana looked over her shoulder at Skylar, who had come out of the bedroom with his grandmother. "Is that the boy?"

"What is it exactly that you want to know?"

"You have in your possession a series of journals kept by Chester Williams, journals in which he describes in detail killings and acts of violence committed by himself and his followers. You're also the one who discovered severed body parts that Williams cut off of his victims for his own personal use."

"Yes," she admitted.

"Can you tell me of any unusual or unexplained occurrences that have happened in or around the Williams house recently?"

She frowned. "What is this? What's going on?"

He looked her in the eye as the other agent got out of the car. "Have you seen any ghosts or spirits, Mrs. Connor?"

She paused for only a second. "Yes." Jolene exhaled deeply. It was a relief, somehow, to be able to unburden herself, to explain what she'd seen and experienced to someone in a position of authority. Both agents came inside and sat down, and although she had done her best up until this point to keep the worst of it from Skylar, she spoke freely now in front of him, knowing that it was time for him to learn what was going on. She handed the diaries over to Saldana when she was through describing what was in them. "Here," she said.

"I would like you to accompany us to the house of Chester Williams," the agent told her. "I want you to show us where everything occurred."

"I'm going, too!" Skylar announced.

"No, you're not," Jolene told him. "You stay here with Grandma."

"I have to go. I have to be there. I'm the one it talks to."

I'm the one it talks to.

She suddenly felt chilled. "I don't want you anywhere near that house, do you understand me? You—"

"Who is 'it'?" Saldana asked Skylar.

"I don't know. But I dreamed about that old Chinese guy who kidnapped me, and I dreamed about that Williams guy, and then I was in this dark place and this really big . . . thing"—Jolene saw the shadow of fear pass over his face—"talked to me and said the only way to stop all this was to destroy the house."

"All 'this'? All what?"

"I don't know. All the stuff you're here about, I guess. All the stuff you're supposed to stop."

The two agents looked at each other. "He's coming with us," Saldana said.

"No, he's not," Jolene insisted.

"He's coming with us."

Thirty-two

In the Passenger Car

Time was fluid in here. Dennis knew, objectively, that it shouldn't take more than a day to reach their destination if they really *were* riding on a train. But sometimes it felt as though he'd been in here over a week—and sometimes it seemed that only hours had passed by.

They made no stops, at least not to his knowledge, but other people wandered into the passenger car periodically. People like himself. Living people. Chinese people. They seemed as confused as he had been upon entering, and, as with him, the ghostly man sat next to each of them in turn and *explained* things, showed them scenes outside the blackness of the windows.

Afterward, the newbies came to sit by him, either drawn by his warmth or repelled by the others' cold.

What was happening was wrong, Dennis knew. He recognized the reason for the rage, even felt some of it himself. The desire for revenge was understandable and perhaps even justified given the circumstances, but two wrongs didn't make a right, and no matter what various religions said, the sins of the father should *not* be visited upon the sons.

Not everyone agreed. One of his fellow travelers

was a college professor from Denver, another an elderly housewife from Oregon who reminded him of his mom, and both of them believed retaliation was entirely appropriate. They had been told and shown the same things he had, but it seemed that they had known already. Like the old man he had seen in the Selby cemetery, they had been practicing rituals handed down from their parents and grandparents, rural rituals from old religions that were intended to lead to the very end they were experiencing now: the resurrection of the dead. Their people had been grievously wronged, the professor said, not merely exploited but murdered because of their ethnicity, and those who had died deserved the chance to strike back at the society that had fostered such hatred. Whatever punishment might be meted out was more than deserved. Dennis definitely did not agree, and he thought perhaps it was a generational thing, or maybe it was because he considered himself more American than Chinese. He was relieved when another young man—a medical student from Las Vegas—seemed to be just as clueless and horrified as he was.

The odd thing was that none of them seemed to be freaked-out by the fact that they were riding in this phantom train—himself included—and he wondered if the others had experienced the same sort of subliminal pull that had compelled him west, that had led him from state to state, town to town, and finally to here. He wondered if, like himself, they looked at this dark ride as the logical continuation of a journey they had already been on.

At some point, the train would reach its final destination. Probably sooner rather than later. He was not exactly sure what would happen there—well, he knew *what*, although he did not know *how*—but he realized that he needed to find some way to stop it. He thought of what he'd seen out the windows. An army of Native Americans was waiting for them at Promontory Point. Aligned originally against the white society that had abused them both, the Native Americans had gone from allies to enemies over generations due to the all-consuming hunger of the Chinese dead. Dennis had no idea how the men of the tribes had discovered that it would happen at the Point, the burning place, or what was behind their gathering; all he knew was that if they failed, the dead would have free rein and no one would be safe. He could not allow that to happen. In school, in the ethics class he'd taken the semester before dropping out of college, there'd been endless discussions about how choosing not to act was still a choice and choosing not to act against evil made one complicit in that evil. They had all sworn that were the opportunity to arise, they would take a stand no matter what the personal consequences.

Now he had the opportunity to act on that promise.

If he could only figure out how.

He wished Cathy were here. His sister might be young, but she was smart and good at thinking on her feet.

On an impulse, he tried his cell phone, but it didn't even turn on. There was no light, no beep, nothing. He pressed his face to the window. On the other side of the glass, no historic scenes were replaying themselves for his benefit. There was only darkness.

"Dennis."

He looked over at Malcolm, the medical student. "Yeah?"

"You think it's all true?"

Dennis nodded. He did. Like that of any other minority group, the known history of the Chinese in America was pretty bad. To discover that it was even worse and more brutal than he'd been led to believe was not exactly a shocker.

"But it's still not worth retaliating for?"

"Against people who had nothing to do with any of it and don't even know what happened? No." He frowned. "Why? Are you changing your mind?"

"No. No, not at all. It's just that . . . why are *we* here? What do they need us for? What do we bring to the table? You know what I'm saying? There must be a reason. But . . . what is it?"

"I don't know," Dennis admitted.

"It worries me," Malcolm said.

Dennis nodded. "Yeah. Me, too."

Thirty-three

Promontory Point, Utah

What surprised Angela most about the gathering was its size. The shots on television had not done it justice. There it had looked like the crowd of an ordinary football game behind the reporter. Viewed here from the road, however, there seemed to be enough people to fill five or six stadiums. The sight was impressive . . . but also a little creepy. The fact that this many individuals had suddenly, inexplicably and simultaneously walked out on their ordinary lives and used whatever means necessary to get to this place left her feeling not only frightened but overwhelmed. If whatever they were dealing with had the power to summon thousands of people over such a broad geographic area, they had no hope in hell of combating it. They might as well turn tail right now and run as far away from here as they could get.

The car approached the edge of the gathering. A brown sign by the side of the road read GOLDEN SPIKE NATIONAL HISTORIC SITE. Somewhere in the middle of this massive assemblage was a visitors' center, were roads and parking lots that led to the structure, but the amorphous nature of the crowd and its incredible scale had engulfed those permanent fixtures and temporarily changed the topography of the land. She could not tell where anything was located.

Derek pulled next to a CNN news van. A satellite dish atop a long pole protruded from the center of the van high above the gathered throng. Black wires and cables ran in bunches from within the vehicle's open center door outward into the crowd.

"The train's not here," Derek said.

"Yet," Angela emphasized. For she felt certain that it would be. And soon. She had no clue as to why it was late or what detour it could possibly have taken, but she knew in her gut that the corpse-hauling locomotive would arrive. This was where it was headed; this was its destination.

She unbuckled her seat belt and got out of the car. Her legs hurt from being cramped in the same position most of the day, and she stretched gratefully, thankful to have freedom of movement once again. As Derek, his mom and his brother got out of the car, she walked over to the news van to see if she could find out what was happening. Poking her head in the open door, she saw banks of electronic equipment and a row of six small television screens showing six different shots of the crowd, but no person inside the vehicle. She glanced from one screen to another, looking for some kind of clue, something that would give her an idea of where to go and what to do, but there were only scenes of campers and crowds, people milling around.

"Can I help you?" someone asked behind her.

She pulled her head out of the van to see a cleancut young man only a few years older than herself carrying what looked like a video camera and an extra length of coiled cable. "Uh . . . ," she stammered, caught off guard. "I, uh, was just wondering . . . uhm . . . no," she said. "Sorry." She moved away to let the man into the van.

"What now?" Derek asked, coming up next to her.

"I don't know," Angela admitted.

"These are close quarters. If that train gets here, if those . . . zombies come out and that mold starts infecting people?" He shook his head. "It would spread really fast."

She'd been thinking the same thing, but she had no idea what they could do to prevent any of it. She felt helpless, powerless, useless.

"Maybe we should leave," Derek's mother suggested.

His brother, Steve, nodded nervously. "Yeah."

"No," Angela and Derek said simultaneously.

They looked at each other and smiled. *Where there's humor, there's hope,* she thought. She wondered what her parents were doing right now, wondered what they would say if they knew she was here and why. She hadn't talked to them for the past two days. For all she knew, they thought she'd been kidnapped, and were calling Flagstaff police to send a search party after her.

The sun was starting to go down.

"What do we do about sleeping arrangements?" Angela asked. "I don't think there are any hotels around here."

"I don't even think there's a bathroom," Steve said.

Derek shrugged. "I guess we'll just sleep in the car."

The temperature was dropping, too.

Angela looked around at the crowd of Native Americans. They all seemed to be men, but they were old and young, fat and thin, crew cut and ponytailed. One thing they had in common was that they completely ignored one another. The communal spirit usually present at large events like concerts and football games was absent. It was as if thousands of individuals with absolutely nothing in common and no interest in one another happened to find themselves in the same place at the same time.

Between the crush of bodies, she thought she saw a portion of railroad track.

It's coming, she thought. *It will be here tonight.*

She said nothing to Derek. But when he took her hand, she squeezed it tightly, hoping to stop her trembling.

The second day passed slowly. They had run out of things to talk about and none of their immediate neighbors seemed in the mood for discussion, so mostly they sat around silently and waited. Henry wished he'd brought some reading material, but he hadn't and no one else had either. He could have spoken to reporters, given them his take on the situation for broadcast. But he had a career to think of after all of this was over, and it was more important to maintain his credibility than provide himself with diversions. Toward the middle of the day, he hiked around a bit, surveying the surroundings and trying to strike up conversations with other sojourners to no avail. He returned hot, tired and frustrated.

Lookiloos arrived, conspiracy buffs and New Age ninnies attracted by stories on the newscasts who'd come to see for themselves what was going on.

"They're in for a surprise," Wes said simply.

The others nodded.

The temperature dropped as the sun went down. Shadows grew long and then blended into the darkness as dusk became night.

Henry'd had a lot of time to think things over, to ponder what he'd learned and what he'd been told. It seemed to him that the Native American peoples had had a symbiotic relationship with the Chinese massacre victims from the beginning. Since both had been exploited by white men and the railroad, their interests converged; they each had a vested interest in taking revenge on their persecutors. The Chinese even seemed to have adopted some of the native beliefs for their own purposes. He recalled the first time he had dreamed of the twins and then when he had initially seen their shadows. They had revealed themselves slowly, seducing him, and while he had known nothing about them, and had found them profoundly alien and frightening, the shadows had from the beginning acted as though his capitulation was not only inevitable but preordained. He understood now that the shades had been gaining strength for well over a century this way, and Henry had no doubt that initially the arrangement had been agreed to by shamans or chiefs or even the native peoples themselves. But over the years, knowledge of any such pacts had been lost and forgotten, and the current generation not only resented and objected to being used but rejected the very premise of the massacre victims' resurrection. What was past was past. And wrongs could not be avenged, only righted.

From somewhere in the night came the sound of a train.

The hair prickled on the back of Henry's neck and arms. The mournful cry of the whistle was familiar . . . yet there was an added dimension to it, a fullness, an eerie haunting quality that gave it far deeper resonance than expected. Around him, people were getting uneasily to their feet, their faces blanched, their eyes filled with fear.

It was coming.

The ground rumbled as the train approached. The air shifted, growing warm, then cold, pressing forward and backward, though it was not wind and disturbed very little. Even the thin hairs on the top of his head remained unmoving as great blocks of air were displaced. He had no idea from which direction the train was coming or where it would eventually stop. He knew only that the waiting was over.

The whistle sounded again, and this time it resembled the crying of a beast.

The wheels on the rails emitted a monster's roar.

And then they saw it. From the edge of the plain to the east came a hulking black shape that sped along the tracks toward them, a vortex of darkness that seemed to suck into it all of the ambient light from the moon, the stars and assorted flashlights and lanterns. It looked like a train.

Looked like a train.

But wasn't.

As it grew close, Henry could see that the massive object hurtling toward them was made of writhing bodies, hundreds of them, covered with what looked like black mold and contorted into impossible shapes that fit together like parts of a jigsaw puzzle. The portion of the crowd that had gathered near the tracks was parting, people frantically dashing to one side or the other in order to get out of the way, leaving behind tents, cars, coolers and chairs as they tried desperately to get as far away from the onrushing train thing as they could.

He knew without being able to see faces that the squirming bodies were Chinese. They had built the rails and now they were using them, gathering victims from across the country and bringing them here, to the site of their greatest triumph and greatest tragedy.

The giant black shape did not brake or slow down or gradually halt. It did not have to follow the traditional laws of physics. All of a sudden, it simply stopped. There were none of the after noises associated with real trains, none of the steam hissing or mechanical clanking. It sat there in the center of the gathering, at a standstill, ominous and silent.

The bodies were no longer moving. Although they'd been constantly writhing while the train was in motion and had appeared almost alive, they were now very definitely dead. Their eyes were closed, and the layer of thick black mold that coated them bound them together and sealed them in like a cocoon.

News crews were yelling, shouting, hauling equipment, shoving their way past people, moving through the crowd to get to the train.

Or trains.

For there was another one now, coming from the opposite direction. This one was silent and shadowy, and Henry shivered as he saw the silky way it moved along the tracks. It reminded him of the twins. It may have resembled a mechanical object, but as impossible as it seemed, there was something sensual and seductive about the oversized form.

The two trains bumped, touched.

He and the other Papagos made no effort to move any closer. Indeed, most of the individuals on the periphery of the crowd remained where they were, and quite a few of the men who'd been closer to the tracks were now moving outward and away, trying to distance themselves. It was only the news crews and the tourists who were excitedly rushing forward, who appeared not to understand the seriousness of the situation—or the danger.

They all seemed to be white, Henry suddenly noticed.

They were the enemy.

As if on cue, the Others came. They did not emerge from either train, did not come out of the sky or the ground. They were just there one moment, moving through the throng of people, on the hunt. Henry did not know what they were, but these were the beings responsible for the killings, for the deaths, for slaughtering Laurie Chambers and Ray Daniels. They had no shapes to speak of and appeared to be formed from fungus and claws. He wasn't even sure how they moved; they seemed to sort of roll and scuttle at the same time. But he was afraid of them, and he instinctively moved back toward the pickup truck, his heart hammering in his chest as though it were about to burst.

One of the creatures reached a young man and woman. College students. The girl had an expensive still camera with a telephoto lens, the guy a palm-sized video recorder. They were capturing events for a college newspaper/TV station, for a class, for their own personal interest or perhaps because they hoped to sell the shots to another media outlet and make some money.

The creature sliced off their heads.

It happened in an instant, before they could even cry out. A shapeless smudge of fungus with razor-sharp talons lashed out and in one quick move cut through first the guy's neck, then the girl's. Both bodies took one extra step before crashing into each other and collapsing in a heap, blood geysering from their severed arteries while their heads landed on the ground. The people around them shouted and screamed as they were splashed with the spurting blood.

Henry felt an ice-cold sliminess slide against his back. It passed through the thick material of his shirt like it wasn't there and for a brief frigid second it seemed as though a gigantic raw oyster were being drawn across his skin. He spun around and saw one of those creatures passing right next to him. Even this close, he could see no details in the blackness, only the vague fuzziness of the mold and the occasional sharpness of randomly jutting claws. It sped by quickly, and he stood stock-still, afraid to move, those around him doing the same until the monster had disappeared into the crowd, into the night.

Henry backed away.

The creatures were everywhere, attacking the tourists, the reporters, the cameramen, the technical workers on the news teams. He saw arms lopped off, stomachs rent, people torn apart, as the black shapeless figures passed through the crowd. Oddly enough, what brought it home to him, what made it seem truly real, was the fact that famous people were being killed. Both NBC and CNN had well-known national correspondents on the scene, and to see them die so gruesomely, these men and women who had been on his television countless times over the years, reporting from crime scenes and trouble spots as he'd been eating his dinner, made him realize that this was actually happening.

And yet the men of the tribes remained untouched.

It wasn't fair, and while he was one of those spared, he felt the unjustness of it, knew it was wrong and felt guilty about it.

This had to stop.

He glanced over at Wes, Milton, Antonio and Jack. They and the group of Pimas next to them looked as stunned, sickened and abashed as he felt.

And still more trains were coming.

The air was moving again. Not wind but the same sort of huge displacement that had heralded the previous arrival. There was already chaos in the crowd from the murderous attacks, but it grew worse as survivors began running frenziedly about, trying to anticipate where the next locomotive would be coming from. For railroad tracks were springing up beneath their feet, rising out of the hard earth, an impossible crisscrossing network that seemed to extend in every direction. Henry nearly fell over as rails and ties pushed up from the ground, and he looked frantically both ways to make sure nothing was bearing down on him.

The dark murderous entities that had been rushing wildly through the crowd and tearing people apart seemed to have disappeared, although perhaps they'd only moved on to another section of the huge assemblage. This area was on a slight rise, and Henry could see all the way to the original tracks. It was dark out there and he couldn't be sure, but it looked to him as though some of the creatures were merging with the eastbound train, the shadow train, not climbing aboard but being *absorbed* by the locomotive, becoming part of it.

And the train grew darker, more solid.

Fresh screams arose from the south as the new locomotive arrived, barreling through the throng on one of the emergent tracks, running over dead bodies and shoving other people out of its way, sending them flying. Despite its tangible concrete presence, this train, too, made no sound, and though smoke seemed to be belching from its chimney, Henry saw as it sped by that the smoke was comprised of shadows, the hovering forms of those seductive shades who'd been violating his people.

His people.

How quickly he had come to identify himself as Papago after years, decades, of seeing himself as Caucasian and thinking of his father's story as nothing more than a fanciful rumor.

A hot wind engulfed him as the behemoth passed, smelling of sulfur and death, blowing the long hair of the men around him and causing his own shorter hair to whip backward painfully. He saw blood and bits of flesh both on the scoop in front of the engine and spinning around on the wheels. In the passenger cars that followed, the countenances that stared out were rotted and skeletal, the faces of corpses long dead.

From the north, a fourth train emerged from the night, this one seemingly more ordinary, although any real determination was impossible to make at this distance. Its sound and appearance were those of a traditional locomotive, but it *was* arriving on one of the spider's web of new tracks rising from the plain, so it couldn't have been anything close to normal. Like the others, it drove through the multitudes, over stray individuals, heading directly for the heart of Promontory Point—the spot at which the golden spike had been driven.

Just as they had in 1869, when the lines met and the transcontinental railroad was born, two trains faced each other on the original east-west tracks while a huge crowd watched. This time, however, two other trains on a pair of the newly emergent tracks faced each other from the north and south as well. It was an awesome and frightening sight. The four engines looked like gigantic creatures holding a conference, and in a way, Henry supposed, that was exactly what was happening. For these were not mere vehicles in which passengers were being carried; they were entities of their own, created for a specific purpose, incorporating yet superseding the corpses, shadows, ghosts, mold and whatever else made up their individual components. He had no idea what came next, but it was not hard for him to imagine the four locomotives merging into one, forming a single supernatural force capable of crisscrossing the nation in endless pursuit of vengeance.

The ground rumbled again. None of the trains were in motion, but there was movement beneath the earth, as though something was attempting to break through to the surface, and he imagined an army of corpses emerging from the soil, their skeletal faces frozen in expressions of rage and hate.

Henry smelled smoke, felt heat, although whether it was coming from under the ground or from the engines themselves he could not be sure.

This was it. This was what they'd come for, what the shamans had predicted. It was time for them to take a stand, to align themselves against the trains and the rapacious dead, to reclaim for themselves the power that the Chinese had appropriated. A shudder seemed to pass through the crowd. Only it wasn't exactly a shudder. It was more like a collective shift, a uniform movement that seemed almost choreographed in the way it migrated from one side of the gathering to the other.

Henry felt Wes reach for his hand, and he reached out to hold Milton's. Who in turn grabbed Antonio, who . . .

It spread like a wave through the gathering, and Henry watched as all of the disparate individuals who had heretofore resisted any and all attempts at social connection formed a sort of human chain, linking themselves physically with one another, with every pilgrim who had made his way to the Point. *This* was why they were here. There was a calming effect as he stood between the two men, holding their hands, a soul-soothing emotion that radiated through him as though conducted by the hands holding his, and it felt at once comforting and cleansing.

Along with this came a chanting, words he did not recognize and did not know but that he picked up through simple repetition of the syllables. He joined in, starting hesitantly but growing louder, stronger and more confident with each round of verse. Many of the other men seemed unfamiliar with the words as well at first, and he wondered from which tribe the chanting had originated. He had the strange feeling that it was not from any tribe, that the words were in a language familiar only to shamans, and the thought made him recite more forcefully, suddenly certain that doing so would give the words power.

The calming influence was superseded by an energizing force that likewise seemed transmitted by the hands of the men around him. Transmitted and amplified. He was suddenly filled with the desire, the need, to confront the trains and whoever or whatever lay behind them.

It was time to fight back.

Thirty-four

On the Passenger Train

The train lurched.

It had stopped seconds before, and while Dennis could still see nothing out the window, there seemed a slight lessening of the darkness, as though the outside world had caught up to them and was gradually coming into focus. The lurch was strange, jarring and definitely unplanned. Even a couple of the ghosts were thrown forward, and the identical expression on their formerly blank faces was one of confusion. Instead of growing more corporeal, as planned, they seemed to be growing less solid, and it was clear that this was a development that had not been expected.

Dennis stood, as did Malcolm, but it was difficult to do so. Something about the railroad car had changed. It was less solid than it had been, weaker. If before they had been cocooned within the substance of the train, now that cocoon was slipping, shrinking, tightening around them, trapping them.

There was another hard lurch, as though they'd been hit from behind, and the dead surrounding them flickered off and on like lightbulbs.

They needed to get out now, Dennis knew, or they might not be able to get out at all. Even the professor from Denver and some of the people who'd been craving revenge were now frightened and desperate to leave the train. The dead remained in place, unmoving, their faces betraying the fear they now felt. All of the living people were making their way up the aisle toward the exit. It felt to Dennis as though they were slogging through water, so thick did the air seem to be, and he carefully kept his hands at his sides after accidentally touching the back of a seat and feeling a hairy sliminess that made his skin crawl with revulsion.

He reached the door and tried to open it, but the latch pressing against his hand did not retain its shape or function and squished out from between his fingers like rotten black gelatin. Crying out in surprise and disgust, he flung the bulk of the mess onto the ground, wiping the rest on his pants, rubbing his skin compulsively against the material until he was sure it was completely gone.

Malcolm had passed through the connector to the car in front, and Dennis cut in front of the professor and followed.

Only the car wasn't there.

The connector remained the same as it had been when they'd initially entered, but the first passenger car had been replaced with what appeared to be a grotto made from mold and mud. Faces peered out of the walls, faces that looked vaguely familiar, that had no doubt been the passengers they'd passed on their way in, but they were frozen in expressions of agony. It was how they'd looked at the second they'd died, Dennis realized, and he understood that whatever process had brought them to this point was reversing itself. The dead were reverting to their previous forms. If the rest of them did not get out at this instant, they could be trapped here forever—wherever *here* was.

Malcolm backed up and so did he and so did the professor. The housewife and a computer programmer, meanwhile, had found a way to open the door. The slimy goo that had been the latch was still lying in globs on the floor where he'd thrown it, but the rest of the door had somehow remained intact and was sliding open. Through the doorway, they could see night sky and what looked like thousands upon thousands of people holding hands and chanting on a desert plain.

Promontory Point, Dennis thought.

This was where it had all begun, and this was where it was destined to end.

Other trains were here, he saw, other railroads carrying more of the wronged, the massacred, the dead.

The programmer and the housewife stepped down, went outside.

Taking a deep breath, Dennis followed.

Thirty-five

Bear Flats, California

They pulled up in front of the Williams place in the FBI agents' car: the two agents, Skylar and Jolene. Her mother remained back at the house in case Leslie showed up. Their headlights shone on another car already parked in the circular drive and on two more identically attired agents who stood with Ned Tanner and an officer she didn't know, who were obviously waiting for them to arrive.

Jolene got out of the backseat, holding tightly to Skylar's hand. She still didn't want him to be here, but she recognized that he was connected to all of this in some strange way she did not understand. Even if she tried to keep him out of it, he was involved, and the safest thing to do was keep him with her at all times.

Ned smiled a greeting, and Jolene nodded back, walking over. The four agents met by the other car and briefly conferred before splitting apart. Saldana seemed to be the man in charge, and he approached the police chief. "You have the key?"

Ned handed it to him.

"I'd like to see the spot where Mrs. Carter was killed."

"It's in one of the bedrooms."

"Show me." The agent motioned to Jolene and Skylar, indicating that they were to come, too.

Ned instructed the other Bear Flats officer to stay outside while the rest of them entered the house. Just inside the doorway, someone flipped on the lights. It looked the same as it had two days ago, when she and Leslie had come back for the diaries, but the atmosphere was different, stranger, more sinister and overtly threatening, the way it had been the day Anna May had been murdered.

And Skylar had been naked in the cellar.

She didn't want to think about that.

"Ow!" Skylar said. "You're hurting my hand!"

"Sorry," Jolene said. She'd been unaware that she'd been squeezing so hard.

Ned led the way up the stairs. Darkness lay at the top of the steps, and no one seemed to know where the light switch was. There was some fumbling around by Ned and one of the other agents, and Jolene was filled with the irrational certainty that the two of them would be engulfed by the darkness and eaten by whatever was hiding in there. Her breathing grew shallow, and she had to make a concerted effort not to squeeze Skylar's hand too tightly.

Then Ned found the switch and the upstairs hallway was illuminated before them. Everyone was here, everyone was fine, but the sense of dread did not dissipate. If anything, it became stronger as they approached the bedroom. Jolene remembered the loud thump they'd heard from downstairs when Anna May's body had hit the floor. She recalled with perfect clarity the way the old woman had been not only beaten, her head nothing but a bloody pulpy mess, but slashed open, the gashes in her legs so deep that the white of bone was visible through the red of flesh.

"I don't think I closed that door," Ned said in front of them, and Jolene could tell that he was scared, too.

He pushed open the bedroom door.

They stood there, looking in, flashlights shining on blackness. The interior of the bedroom was now completely covered with mold. It was impossible to tell whether the black fungus was consuming the room or transforming it, but it was no longer merely a faint shadow on the walls. A thick layer that looked like the fur coat of an animal grew over every available inch of space—floor, ceiling, furniture—erasing distinctions and imposing uniformity. The enclosed area looked less like a room now than a cave.

No. Not a cave. There wasn't the haphazard naturalness that a cavern would possess. Instead, the metamorphosed walls possessed an almost mechanical aspect, and she thought that it looked more like a boiler room or . . .

Or the cabin of a train engine.

Even the FBI agents seemed caught off guard by the condition of the room.

"Where was the body?" Saldana asked. The police chief pointed. Neither made an effort to enter.

Jolene pulled Skylar away from the doorway, back down the hall. From somewhere else within the house came the faint sound of laughter. It was muffled, hard to hear, its source impossible to pinpoint. Though the tone was a deep masculine baritone, there was something flighty and vaguely feminine about the cadence, and the juxtaposition sent a shiver down her spine.

"Ow!" Skylar said.

"Sorry," she told him, loosening her grip.

"Where was your son found?" Saldana asked. "I want to see that basement."

They descended the stairs, none of them remarking upon the black room they had just left, and Jolene found herself more frightened than she had been before. Whatever small confidence the authority of the FBI had instilled in her was gone. Saldana and his men could not have learned much from their brief look at the bedroom, and they certainly hadn't accomplished anything. Which meant that the agents were as lost as she was in the face of this horror.

Still, they all went down to the basement, although she and Skylar ventured no farther than the bottom of the steps in case they had to make a quick getaway.

The door in the floor was closed. Ned again expressed surprise at that, since he was the last person who'd been in here and it had been open when he'd left yesterday afternoon.

Saldana pointed. "That's it? Down there?" His voice was not quite as loud as it had been, as though in deference to this place.

Jolene nodded, not trusting herself to speak.

"And there's no other entrance or exit?"

"None," Ned said. "I checked myself." He was about to pull open the trapdoor when from beneath the thick wood came an indistinct scratching followed instantly by the sound of wood hitting wood.

Someone was down there.

As one, the FBI agents and the police chief drew their holstered guns. Jolene's heart was pounding so hard she could barely hear over the thumping in her ears. She backed up, holding tightly to her son, retreating slowly up the steps. She thought of that low terrible space with its dirt floor, its foul smell and that single bookcase in the center. It had been ghastly enough in the middle of the day. At night, it seemed more terrifying than anything she had ever encountered or could ever have imagined, and the thought that Skylar had had to spend even a second alone in that dark horrible space filled her with anguish.

Ned and the FBI agents had formed a ring around the trapdoor, their drawn weapons pointed at arm's length at the wooden hatch. Saldana nodded to the agent closest to the handle, indicating that he was to pull the door open. He was Asian, Jolene noticed for the first time. She wondered if he was of Chinese descent.

As before, the spring-hinged door came up fairly easily, and for a brief moment she saw the top of the primitive ladder.

Then the agent was gone.

She could not tell if he *fell* into the opening or was somehow *drawn* in. All she knew was that one second he was standing next to Saldana and the next he was tumbling into the blackness with a short surprised scream.

The trapdoor slammed shut.

The screaming continued.

Grew worse.

Jolene yanked Skylar's arm, pulling him the rest of the way up the stairs. They had to get out of here. Now.

"We have to destroy the house!"

She stopped. Her son's declaration was so loud, so authoritative, so unlike his usual quiet voice, that for a brief second she thought he might be possessed, thought something else might be speaking through him. But when she peered down at his face, illuminated by the light from the kitchen above, she saw only Skylar, and while the look of determination on his features was far more intense than usual, it was definitely his own.

A hint of exasperation crept into his voice, as though he knew ahead of time that he wouldn't be taken seriously because he was a kid, but when he spoke it was with the same strength. "Trust me. I know what we have to do."

"We can't—" Saldana began, his eyes never leaving the closed trapdoor.

"It's the only way to stop it!"

Muffled laughter sounded from the lower cellar, a deep evil chuckle that was accompanied by a strange *juicy* sound she could not quite recognize. The screaming had stopped.

"We have to destroy the house!" Skylar's voice was more whiny now than authoritative. "We have to burn it down!"

Jolene pulled him into the kitchen. She didn't care what the rest of them did, but she was taking her son and getting out of this fucking building.

The two of them dashed through the kitchen, out into the first-floor hall, through the foyer and out the front door.

"Jolene! Skylar!"

It was her mother's voice.

Jolene pulled her son down the steps, running into the drive. She squinted against the patrol car searchlight until she found her mom. And Leslie. The two had driven here in Leslie's Toyota and were waving them over.

"Jolene!" Leslie called, her voice filled with relief.

"Is everything all right, ma'am?" It was the officer who had remained outside. Jolene had no idea how to answer that—so she didn't. She continued running.

"Skylar!" Her mother took him from her, hugging the boy and holding him close.

He pulled away. "We have to destroy the house!" he repeated in a tone of supreme frustration. He was almost crying. "It's the only way! We *have* to!"

"He's right. He knows."

Jolene looked at her mom. Was this the same woman who'd angrily told her and Skylar that they hadn't seen *anything* at the window? How could she have come around so quickly—and without even having seen what was inside the house? Jolene wasn't complaining, but she didn't understand. She loved her son, but even she hadn't been entirely persuaded until only a few moments before.

Leslie opened the trunk of the car. In it was a pile of dirty rags and a case of whiskey she had obviously brought from the restaurant. "We can make Molotov cocktails."

Leslie had been convinced, too.

"Chief!" the policeman shouted.

Jolene looked up as Ned emerged from the front door, battered and bloody, his clothes torn.

He was alone.

He staggered down the porch steps, leaning on a post for balance as the waiting officer rushed to offer him assistance. No one came out of the house behind him, and Jolene knew without having to ask that the four FBI agents were dead.

"Stay here!" she ordered, and started across the drive to help. She changed her mind halfway over and quickly hurried back. "Stay together!" She grabbed Skylar's wrist. He was already holding his grandmother's hand, and with Leslie running alongside, the three of them made their way over to the patrol car. Within the house, lights seemed to be flicking on and off at random.

"Are you okay?" Jolene asked the police chief.

His eyes were filled with agony. "They didn't make it."

"We have to destroy the house!" Skylar shouted.

"He's right," Ned said, breathing heavily and with difficulty.

"I brought a lighter and rags and bottles of alcohol," Leslie offered. She seemed to realize that what she was proposing was illegal, was in fact arson. And premeditated arson at that. She glanced quickly from the police chief to his underling.

"Then let's burn the place down," Ned said.

The chief was in pain and seriously injured, but through sheer determination he hobbled across the drive to Leslie's Toyota. He looked into the open trunk and nodded approvingly. "Joe," he said to the other officer. "We have five gallons of gas in those emergency canisters in the trunk of the car. Get them out."

The policeman hurried off. Ned tried to lift up the carton of whiskey bottles but couldn't do it, so Leslie lifted it out for him "Go take it over to Joe," he said. "Set it down in front of the porch. I'll get a couple of rags. All we need is one incendiary device. We'll douse the place first, then set it off."

Jolene found herself wondering what would happen once this was all over. *If* it was all over. There would be four murdered FBI agents in a house burned by an arson-set fire. Under Ned Tanner's orders, the Bear Flats Police Department might not come to any conclusions, but with feds involved, she had the feeling that there would be outside investigations into the deaths.

They couldn't worry about that now. The important thing was to destroy the house.

She watched with her mother and Skylar as Joe hauled out the gas cans and Leslie began unscrewing the caps on the bottles. They worked fast. Under Ned's instructions, Joe dashed briefly into the Williams house carrying two canisters of gasoline. Jolene held her breath until he emerged empty-handed a moment later. He then went over to the north side of the building, broke one of the windows, poured gasoline inside and threw the can after it. He did the same thing in another ground-floor room on the south side of the house.

Ned tried throwing a bottle through the open doorway but succeeded only in tossing it onto the porch. It didn't even break. He quit instantly, not wanting to waste their limited resources, and Joe began pitching bottles through the doorway and then through an open window on the upper floor.

The house was dark now, no lights were on, and it felt to Jolene as though the building lay there waiting, like a predator preparing to pounce. She pulled Skylar back a few steps.

There were only two bottles left. The police chief took a long swig out of one, handed it to Joe, who did the same before passing it back, then pressed one of the rags through the bottle neck. He took the lighter from Leslie. "Stand back!" he ordered.

Joe held the bottle while Ned lit the rag.

"Now!" the chief yelled.

The policeman threw it through the doorway, and there was a whoosh of hot air and a sudden roar as the foyer went up in flames. Jolene didn't know what Joe had done on his quick trip inside the house, where he had dumped the gasoline, but he'd obviously known what he was doing because the building was instantly ablaze. There was a loud metallic thump, then the tinkling shatter of glass as one of the gas cans smashed through the picture window in the sitting room and came shooting out toward them, hitting a pine tree and bouncing to a stop next to the police car.

They all backed up.

The second bottle had been saved in case the first wasn't enough to start a fire, but that wasn't necessary.

Flaming drapes blew outward through the broken picture window, accompanied by billows of black smoke. The sitting room and the foyer were hellish infernos. Another window shattered. And another.

They stood staring, the night darkening around them as the fire grew brighter, moved to other rooms, came onto the porch where Ned's unbroken bottle had landed, touched the shake roof.

Jolene thought she heard a cry of rage from somewhere deep within the blaze, a crazed infuriated bellow that blended with the roar and crackle of the conflagration. Would the fire reach the cellar? she wondered. Even in the upper basement, there wasn't much to burn. Although it seemed highly unlikely that the flames would penetrate the trapdoor, a living person would still suffocate down there from lack of oxygen and probably die of smoke inhalation.

But whatever was down there was neither living nor a person.

Perhaps the heat from above and the weight of the collapsing house would crush the cellar until it was nothing but a pit full of smoldering ashes.

Skylar looked up at her. "He wasn't in the basement," he said, as though reading her thoughts. "Not really. He was in the whole house."

She hoped he was right.

And as she watched the fire, held tightly to his small hand and heard once again that bellow of rage, she thought that he probably was.

Thirty-six

An old guy who looked like a prospector with three cameras hanging around his neck lay butchered at her feet, his torn, broken body covered with blood and vomit.

Her vomit.

Angela wiped her mouth, her stomach still feeling queasy, the stench of death strong in her nostrils. All about her were the dead and dying. She had no idea what that *thing* was that had come through here, all wild claws and silent destruction. She knew only that it was made of mold, the same black mold that had been transferred to her by the corpse in the tunnel, that had taken over Babbitt House and corrupted her roommates.

But just as in Flagstaff, she was apparently immune. The mold had no effect on her. As far as she could tell, it had no effect on any of the Native Americans either.

It affected only white people.

The conclusion appeared inescapable. In Flagstaff, it turned them into raging bigots. Here, it slaughtered them with abandon. Angela could only assume she had been spared because she was of Mexican descent, a minority.

As crazy as everything else was, the concept of a politically correct monster seemed the most ridiculous and hardest to believe. How else to explain what had happened, though? The Chinese dead and their cohorts had spared her and all of the Native Americans but struck down with fury the Caucasian camera crew from CNN. Did that mean . . . ?

She looked around frantically until she saw in the crowd the familiar face she'd been searching for.

Derek.

He was still alive.

They'd been separated in the melee, and she was irrationally, exuberantly grateful that he was unharmed.

She recalled the photo of Derek's father she'd seen in his house, Mrs. Yount standing next to a man considerably darker than herself.

Derek saw her the same instant she saw him. He ran over, giving her a hard, desperate hug. Her heart skipped a beat, and she was suddenly suffused with a feeling of dread. Where was his mom? And his brother? She hugged him back and could tell from the lurching of his shoulders and the tight way he pressed his face into her hair that he was sobbing.

No, she thought.

Yes, she knew.

Around them, as if on cue, perhaps following the same instinct that had led them here in the first place, the Native Americans joined hands and started chanting. It reminded her of that Hands Across America thing her parents had done before she was born, although there seemed something vaguely religious about it as well. Many of the men's eyes were closed, and it looked to her like they thought they were going to die and had decided to passively await their fate, the hand-holding and chanting demonstrating their acceptance of death.

As two heavyset men moved to join the line of hand-holders, Angela saw, lying on train tracks behind where they'd been, the body of Derek's mother slit open from throat to groin, her bloody innards spilling onto the railroad ties. Sickened, she looked away, trying hard not to throw up, though she doubted there was anything left in her stomach to disgorge. She felt a distressingly deep void within her, an aching hole that threatened to grow wider and wider until whatever self she had left fell in and disappeared. It was like a sharp stab to the soul to see her friend's mother that way, and to know that his little brother lay somewhere around here as well, murdered and mutilated.

She started praying. It was conditioning more than anything else. Habit. Praying made her feel better, gave her comfort in time of need.

Always before when she'd prayed, there'd been uncertainty behind it. She'd sent out her wishes and gratitude *hoping* they would be heard. But this time to her complete and utter shock there was an immediate connection. She was filled with the unexplainable yet irrefutable knowledge that she was speaking directly to an entity that heard and understood her.

Only . . .

Only she was not sure it was God.

It was powerful, no doubt about that. But she *sensed* things about this being, and its attributes were definitely not those she associated with the Almighty. It was close by, for one thing, not an omnipresent force but a specific entity existing within a clearly defined space. For another, it seemed offended somehow,

angry, filled with the sorts of petty human emotions
that should be beneath a deity. Not that the Lord
himself hadn't exhibited the occasional pettiness and
petulance from time to time—but that was when he'd
been a young God, in the Old Testament, just learning
the ropes and trying to figure out the boundaries between himself and his creations.

This thing wasn't young.

She was afraid to stop praying, afraid the connection
would be lost. The entity to whom she was talking
might not be a god, but she felt safe in its company,
protected by her communion with it. And the more
she spoke, the more she opened herself and made
explicit her fears and wishes, the closer she seemed to
come to this awesomely powerful being. She had the
impression that it knew who she was, that her coming
here had been arranged or somehow preordained, although that made no sense and she could not imagine
how she could help, what possible use she could be,
what she could bring to the table.

Derek was still hugging her, leaning on her, sobbing
and holding her tightly. Her hands were clasped behind his back, her eyes closed as she prayed.

There was movement beneath her feet, accompanied by an audible rumbling, and at that, her eyes
snapped open. As a native of Southern California,
she'd lived through her share of earthquakes, and
those experiences had made her wary and alert to any
seismic phenomena, instinctively ready to bolt or seek
cover at the first sign of geologic instability. This
wasn't an earthquake, though. She knew it immediately. The second her eyes opened, she saw a figure
beginning to coalesce from the land surrounding them,
elements of earth and sky coming together to form a
single beast, as though the substance of each compo-

nent making up this plain was being drawn particle by particle from its inanimate source by an invisible force and shaped into a monster.

But *was* it a monster?

It drew itself upward from the ground, rising as tall as a building into the still night air, illuminated by the light of the recently risen moon. It was indeed horrible to look upon, this thing of rock and sand and cloud and brush. Recognizable ingredients had been put together in such a way that the end result was not only unfamiliar but profoundly disturbing. At the same time, she was not afraid of it. She faced the massive figure. There were no arms or legs, but there was very definitely a face. It hovered somewhere in the middle of the thin wavering form: ancient angry eyes, a beakish nose, a lipless maw that was at once overlarge and tightly constricted. Yet despite the being's hideous appearance and overwhelming size, she was not really frightened. Awed, yes, but not scared.

She could see through it. Despite its makeup, the creature did not have the heft of solidity, was more apparition than physical presence. Had it been summoned by those chanting men? Was this an agent of protection, some sort of Native American deity they had conjured in order to save them from the dark forces that had drawn them here?

Angela didn't know. All she knew was that this was the being to whom she had been praying, or, rather, the being that had intercepted her prayers.

The spirit of America.

She wasn't sure where she'd heard that phrase before or to what it referred, but the description came closer than anything else to describing the thing that now loomed above the plain.

Derek had pulled away, either the tension in her body, a change in the atmosphere or some sixth sense alerting him to the fact that there was something behind him, and he turned to look. He was scared, but, like herself, not as scared as he should have been given the thing's size and appearance.

The spirit of America.

It might be wrong, might even be blasphemous, but once more Angela closed her eyes and folded her hands.

She began to pray.

The connection was there again instantly, an intimate sharing that was even stronger this time. She had a hard time associating such a delicate process with the monster towering above them. On the other hand, Angela had no problem relating the anger she sensed back to that formidable figure. It was a fury borne of betrayal, a wrath directed at those who had overstepped boundaries: the Chinese, the corpses, the black mold. This was a being that had been here since before there was a country, since before there were people. She had no idea what it was, but the appellation she'd come up with—

spirit of America

—rang true to her, as trite and ridiculous as it might sound, because she sensed within the being a feeling of stewardship toward the land and, perhaps, the people who inhabited it. What the spirit required, she felt, what it demanded within its purview, was balance, an equality of opposites. It could not allow the evil behind the trains to run rampant over the land.

That meant the entity was on their side. This time. But she understood that that might not be the case in the future or may not have been in the past. It was a temporary convergence of interests, and she was thankful for that. Despite the nonthreatening connection she enjoyed with the

spirit

she understood the potential horror of such power, and knew from the monstrous appearance of the being, a sight that had been permanently etched into her brain, that it had the capacity to be far, far worse than the black trains and their cargo of vengeful dead.

One of the trains blew its whistle, a sound not mournful but chilling. Instead of a long sustained blast, however, the noise was cut off almost as soon as it started.

She opened her eyes, though her hands remained clasped and her mouth kept whispering prayer.

The gigantic figure grinned, its teeth dark in the moonlight and resembling sandstone.

And for the first time she was truly afraid.

Dennis emerged from the passenger car feeling numb and somewhat out of it, as though he'd been anesthetized in preparation for an operation and had only just come to. His vision seemed blurred, his thought processes murky, and when he stepped onto the ground behind the housewife, he did so slowly with legs that felt thick, unwieldy and not his own.

Malcolm followed him out. Then came the rest of the living. The dead remained on board.

There was a maze of tracks on the ground before them and what seemed to be a labyrinth of locomotives, huge black engines that were all different—yet all related. One, he saw with horror, was made of corpses, hundreds of them, covered with mold and forced into the shapes of headlights, catwalks, steel plates and doorframes.

It was difficult to walk, but one beneficial by-product of his deadened state was the fact that the fear he should have felt remained subdued, tamped down. Intellectually, he recognized the magnitude of the terrible scene that greeted him, but emotionally it did not register, and his heart was not jackhammering into overdrive the way it otherwise would have been.

He stumbled toward the front of his train where it met three others, all four seemingly from the different directions of the compass—north, south, east, west. He bent down, dropping to one knee between two crisscrossing tracks, and scooped up a handful of dirt in his palm. He felt the dirt, smelled it, touched it to his lips. There was blood mixed with this soil, the blood of his people. Chinese immigrants had been massacred at this spot, and that was a stain that would never go away.

He let the dirt fall, slipping through his fingers.

He *had* been summoned, Dennis realized, but it had not been by the ghosts of his people, as he'd originally thought. Most of them were caught up in this revenge play just like himself, not intentional warriors but conscripts, drawn into battle by forces beyond their control and probably beyond their ken. Despite the fact that he had been welcomed onto the train, expected even, that had not been his destination, merely his mode of transportation. Perhaps those in the passenger car had expected him to join their fight, had thought that all of the living people they were picking up would devote themselves to bringing retribution to white America, but that had not happened.

No, something else had led him here, had called to him across the miles and through the years.

And then he saw it.

In back of the locomotives, *above* them, towered a strange and dreadful figure he recognized from his dreams. It was the being that had summoned him here, the one whose triangular head he'd seen behind the wall of smoke at the end of the road, the one in his nightmares who had always been in the background, watching, waiting, beckoning him forward, its dark shifting form visible in the sky, above the trees, above the mountains.

Just as it was now.

If the trains were variations on a normal object, bastardizations of known machines, this was something else entirely, a form so singularly horrific and profoundly strange that had he not dreamed of it before, his brain would have been able to find no correlations or comparisons.

And yet it belonged here. As alien as it seemed, it was clearly a natural part of this land, like the mountains and the sagebrush and the rocks and the air. It was a creature of this place, had been here long before this country was settled, and would remain here long after their civilization crumbled to dust.

Dennis looked up into the moonlit sky at the wavering form. Waves of anger and displeasure rolled from it, emotions he understood but that nevertheless frightened him because their origins in this instance were so fundamentally inhuman. It had called him here, brought him to this place in hopes that he could help stop the seemingly inevitable progression of the vengeful malediction. As huge and powerful as the entity might be, it was impotent. At least in regard to this. It could not stop the retaliation to come or it would have nipped it in the bud long ago. All it could do, apparently, was draw to it people it thought could derail the process.

But what was he to do? What *could* he do? All of this had been put into motion by a freakish convergence of circumstances, by a curse spoken in the right place at the right moment that had burgeoned into a movement now entirely uncontrollable. He could not stop it. He had no power and knew no spells. There was no way anything he did could have the slightest effect on what was essentially the biggest class-action proceeding of all time.

Malcolm and the others were standing close behind him, frightened by the hellish landscape in which they found themselves and uncertain of what to do, looking to him for guidance. Dennis, too, was lost, and for a moment he simply stood there, breathing in the smoky fumes and staring up at the angry face in the sky.

Except the face wasn't all angry. The mouth was smiling. It was a horrible smile, and the teeth reminded him of cactus, but it was a smile nevertheless, and it was directed at the thousands of Native American men who stood on the Point, linked together and winding around the trains over the land like an endless snake, chanting.

Had they conjured up this being, this monster, this . . . spirit?

Spirit.

Yes. That's what it was.

The last of the line stood directly in front of him, a short man nearly as wide as he was tall with shiny black hair that from the rear made him look Chinese. Dennis swiveled his head, trying to discern the successive links in the chain, but the line of people was as tangled and complicated as the railroad tracks beneath their feet and it was impossible to tell where it went after the first crossing.

Chain.

Everything that had led them here was part of a chain, a chain of events set in motion well over a hundred years ago. He was part of that chain, and he grabbed the hand of the squat man, then reached around and held Malcolm's hand. For a brief second, he worried that Malcolm might think he was gay— years of social conditioning didn't just disappear, even in a time of crisis—but then Malcolm grabbed the hand of the professor from Denver, who grabbed the housewife's hand behind him.

Dennis considered joining the chant, imitating the words being spoken all around him and echoing to the skies, but it did not feel right. Next to him, Malcolm started his own chant in Mandarin, something that sounded like a prayer to the ancestors, and Dennis followed suit, speaking in Cantonese, repeating the first thing occurring to him that sounded anything at all like the rhythm of the chant: an old nursery rhyme his mother had taught him as a small child. Behind them, the others began doing the same, chiming in with their own personal contributions.

It felt good to be doing this, but it didn't seem to have any real effect. On impulse, he glanced back and saw the end of the line. All of the living were attached, were connected, but . . . but something was wrong; something didn't look right.

The gap.

Yes. There was a gap at the end of the line between a long-haired young man and the train. A missing link in the chain. He was just standing there, right arm dangling uselessly at his side, while the passenger car stood less than a foot away.

The two needed to touch: the line of people and the train. He knew it instinctively, although the feeling was reinforced by that spirit in the sky. Along with the waves of anger and displeasure he sensed from the gigantic being came an understanding, a knowledge that these two opposing forces had to connect.

And it could be done only by someone Chinese.

There were a lot of factors at work here, a whole host of individual actions, links in a chain, that taken together constituted a unified movement, a surging riposte against the power of the past. He looked up at that face in the sky and felt like a game piece on a chessboard. The Native Americans had not conjured up that monstrous spirit, he realized. It had led them here just as it had him.

He let go of the short guy's hand and pulled Malcolm closer, placing the two men's hands together. Neither objected and neither stopped chanting, and indeed Dennis realized he himself was still repeating the nursery rhyme.

He dashed over to the long-haired young man, took the man's right hand in his left . . .

Then shoved his own right hand against the side of the passenger car.

The results were immediate. What felt like a bolt of electricity passed through him, although whether it was going from the train to the people or from the people to the train he could not be sure. He knew only that the energy using him as a conduit was powerful, would no doubt, in other circumstances, fry him until he was nothing but a charred pile of ash.

The three other trains started rolling, backing up, trying to escape. If they had succeeded in moving any length of distance, they would have crashed through and broken some portion of the chain, but already they were dying, stalling, stopping. The closest lost its substance, lightening into a shadow, then faded into the surrounding night. The engine and passenger cars next to it melted like ice cream, the black mold that was this railroad's essence seeping into the rails and ties beneath it. The train made from bodies, the one he suspected was the true train, the father of all the others, got a little bit farther along its tracks, but the figures that made up its components were wailing in agony and gnashing their teeth, squirming about in obvious torment. Those who were the wheels went first, collapsing, falling sideways off the tracks, causing everyone above to disengage and revert to their normal shapes, hundreds of bodies raining about and sliding down the slight slope. They, too, were covered with mold, and the mold melted off them, oozing into the ground. Beneath the black fungus, the dead were little more than ragged corpses, and in a matter of seconds they came apart, as though it was the mold that had held them together individually as well as collectively. Suddenly bones were everywhere, and Dennis saw one skinny Native American man, grinning and chanting, kick a skull across the ground as though it were a soccer ball.

This all happened simultaneously. His own train stayed intact a little longer, perhaps because he was touching it—either drawing power from it or putting power into it—but finally it, too, succumbed, breaking into pieces as though the bolts that had held it together had all disappeared. The panel he'd been palming dissolved beneath his hand, turning into a powder that felt like crumbling dirt, and he wiped it on his jeans.

Other men were kicking bones now, and Dennis felt a small flash of anger. That wasn't right. He looked up, and the figure towering above them seemed more solid now, as though the demise of the trains had granted it strength. It grinned at him, and his anger faded. The face of the thing was still hideous and terrifying, but, damn it, its smile was infectious, and as creepy as it might seem to someone looking on, Dennis stared up at the spirit and grinned back.

As a park ranger, Henry had to be familiar with a host of Native American beliefs, particularly those held by the older lost cultures who had settled the Southwest and left their mark upon the land in the form of ruins, pueblos, drawings and carvings. But despite the rumors and suspicions concerning his own ethnicity, he had never really felt kinship with any of those beliefs.

He still didn't.

He was like a foreign visitor here, but he could not fail to recognize the power and efficacy of what had just happened. Coming together, holding hands, chanting the shamanistic words, had not only exorcised the shadows that had been plaguing them; it had somehow made the trains either disappear or fall apart. There was no doubt in his mind that, given more time, those locomotives would have drained dry every man here and gone on to kill who knew how many others over who knew how many years, the Chinese dead cutting a broad swath across the land in their quest for vengeance. Would white America even have known how to handle such a scenario? Would police and other law enforcement agencies have been able to figure out that there was something supernatural afoot, or would they have doggedly continued looking at everything in a literal fashion, refusing to see associations, assuming all of the deaths were random and unconnected? It was impossible to tell, but it was a moot point anyway. The trains had not progressed to the next level.

They'd been sent back to hell or wherever it was they belonged.

Henry looked down. The tracks were glowing beneath his feet, glowing, not white, yellow, blue, green or any of the other colors associated with luminescence, but black, the gray steel rails radiating a jet darker than obsidian and somehow sharper than any hue was meant to be. He wondered if, from above, the tracks formed some sort of pattern. He looked up—

And saw a face.

It was a terrible visage that looked down upon the scene below it with a mixture of approval and disgust.

The spirit of the land, he thought instantly, but it was such a stupid cliché that he pushed it out of his mind.

His shoe felt hot, as though the section of railroad tie touching it were made of lava, and he jumped aside, finding sandy ground, trying not to touch any of the tracks. Other men were hotfooting it, too, some of them crying out in pain.

The tracks disappeared the same way they'd come in, sinking back into the ground; only this time, Henry noticed, they seemed to disintegrate as they submerged, not going under the dirt but becoming part of it, as though they had been conjured forth from native elements and were reverting to their natural state.

Henry looked up again at the face in the sky and saw that it was more than just a face. There was a body as well, although its components were parts of the surrounding landscape, which made it difficult to see. It was a creature of some sort. A monster, he wanted to say, but that was not right. This was something to which he felt connected, and he found himself thinking of all of those spirits and desert gods the old tribes had worshipped and to whom they had often appealed for assistance. He'd always assumed such stories were the way a primitive people would explain natural phenomena they did not understand, but for the first time he found himself wondering if there were not more things under heaven and earth . . .

Wes clapped him on the shoulder, grinned at him. "It's over, man. I think that's it."

"I think so, too," Henry said. He pointed up at the sky, intending to show Wes the creature towering above them, to ask whether he knew what it was, whether it was some sort of native deity or earth spirit that had been conjured by their chanting. He had the feeling that it was something else entirely, that they had not conjured *it* but rather that it had brought *them* to this place. "What do you think—?" he began.

But the figure was gone.

By the time Rossiter arrived, it was ending. He saw only the thing in the sky and the black tracks sinking into the ground and *those* nearly made him turn tail and run like a pussy. He was thankful to have missed the action this time, and he could tell from the body language of the agents surrounding him that they felt the same. They stood on the hillock next to their cars, and tried to make sense of the chaos in front of them. No one said a word, and Rossiter realized that the other men were afraid to do so. They were silent out of deference. He was the expert here, he was the boss, and the knowledge made him stand taller.

He looked out at the tremendous gathering, doing his level best not to glance upward and see that moon-lit monster face. It was impossible to judge the size of the crowd in the darkness, but there was a sea of bodies out there. It looked like one of those marches on Washington. Many of the men seemed to have been holding hands, and that seemed odd. Was there some sort of religious element here?

He didn't know, but he'd find out soon enough.

Rossiter breathed deeply, thought he smelled smoke beneath the dust. And mildew.

What the hell was Saldana doing? he wondered. The other agent hadn't checked in at the appointed time, and that had already been—Rossiter consulted his watch—a half hour ago. He wanted to believe that it was because the man had forgotten, a lapse for which

Rossiter would happily chew out his ass, but until that point, Saldana had been as regular as clockwork.

Something had happened in Bear Flats.

Maybe it had and maybe it hadn't. He didn't want to think about that right now. All he knew at this moment was that out here at Promontory Point it was finished. And it looked like the good guys had won. His mind was already concocting cover stories, bland explanations that would mollify the press and satisfy the public. A train crash, he was thinking. An accident involving two locomotives. Once he and his men conducted a few queries, took some photos and video and got a handle on what had happened, he would report back to Horn and the president.

He smiled to himself.

This time he wouldn't be pushed back into the closet.

This time he would get his promotion.

Epilogue

Canyonlands National Park, Utah

The seasons changed, the crowds returned, and it was easy to forget sometimes that any of it had ever happened.

Henry gave ranger talks, guided visitors to some of the more popular sites, narrated occasional evening slide shows in the campground, caught up on paperwork in the back office of the visitors' center. In short, he went back to his normal life.

For the most part.

But the nights were long, and on cold late evenings he sometimes found himself glancing nervously around his cabin, unnerved by the number of shadows gathered in the corners of the primitive space, half expecting one of them to move. And whenever he looked west, past Ray's cabin, and remembered the train they had seen there, it was as if it had happened just yesterday. The feelings returned full force, and he was engulfed by a fear so profound that he could not stop shaking.

Raul and Stuart were gone. Raul had transferred to Bandolier, while Stuart had quit the park service entirely. Healey had taken an early retirement, and while Henry couldn't say he was sad to see the supervisor go, he had to admit that he missed the freedom he'd had under the man. The new guy was far more efficient and much better qualified, but he was also a stickler for procedure and kept a far tighter rein on the rangers than they were used to. Healey had always acted like a hard-ass, but he was so incompetent that his orders could be safely ignored. Not so with the new guy. But maybe time would change that.

If he'd expected to become more spiritual after what he'd experienced—or even more Indian—well, that hadn't happened. He was too old and set in his ways, Henry supposed. He was what he was, and events that no doubt would have been life altering had he been twenty or thirty years younger now left him battered and bruised but essentially unchanged.

Life went on.

In February, before the start of the spring rush, when one could travel for days through the park without encountering another soul even on the most popular roads and trails, Henry found himself alone in a secluded canyon while patrolling the northeast quadrant. A box canyon. It bore no resemblance really to the canyon with the petroglyphs where he'd encountered the twins, but he stopped his Jeep nevertheless and got out, searching the rock walls and the narrowing expanse of sand before him. It was late afternoon, the sky hidden behind shifting layers of dark overlapping clouds, small traces of sunlight penetrating periodically from the west. He hadn't expected to find anything, but on the cliff face to the side of the Jeep, he saw what looked like the shadow of a voluptuous woman. It was a random confluence of shapes that together happened to resemble a person, and he could even spot the individual sources that contributed to the head, the breasts, the legs, but he pulled his pants down anyway and tried to masturbate.

He stroked slow, then fast, but it wasn't happening. He couldn't get even the slightest bit hard, and after a minute or two, he began to feel ridiculous.

He pulled his pants back up.

It really was over.

After work, he headed into Moab, to the Boy Howdy. Ector was supposed to meet him at the bar, but his friend hadn't shown up yet, so Henry ordered a beer and staked out a small table along the east wall. At the end of the counter next to him, two men, one overweight, one underweight, both wearing painter's overalls, were talking loudly enough to be heard over the television.

"I was at that Indian powwow a few months back," the fat guy said. "You know the one up at Promontory Point that was all over the news?"

"Really? Did you see the accident?"

"Front-row seats," the man bragged. "Those trains came at each other like two bulls out for blood. People were tryin' to get out of the way, but it was a mob scene. Reporters were gettin' trampled. Indians were runnin' in all directions, tryin' to get away from the tracks. . . ."

Ector arrived, squinting into the dimness.

Henry waved him over.

"Yeah," the man said, "it was like those engineers had it in for each other. They just kept acceleratin' until—*bam!*—the trains hit. Shit was flyin' every which way. . . ."

Henry couldn't help smiling to himself.

Ector walked up, slapped a hand on the table. "Hey."

"Hey, yourself," Henry replied.

". . . and those two trains were . . ."

He was still smiling. "Have a seat," he said. "Have a beer."

Seal Beach, California

Dennis stood at the end of the pier, looking not out at the ocean but back toward the shore and the solid row of contiguous houses that faced the beach. Within the past week, dump trucks, bulldozers and a cadre of uniformed men from the Army Corps of Engineers had built a sand berm in front of the houses in order to protect them from the waves of winter storms, but today's weather was nice, and mothers with their preschool children were walking, running and playing atop the giant hill of sand. Inland a few blocks, his mother and sister were, against his wishes, cleaning his apartment. They were out here only for a short vacation, in order to see for themselves where and how he was living, but Cathy had already told him she wanted to move out West, and he knew that with both of her children living here, his mother would follow.

As he had every day since his arrival, Dennis marveled at California's amazing weather. In Pennsylvania right now, the temperature was well below freezing and dirty snowdrifts were piled high along the roads like walls. Here it might as well be summer. On both sides of the pier, young men in wet suits were waiting on surfboards for waves to catch, and on the beach several couples as well as one very hot teenage girl were lying on blankets, catching some rays, while a tourist family ate lunch out of a picnic basket. Two small children ran up and down the shoreline, chasing seagulls and screaming.

It was a world away from Pennsylvania and a universe away from what he now thought of as his road trip through hell.

Unlike the other people at Promontory Point, he and his fellow passengers had been stranded by the destruction of the trains, left on that plain in Utah with no transportation and no way to return to their starting locations. His own car was way back in Milner, Wyoming, and if it hadn't been for a Sioux man with an old Pacer heading back home to Montana who offered him a ride, he had no idea what he would have done.

They hadn't spoken on the return trip, he and the Sioux man. There might have been a couple of exchanged sentences along the lines of "Let's get something to eat" or "I'll drive if you're getting tired," but for the most part there were hours and hours of silence as they drove north through plains and past mountains. It wasn't an uncomfortable silence, but it wasn't exactly comfortable either, and to Dennis the trip seemed very, very long.

He arrived in Milner midmorning, after a long nap, and he was grateful for that. He didn't want to see Carl Fong or his buddies, wanted only to escape cleanly and quietly, and he settled his bill at the motel, packed his stuff, got in his car and drove away, heading toward the coast.

He had a lot of time to think on the road.

But he avoided that.

Dennis turned, looked out at the ocean. A lone sailboat was heading toward Long Beach, and beyond that, silhouetted by a thin layer of white smog, he could see the blocky shape of a cargo ship waiting to dock at the port. A few days ago, there'd been a story on the news about illegal Chinese immigrants who'd been smuggled in the hold of one of these cargo ships but captured upon inspection. Although there wasn't as much resentment toward Asian illegals as there seemed to be toward those from Mexico—who weren't even granted the status of human but were referred to as *aliens*—darker races still seemed to provoke the ire of white America. There never seemed to be much of an outcry against immigrants from Caucasian countries.

He thought of that professor from Denver and the housewife from Oregon who had believed so strongly that retribution was necessary, violence justified, against the descendants of those who had persecuted their people. It was an insane and untenable position, the type of attitude that had led to wars and instances of ethnic strife throughout the world.

And yet . . .

And yet he could see their point.

He thought of the looting and lawlessness that inevitably followed large-scale disasters. The veneer of civilization was thin. Anger and violence were always near the surface, even in seemingly peaceful rational individuals.

He recalled that giant . . . *thing* . . . he'd seen towering over the plain.

Sometimes it was only outside intervention that saved people from themselves.

"'Scuse me." A dark squat man carrying a fishing pole, a tackle box and a bucket pushed past him to stake out a spot by the pier's railing.

Dennis started walking slowly back toward shore, enjoying the feel of the offshore breeze against his face. He looked up at the clock tower on top of the police substation. It was getting close to lunch. Already he could smell Mexican food from Taco Surf, and as he drew closer the scent of baked goods came to him from the bakery.

Maybe he'd take his mother and sister out to lunch. His mom moaned and complained if they ate anything other than Chinese food, but this was his chance to try and broaden her horizons.

From somewhere far off came the sound of a train whistle, and Dennis stopped in his tracks, heart pounding, the hairs bristling on the back of his neck. For a moment, he was frozen, his breath caught in his throat, his eyes wide with fear. But then he forced himself to exhale, forced his eyes to blink, forced his feet to walk forward, and within a few seconds he was back to normal. Glancing up at the slightly smog-tinged sky, he took a deep breath. Once again, he thought of the—

spirit

—that he'd seen looming over Promontory Point. What had really happened there? What exactly had they prevented? Was it all over for good?

Or were the professor and the housewife, along with other Chinese Americans throughout the country, resuming their blood rituals in hopes of once again raising the dead?

He didn't want to think about it.

And he wouldn't.

Dennis reached into his pocket, pulled out his cell phone and dialed the number of his apartment. After three rings, his sister answered, and he told her to stop whatever she was doing, grab their mother and meet him at Taco Surf in ten minutes.

"Is that Mexican food? You know Mom won't—"

"Hey, this is California."

He could almost hear his sister's smile over the phone. "And if we're both going to be living here, she'd better get used to it."

"Exactly." He gave her directions on how to reach the restaurant from his apartment.

"We'll be there," Cathy said.

Feeling happy, feeling good, Dennis closed the phone, put it in his pocket and strode off the pier onto the sidewalk. Instead of walking up the left side of Main Street to the restaurant, he started up the right side toward the liquor store.

He wanted to get a lottery ticket and a newspaper before his mother and sister arrived.

Bear Flats, California

It was not where she'd expected to be, not even where she was sure she wanted to be, but Jolene found herself working for the Bear Flats Police Department as an adjunct officer, a position created for her until she could find the time to undergo training, pass the test and become official. With her background, a career in law enforcement might have seemed a natural, but the truth was that she'd never considered such a move until Ned brought it up to her a week after the charred ruins of the Williams house had been razed. The police chief hired her, she supposed, because he knew that she could function well under extreme pressure. And because he needed her. There'd been one death and two defections, and the loss of even one person in a department this small had major repercussions. It was no more than the usual turnover, Ned tried to reassure everyone, but they all knew that wasn't the case.

The Williams place might have burned to the ground, but its influence lingered.

She needed the money and was happy to be employed. Leslie had offered to find her something to do at the restaurant, but that would have been a make-work pity position, and she would have accepted it only as a last resort. Her mother had said she and

Skylar could remain at her place indefinitely—and the three of them *had* been getting along extremely well, particularly with the moratorium on drinking—but the quarters were still too close, the situation too stressful, and she needed to assert her independence and try to start a new life.

It was Ned's wife who'd found a place for her and Skylar to live. Lottie Tanner was in real estate, and though Jolene hadn't said anything to her, Ned must have, and she located a cabin for rent just down the road from Leslie's place. There was only one bedroom, but the cabin was furnished and the sofa in the living room folded out into a bed. Rent was cheap. It was not someplace where they could live permanently, but in the interim, while she decided what came next, they had a roof over their heads.

Even more important than her finding a place of their own, the divorce had become finalized.

It should have been messy, should have been complicated—she and Frank had a son together, after all—but Frank had been neither as intransigent nor as vindictive as she'd expected him to be, and they'd been able to do it all through lawyers, without meeting face-to-face. He'd even agreed to pay child support and waive all visitation rights, although this was not something she'd shared with Skylar. Jolene suspected he had someone else on the line already, and in a way she was glad. It took his focus off them, left them free to move on.

The truth was, Jolene hadn't discussed much of *anything* with Skylar since . . . since everything had happened. Her son had always been somewhat close-mouthed and reserved, keeping his emotions to himself, but she'd prided herself on the way she shared everything with him, kept him in the loop, maintained a close relationship despite the circumstances of their

lives and his natural disposition. In the wake of their
experience at the Williams house, however, she'd
found it easier to avoid certain subjects, to *not* talk
about what they really *should* talk about. She felt
guilty about that, but she still couldn't bring herself
to break the pattern.

Three o'clock rolled around. Jolene got off work,
picked up Skylar at school, and the two of them
stopped by her mother's for a moment to say hi and
pick up some hamburger casserole for dinner before
heading home. Inside, the cabin was quiet, too quiet,
and Jolene quickly turned on the television so they'd
have some background noise.

Skylar shut it off.

She looked at him in surprise.

"Mom . . ." He started to say something, then
changed his mind, looked down at the floor.

"What is it?" she prodded gently.

"It's . . . I just . . ." He shook his head.

Jolene walked over, put a hand on his shoulder.
"Tell me."

Skylar looked up at her. "Are we going to stay
here?" he asked. "Are we going to live here for
good?"

Jolene had not made a decision about that, although
she realized almost instantly that the decision should
not be hers alone. These were important years for
Skylar, and after all that he'd endured, he deserved
to know what they were going to do, where they were
going to live. He needed some stability in his life. "Do
you . . . ?" she began, but in his eyes she already saw
the answer to the question she was about to ask. She
thought about her mother and Leslie and her job and
Skylar's school, where he'd already made a little
friend. "Yes," she told him, meeting his gaze. "We
are."

He hugged her tight, and she could tell from the way he hung on, pressing his face into her side, that he was crying. "Good," he said, and beneath the tears she heard gratitude. "Good."

Flagstaff, Arizona

What surprised Angela most was that she didn't go back home.

Despite everything that had happened, despite all that she'd gone through, all the horror she'd seen, she didn't go running back to Mommy and Daddy, didn't retreat into the safety of the familiar and the bosom of her family. She stayed and toughed it out.

Like an adult.

Although she'd decided to remain and finish out the semester, after that, anything was possible. She could stay; she could return home; she could transfer somewhere else. For now, though, the discipline and stability were necessary for her to work through all that she'd experienced.

Angela sat in the quad, watching students pass by. She and Derek both had a free period right now, but neither of them had made an effort to meet up with each other. It was an anniversary of sorts, two months since the night at Promontory Point, but it was not something that either of them felt like celebrating or even talking about.

She was surprised that the two of them hadn't become an item. In movies and books, males and females thrown together under traumatic circumstances invariably became lovers, although it was impossible to say how long those liaisons lasted after the credits rolled or the book covers closed. In the back of her mind, she'd half expected that to happen to them. Conditioning, she supposed. But instead the opposite seemed to have occurred. After it was all over and done, the intimacy they'd shared seemed to pull them apart rather than draw them together. They were awkward with each other now, both seemingly embarrassed by the sides of themselves they'd exposed, and while neither of them had dropped Dr. Welkes' class, they made no effort to sit together.

Derek definitely bore the brunt of the fallout. Dealing with what had happened was tough on her, but he'd lost his mother and his brother. She'd endured nothing compared with that. He was relying more on his old friends than her for support, Angela knew, and as guilty as it made her feel, she was grateful for that. She wasn't ready to be sucked into that emotional hurricane right now, and she didn't think she was strong enough herself to be someone else's rock.

Who knew, though? In time . . .

For now she was content to attend classes, study and continue on with the responsibilities of being a full-time student.

Not that there weren't scars.

Occasionally, she found herself glancing around at the other young men and women in her classes, in the library, in the student union, at the pub, wondering if they had been in the crowd cheering the lynching of Edna Wong. She tried to tell herself that even if they had, it was the mold that had made them do that, that had affected their behavior. But the ethos of personal responsibility was too strong within her, and it was impossible for her to completely absolve those who had murdered Edna.

Which was one reason why she thought she might transfer to another college next semester.

Maybe somewhere in New Mexico.

She liked the Southwest.

Her cell phone rang, and Angela answered it. "Hello?"

It was her mother. She was grateful to hear her mom's voice, and it felt relaxing and comforting to speak Spanish, despite the looks of disapproval it engendered on the faces of some of the passersby. They talked for a while, about nothing really; then her mom said she had to make lunch, and hung up.

Angela put the phone back in her purse and looked up. The campus seemed to be getting foggy. Buildings on the opposite end of the quad were light and getting lighter, bulky outlines behind a sheer wall of white.

It wasn't fog. It was snow.

She still was not used to seeing snow fall—in Southern California, snow was something that happened up in the mountains, not on the ground—and as the flakes became larger and more obvious, as the underdressed students around her began hurrying toward their indoor destinations, she stood there smiling up at the sky, the snow hitting her face and melting against the warmth of her skin.

She opened her mouth, ate a few snowflakes, then walked slowly toward her next class, looking around her at the pale silhouettes of the hulking NAU buildings, marveling at their beauty.

Maybe she wouldn't transfer to another school.

Maybe, she thought, she would stay.

About the Author

Born in Arizona shortly after his mother attended the world premiere of *Psycho,* **Bentley Little** is the Bram Stoker Award–winning author of sixteen previous novels and *The Collection,* a book of short stories. He has worked as a technical writer, reporter/photographer, library assistant, sales clerk, phonebook deliveryman, video arcade attendant, newspaper delivery man, furniture mover, and rodeo gatekeeper. The son of a Russian artist and an American educator, he and his Chinese wife were married by the justice of the peace in Tombstone, Arizona.